Once inside her ap

sofa. Barnaby fussed ar

straightening her skirt. "He'll be all right. Let not your heart be troubled. John 14, verse 1. Joseph's a tough old bird. I was planning to ask him to help with the hunt. That'll perk him up. I'll ask him tomorrow. He should be fine by tomorrow. Do you want a drink? Water? Hug?"

She looked up at him, and her eyes filled with tears. "Oh, Barnaby."

That was enough. He sat next to her and gathered her into his arms. She laid her head on his chest. In between hiccups, she whimpered, "Joseph is really my only friend here. I inherited the shop three years ago and spent the first year getting it back up and running. I haven't had time to meet anyone else. My family's gone and I…I have so many responsibilities. And now Joseph…" Her hand lifted, then dropped.

Barnaby pulled out a tangerine handkerchief printed with garden gnomes and wiped her nose. "There, there. He's not your only friend, you know." He squeezed her. "You have me."

She gazed at him. His lips slowly descended upon hers.

Hidden Gem: The Secret of St. Augustine

by

M. S. Spencer

This is a work of fiction. Names, characters, places, and incidents are either the product of the author's imagination or are used fictitiously, and any resemblance to actual persons living or dead, business establishments, events, or locales, is entirely coincidental.

Hidden Gem: The Secret of St. Augustine

Contact Information: info@thewildrosepress.com

Cover Art by *Tina Lynn Stout*

The Wild Rose Press, Inc.
PO Box 708
Adams Basin, NY 14410-0708
Visit us at www.thewildrosepress.com

Publishing History
First Edition, 2022
Trade Paperback ISBN 978-1-5092-4035-7
Digital ISBN 978-1-5092-4036-4

Published in the United States of America

Dedication

To my father,
who lived on Aviles Street above an antique map store
and introduced me to St. Augustine.

To [illegible]

Happy reading!

[illegible]

Chapter One

But when a young lady is to be a heroine…something must and will happen to throw a hero in her way.

—Jane Austen

Mind Over Matter, St. Augustine, Monday, June 4

"Can I help you?"

The tall young man dressed in canary yellow chinos and a polo shirt embroidered with tiny Barbie dolls snapped his hand back from the book on the display shelf. "Um, no. Thanks. Um. Just looking." He backed away from the case, wiping his hand on his back pocket.

Philo cast a quick glance at the table. *Oh God, not another treasure hunter.* "Were you interested in Byron Preiss's *The Secret*? Is it because one of his twelve gemstones may be hidden here in St. Augustine? It's not the only treasure the city has to offer, you know."

"I know that. Of course I know that. I happen to be a…professor. Yes." He blinked. "Of…of…er…history. So I'm acquainted with all the treasures of St. Augustine." With an inauthentic flourish, he pressed his hand firmly on the book. "Including this one."

Philo had some difficulty accepting the bit about being a professor. The man seemed indecisive. In her experience, academics were usually overly sure of themselves—cocky even. With her store situated only a few blocks from Flagler College, she dealt with them daily. "Do you teach at Flagler?"

The man's bristly russet eyebrows went up, revealing deep green eyes. He opened his mouth and closed it again. "Yes. Yes. I do. Teach there."

She couldn't help it. "Are you positive?"

His chin jutted forward aggressively, although Philo had the impression he was only posturing. "Yes. Don't you believe me?"

"Well, you seem a little hesitant."

He took a step toward Philo. His eyes roamed over her for a long, speculative moment. Apparently satisfied, he said diffidently, "Actually, I'm only an aspiring professor. I'm conducting a summer seminar here while I work on my dissertation."

"Dissertation? What are you studying?"

"Never mind. Not important." He went on hastily. "This is my first visit to St. Augustine. I can't believe I'm actually living in the oldest city in continental North America." He looked through the dusty front window to the cobblestoned road outside. "And I just sauntered down the oldest street. I read that Aviles Street has been in use since the 1600s. It makes me feel like Rip van Winkle…only in reverse." His smile transformed what had been a serious face into a glorious burst of joy.

Wow. Philo took a deep breath and waited until she was confident her voice would be steady. "So you're a graduate student." *Better than a professor, but not by much.* Raised in a household of teachers, Philo had had her fill of academics. Since she dropped out of the doctoral program in anthropology, she had not taken so much as a pottery class and considered herself a fortunate refugee from the ivory tower. Her glance swept the piles of books and racks of maps that cluttered her shop. *That doesn't mean I have to stop reading, though.*

"Yes, yes. I am that. Graduate student. Barnaby Swift at your service. And you are Philo Brice."

The statement rattled her. "How do you know that?"

He pointed at the entrance. The door stood open. Etched into the glass were the words:

Mind over Matter
Rare Books & Maps
13 Aviles Street
Philo Brice, *prop.*

A white card had been taped below the name:

Summer Hours: Monday & Friday, 12 PM to 5 PM.

Barnaby resumed without acknowledging the conversational detour. "Have been for five years. A grad student. Not the record. Oh, no. That was achieved in 1975 by one Zalmay Tinderstone. It has yet to be broken." He curled his lip. "In fact, the man is *still* working on his thesis. Some obscure medieval Islamic poet. I hear it's going on two thousand pages now." He broke off. "Where was I?"

"Talking."

He didn't appear to hear her. "Nowadays they set a time limit on dissertations. I still have two years to go before they expect to see actual pages, which is lucky because I'm practically destitute and have to work for my supper. Flagler College pays really well—did you know that?"

"I—"

"They don't advertise the fact, but they must have a hell of an endowment. Old Man Flagler was one of those robber barons, wasn't he?"

"No! Well, yes, but—"

"I shouldn't have used that term, I suppose. It's loaded. As I understand it, he single-handedly brought eastern Florida into the modern world." He paused expectantly.

Philo was surprised into answering. "He wasn't the only one, but he did do a lot for the state. He built five grand hotels from St. Augustine down to Miami, plus a railroad that ran from Jacksonville to Key West. It ferried people to south Florida and delivered oranges to the north. You could say Miami owes its existence to him. So does the citrus industry." Having given her speech without taking a breath to foil any attempted disruption, she took a great gulp of air.

He said indifferently, "Oh, well, that's all to the good. I'm grateful for his efforts, as assuredly are many others, from the bikini-draped spring-breakers to the dust-covered farmers." He plucked a cell phone from his shirt pocket. "I *am* lucky to be here. I could be in New Jersey, slaving at a desk in a library lit only by green-shaded lamps. I know it's called the Garden State, but really most of it isn't. A garden. More like smokestacks, warehouses, and grim-faced commuters. So here I find myself in the city of dreams, living on a pittance, braving the tourists, and taking lots and lots of pictures. Want to see some?"

"Huh?" Philo realized she'd missed the last few sentences of Barnaby's speech, lost in the rising and dipping waves of his rich baritone. She focused again on his face. *Hmm.* A face to match the voice, she thought with approval. The aforementioned verdant eyes went with a brush load of appealingly auburn hair, topping a youthful, rather thin face, currently moving like an animated cartoon.

"Photos. Want to see some?" He held out his phone, his eyebrows bobbing like Groucho Marx's.

Uh-oh. Could this guy be a pervert? "Of what?"

He thumbed an icon. "So, here's the Bridge of Lions. That's just around the corner from here." He flicked a finger across the screen. "And here's a shot of the Castillo de San Marcos from the air. Snapped it on one of those helicopter tours of the city." He whistled. "It was a dandy trip, even though the din from the rotors made it impossible to hear the guide. I suppose I should have sprung for the earphones, but they were ten bucks."

As opposed to the helicopter ride itself. Which last time she checked cost sixty.

When Philo didn't respond, he flipped to another photo. "And this here's the Fountain of Youth." He gazed dubiously at it. "Kind of a bust, if you ask me. Turned out to be a tiny spring with the most unpalatable water I've ever tasted." He flicked past some more images. "Aha. Now *this* was the highlight of the tour. I jumped off the little train here."

"Train! I thought you were on a helicopter."

"Huh? No, the train was after the helicopter. Weren't you listening?" He raised his eyes to her. "There's a bright red open-car trolley that goes to all the sights. You can hop on and off whenever it takes your fancy. I paid the exorbitant price for a ticket, but I could have just walked beside it and listened to the fellow's spiel for free. You could hear him at least a block away." He tapped his lip. "Maybe the helicopter pilot should get a megaphone too. I wonder if they have a suggestion box?"

Philo was moved to ask, "You were going to show me the highlight of the tour?"

"Oh, right. I'll just refresh." He fiddled with the phone, then held it up for her. The screen displayed the front of the local hot sauce shop on St. George Street.

"That's it? The Pepper Palace?"

"Yes, indeed. Don't you love the variety, the unconventional ingredients…even—no, *especially*—the labels? And the names are so creative. They're more imaginative than microbrews." He grinned. "Also, they go very well with beer. Do you like spicy food?"

Philo blinked. "Uh, I guess so."

"Would you like to have the best chili in St. Augustine?"

"Excuse me?"

He said patiently, "Chili. Best. St. Augustine. Are you with me?" He rose on his toes.

"Uh…"

"Okay, I'll pick you up here, shall I? When do you close? Oops. My bad. It's right there on the sign—five o'clock. See you then. Oh, by the way, name's Barnaby. Barnaby Swift."

And he was gone before she could point out that he'd already introduced himself. *But will he remember* my *name?*

She puttered around the store for a couple of hours trying not to think of the unusual young man who had invited her to dinner. *He did invite me to dinner, didn't he?* She passed the Preiss book lying open on the table. *He said he was familiar with* The Secret. *So why did he seem mesmerized by it?* She picked it up and took it back to her desk. The blurb on the back cover said:

"In 1982 Byron Preiss published *The Secret: A Treasure Hunt*. The year before, he had traveled to twelve spots in the United States (and possibly Canada), at each of which he buried a ceramic box or casque. Each casque contained a small key that could be redeemed for one of twelve jewels Preiss kept in a safe deposit box in New York. To find a casque, the seeker had to match one of twelve paintings to one of twelve poems. Between them they held all the clues to the key's location. Once he found the casque, he would be rewarded with the gem depicted in the painting." At the bottom was a link for a website called simply *Thesecret.com*. "*Hmm.*" Philo typed in the link and clicked Enter.

According to the home page, the riddles had stumped people since the 1980s. A global club of seekers had grown to thousands—with their own Facebook groups and online podcasts—and the competition had become fierce. They were an idiosyncratic bunch—fanatically dedicated to deciphering a decades-old mystery. Since the book was published, only three of the twelve hiding places had been uncovered.

Under the tab marked "Images" she found a running research file, to which members added their findings, queries, and guesses. Each painting had its own screen, with the poem generally recognized to be its match alongside.

The paintings were intricate, chock-full of allegories and hints about the hiding places of the casques. She turned to the first one, depicting a dark-haired woman before a tall mountain range. A rose sat on a table next to her, and her long gown was embroidered with a sinuous dragon. The consensus seemed to be that the picture—linked to Verse Seven—referred to San Francisco, but so far no one had discovered the burial site.

Many of the participants were convinced that the sixth box—with a sapphire as the prize—was in St. Augustine. *So is Barnaby Swift one of those seekers, engrossed by the hunt for a jewel?* There was only one way to find out.

When she checked her watch, she was shocked to see it was a quarter after four. She shot the bolt on the front door and went up the back stairs to her apartment to change.

Lessee—what is the proper attire for a first date at a chili joint? She caught herself looking in the mirror. *What are you talking about, Philo? First date, indeed. You don't even know the guy. He could be a serial killer…or a socialist!* She drew the cream-colored shirtwaist dress she usually reserved for dental appointments over her head. *Not too short but still sets off my one redeeming virtue.* The rest of her might be on the dumpy side, but she knew her legs were spectacular.

If pressed, she would admit she also liked the cozy brown eyes she'd inherited from her father. Her hair was a nice honey blonde, albeit too thick and frizzy for her taste. She wound it into a knot at the nape of her neck, brushed her teeth, and spent ten minutes deciding which shoes to wear. *Something with heels. He must be six three—I don't want to have to crane my neck to see his face.* On the other hand, considering his references to an impecunious condition, she had a feeling they'd be walking. She settled on a pair of ruby red flats. As she slipped them on, she clicked her heels together. *For luck? Or something else?*

Chapter Two

A little bad taste is like a nice splash of paprika. We all need a splash of bad taste—it's hearty, it's healthy, it's physical. I think we could use more of it.

—Diana Vreeland

Mind over Matter, Monday, June 4

At five o'clock Philo descended to the store and unlocked the front door. Barnaby stood outside, holding a newspaper over his head. He wore a kilt, sporran, and a white ruffled shirt. *The Converse high tops are a nice touch.*

He peered at her. "You have donned new attire. Do you live in the store?"

"No, I have an apartment upstairs."

"Ah. Do you own an umbrella?"

She countered, "Do you know my name?"

He gave her a startled glance. "Did you need reminding?"

"No, but…" She threw up her hands, at a loss.

"It's Philo Brice." He came in and gestured toward the entrance. "Says so, right there. I'm glad you brought it up, though." He framed her face with his fingers. "Curly locks, cinnamon-toast eyes, a perfectly shaped nose if you disregard the slight bump on the bridge, and a rosy complexion. I deduce English stock. However, the only Philo of whom I'm aware is Philo of Alexandria—

a Greek Jew and therefore of swarthy appearance. So whence the moniker? Or is it an eponym? Did your parents wish for a boy? A philosopher?"

Philo thought about laughing but decided against it. "I'm named after the island. Since our last name was Brice, my father was curious to see how many people made the connection." She waited.

"Not sure I…wait a minute. Philo Brice. Island." He pinched his lips together. "Nope. Never heard of it. And I pride myself on my knowledge of obscure geographical nomenclature."

"I'll give you a hint. It's in the middle of Lake Raccourci, in the Gulf of Mexico."

"Aha. Lafourche Parish, Louisiana. Southwest of the Big Easy. Lovely region of islets and bays. Good fishing. Now why am I not acquainted with this particular atoll?"

"Probably because it's partially submerged. Also, it's uninhabited except by shorebirds."

"Ah."

She felt the need to explain. "My father loved maps and spent his life studying them." She waved her hand at the racks and cases in the store. "He named each of his dogs—and me—after an island. Philo's not bad; I was almost Faroe." She grimaced.

Barnaby promptly recited, "The Faroe Islands. Situated in the North Atlantic, midway between Norway and Iceland." He concentrated, his brow furrowed. "Eighteen islands, plus some seven hundred skerries. Skerry: a rocky outcrop. Like your Philo Brice, populated solely by birds and seals. They speak an ancient Norse language. The people, not the seals." He frowned at her. "It would have been an odd name for a girl."

"No stranger than a sand bar that only emerges fully at low tide and is covered in guano."

"I see. Well, I'll give it this: Philo is a great word for a crossword clue, but your pop would have been better off choosing Kilda. Or Skye. Much more feminine. Philo…" He frowned. "I'll have to think about that. Now, umbrella?"

"You don't want to come inside?"

"And miss our reservation?"

Maybe it's not a joint. Philo suddenly felt underdressed, but considering the way Barnaby was tapping his foot, she didn't think he'd appreciate it if she insisted on changing. She retrieved two umbrellas, and they walked in the light drizzle across the Plaza de la Constitucion and up St. George Street. Thronged with tourists even at that hour, they passed T-shirt stores and gift shops interspersed with museums and ancient buildings. The smell of popcorn and stale beer always depressed her. *It's like an amusement park instead of a significant historical site.*

"The oldest continuously inhabited city in the United States, right?" Barnaby didn't seem to notice the crowds of overweight, perspiring people wearing tops providing as much private information as their Facebook pages did. "There are those who argue San Juan, Puerto Rico, is older, but I contend that's a consequence of the indefatigable activities of Ponce de León. He sailed back and forth between Florida and Puerto Rico like one of those windup bathtub boats, leaving settlements behind like so many European cow pies."

Philo just nodded her head.

"Oh, look. That's the Oldest Schoolhouse." He paused in front of a dilapidated wooden structure to read the plaque. “Says here it was established in the eighteenth century by a Minorcan named Juan Genoply to teach little Minorcans. Huh. Who’da thunk there would be that many immigrants from one tiny island in the Mediterranean?” He glanced at Philo. “Did your father ever consider calling you Minorca?” He didn’t wait for her to reply but kept walking and talking. “There’s an awful lot of ‘oldest’ stuff here, isn’t there? Oldest House, Oldest Drugstore, Oldest Jail, Oldest Schoolhouse. So how do they know it’s the oldest? And the oldest of what? Schoolhouses in America? In the world? Were you raised in St. Augustine?”

The abrupt question caught her off guard. “No. I grew up on the west coast of Florida. Near Sarasota.”

“How’d you end up here?”

“My father and mother divorced when I was eight. Dad moved here twenty years ago and, after he retired from teaching, opened Mind Over Matter. He left it to me when he died.”

“Wow. How lucky can you be?”

In fact, she had viewed it as a burden and a curse at first, but in the last two years had come to enjoy the work and the customers. People were fascinated by the beautiful old maps and artifacts she displayed. “I didn’t think I was, but I’m getting used to it.”

“Great.” Barnaby stopped to survey the street, took a tentative step, and halted again. He whirled around and trotted back the way they had come. “Ah, here we are. Thought for a minute I’d misplaced it.” He led Philo down an alley she’d never noticed before to a tiny restaurant—little more than a hole in the wall. A chalkboard hung in its grimy window. Scrawled on it were the words Welcome to Flora’s. “Let’s see what the specials are." He read. "Well, how do you like that? Chili's on the menu. *Again.*" He held the door for her.

The interior was painted a garish turquoise. Two wobbly Formica-topped tables took up the open space. Pink vinyl stools lined the counter. A woman supported herself on its scratched and stained surface, folds of fat cushioning her elbows. On the steel shelf behind her stood a large coffee urn and a cake stand piled with dusty-looking churros. *How on earth did she wedge herself into that cramped space? She has to weigh four hundred pounds.*

Barnaby strode up to the woman. "You must be Flora. Reservations for two at six, under Swift. I know we're a trifle early, but could you squeeze us in?" Flora stared silently at him. He said heartily, "Well, then. Two bowls of your finest chili please, with all the fixings. You want a beer?" This last to Philo.

"Thanks."

He walked over to a refrigerated display case and pulled two bottles out. "Dos Equis. Excellent."

They sat at one of the tables, and Flora brought out two soup bowls filled with a dark red mess, along with a tray of chopped onions and peppers, and grated cheese. She plunked a basket of fresh tortilla chips in between the bowls. "*Buen provecho.*"

Barnaby pulled a small bottle from his pocket. "I always carry my own hot sauce. A blend of pineapple, serrano chilis, and chipotle, with a hint of chocolate." He poured a generous amount over his chili.

Philo took a tentative bite of hers. Her eyes opened wide, and she almost spit it out.

Barnaby handed her a napkin, concern coloring his face. "Whatever's the matter?"

She wiped her mouth and whispered, "This is vile."

"It is?" He gazed at his bowl. "I'm from Pennsylvania. I've only tasted the canned variety." He swished his spoon in the glop. "Is it supposed to have these little pellets in it?"

"Those are beans."

"Well, I never. I thought legumes in chili were a no-no."

"Only in Texas. Most other American recipes call for the addition of beans."

"Why are they taboo in the Lone Star state?"

Philo was only flummoxed for an instant. "Because Texans won't let anything come between them and their beef. Beans are filler. No cowboy worth his rawhide will admit he can't afford meat." *And if you believe that, I have a bridge of lions to sell you.*

"Oh." He dug into his chili. "So, is there meat in this?"

She reluctantly took another bite. "Maybe."

Barnaby swigged his beer. "Well, it's definitely filling anyway. Eat up, and I'll take you for ice cream."

Philo felt the beginning pangs of uneasiness. Yes, Barnaby was really cute, and she rather liked his staccato style of speech, but a man with no taste buds…*that could get old quickly.* She finished what she could of the chili and had another beer. Barnaby pulled a five-dollar bill out of his wallet and left it on the table. *So…that whole meal cost less than a pair of helicopter headphones.* She examined her escort with wary eyes. *A real big spender, as sweet Charity might say*. But then she took note of the glossy hair flopping across his brow and the stately aquiline nose, its tip upturned just a smidgen. *Still…very cute.*

They returned to St. George Street and strolled a few blocks to an ice cream parlor. Barnaby ordered two scoops of butter brickle ice cream in a sugar cone. Philo chose a scoop of coffee with sprinkles.

He took a lick lap around the top scoop. "My favorite flavor. It's hard to find nowadays. When I was in college and we had to pull an all-nighter, we'd go to this diner in the suburbs. Their specialty was a butter brickle sundae with hot butterscotch." He closed his eyes and smacked his lips. "Ah, salad days."

"Salad days? I thought you said it was ice cream."

He walked around her, inspecting her head. "Just checking that it's screwed on. 'Salad days' is an expression for the good old days. Halcyon days. Heyday. Days of yore. Get it?"

Philo didn't bother to reply. Opening her coin purse, she said briskly, "My treat." They found a bench outside and sat down. "You were going to tell me about your dissertation."

"I was?"

Short term memory loss? Or a phony? "What school?"

"Princeton. But let's not talk about that. I want your advice."

Aha. My new friend has something to hide. "Okay."

"I'm conducting a four-week seminar on historical methodology for six Flagler students. They're rising seniors, majoring in one or another of the social sciences. The first day or so I'll be teaching them about research methods—library, field, experimental. Then I plan to let them apply what they've learned. So I thought, why not send them on a treasure hunt?" He looked at her anxiously. "What do you think?"

"You mean, *the* treasure hunt? Byron Preiss's *Secret*? Is that why you were lurking around the book?"

Barnaby nodded vigorously. The ice cream fell out of his cone and landed on his shoe. He regarded it, clearly confounded.

When he showed no sign of recovering, Philo took charge. Handing him her cone to hold—"You eat it, you pay for it"—she went inside, pulled a wad of napkins from the container on the counter, came out, and wiped the mess off his foot. While she worked, his tongue took a surreptitious swipe at her ice cream. "I saw that!" She handed him the dirty napkins and took her cone back.

Once again, he went on as though there had been no interruption. "See, I want them to use the methods we discuss to solve the secret of the stones. The sixth image in the book is almost universally deemed to refer to St. Augustine. My objective is to set them the task of finding the casque using their powers of extrapolation and perscrutation." He glanced at her dazed face. "If perforce you find yourself without your trusty pocket thesaurus, that means detection."

"It's a great idea. I—"

"Good, good. Finished?" He clapped his hands and stood up. "That must be it. I think I'd really better make that phone call now." He walked briskly away and rounded a corner. A minute later he returned. "Ready?"

Philo decided that it was rather restful not to have to come up with clever dialogue, or even make a decision. "Where to?"

He checked his watch. Philo was amused to observe it was black plastic with a picture of Goofy on it. "I'll take you home. Early day tomorrow."

"Oh? What do you have on?" She felt a brief, unaccustomed disappointment. *I should be relieved. At least there's still time for a real supper*.

"Not me. Us. I've seen St. Augustine from the air and by train. Your shop is closed tomorrow. I propose we take a walking tour of your fair city, starting with the Castillo. I'll meet you at the Bridge of Lions at eight thirty sharp." He lifted one foot. "Wear comfortable shoes."

Well, I'll be damned. She couldn't think of anything in response, and they continued down the street to the central plaza.

As they passed under the old wooden archway leading to Aviles Street and her apartment, sirens rent the air. Barnaby pointed down King Street toward Cordova Street. "They're coming from there. Hurry." He started to drag her down the sidewalk.

She resisted. "What are you, some kind of ambulance chaser?"

"No, no. What a funny thing to say. No. Don't you hear them?"

"The sirens?"

"Yes."

"So?"

"So…I'm thinking they found the body."

Chapter Three

Everyone has a photographic memory, some just don't have any film.

—Steven Wright

Lightner Museum, Monday, June 4

"Body? What body?"

"The one in that strange building up there. Big open atrium with galleries. Makes you feel like you're in the belly of the Ark."

"Oh, the Lightner Museum. You're talking about the swimming pool."

He eyed her like she was two cards short of a full deck. "I don't recall getting wet. I stood there for maybe fifteen, twenty minutes." He closed his eyes, then opened them. "No, I'm sure there wasn't any water. Just a big room, like a concert hall. There were potted palms scattered about and some café tables. Didn't really fill the space."

Philo said impatiently, "Of course there's no water *now*. In the early 1900s, it was the world's largest indoor swimming pool. The building was originally Flagler's Hotel Alcazar, and the pool was its featured attraction."

"Oh." He tugged at her sleeve. "Are you coming?"

Up ahead she could see flashing lights. As they drew near, a line of yellow police tape barred the way. Beyond it, squad cars and crime scene vans were parked nose to tail. An ambulance—its back doors open—stood at the side entrance of the museum. Barnaby shouted at a man wearing a jacket with the words *Forensics Unit* emblazoned on its back. "Hey, you! Did you find it?"

The technician stopped and turned around. "Find what?"

"The body, of course."

He approached Barnaby and looked him up and down. "You a reporter?"

"Gosh, no."

"Then how do you know about the body?"

"I called it in."

The man lifted the tape. "Oh yeah? I think the lieutenant might want to have a word with you."

"I'm sure he does, but first I must escort my friend home. I'll be back in a trice, and—"

The agent took a firm grip of Barnaby's forearm and hauled him toward one of the police cars. Philo wasn't about to miss out on whatever tale Barnaby had to offer. She followed, trying to look both unobtrusive and official. It worked; she was able to keep up with the two men and thus listen in on a remarkable conversation.

The tech rapped on the window of the squad car. "Lieutenant Tolliver, this here fellow says he's the 9-1-1 caller."

"Oh yeah?" A paunchy man in a frayed polyester jacket that didn't match his voluminous slacks slouched out of the car. The stumpy cigar between his fingers glowed in the dark. "What's your name?"

Barnaby rose on his toes. "Do you law enforcement personnel always preface your remarks with 'Oh, yeah'? If so, it implies a lack of confidence, or worse, of imagination."

"Oh yeah?" When Barnaby didn't respond—Philo presumed because he felt he'd said it all—the detective repeated, "Name!"

"Is that important? Aren't you more interested in my statement?"

Tolliver bellied up to within two inches of Barnaby. If he meant to intimidate, it failed, as Barnaby gazed obstinately over the top of his head. He soldiered on. "First things first. Name?"

Barnaby set his lips tightly together. "As an American citizen, I'm entitled to my privacy—and that includes remaining anonymous when reporting a possible crime."

Tolliver's face turned purple. He gestured at a uniformed cop. "Sergeant Landman?" When the officer approached, he said curtly, "Cuff him, Steve."

"Hey!"

The sergeant asked, "What's the charge, Lieutenant?"

"Interfering with an investigation. Intent to convey false or misleading information."

"Hey!"

Barnaby seemed to have lost the power to utter more than a single syllable. In any other circumstance, Philo might have rejoiced, but she knew now was not the time to rig for silent running. "Lieutenant? Sir? His name is Barnaby Swift. He teaches at Flagler."

"Oh? And you are?"

"Philo Brice. I own Mind over Matter, the bookstore on Aviles Street."

"And what can you tell us about this event?"

Ulp. "Nothing. I've only just met Mr. Swift. We had dinner tonight and were coming home when we heard the sirens." She didn't look at Barnaby, but she could hear his snorts and whinnies. *He'd better not be mad at me. I'm saving his butt.*

Tolliver turned to Barnaby. "Don't tell me. You didn't actually *make* the call. You're one of those nosy parkers. Well, this is a crime scene, buster." He waved a grouchy hand at him. "Now get out of here."

Barnaby stammered, "But…but wait. I can tell you about the…the victim."

Tolliver spun around. "What did you say?"

He took a deep breath. "I think I saw it happen."

The detective spat. "Oh, for Christ's sake. Come with me." He led Barnaby and Philo into the museum. Police swarmed the interior, currently lit by searingly bright floodlights. The chamber rose three stories, framed by open galleries. From where they were standing, the cement floor sloped gradually upward to the far end.

Barnaby whispered, "Now I see it. We're in the deep end of the pool, aren't we?" His eyes went to the top gallery. "Did they have a high dive?"

"I think they had a swing."

He whistled appreciatively.

They passed a hostess station, unattended. A sign said Welcome to the Café Alcazar. Tolliver indicated a small wrought iron table in a corner. "Sit." They sat. He pulled a chair from a nearby table and sat down as well. Sergeant Steve leaned against a column, arms folded.

Tolliver paused in thought, then suddenly barked, "Why weren't you here when we arrived?"

Barnaby's mouth, which had opened—Philo feared to release a stream of nonsense—snapped shut. Inspiration dawned. She glanced at Barnaby. "That's who you called at the ice cream store, wasn't it?" Before he could respond, she turned back to the lieutenant. "We were halfway up St. George Street. When we heard the sirens, we rushed back as fast as we could."

Tolliver scratched his head. "If you weren't here, how did you know there was a victim?"

Philo prodded Barnaby. "Tell him."

Barnaby muttered something.

"What?"

"It's not that easy. He's going to think I'm crazy. Or guilty."

"Just tell him whatever it was you saw," she said encouragingly. *I hope I'm not signing his arrest warrant.*

"All right." Barnaby sighed loudly. "I was supposed to meet someone here at four thirty. When I arrived, the place appeared to be empty, and I figured he'd skipped out." He sniffed. "I should have known. He seemed a bit spacey on the phone. Probably just another charlatan."

Charlatan? What is Barnaby involved in?

"What were you meeting him about?"

"That's not important."

Tolliver looked like he was going to insist, but said merely, "Go on."

"I waited fifteen minutes, but he still didn't show. I had a date"—he touched the back of Philo's hand—"and didn't want to be late, so I left."

"While you were waiting, did you look around?"

Barnaby suddenly blushed. "Not…not really. I mean, I went…er…"

"To the men's room?"

"Yeah. To freshen up." He averted his gaze from Philo. "It was almost five when I finished, so I hightailed it out the side door. And that's when I saw it."

"It?"

"This big object falling. It must have come from one of the upper galleries. I only caught a glimpse."

"And you didn't stop and look?"

He shook his head. "No. I assumed it was a trash bag. You know, the cleaning lady didn't feel like lugging it all the way down the stairs and threw it over the balustrade. I didn't want to—couldn't—be late for my date."

The detective listened, brow creased. "Okay. Then what made you change your mind?"

"Oh. Well. Here's the thing." He paused and closed his eyes. "We were eating ice cream on a bench in front of one of those souvenir shops. You know, the kind with T-shirts and bumper stickers and little shot glasses." He elbowed Philo. "I knew a girl who collected them. She was a teetotaler." When she didn't reward him with a laugh, he resumed just as Tolliver was signaling to Steve. "Then there was my cousin's husband. He collected beer cans. He stacked the cans like wallpaper along an entire wall in his basement. When he'd covered that wall floor to ceiling, he—"

"Started on another wall?" The sergeant named Steve seemed fascinated.

"He opened his own brewery. I asked him if it was to have a ready supply of wallpaper for the rest of his house. What do you think he said?"

"What?"

"He said, no, it was to have a ready supply of beer for the rest of his life."

"Huh." Steve leaned back again, disappointed.

After a minute, Barnaby continued. "I had suffered a slight setback with my cone, and Philo here kindly went for help. While she was gone, I amused myself by looking through the window. This little girl was reaching up for a teddy bear and accidently knocked it off the shelf."

This was met with puzzled silence. Finally, Tolliver asked, "Window? Little girl?"

"At the T-shirt emporium."

Philo knew Barnaby longed to say, "Try to keep up, would you?" but thankfully thought better of it.

Tolliver patted his holster. It had no effect on Barnaby. "Uh-huh. And?"

"Well, I got this image—one of those repressed memories. You know, like under hypnosis, when something resurfaces that happened to you when you were three? I did that once." He smiled at Philo, his eyes sparkling. "We were at Coney Island and there was this booth and the man said he could hypnotize me for a dollar. So I borrowed a buck from my brother…" He cast a nervous glance at the cop. "Well, actually, I nipped it from him. Only thing I ever stole in my life. Honest, Officer. And besides, Nicky took my bike without asking and wrecked it trying to fly off a cliff, so that dollar was partial payment." He began to grumble. "Never did get another bike. Nicky got a record player *and* a scooter, but no…"

Tolliver got up and walked away. Steve gallantly stepped up. "Um, Mr. Swift? You remembered something?"

"What? Oh yes. I could see it in my mind's eye—" He winked at Philo, then abruptly straightened. "An engram. That's the word I was searching for. An engram."

"Engram. Got it."

"That what I'd seen falling was a body. I hadn't focused on the object then, but now I feel sure it had legs and arms, just like the teddy bear. Only these were flailing. So, naturally, once it sank in, I called you folks." His last words were flush with self-congratulation.

Tolliver sat down again and put his beefy hands on his knees. "That's all? You done?"

Philo held up a palm. "Lieutenant Tolliver? I have a question."

"*What*?"

"Could he take a look at the body? Maybe it's the person he was supposed to meet."

Tolliver scratched his head. "Miss Brice, I should offer you a job. Mr. Swift? Will you come with me?"

Barnaby shot a look at Philo that made her shiver. *Did I do the right thing? He obviously has secrets.* He'd lied at first about who he was. He refused to tell her the subject of his dissertation. And now this. *Maybe I should go home before I get sucked in deeper.* She began to edge away, but Barnaby caught her hand.

"Please don't leave. I may need a comforting shoulder. Or bail money."

The lieutenant preceded them to the waiting ambulance. Barnaby climbed inside with him. A minute later they emerged. Tolliver pulled out a notebook. "Okay, spill. You say his name is Robert Cottrell. How do you know him?"

"We were pen pals."

"What, you mean like on email or Gab?"

"No, real pen pals…as in writing letters to each other. With a pen."

"Don't get smart with me, Swift." He licked his pencil. "If you hadn't met face to face, how did you know what he looked like?"

Barnaby's eyes flickered. "He…uh…sent me his photo. So I could pick him out of the crowd."

"A photo, huh." The detective peered suspiciously at him. "You do know how to use a computer, right?"

"Of course." Barnaby gave him a baffled look. "Don't you?"

"We're not discussing me. Now, once again, how do you know him?"

"Mr. Cottrell and I were members of a club."

"A club?"

"Yes."

"What kind of club?"

Barnaby's mouth twisted. Philo supposed he was coming up with another whopper. "We…uh…we swap stories about ghost sightings."

"Really."

Looks like the good detective has his number too.

"Yeah." Barnaby warmed to his narrative. "He wrote me that he had evidence an apparition was haunting this building. He wanted to show it to me."

Tolliver rubbed his eyes. "Let me guess. Ghost spoor?"

"Um. Yes."

Chapter Four

The wardrobe is always the last piece of the puzzle. When you step into the clothing, that's the final step to figuring out that character.

—Mia Wasikowska

Lightner Museum, Monday, June 4

Tolliver stood. "Okay, thanks for the identification. It confirms the license we found in his wallet. Leave your contact information with Sergeant Landman. I'll be following up with you later." He flipped a finger at Steve, who wrote down Barnaby's number.

When the policemen had gone back inside the building, Barnaby blew out his cheeks. "Come on, Philo." He ducked under the yellow tape and trotted down the street. Once they turned a corner and were out of sight, he broke into a run. Philo couldn't keep up, but when she reached the shop, he was waiting.

"My lady."

"My lady, my eye. What was that all about?"

He contrived to look innocent. "I presume you're referring to my ghost club."

"Was *any* of that farrago true?"

He drew back. "Well, I like that. Here I've welcomed you into my confidence, broken bread with you, cast my affections before you like pearls before…er…a swan, and this is how you repay me? Where is the trust I so richly deserve?"

Philo, rather than being intimidated by this rant, was enchanted. And perplexed. "What on earth are you talking about? What confidence?"

"I told you—" He broke off and spoke to the indigo sky sprinkled with brilliant white asterisks. "I told her, didn't I? That I was considering using *The Secret* treasure hunt as an educational tool for my young scholars." His eyes seized upon hers. "Mr. Cottrell claimed to have some information."

"Cottrell…the dead guy." She put her hands on her hips. "Well, why didn't you tell the police that? Why go on about some stupid apparition?"

He was affronted. "I'll have you know ghosts exist and walk among us all the time." As if to prove it, a tiny dust devil skirled up at Philo's feet and dissolved when it reached her face.

She waved the motes away. "The truth now. Were you there to see a man about a ghost or a treasure?"

"Well, I wasn't there to see him about a dog."

"Barnaby!"

"All right. I made up the ghost. At least this particular ghost. Although…" He rubbed his chin. "I'm betting in a place like that—a luxury hotel frequented by the elite of the city, some of whom indubitably drowned in the pool—all kinds of ghosts drift in and out."

"Barnaby?" She was feeling cold and tired.

He touched the goose bumps on her arm. "You're chilled. Look, I'll tell you all tomorrow. I know I said the Bridge of Lions at eight thirty, but you could use some beauty sleep—it might revive your customary ruddy glow. I'll pick you up here at ten."

"For what?"

"How soon they forget! For our excursion. Together we shall tour the monuments of this magnificent old burg. It will be grand." He looked her over. "I would suggest a fitted dress—something to accentuate those comely curves of yours. Perhaps in a light teal—it would set off your porcelain epidermis to a T. No, strike that. A deep, rich coffee color to match those liquid mocha eyes." He touched the messy bun at the back of her head. "May I ask how long your xanthic tresses are?"

Philo took a step back. "What?"

"Apparently vocabulary isn't your strong point. How about flaxen? Saffron? Blonde? Yellow?" When she remained silent, her mouth open, he sniffed. "Oh well, perhaps someday you will favor me with a view of said tresses. So, ten?"

I think a quick escape is best. "Ten it is." She whirled and ran down the alley to her apartment house door. She heard his whistle start up, then fade away. She recognized the tune. "*Waltzing Matilda.*"

****

Philo's apartment, Tuesday, June 5

The sun streaming through the open window woke Philo up. "Oh geez, it's late!" She threw off the covers and skipped to the kitchen. "I'm coming, Delilah!" She pulled a package wrapped in wax paper from the refrigerator, plucked two tiny mouse bodies out, and carried them into the bedroom. Occupying one wall was a fifty-gallon aquarium furnished with branches and moss. A variegated kingsnake, striped red, black, and yellow, lay curled in a ball in the water dish. "Delilah! Get out of that bowl. You know it's for drinking." The snake uncurled to her full two-foot length and glided over to the glass. She lifted her head and knocked gently on it.

Philo reached in to retrieve the snake. Delilah wound around her arm and squeezed affectionately. "Who's my sweet 'Lilah?" Philo let the snake slide back into her nest and laid her breakfast on the moss. "Lookee here, honey—two nice fresh pinkies for you." The snake glided over, her tongue flicking at the food.

She answered a knock to find one of the two other tenants of her building standing on the mat. As usual, Ida Kink was in a foul mood. She wore pajama bottoms and a torn T-shirt, any support apparatus beneath it manifestly absent. Which was unfortunate, since her bosom reflected the weight of all sixty-eight of her years. In her hand was a copy of the St. Augustine *Crier.* "They put my paper in your mailbox *again.*" Her tone was accusatory.

"Sorry. Don't know why they keep making that mistake. I don't even have a subscription."

"*Humph.* You'd better not be sneaking a free read, that's all." The woman stuck the newspaper under a sweaty arm and marched down the hall.

As she turned to go back inside, her other neighbor opened his door. "Ah, I thought I heard your mellifluous voice, Philo. Good morning! You're looking ravishing as usual."

"Hello, Joseph." Philo was not surprised to find the eighty-year-old impeccably garbed, although lately he'd mellowed a bit and allowed her—but only on Sunday mornings—to see him in a silk dressing gown. Today he was in full lawyer regalia—a charcoal pinstripe suit and tartan vest, with blue socks and matching handkerchief. "Are you going somewhere?"

"For a stroll, my dear. Just for a stroll. Have to keep the old ticker cranking, you know." He gave an elaborate sigh. "How I miss those thrilling days when I was up at dawn preparing my defense for some unlucky soul who found himself on the sinister side of the law." He peered at Philo from under bushy white eyebrows. "You haven't been accused of a prosecutable offense lately, have you? It would do the old man good to have a case now and then."

"Not recently." Philo gave a little hiccup as the events of the night before galloped across her memory. "Although *someone* may need a lawyer." She pointed at the paper in his hand. Splashed across the top was the headline "Body Plummets to Bottom of Dry Pool, Crushing Potted Palm."

His eyes widened. "Oh dear. When did this occur and where?"

"In the Lightner. Last night."

"How do you know? Was it on the radio?"

"I was there."

Joseph took a step back. "You saw a man die?"

"Oh, no. He was already dead." When this seemed to distress Joseph even more, she said hastily, "I was passing the building when the police arrived. I…uh…talked to them."

"You *what*? No, my dear, I must insist. As your solicitor, I order you not to say another word to the police until you've conferred with me."

Philo thought he was joking, but his expression was sober. "I didn't do anything you have to worry about. They were more interested in what Barnaby had to say."

"Barnaby?"

Shoot. Joseph knew her parents were dead and as such often adopted a fatherly attitude, particularly on the subject of the men in her life. "My date. We went out for"—*gulp*—"chili."

"Chili is no excuse for manslaughter. I don't want you associating with people who consort with dead bodies. I'm putting my foot down."

"Oh, he wasn't involved. Not really, anyway." *Uh-oh.*

Joseph zeroed in on her misstep. " 'Not really'? The police questioned him? What for? Philo—"

Behind her the telephone began to ring. *In the nick of time.* "Sorry! Have to get that. Talk to you later." She backed inside and slammed the door.

When she picked up the receiver, a buoyant voice trilled, "Good morning, Carmen Sandiego! Ready for the next mission?"

"Barnaby?"

"*C'est moi, c'est moi*, I blush to disclose."

"How did you get my number?"

"Questions, questions. Don't you want to know what I have planned for us today?"

She wavered. *Joseph could be right. Do I really want to be alone with him? Just because he has alluring tourmaline eyes and a voice I could bathe in doesn't mean he's safe.* She could hear tapping through the phone. *No harm in asking.* "All right, what?"

"I have mapped out a full day of sightseeing for us. You shall be astounded and amazed. As the peerless ringmaster Johnathan Iverson used to intone, 'Ladies and gentleman, boys and girls, children of all ages, get ready for the Greatest Show on Earth!' "

"What about your class?"

"Turns out it doesn't start until next Monday. I have to put together the syllabus and reading list before then. And research the clues."

"Clues?"

"Yes, yes. I told you yesterday. The quest. *The Secret*. The treasure. Weren't you listening?"

Philo gave up. "All right. Are you coming to pick me up?"

"I'm at your gate."

"Well, you're just going to have to wait there. I'm not dressed."

"You're unclothed at this hour? Heavens. I didn't know I was dating a slugabed, an idler, a lazybones. The modern equivalent of Zola's *Nana*, the courtesan. I'll have to reconsider my strategy."

"I'll be down shortly." She hung up. *What did Barnaby say I should wear? A teal dress?* Hmm. *Some day when I have time, I'll shop for one.* She drew on a short, olive-colored shift that brought out the hazel flecks in her eyes and brushed her hair. As she reached for her purse, her stomach growled. *Breakfast! I almost forgot to eat!* She checked the clock. *Two minutes, tops.* She cut a wedge of quiche and stuck it in the toaster oven. She had set a mug under her one-cup coffee maker when she heard a noise in the living room.

"Says here they know who the victim is, but that's about it."

"Barnaby?"

Her new friend walked into the kitchen holding the *Crier*. Today his togs of choice were a set of surplus army fatigues, a cowboy hat, and flip-flops. He read from the front page. " 'Robert Cottrell owned Granada Liquors on Valencia Street. He was seventy-six. A member of the Kiwanis and Trinity Episcopal church, he leaves behind a wife, Harriet, a son, Norton, and a dog, Clem.' " He looked up. "Without his beloved master, whatever shall happen to poor Clem? Will he eke out his life guarding Robert's tomb like that Scottish terrier, Greyfriars Bobby? Or perhaps…" He beetled his brows at Philo. "Are you amenable to adopting the mutt? That would definitely beef up your good karma. It could mean the difference between coming back as a gnat or a butterfly."

Philo heard none of this, distracted by a sudden scary thought. *Is Joseph right? Is Barnaby dangerous?*

Barnaby put the paper down. "What's the matter?"

"*How did you get in here?*"

Chapter Five

Wow, this place is amazing! It's like Disney World, only it's real!

—Anonymous St. Augustine visitor

Philo's apartment, Tuesday, June 5

"Who, me? That nice gentleman from across the hall saw me trying to pick your lock and used your spare key to let me in. You really should find a less traditional hiding place. The transom is too, too obvious." Barnaby scratched his head. "Perhaps behind the macramé hanging in the hall? Or under the pot with the plastic tulips?" He inspected her dress. "Nice color on you. May I have a cup of coffee?"

What the hell? Philo handed him the mug and got another down from the cabinet.

"That quiche looks delicious."

"Yes, it does." She put it on a plate and cut herself a large forkful. "*Mmm.*" She expected him to continue pestering her, but instead, he pulled a candy bar from his pocket and started to unwrap it. "You're not going to eat *that* for breakfast, are you?"

"This? It's quite nutritious. Nuts are high in protein and antioxidants; the coconut abounds in selenium and manganese, and the chocolate provides the minimum daily requirement of pleasure." He took a bite. "The Flagler College commons was closed, and I'm afraid I'm a little short after our date. I don't get paid until next week."

"Oh, for…Here." She handed him the quiche and cut another slice. "So what else does the article say?"

"Not much. Robert Cottrell fell from the top gallery. Even though a tree broke his fall, he still sustained fatal injuries. I suppose landing on the concrete floor didn't help." He read on. "Thank God—the police only say they interviewed several unnamed bystanders. They don't mention me."

"They may be saving you for further questioning."

Barnaby blanched and dropped his fork.

She went on. "That reminds me: you promised to explain why you didn't tell Lieutenant Tolliver the real reason for your rendezvous with Mr. Cottrell."

"Isn't it obvious?"

"Not to me."

"I've discovered this treasure hunt is a cutthroat business. I expected to send the students on a lighthearted quest, which would provide them with a field guide—a vade mecum, if you will—for their future research efforts. Working in teams, they would pore over the clues, explore the sites, and come up with the solution by the end of term. Instead, I find a dark underworld of conspiracies and confidences, of rivalries and deadly games. People are what you might call bewitched by Preiss and his pictures."

"It wouldn't have anything to do with a fortune in precious stones to be won?"

"No, I don't think so. Most of the jewels are semiprecious and therefore not worth a lot in monetary terms. Let's see…there's an aquamarine, a garnet, a sapphire—that's the one in St. Augustine…The only other one I remember is an opal. The players—they're called 'seekers'—are generally more interested in unraveling clues and finding the solution. At least the ones I've communicated with." He shook his head. "It's amazing how engrossing a simple puzzle can be."

"I see. And you have plunged headfirst into this underworld?"

"Of course. I have to reconnoiter the battlefield before I allow the little darlings to parachute into it." He sipped his coffee. "Most important right now—besides scoping out the sites—is to ascertain if Mr. Cottrell was murdered."

"Murdered!" Philo felt her throat tighten. "What would make you think that?"

"As I said, this *Secret* stuff is no walk in the park. Another seeker may have wanted to silence Cottrell. Or get him out of the way."

"Could it…could it be related to whatever you were meeting him about?"

"Not sure yet." He rapped the newspaper. "According to the article, the police have very little evidence to go on. And so far no discernable motive. At this point, they're leaning toward a verdict of suicide. I'll let them do the snooping into his private life. It's only fair they have some of the glory."

"Well, if they determine it's a case of homicide instead, let's hope they don't fixate on you."

"I'm much too insignificant for that." He rose and put his cup in the sink. "You ready?"

"For what?"

He rolled his eyes, but softened it with a grin. "We are about to venture into the wilds of La Florida. Don't forget your purse."

When they reached the street, he unlatched a shoulder bag and rummaged through it.

"You have a *man* bag?" Philo smirked.

"I'll have you know this is a gender-neutral satchel. If you bought one too, we could match." He plucked at his camo shirt. "While we're at it, we should consider coordinating our outfits as well."

Not for the first time, Philo found herself speechless.

Barnaby unfolded a map of the old city. "All righty then." He pointed to their left. "First, the Governor's House."

"I know."

He swung his finger to the right. "Over there, the Bridge of Lions."

"I know."

He pursed his lips. "You're not being helpful. Of course you recognize these structures—you live here."

"Well, what do you want from me?"

He answered patiently, "In case you've forgotten, we're looking for likely spots for the treasure. I assume it's in a public place, one that's remained relatively unaltered for the last forty years. And one that fits the clues in the poem. You read the book, right?"

She hated to admit it. "Some of it, yes. Yesterday afternoon, after you left the shop."

"Good. Now, put your oar in the water, gird your loins, sink your teeth into it. You may employ your own idiom if you have a particular favorite. What other historic sites dot this metropolis?"

"Hundreds. The place is crawling with them—from the sixteenth-century Spanish sites like the Fountain of Youth and the Castillo de San Marcos, to the nineteenth-century palaces of Flagler's Gilded Age."

"*Hmm.*" He tapped his teeth. "I propose a whirlwind tour before we start whittling down. I've already walked the Bridge of Lions. Did you know it was built in 1927 by a developer, just so people could reach his new housing tract?"

Philo started walking across the square.

"Where are you going?"

"To the trolley stop."

He loped after her. "Good idea. I wasn't looking forward to schlepping all over the city. How much money do you have?"

She shook her head. "I'm not paying for you, if that's what you expect. This is your junket."

He emptied his pockets and cocked his head like Charlie Chaplin. Seeing that resistance was futile, she sighed and opened her purse. "I happen to have a couple of train tickets I bought for my friends from North Dakota. We'll use them."

"What made your northern friends unworthy of your largesse?"

"It wasn't their fault. A late spring blizzard hit Fargo. By the time they dug out, the spring floods had begun. They'll come next year."

They waited at a stop on St. George Street until a five-car, open-sided trolley came trundling by. It took them down Cordova Street past the Memorial Presbyterian Church, stopping at the entrance to an elegant red-trimmed stucco building. The tinny voice of the tour guide rose above the rumble of the train's engine. "This imposing Spanish Renaissance edifice was Henry Flagler's first hotel in St. Augustine, the Ponce de León. Flagler, who partnered with John D. Rockefeller in Standard Oil, discovered the salubrious winter climate of Florida in the 1880s. The hotel is now home to Flagler College."

Barnaby opened his satchel and dug out a packet of flyers, held together with a rubber band. He pulled one from the middle marked Flagler College. "Says here the student dining hall was the former ballroom. It has striking Tiffany stained-glass windows, carved wooden chairs, and gold-leaf ceilings. Must be splendid to be a student."

"I imagine they let the faculty inside too."

"I hope to find out before my next meal."

As they drove past the Lightner, Philo noticed a remnant of yellow tape fluttering in the gutter. "How do you think the investigation is going?"

"For some inexplicable reason, I have not been made privy to Detective Tolliver's recent progress, if any."

Several people got off at the distillery, more at the chocolate factory. There were very few left as they rode back down King Street and turned right onto Aviles Street. The trolley bumped and swayed on the uneven bricks. Tourists walking down the middle of the ten-foot-wide street scrambled to get out of the way. Barnaby pointed out Philo's store as they passed it—rather unnecessarily, in her view.

The trolley went down a side street and hung a left onto the riverside boulevard, which took them past the huge stone walls of the Castillo de San Marcos and finally to the Fountain of Youth. At each stop, Barnaby hopped off and took photographs. By the time they reached the Fountain of Youth, it was lunchtime. "There's a sports bar over there. Let's try that."

Barnaby offered to pay, leaving Philo both awed and charmed, until she read the chalkboard. "BOGO DAY: Buy one get one free."

They ordered beers and hamburgers and sat in the dark bar looking out at the sunny street. Across the way was a park with a children's playground. Barnaby squinted. "Hey, look! There's a merry-go-round!" Kids swarmed the antique horses, squealing in delight. "I haven't been on one of those since my brother and I rode the one on the National Mall. Want to go for a ride?" Barnaby was practically panting.

"You have to be under four feet tall."

"Really? So unfair." He paid the cashier. "Let's go take a look anyway." He sprinted across the street, barely avoiding the cars. By the time Philo caught up to him, he was standing at a fence watching the children climb off the slowly revolving ride and run to their parents. "Aren't the horses fabulous! See that one?" A beautiful white mare, its neck arched, its saddle gleaming with gilt, flowed past, rising and falling on its pole. "Ooh, and that one." A dappled gray and carmine stallion, its mouth open as if it were whinnying, came into view. It was painted with silver armor. "It looks like a war horse."

"They've even got a painted pony."

Barnaby frowned. "They're all painted, Philo. You *do* know these aren't real horses?"

"I meant the pinto there." She pointed at a horse covered in large splotches of chestnut and white. "They're sometimes called painted ponies."

The carousel picked up speed. The horses flashed past, moving up and down in time with the music. When it finally came to a stop, Barnaby turned back toward the street. “I’ve got to go download these pictures from my phone. You coming?”

“Where are you going?”

“Your place.”

“Oh, then, I don’t mind if I tag along.”

They caught a public bus that took them to the square. Barnaby led the way to Philo’s apartment. When she graciously consented to unlock the door, he barged in, stopping short in the living room. “Where’s your computer?”

She led him to a recess off the dining room, where an antique desk littered with catalogues and books faced the window. Barnaby sat down and proceeded to download the hundreds of shots he’d taken. Every so often he’d jump up and crow, then peer closer at the screen and drop back into the seat. Philo busied herself in the kitchen. It was nearing five o’clock when she came out to the study and looked over his shoulder. “Anything grab you?”

“Oh, yeah. Everything.” He slumped. “Where do I send my students? Ripley’s? The Fountain of Youth? The Castillo? For all I know, the treasure could be buried in a vat of chocolate at Whetstone’s.”

“Or in a whiskey barrel at the distillery.”

“You’re not helping.” He looked up at her. “Are you having fun?”

Philo blinked. *I am, aren’t I?* “Yes.”

“Do you mind if I kiss you?”

“What?”

He stood up, pulled her into his arms, and gave her a mighty smack. “Been meaning to do that since this morning. You’re a good sport, Philo.”

Doesn’t get more romantic than that. “Ur, thanks.”

He gathered up his phone and a thumb drive he'd apparently commandeered. "Gotta go. Will you be here when I get back?"

"I live here, Barnaby."

"Oh, right." He kissed her again, and left.

Chapter Six

The nice thing about doing a crossword puzzle is, you know there is a solution.

—Stephen Sondheim

Philo's apartment, Saturday, June 9

Philo didn't know whether Barnaby would return in five minutes or five days, so she wasn't too worried when he failed to appear on Wednesday, or even Thursday. Friday she had to man the shop. Summer had returned with a vengeance, and customers swarmed into the tiny store, most likely to get out of the sun roasting the cobblestones of Aviles Street and anything walking on them. It wasn't until Saturday morning, with no word from him for four days, that she was forced to entertain the possibility that he had left her life as abruptly as he had entered it.

She finished her coffee and walked to the corner newsstand to pick up a newspaper. When she read the headline, she had an inkling of what may have precipitated his disappearance.

Splashed across the front page in forty-eight-point Franklin Gothic was this: "Extra! Corpse's Wife Dead Too—Suicide Pact or Crime Wave?" *Couldn't be.* She took the paper inside and laid it open on the kitchen table. The article was above the fold.

"Harriet Cottrell, wife of Robert Cottrell, recently deceased, was found dead early this morning at the Fountain of Youth. Police state that she drowned in the Spring House, but do not elaborate on how she got inside. The park is closed and padlocked at night, with security cameras and guards. At the press conference, Carl Harris, the manager, explained that it is common to catch treasure hunters or tourists trying to sneak into the compound. Police have obtained the surveillance tapes and are reviewing them. They are as yet unwilling to make any connection between Mrs. Cottrell's death and that of her husband five days earlier. Robert Cottrell fell from the top gallery of the Lightner Museum on June 4.

"This article will be updated online as more information is available."

She raised her eyes from the text. "Where the hell is Barnaby?"

"Right here."

Philo jumped. "What are you, some kind of magician who can shrink yourself and slip through the keyhole?"

Barnaby—decked out in madras Bermuda shorts and a British army uniform shirt complete with epaulets—gestured behind him. "The door's wide open."

"But the gate downstairs is locked."

He grinned. "Oh, I picked up a trick back when I lived in Chicago. You press all the buttons repeatedly until some kind soul buzzes you in."

"There are only three of us in this building."

"Then I got lucky. That nice old gentleman in the tartan waistcoat who let me in last Tuesday answered the tocsin. I believe his name is Brighton. We passed the time of day before I took my leave in order to brighten your spirits with my presence. Say"—his eyes sparkled—"played that card rather skillfully, didn't I?"

I'd better have a word with Joseph before he opens the borders without screening arrivals again.

Barnaby moved around her and cast an eye at the broadsheet. "Looks like it's all over the tabloids."

Philo felt a twinge of fear. "You already knew about Mrs. Cottrell?"

He nodded. "I was there."

"*Again*? You're beginning to concern me. At the Fountain of Youth?"

"Yes. See, many seekers believe the sixth casque is buried somewhere in the park."

"And what does this have to do with Harriet Cottrell?"

"Both Cottrells were deeply engaged in the hunt. They were on the forum."

"Forum."

"The St. Augustine forum. One of many Facebook groups dedicated to solving the puzzles. That's how I met Robert."

"Did you know Harriet, too?"

"I didn't know either of them, at least not well."

Philo thought of something. "You had arranged to meet Robert. Did you do the same with Harriet?"

"Uh-huh. The brochure had been returned to her after the autopsy, and she said she'd be happy to share it with me. I think Robert told her I wasn't a threat. Damned decent of him."

"Brochure?" *He's like ketchup. I have to turn him upside down and pound the information out of him.*

"Yes. A pamphlet that Robert was sure held a major clue. He found it in a filing cabinet in the basement of Proctor Library at the college. The police retrieved it, along with his wallet, from his body. When I called Harriet to offer my condolences, she volunteered to let me see it."

"When were you supposed to meet?"

"Yesterday evening at six."

"At the Fountain of Youth?"

"At the entrance."

"But why there?" She shook the paper. "It says here the park closes at five."

"True. Actually, our original plan was to get together at Ripley's—or rather, at a bar next to it. She called at five thirty to tell me she was on her way. I was just setting out when I got a text from her asking to meet me instead in front of the Fountain of Youth. She was super excited. I know because the text was all in caps." He stopped. "Is that coffee?" He pointed at the mug in Philo's hand.

She silently handed it to him.

"Thanks. See, most of the players claim the casque is a clue."

"A clue? Isn't the casque the object of the search?"

He frowned at her. "I thought you had informed yourself on the topic. Never mind. I can see that I shall have to walk you through it." He settled himself on the kitchen chair and sipped his coffee. "In 1909 a gardener at the Fountain of Youth was clearing brush around the spring and dug up a silver capsule shaped like an egg. Inside was a parchment dated 1513 documenting Ponce de León's arrival and mentioning a spring with 'sweet' water. The presumption is that Preiss thought it would be amusing—or maybe muddy things up—to bury his own casque nearby. Me, I'm skeptical. It's too easy."

Philo sat down with her own mug. "Why shouldn't it be easy?"

"Remember, this quest has been going on since 1982. If it was easy, all twelve boxes would have been dug up long ago. No, I'm sure it's somewhere obscure—or out of the ordinary, like a parking lot or under the Bridge of Lions."

Philo got up, put two slices of bread into the toaster, and cracked two eggs into a skillet. "You said you were originally going to meet at Ripley's. Why the change?"

"The better question is, why Ripley's in the first place?"

"All right, I'll bite. Did Harriet give a reason for choosing it?"

"No."

Philo waited. Finally, she prompted, "So…why were you meeting?"

"To deliver the brochure. Duh." He paused. "When she changed her mind at the last minute, I wasn't able to ask her if the venue held some significance. Because, well, she was dead."

"She had obviously come across a new clue."

His brow cleared. "Yes, that's it."

She decided to let him off the hook. "Okay, you received an enigmatic text from Mrs. Cottrell and raced up to the Fountain of Youth."

"Cantered. It was more of a canter, but yes. I cantered along up to the park. Sure enough, it being after five, it was locked up tight. I could hear the whirring of video cameras overhead." He raised his eyes to the ceiling and ducked dramatically. "Say, do you suppose they use drones? That would be nifty. And really enhance the security." When she didn't react, he went on. "I hear folks are always trying to get in there, even though it's private property. The city wants to designate it a historic site and has tried to wrest it from the owners for decades, to no avail." He swiped one of the pieces of toast before she could stop him. "How extraordinary it must be to own a tourist attraction." He looked at Philo as though he expected an answer.

"Uh."

He took a bite. "So, I'm loitering there when I hear a screech."

"A screech. From Harriet?"

"It sounded more like a great blue heron—sort of a rasping squawk. I had no idea where Harriet was. I assumed she couldn't get inside either, what with all the security, so I backtracked to the bar to wait for her there. After an hour or so, I gave up and went home."

"If the screech came from her, you might have actually heard her dying."

"Operative word: 'if.' According to the article, she drowned. I don't think you can screech when you're drowning." To illustrate, he opened his mouth and made a gagging sound. "See? Is one of those for me?"

She slid one of the eggs onto a plate and handed it to him. "So this happened last night. What have you been doing since Tuesday?" She hoped her tone was as casual as his.

"I *told* you. I've been printing the photographs, writing the course syllabus, and putting together a reading list." He frowned at her again. "Perhaps we should get your hearing checked."

"My hearing's fine. It's your communication skills that are lacking. I can't imagine how you do in a classroom."

"Hey! My students love me. Why, a young lady once told me I was like the Pied Piper of Hamlin—leading them into a life of high adventure."

"How old was she? Four?"

"Twelve. She was one of my charges at summer camp."

"So I see you've been gainfully employed at least once in your life."

His nose went up. "I'll have you know I was there for three summers—ascending to the rarified rank of senior counselor. I even won an award for most pounds shed by my unit."

"Wow." Philo took her plate to the table and sat down. "Let's see the photographs."

"Not yet. I actually came by to get that copy of Preiss's book. Do you still have it downstairs? I need to take a magnifying glass to the sixth image."

"That's the one that refers to St. Augustine, right?"

"The very one. I found it online, but I couldn't get the damn thing to zoom in. Are you done yet?"

She held on to her plate to keep him from snatching it away. "In a minute."

When she'd finished her breakfast and rinsed the dishes, they descended the stairs and entered the shop through the back door. Barnaby went straight to the table. "It's not here."

"That's odd. I saw it yesterday when I opened the shop." Philo scanned the other tables. "Someone must have bought it. I had quite a crush of customers toward the end of the day. I'll order another." She went to her desk. Barnaby wandered the shop displacing books and rearranging the maps. She was about to remonstrate when she saw movement outside. "Someone's out there."

"Shop's closed."

"I know that," she snapped.

Just then a heavy knock sounded.

"Police! Open up."

****

Mind over Matter, Saturday, June 9

Philo watched as they led Barnaby away. She was terrified. She may not have known him long, but she'd developed something of an affection for the lunatic. The officer had been soothing. "We just want to ask him a few questions, miss. He's not under arrest."

Barnaby had given her a gloomy smile before sliding into the back of the squad car.

Two hours later she looked up to see his face plastered against the store's glass door. She ran to open it. "Are you okay? They let you go?"

He attempted to enter jauntily but gave up, staggered to a chair, and sank down on it. There he sprawled, arms and legs flopping like a Raggedy Andy doll. "It was *ghastly*."

"They didn't beat you, did they?"

His jaw dropped. "Beat me? This isn't North Korea. No, I was treated with the proper respect due any American citizen."

"Then what was so ghastly?"

"The police station. It smelled like Kung Pao chicken and sweat. And it must be the last place in America where you're allowed to smoke indoors. The good lieutenant puffed on his cheroot the entire time I was there." He sniffed his collar and wrinkled his nose.

Philo's patience was beginning to ravel. "You can wash later. Why did they take you down to the station?"

"Well, it turns out those security cameras pick up pedestrians who happen to be standing on the street outside, minding their own business. My mug appeared on the screen. Unfortunately, Lieutenant Tolliver recognized me from last Monday. He probed me unmercifully, yet so skillfully it didn't leave a mark. I was forced to confess."

"About *The Secret*?"

"Yes. I told them the Cottrells were involved. I explained about Preiss and the images and that I was planning to set my students on the track of the casque, but only as an academic exercise." He pouted. "They thought it was funny."

"Why would you care? You're not getting carried away with this, are you?"

"Me? Not at all. There are just too many wackos out there. One might mistake me—or one of my kids—for a seeker, and try to dispose of the competition."

"So do the police think the Cottrells' deaths are connected to the cult…er, I mean, the club?"

"Maybe. Well, the investigation into the husband's death is still wide open, but in the case of the wife, the working theory was accidental death, at least when I left. They surmise that Harriet was digging in the spring for the casque—and somehow got stuck under the grate. There's some merit to the explanation, since they found a trowel near her."

"But the newspaper article said she drowned."

"She did. In the water." He wiped away an imaginary tear. His voice broke as he whispered, "Perhaps with Robert gone, all she had left was the quest."

Philo dismissed his theatrics. "Why don't they think Robert's death is related to Harriet's?"

"In his case, while they haven't yet ruled out suicide, there's evidence it had more to do with a nasty business dispute. A corporation wanted to buy out their independent liquor store, and Robert was balking. He called the police several times, complaining that the company was utilizing some rather unorthodox tactics."

"What—are they gangsters or something? Mafia?"

Barnaby reared back. "No, nothing like that. They're just hard-charging businessmen. I know Axel can be tough, but he'd hardly stoop to murder."

Philo paused, her coffee hovering below her lips. "Axel?"

"Axel Zimmer."

"He's the head of the corporation? And you're on a first-name basis with him?"

"Er…see…he's my former boss."

Chapter Seven

...in the middle of Little Italy little did we know that we riddled some middleman who didn't do diddily.

—Big Pun

Philo's apartment, Saturday, June 9

"Your boss? So, you've had at least *two* paying jobs in your pathetic life. What did you do for him? Massages?"

"Sheesh, Philo. Have some faith in me."

"I don't see why I should. I've known you all of five days."

Barnaby stood and paced. He paused before a large map of the western Caribbean. A tiny island was labeled "Providencia, Once Home Port for the Pirate Harry Morgan."

"Providencia. Huh. I think I have a T-shirt from there."

Philo drummed her fingers on the mug. "Axel Zimmer?"

Barnaby faced her. "The summer before my senior year in college, I was an intern for the Millstone Brands company. I was assigned to shadow the president, Axel Zimmer. He's an awesome guy—started his business at age twenty-one and was a millionaire by thirty."

"And what is his business?"

"Boutique liquor. He inherited a distillery from his father—they're from Wisconsin. Don't ask me why they didn't make beer like everyone else in Milwaukee. Anyway, he ran across a chef who had a collection of old family recipes for flavored vodkas and hired him to develop them for the market. Not for the mass market. Oh no. Not even for premium customers. For the *nosebleed* section of the high-end market." He pivoted and paced back to Philo's desk. "It's mind-boggling what people will pay for a fruit drink with high alcoholic content if it's sold in a fancy bottle and advertised in gourmet magazines. You got any food? I'm starved."

"No. Why is Zimmer interested in a dinky store in a small town in Florida?"

Barnaby clutched his belly. "No?"

"No."

He waited one more minute before giving up. "Once he got his product line up and running, he expanded from restaurants to liquor stores. The Cottrells were purveyors of the most exclusive alcohol brands in the Southeast."

She poured more coffee into her cup. "You say he went after them. Why didn't he just ask them to stock his brands?"

"That's not how he does business. He likes to have complete authority over the process from source to retail. It eliminates the middle man, resulting in more profit for him and better quality control for the customer."

"So he made them an offer, and they turned him down?"

"Yes. From what I gather it was a great deal of money, but the Cottrells weren't willing to sell. The store's been in the family for three generations. I'm afraid their refusal didn't sit well with Mr. Zimmer."

"What do you mean? Did he threaten them?"

"Not exactly, but soon after their rejection of his offer, the front window was smashed and they received several threatening phone calls. Robert suspected Zimmer or his minions."

"Did he report it?"

"He did. The police came and took their statements, but that's all. Robert's death has inspired them to take a second look."

Philo thought of something. "Do the police know of your relationship to Zimmer?"

"No, and I'll thank you not to tell them."

"So they only questioned you because you happened to be on the scene when both Cottrells died?"

"Yeah, but I overheard the officers talking about Millstone Brands. The police must be trying to trace a link between the vandalism and the deaths."

And if they were aware of Barnaby's acquaintance with both Zimmer and Robert Cottrell, he would inevitably become a suspect. She thought of something. "How do you know about the threatening phone calls? You no longer work for Zimmer. If the police didn't tell you, who did?"

"Cottrell."

"Robert? Did *he* know you worked for Zimmer?"

"Yes. When he let it drop about the harassment, I told him about my internship. I promised to contact Axel—tell him what was going on. He may be a tough sonofabitch, but I can't believe that he would be a party to those kinds of shenanigans."

Philo put her cup in the sink. "Let's go next door and get some sandwiches."

They ordered Cuban sandwiches to go, and Barnaby, after a nudge from Philo, sprang for two cans of Pabst Blue Ribbon. They took them back to her apartment and settled on the balcony.

Philo waited until Barnaby had a mouthful of pork and Swiss cheese before demanding, “Okay, come clean. Why were you meeting with Cottrell at the Lightner?”

He chewed just slowly enough to annoy her. “You are altogether too mistrustful. It’s not healthy.”

“The truth now. What was the purpose of your tête-à-tête on June fourth? Was it the business or the treasure?”

Barnaby hunched his shoulders. “Honestly? Both. I’d contacted him initially about *The Secret*. We met in his store. As we were talking, he got a phone call. The caller didn’t identify himself, but from Cottrell’s reaction, he was making more threats. When Robert hung up, he told me what was going on, but it was the mention of the corporation’s name that freaked me out.”

Philo had been struggling to put her finger on what was wrong with Barnaby’s story. At last it hit her. “Wait a minute. You told Lieutenant Tolliver you’d only communicated via snail mail.” *Another untruth. Is he a compulsive liar or is there a method to his madness?*

Barnaby shrugged. “Yes, I fudged a bit on that. I was afraid the whole Zimmer thing would come up, and Tolliver would decide to put me under a microscope. I worried he wouldn’t like what he saw.”

“A slimy, squiggly paramecium?”

“A possible suspect.”

“What did Robert do when he learned of your affiliation with his enemy?”

“He begged me to contact Axel and see if they would lay off the bullying tactics.”

“And you did.”

"I did. Axel was furious. He promised to look into it."

"And you believed him?"

Barnaby wouldn't look at her. "It was worth a try. I was as surprised as anyone when Axel got back to me. He said he'd fired a vice president and that if Cottrell was open to it, Axel would be happy to meet directly with him. He apologized for the strong-arm stuff."

"So you went to the Lightner to convey the message to Cottrell."

"Yes. Harriet was adamant that they not sell and refused to even negotiate, so Robert requested I choose a neutral location. He told me he was ready to cash in on Axel's offer. He belonged to several online mystery groups and wanted to devote his time to them. In return for my help, he promised to bring me the evidence he had of the casque's location. I gave him my word that whatever my students found we would share with him."

"Evidence?"

"The brochure." He drained the last drop of beer from the can. "The fact that he wanted to cash in puts the kibosh on the suicide theory, doesn't it? Maybe it *was* an accident." He wiped his mouth on a napkin and stood. "Now if you'll excuse me, I have to get back to work. Classes start Monday."

"Oh, yeah. Sure." Philo felt unexpectedly let down. "I won't see you again, then."

His face fell. "You don't want to see me again? What about tomorrow? The picnic? The beach?"

"What picnic? What beach?"

"I thought you'd like to have a day off just to laze around and sip a mai tai. Or a planter's punch. Or whatever cocktail goes well with a little umbrella. I keep a box of those handy for just such an occasion."

Philo made an effort to be offhand. *He may be a serial liar to others, but I can't pretend a day with him doesn't make me giddy.* "That sounds fine."

"Okay. We'll take your car. Do you have a picnic basket? Any more beer?"

She had to giggle. "Tell you what—I'll put together food and drink. You find a bathing suit."

"Perfect. I'll be at your front door tomorrow at noon."

****

Anastasia State Park, Sunday, June 10

Sunday turned out to be a sunny, dry day—perfect weather for their outing. Barnaby showed up in a one-piece blue-and-white-striped Victorian bathing costume and rubber water shoes.

"You're going to wear that in public?"

"Heavens, no. That would be indecent. I shall save my sartorial splendor for the beach." He pulled on an old mackintosh and belted it.

She looked at him askance. "Just don't flash anyone."

They drove Philo's Fiat over the Bridge of Lions to Anastasia Island and down A1A, passing the St. Augustine Alligator Farm Zoological Park. The sign on the entrance shouted Open Every Day! Crocodile Crossing on a Zip Line! Python Drop! Fun for the Whole Family!

Barnaby watched as a school bus turned in at the entrance. "Have you ever been there? I hear it's one of the earliest Florida tourist attractions—entertaining hordes of ghoulish thrill seekers from New York and Ohio for generations."

"My father took me once. It's an offbeat kind of place. The main attraction is a big mud pit teeming with alligators."

"Wow—I'm guessing that's how they came up with the name for the park. Do they keep them ill-fed to make them aggressive?" He snapped his jaws loudly.

"Oh dear, no. As I recall they seemed more bored than bellicose."

Barnaby had already lost interest. "There's the exit for Anastasia State Park. Quick, quick—cut that minivan off."

"Why?"

"Because they will undoubtedly take up two parking spaces. And then, while we're circling the lot fighting for the last open slot, the doors will open to release a family of eight, most of whom already have sticky fingers and dirty diapers. They will set up vast cabanas that obstruct the view of the water, grill stinky sausages, and turn up the volume on a humongous boombox that plays the theme from Sesame Street and the one for that purple dragon until we want to stuff corn cobs into our ears. We need to snag a spot as far away from them as possible."

Philo parked under a tree, and they lugged the picnic basket and cooler for what she loudly declared to be at least two miles to a small cove. To make sure her objections hit home, she went for a swim while Barnaby set up camp.

By unspoken mutual consent, they did not mention either the treasure hunt or the deaths for the rest of the day. After lunch, Philo lay back on a towel and let Barnaby's nimble banter dance over her like the fingers of a concert pianist. *I know he's a cheapskate, but he's an adorable cheapskate.* She cracked an eye open. *And so cute.*

"The beer's gone."

She roused herself. "I brought two six-packs. How many did you drink?"

"Enough that there aren't any more. Shall we go?"

She rose and stretched. "What a marvelous idea this was! It's been such a relaxing day."

"Yes, yes. Grab that towel. I've packed up the basket." He seemed in a rush.

Did I say something wrong? Philo reviewed the recent conversation. *I don't see how. I hardly got a word in edgewise.* She gathered her things, and they headed back to her car.

Barnaby was uncharacteristically quiet on the drive back. As they approached the bridge, he suddenly yelled, "Pull over!"

She braked, provoking an indignant toot from the man in the car behind her. She turned off the road into an alley and stopped. "What is it?"

"This'll only take a minute." He slid out of the car and disappeared down the embankment. Just as Philo began to think she should cut the engine, he reappeared. "Okay, that's a no."

"What is?"

"The bridge. It's on my list of potential hiding places for the casque."

"You mean, underneath it?"

"Yeah. One corner of the image shows what looks like a bridge. Or it could be a big fish." He clucked his tongue. "Or a turtle. Hard to tell."

"Image."

"Yes. Image Six, the one thought to relate to St. Augustine."

"Oh right, *The Secret*. Have they figured out which verse it goes with?"

"Verse Nine."

Philo made a mental note to have another look at the website.

The late afternoon weather had turned humid and hot. They trudged upstairs. Philo turned at the door, thinking Barnaby would take his leave. Instead he said diffidently, "May I come in?"

Maybe he's not in such a hurry. "Okay."

He took the basket to the kitchen and returned to her. The sand coating Philo's skin itched, and her bathing suit chafed. "Well, thanks again for a lovely day. I think I'll go take a shower."

He didn't move. "Philo?"

"Yes?"

"I'd like to kiss you again. I have lots to do tomorrow, and I can't see you until the evening. It would sustain me." He bent slightly forward, his hands balled tightly.

She plucked at her suit. "I, uh…Okay."

He must have noticed her squirming, for he said gently, "You want to take a shower first. I'll wait." He sat on the couch.

Philo dithered. She badly wanted to peel off the suit, but the thought of Barnaby sitting in the living room while she was naked—even if he couldn't see her—made her very self-conscious. "Tell you what, why don't you kiss me first."

He considered this. "Very well."

The kiss was just as good, if not better, than their first one. She began to revise her next move. As she reached for his neck, a little stream of sand dribbled onto the floor. "Oops."

He stepped back and brushed the grit off his raincoat. “I do believe I have enough to savor, at least for the next twelve hours. I shall descend upon you tomorrow at six.”

She opened her mouth, but he was already out the door.

Chapter Eight

Forsaking the sun-tanned Riviera, water Dracs, playful-as-porpoises, and the languid, amorous Fadas found contentment upon the hot southern shores of the New World, amidst pink, long-legged birds and high, swaying palms.

—Byron Preiss, The Secret

Mind Over Matter, Monday, June 11

Philo's Monday was consumed with customers. The tourist season was in full swing, and large groups of tired Midwesterners took over Aviles Street, oblivious to the fact that, despite its cobblestones, it was a real street on which real cars needed to drive. When some poor van driver finally lost his temper and honked at them, they'd dive for the sidewalk, and sometimes all the way through the door into her shop. This often resulted in some confusion. Philo put it down to the fact that hers was one of the few nongift shops in the city.

Joseph stuck his head in. "And a good afternoon to you, my dear. Where is your gallant this day?" He pronounced it "ga-LANT."

"Gallant?"

"An old-fashioned term for your beau, Mr. Swift."

"What makes you think he's my boyfriend?" *Although the term does have a nice ring to it.*

"He told me."

"Oh, really? *Humph.*"

"Well?" Joseph waited, a smile on his face.

"His class starts today. He's teaching a seminar on historical methodology at Flagler."

"He's on the faculty?"

She shook her head. "Just a summer job. He's writing his dissertation at Princeton."

"Ah. He seems a creative sort of fellow. Historical methodology, you say? How does he plan to attack it?"

"He's going to send his students on a scavenger hunt." She swatted futilely at a fly. "Would you mind shutting the door?"

"Oh, sorry." Joseph came all the way in and sat down next to Philo's desk. "A scavenger hunt? That could be a challenge. What will they look for?"

She turned the monitor screen—on which she'd brought up a web page dedicated to *The Secret*—toward him. On it appeared the image numbered six. Next to the image was a short verse full of vivid, albeit obscure images. "This is one of twelve images and poems that make up Byron Preiss's book *The Secret*. They are puzzles that give clues to the whereabouts of twelve urns, buried somewhere in North America. Once you match an image to the riddle, you're supposed to decipher the symbols in both and locate the urn."

"And what does this urn hold?"

"The key to a vault where Preiss stored twelve precious gemstones." She pointed at the screen. "This is the text they believe refers to St. Augustine."

Joseph's eyes lit up. "So the one who solves the puzzle wins a jewel?"

"Yes. St. Augustine's is a sapphire."

"I love puzzles." He leaned forward and examined the screen. "*Hmm*." After a minute, he straightened and rubbed his eyes. "Whew! I think I prefer crossword puzzles. They're more dependent on knowledge than visual skills." He grinned. "And I'm a virtual fount of knowledge."

"Where are you off to today?"

"I'm heading to the market. May I procure something for you? Strawberries? A naughty little Pinot Grigio?"

"No, thanks."

It was close to five o'clock when Joseph returned to Mind Over Matter. "Ah, there you are."

"You sound surprised. This is my shop after all." She smiled at the old man. "Why are *you* here?"

"To confess." He lowered himself onto a chair with a groan and leaned his cane on a table covered with navigational charts. "I am intrigued by this *Secret* affair. I repaired to the public library to acquaint myself with the subject, but instead of answers I found more questions. Apparently, Mr. Preiss simply enlisted his friends to paint the pictures and write the riddles. It is not some deep-thinking cabal of great mystics as I at first presumed."

"So?"

"So how did a bunch of amateurs create a scheme so complex and elaborate that no one in over thirty years has been able to solve it?"

"You got me. Maybe one of Barnaby's students will break the code." She turned off her computer. "Barnaby says some of these players have been at it for decades. Mr. Cottrell—the man who fell to his death at the Lightner Museum? He wanted to sell his store so he could devote all his time to it."

"And such zeal is distasteful to you?"

"Distasteful? No. Perhaps a little worrisome."

The front bell tinkled. Barnaby walked in. His hair was tousled, and his tie askew. Philo noticed that one of his shoes was untied. She also noticed that his socks were Day-Glo purple with green parrots printed on them. And that they matched his tie. "Bad day?"

"Oh Gawd. I need a drink. Coming?"

Philo pointed at the clock and then at Joseph. "Store isn't closed yet, and I have a customer."

Barnaby nodded at Joseph. "Hello, Mr. Brighton. How's tricks?"

Oh right, they've met.

"Fine, fine. I was just telling Philo that I find myself plunging into the riddle of the casques."

Barnaby reared back. "If you value your sanity, don't go there! I've just had the most horrendous day. I'm sorry I ever thought this project up."

"Oh?"

"I'm happy to explain, but I really need the comfort of a calming libation. Will you join us?" This last to Joseph.

The old man lumbered up, puffing a little. "Thank you, no. It's been a long day. I must say I'm feeling a bit winded. After the library, I had a drink at my favorite watering hole—the Dog and Whistle—before returning home. Met a chap there. Supplies of his favorite Scotch had run low at his neighborhood tavern, and he was scouting out other establishments. Stimulating conversationalist. Well-versed in politics and religion." He chuckled. "Had some novel ideas about the law, too. In return, I regaled him with the story of *The Secret* and mentioned that you were acquainted with the seeker who met his maker last week."

Barnaby gulped. "I'm not sure it's wise to broadcast my association with the wretched affair."

"Oh? I apologize, but I don't think you have to worry. The fellow's not a local." Joseph checked his watch. "Oops, I'm late for my nap." He fluttered a hand spotted with age. "You two kids, hie ye to a tavern. Try the Dog. Or Dos Chicas, if you prefer a speakeasy atmosphere." He winced. "My ankles are acting up after the walk. Think I'll check my mail, then put my feet up. Philo, may I use your back door?"

"Be my guest."

He headed toward the rear of the store and walked right into a table. "Ouch. Didn't see that. Maybe I should cut down on my evening quaff, eh?"

Philo laughed. "Only as a last resort!"

Barnaby surveyed Philo's businesslike linen jacket dress. "A speakeasy, huh. In that case, you should be in a fringed minidress and carry a foot-long cigarette holder carved from the horn of a narwhal. Are you perchance endowed with such items?"

"No, but let's go to Dos Chicas anyway. I hear they've relaxed their dress code, and I'm in the mood for a pink lady."

He executed a two-step. "If you meet one, shall I bow out gracefully or do you propose a threesome?"

"We'll see when we get there. It's on Hypolita Street, about three blocks from here." Philo turned the sign to Closed while Barnaby straightened his tie and combed his fingers through his hair. "Shall we?"

Few people were about—one family of four hogged the sidewalk and they had to step into the lane to go around them. A man with his collar turned up and hands in his pockets brushed past them, then abruptly stopped in front of a beauty supply store, blocking their path. Barnaby gracefully skirted him and went on, Philo in his wake. They had reached Hypolita Street when a woman in a dirndl skirt and down jacket cut them off. Thin as a toothpick, she carried a baseball bat. Holding up her other hand to keep them at bay, she scrutinized first Barnaby, then Philo.

Philo said, “Can we help you?”

Without a word, the woman lowered her hand and swished past them. Barnaby watched her turn the corner. “That was odd.”

Philo shrugged. “St. Augustine has its share of eccentrics.”

“No, I meant the jacket. It must be eighty degrees out.”

“Here we are.” An old stone building decorated in white lights housed Dos Chicas. The large room was outfitted with a mahogany bar, black leather benches, and flocked wallpaper. The overall effect was of a slick, backlot version of a Prohibition-era nightclub.

“Will you look at that?” Barnaby pointed at a mural of a scantily clad woman bending over backward. She had a pistol tucked into her garter and a sombrero hanging from the toe of her six-inch heel. “Reminds you of the *Secret* paintings, doesn’t it? Maybe it’s a clue.”

The bartender glided over and stopped with a squeak. Philo leaned over the bar. “Roller skates? Are they the latest in waiter footwear?”

He performed a pirouette. “Bennie Bolton at your service.”

She applauded. “Single malt please.”

He consulted a list. "I've got Aberlour—heavy on the sherry. If you want more peat, I'd suggest Talisker or Ardbeg."

"How about Glenfiddich?"

"Sorry. We didn't get our regular shipment in this week. It's very popular."

"Okay. I'll have the Talisker. Double. Rocks."

Barnaby gawked at her. "I thought you wanted a pink slushie?"

"I was kidding."

He turned to Bennie. "I'll have what she's having."

Whiskeys in hand, they chose two stools at the end of the bar. Philo piped up before Barnaby had a chance to annex the floor. "Why, thank you for asking. Yes, my day was quite busy. Sold a set of maps tracing the Lewis and Clark expedition and a very expensive atlas to a professor from Purdue. Gave directions to three sets of tourists, and rescued one Ohio man from a gruesome death under the wheels of the red train."

Barnaby turned vacant eyes on her. "I'm sorry, what did you say?"

She took a long sip, savoring the smoky liquid. "All right, spill. How did the students respond to your plan?"

"Oh, are you finished? Your run-on sentence ran on so long I must have dozed off."

Philo didn't care, basking as she was in her victory—temporary though it be—over Motor Mouth.

He waited a minute, clearly hoping she would fret at his indifference. When she didn't, he airily answered. "Everyone loved the idea, of course. They had expected to be shut up in a darkened room for six weeks at the height of summer. Most of the students are from the Midwest or New England—I only have six, by the way, a nice, manageable number—so they jumped at the chance to work in the open air."

A man sat down on the stool next to Barnaby. He didn't acknowledge them, but signaled the bartender. "Shot of Glenlivet and a pint of lager."

Philo nudged Barnaby and whispered, "That's what Joseph always orders."

Barnaby contemplated the man for a minute, then ordered another round. "We spent an hour discussing *The Secret* and Image Six before setting out to identify potential sites."

"I thought you were going to instruct them on methodology?"

"I assigned them reading for tonight. We all felt it would be a better use of the daylight hours to canvass the territory. The students have expressed interest in selecting the sites themselves."

"Where did you go?"

"Well, we tried to go the Fountain of Youth, but it was closed." He winked. "Due—according to the announcement tacked to the portal—to a recent unfortunate event on the grounds."

"Poor Harriet." Philo felt a rush of sympathy. "Are the police still investigating?"

"The guard didn't say. He did tell us the spring was running red…as with blood." He clicked his tongue. "He seemed to relish the effect he had on my kids."

She scoffed. "He was pulling your collective legs. For one thing, she drowned, so there wouldn't have been any blood. And two, if there were, it would have been diluted by now."

"I'm only relaying what I was told." Barnaby pretended to sulk. "Sheesh."

Philo, preoccupied with a new consideration, ignored him. “You know what I think? The police are wrong. It wasn’t an accident. Not right on the heels of Robert’s death. There are too many suspicious coincidences. I think Harriet was murdered.”

Beside her the man dropped the shot glass on the bar, spilling the contents. Silently, he tossed some bills into the puddle, swiveled on his stool, rose, and marched out.

Chapter Nine

This idea of, there's a locked door; how do you open it? You don't necessarily care what's behind it; you're just more excited about opening the lock... It's not about finding the treasure; it's more about defeating the puzzle.

—Harper Reed

Dos Chicas bar, Monday, June 11

"Gee. That was rude."

The bartender skated over and wiped up the mess. "Yeah, he's normally pretty mellow, but we're out of his favorite brand. Plus, you took his usual spot."

Barnaby frowned. "He should have said something. We would have been happy to move."

Bennie cocked his head at Philo. "*Or*...maybe he didn't like all that talk of murder."

"Me neither." Barnaby peered at her. "You don't think it was an accident?"

Philo splayed her fingers. "You told me Harriet refused to sell the store to Zimmer. She was, if anything, even more of an impediment to his plans."

Barnaby sucked in a breath. When he spoke, his voice trembled slightly. "I told you, I know Axel Zimmer. He's no murderer."

Philo could see it would be a waste of breath to dispute the point without further evidence, so she raised her glass. “May I have another?” Bennie took it from her. When he was gone, she said, “Let’s get back to your day. Your group couldn’t get into the Fountain. What did you do then?”

Barnaby popped a peanut in his mouth. “Did you know that in nineteenth-century New York, barkeeps put out bowls of caviar instead of peanuts?”

“I did not know that. Are you saying you took your students to a bar?”

“Certainly not. Not on a school day.” He gave her a disapproving look. “The Fountain of Youth being inaccessible, we decided to walk down the street to the Mission Nombre de Dios. It was founded by Pedro Menendez de Aviles when he landed here, and the first Mass in Florida was celebrated by his chaplain in 1565. A two-hundred-foot cross was erected to commemorate the four-hundredth anniversary of the mission.” He did a quick calculation. “That would make it 1965. Well before *The Secret* was published. So it could be the place.”

“The place? You mean the casque could be buried there?”

“Uh-huh.” He nodded to himself. “Interesting how the Spanish conquistadors lugged their Catholic priests with them on their expeditions. The English were smarter. They made the religious groups do the spadework before sending the redcoats out to reap the spoils. Where was I?”

“The mission.” Philo considered having a third whiskey. This could turn into a long evening.

“Ah, yes. Susie Phelps—she’s from Maine—she’s taken on the Mission as her…uh…mission.”

“What makes her think it’s a likely spot?”

He shrugged. "She liked the park—I think she's Catholic. Remind me to direct her attention to the cross."

Philo had no intention of participating in Barnaby's speculations. "Go on."

He tossed her a suspicious look. "As I told you, I tasked each student with picking a site and studying it for clues."

"Wasn't that their proposal?"

"Sorry? Oh, well. Whatever. So, Susie has the mission, and Kevin's chosen the Castillo de San Marcos. We're all heading there Thursday to reconnoiter. Cleo opted for the Flagler College student dining hall. She says it's incredibly elegant. Haven't seen it yet myself."

"I thought you were going to eat there."

He shook his head. "The school considers it too fancy for teachers and has relegated us to a small, windowless closet they euphemistically label the Faculty Dining Room."

She conjured up the image of an ornate, high-ceilinged chamber. "I've seen the student's hall. Nicest of any college in the Lower Forty-Eight."

"Or even Alaska." He broke off. "Can you imagine being a lowly freshman, eating a breakfast burrito under this vast rotunda covered in frescoes, the morning sun shining through the windows, broken up into myriad colored patterns like a celestial kaleidoscope? I'd feel like a Roman senator…or the Pope. Wow."

He seemed to have lost his thread. Philo prompted, "That's Kevin and Cleo. And the others?"

"We covered Susie too. Although…" He broke off to gaze at the mural with an abstracted air. "The mission's an awfully large complex. I'll let her have it for now, but I think I'll find a different site for her—

maybe one of the oldest whatevers." He sighed. "There are so many choices, and I've only got six students. I may have to spend some time winnowing the list. Or…even better, I can give each of them two cases. *Hmm*."

Philo resisted the urge to pinch him, reasoning that would only slow him down. "That's three. What about the other three?"

"Lessee…Lincoln chose the *Black Raven* because he loves boats. It's a faux pirate ship. Thomas has the Fountain of Youth, although I may divest him of it."

"Why? Something wrong with him?"

"Can't put my finger on it. I don't know him that well yet, but he's got a bit of a hangdog attitude about him. I sense a goldbricker."

"Let's hope you're wrong."

"Besides, the fountain's the most likely location, so I might save it for last and have the entire class study it."

Philo counted on her fingers. "We're up to five. You said you had six students."

Barnaby looked blank for a minute, then slapped his forehead. "Agatha. I keep forgetting her. She ended up with St. Photios. That's a Greek shrine with lots of decorative art."

"Okay." Philo signaled the waiter. "Another, please."

He gave her a disparaging look but brought her a fresh drink. He also made a show of topping off the bowl of peanuts and nudging it toward her elbow.

"What are the students like?"

"A diverse mélange of individuals. Let me see…there's Lincoln Nevers. Super-senior—took a year off to learn shipbuilding, so this'll be his fifth year of college. Kevin Magnusson is from Cleveland. Evidently his parents are associated with the *Secret* hunt, so they were thrilled to have him come to St. Augustine. He says they're particularly keen on the Castillo. That's why he chose it."

"Okay. Next?"

"Thomas 'The Slouch' Doulton. From Iowa. Brickhead."

"You shouldn't call your students names."

"No, I mean he has orange hair. Freckles. Big, floppy ears. Looks just like Alfred E. Neuman."

Philo eyed Barnaby's coppery locks but kept mum. "And the rest?"

"The females. Cleo Marzetti—quintessential New Yorker. Pretty, but a little hard. All angles and too skinny." He pinched Philo's cheek. "I don't care for a woman who doesn't look like she could keep up with me at a buffet table. Now, Susie Phelps…" He smiled. "She's the youngest. Some insensitive hairdresser talked her into an afro. Makes her look shorter." He mused, "I don't think she's ever been in the South before. Seems a little ill at ease."

"And the last one?"

"*Hmm*. I'm not…Oh, right. Forgot her again. Agatha. Agatha Leonardi." He frowned. "I'm not sure where she's from. Mousy. Little squeaky voice. Even shorter than Susie."

Philo ate a peanut. The bartender gave her a thumbs-up. "Have you been to all their sites yet?"

"Only the mission. From there it was a hop, skip, and a jump past the Fountain of Youth (still closed) to Ripley's Believe It or Not. Well, to be precise, some hopped. Some skipped. No one jumped." He whistled. "Anyhoo, we decided to scope it out for future reference.

Expensive little museum. Luckily I'd secured two tickets from the student activities fund. Left the rest outside while Lincoln and I toured the exhibits."

"Is that as far as you got?"

"Uh-huh. It took a while. Did you know they have a stuffed two-headed lamb there? In something called the Odditorium. Lots of pirate geegaws and taxidermy. I think my favorite was the 'fur-bearing trout.' "

"A furry fish?"

"A whole fish covered in fake white fur. Definitely in the 'or not' category."

"Are you going to assign it to one of the kids?"

"The fish? Oh, you mean Ripley's. Yes. Not sure which one yet. Maybe Thomas."

"If you take the Fountain of Youth from him, he'll need something."

"Agreed. Shall we?" As they walked back to Philo's, Barnaby casually took her hand. "Er, tomorrow's pretty free. I'm giving a lecture at four. Your shop's closed, right?"

Something caught in Philo's throat, and she could only gurgle. Barnaby stopped, circled behind her, and clamped his arms around her chest. She bleated, "Wha…what are you doing?"

"Heimlich maneuver. Thought you were choking. Although you haven't eaten anything except that one peanut—did you notice Bennie glaring at you? A bit uppity, but I'm sure he was just concerned for your well-being." He squeezed again. "So I haven't the foggiest what you could be choking on. You're not chewing gum, are you? Gross habit. Makes you look like a cow. I hope you're not into that or I may have to revisit my feelings for you."

She could only gape at him.

He peered in her mouth. "I see from your open maw that you are not in fact masticating what was originally called chicle. Good. Shall we?" He took her arm. "You were saying?"

"I wasn't. What did you have in mind for tomorrow?"

"Perhaps a tad more reconnaissance. If I have to find more than one site per student, I'll have to expand my search. There are so many possibilities in this tiny city. The Oldest House, several Spanish-era houses, the Greek colony thing—"

"You mean, St. Photios?"

"Uh-huh. Although evidently the Greek colony wasn't all Greek."

"No?"

"No. There were Italians, Corsicans, and Minorcans. Only a smattering of Greeks. You remember the Oldest Schoolhouse on St. George Street? Built by a Minorcan." He stopped short, dropping her arm. "*Hmm*. Perhaps that strange tidbit caught the attention of our Mr. Preiss. I think—"

Philo gave him a little shove. "Look!" Blinking lights seemed to be coming from Aviles Street. They hurried down the lane. "Oh, no, that's my building."

An ambulance was parked, motor running, in front of the shop. It was empty, but the gate to the upstairs apartments swung on its hinges. Philo flew up the stairs, trailed by Barnaby.

Joseph's door was open. A paramedic worked on a body on the couch. Philo cried, "Joseph!"

An EMT assisting the paramedic turned around. "Miss? Could you excuse us please?"

Barnaby stepped to her side. “She’s a friend of Mr. Brighton’s. What’s going on?”

Behind them a voice said, “Swift? Don’t tell me you’re involved in a police matter *again*? What have you done now?” Lieutenant Tolliver stood in the hall next to Steve. “I’m going to have to run you in for your own protection. This is ridiculous.”

Barnaby said stiffly, “I beg your pardon.” He gestured at Philo. “I was escorting Miss Brice home. It’s not as though you’ve come across me at every crime scene in the city.” When Tolliver didn’t answer, he looked uneasy. “Have you?”

“Crime!” Philo seemed only able to blurt one word at a time. She craned her neck around the EMT, trying to catch a glimpse of Joseph. “Is he dead?”

“No, miss. Heart attack. Please be quiet.”

They continued to work on Joseph. A few minutes later, the paramedic said, “He’s stable.” He laid out an emergency scoop stretcher, and together they lifted Joseph into it. Barnaby pulled Philo out of the way, and the men carried the stretcher down the stairs. Philo turned to Tolliver. “What happened?”

The detective pulled out a notebook. “What is the victim’s name?”

She answered, her voice tremulous. “Joseph Brighton. I live in the apartment next door. Is he going to be okay?”

Instead of answering, he barked, “Name?”

“Philo Brice.”

“Were you the one who contacted Emergency?” He didn’t say it out loud, but Philo knew he was thinking, *again.*

“No, we just got here.”

The lieutenant touched some numbers on his phone. "Dispatch? We're at 13 Aviles Street. Patient taken to Shiloh General. Who made the 9-1-1 call?...Oh, really? Okay. Thanks." He put the phone back in his pocket. "Patient called it in himself. Said he was experiencing rapid heartbeat, nausea, and shortness of breath. Does he have a history of heart disease?"

"No. At least he never mentioned it. You could check his medicine cabinet."

"Okay..." he said drily. "Or we could pull his medical records."

"Yes, well." Barnaby pushed Philo toward the door. "Carry on, Constable."

Once inside her apartment, Philo collapsed on the sofa. Barnaby fussed around her, plumping the pillow, straightening her skirt. "He'll be all right. Let not your heart be troubled. John 14, verse 1. Joseph's a tough old bird. I was planning to ask him to help with the hunt. That'll perk him up. I'll ask him tomorrow. He should be fine by tomorrow. Do you want a drink? Water? Hug?"

She looked up at him, and her eyes filled with tears. "Oh, Barnaby."

That was enough. He sat next to her and gathered her into his arms. She laid her head on his chest. In between hiccups, she whimpered, "Joseph is really my only friend here. I inherited the shop three years ago and spent the first year getting it back up and running. I haven't had time to meet anyone else. My family's gone and I...I have so many responsibilities. And now Joseph..." Her hand lifted, then dropped.

Barnaby pulled out a tangerine handkerchief printed with garden gnomes and wiped her nose. "There, there. He's not your only friend, you know." He squeezed her.

"You have me." She gazed at him. His lips slowly descended upon hers.

Chapter Ten

Avoid fruits and nuts. You are what you eat.

—Jim Davis

Philo's apartment, Tuesday, June 12

"Oh my God, what the hell is *that*?"

Philo rolled over and rubbed sleepy eyes. "What is what?"

Barnaby sat up in bed, a trembling finger pointed at the aquarium. "That. Is it…is it…?"

"A snake? Yes. That's Delilah." Her pet had uncoiled and was tapping the glass.

"What's it doing? Is it attacking us?" He pulled a pillow out from under Philo and crammed it over his stomach.

"Of course not. She's probably just hungry. She's a scarlet kingsnake. Would you like to meet her?"

He cringed. "Not really. Especially not if she's hungry." He covered his chest with a second pillow. "If I'd known I would be sharing a room with two females, I'd have opted for humans."

Philo started to rise and realized she was naked. She snuggled under the sheets and gave Barnaby a come-hither look. "Forget Delilah."

He reluctantly hauled his gaze from the reptile. "Delilah, huh? I'm not sure which of you is the worse vamp." Nonetheless, he assented to being caressed, maintaining one eye on the other occupant of the room.

An hour later, Barnaby edged toward the door, his back to the wall, keeping as far as possible from the aquarium. "I'll make us some breakfast while you take care of…of your friend."

After Delilah received her weekly intake of pinkies—to the horror of the hero of our story—Barnaby set a plate before Philo and sat down opposite her. "What is this?" She poked at the dish.

"Toad in the hole. See, you make a hole in the bread and drop the egg into it. It's the only recipe I know. Found it on an index card in my English grandmother's desk."

She dug into it. "Not bad."

He picked up his fork but held it motionless in front of him. "I presume these eggs are from a chicken and not from some gelatinous cold-blooded creature?"

"You may."

Barnaby took a bite. "Tell me, how did you come by this wholly unnatural attraction to the class Reptilia?"

"It was the Crocodile Hunter. He was an Australian zookeeper who had an animal show on television. We watched every episode when I was a kid." She sighed. "My first hero."

"Enough. Someday perhaps I shall gird my loins and fondle the animal…but you have to promise me you'll love me forever if I do."

Philo assumed he was joking and didn't respond. "Do you think we'll be able to see Joseph today?" When he didn't answer she looked up. His green eyes were somber. "Barnaby?"

He slugged down his coffee and got up to refill his mug. His back turned, he said lightly, "We can but try.

They seemed to think he'd recover quickly. Shall I call the hospital?"

"Yes, please. He's at Shiloh General."

"Okay." He looked at his phone. "No bars. I'll try in the hall." When he came back, he said, "He's out of ICU. Visiting hours are ten to two." He sidled over to her. "I believe we have enough time."

"Time?"

"Either to play with Delilah or play with each other. Your choice."

I can play with Delilah any time.

****

Shiloh General Hospital, Tuesday, June 12

"Are you feeling better, Joseph?"

The old man opened his eyes. "My dear Philo, aren't you a sight for rheumy eyes! And you brought your young paramour with you. Barnaby Swift, how are you making out with our Philo?"

His cheeks crimson, Barnaby could only manage an inarticulate glug, like the sound a water cooler makes when someone presses the nozzle. Philo spoke for him. "*We're* fine. How about you?"

"Good, good. Have a seat."

Barnaby let Philo sit on the one chair and stood behind her. She leaned forward and patted Joseph's hand. "What happened? You seemed fine when you left us yesterday evening."

He made a wry face. "Actually, I wasn't feeling well, but it didn't seem important enough to mention. When you get to be my age, you have aches and pains twenty-four seven."

"What made you think you were having a heart attack?"

"I was lying on the couch, catching a few winks, when I started having trouble breathing. My heart was slamming against my chest. I sat up and felt nauseous. When spots began to dance before my eyes, I called 9-1-1. They thought I was in atrial fibrillation."

Philo sucked in a breath. "Have you had heart issues before?"

"No, no. In fact"—he thumped his chest—"my primary physician, Doctor Anderson, says I've got a remarkably strong organ. No sign of disease at all."

"Until last night."

"Right."

Barnaby mused, "Something must have set it off—did the ER doctor have any insights?"

He shook his head. "He ordered some tests. I was told he'd have the results by noon." He looked up at the wall clock. "Should be along any time now."

Just then the door opened, and a white-coated man bustled in holding a clipboard. "Hello, Mr. Brighton. I'm Doctor Reagle, your cardiologist. Are we feeling heartier today?" From his expression Philo assumed the joke was part of his standard routine. His red cheeks and brown buzz cut made her think of a cheerful chipmunk.

"Bright as a button." Joseph grinned. "I love my name."

"Well, I'll want to check you out anyway." He turned to the two visitors. "Would you mind stepping outside while I examine the patient?"

Joseph struggled to a sitting position. "Before you do, my friends and I would like to know the results of the tests."

"What? Oh, certainly. Happy to go over them." He read through a couple of pages. "*Hmm*. This is odd. Your blood pressure—normal. Your cholesterol levels—good.

Glucose, fine. No sign of damage to the heart…" He twisted his lips. "You came in presenting with fibrillation, confusion, and some difficulty breathing. Normal signs of a heart attack, but there can be other causes. Had you just exercised?"

"Me? Are you kidding?"

"All right." He made a note. "What did you eat or drink last evening?"

"Nothing. Or rather, I didn't have any supper. I'd gone for my usual tipple at the Dog and Whistle. A shot of Glenlivet and a pint. I came home, had some tea. Then I felt a little drowsy and lay down for a nap. The rest you know."

"Alcohol on an empty stomach. Probably all it was. Still…" He scribbled on the clipboard. "Let's take a listen, shall we? I may want to run a couple more tests." With practiced congeniality, he boomed, "I don't want to see you back here any time soon." He winked at the nurse behind him. "Although I'm betting Mary Lou does."

Mary Lou shooed Philo and Barnaby out. Philo leaned against the closed door. "What now?"

Barnaby checked his watch. "Lunch. Then I have to go prepare for my lecture."

They found a diner near the college and ordered Greek salads. Barnaby took his notebook out. "Let's take a stab at that poem."

"You mean the one that goes with Image Six?"

"Yes."

They pored over it. Barnaby kept circling words or underlining them until Philo reached a hand out and clamped down. "You're not helping." He looked up at her and held her gaze. It was only when a man sat down at the next table and jogged her chair that Philo woke up.

His attention on his menu, the man said casually, "Sorry about that. These tables are so close together, aren't they?"

Philo nodded absently. She was having a hard time focusing on her food, still lost in the deep emerald pools of Barnaby's eyes.

He too was quiet. Finally he put down his fork. "I've…uh…got to get going."

After he left, Philo paid the bill and decided to take a walk. She felt unaccountably troubled. *I've only known Barnaby a few days, but his—I don't know—aura? It surrounds me like an incense-filled cave—sweet, yet provocative.* She couldn't believe she'd slept with him. She was normally a very slow mover. In fact, tortoise-like. When she was fifteen, she'd fallen madly in love with an older man. Nick was seventeen and an Irish romantic. *As in, love 'em and leave 'em.* She'd given him her heart, and he'd tossed it out like the first pitch of a rainy baseball season. After that, she muddled her way through years of bitterness and inappropriate boyfriends. When her father died, leaving her the shop, she didn't hesitate. Pulling up spindly roots, she headed across Florida to St. Augustine.

Once there, she reopened the store and settled into a comfortable, uneventful life, which suited her just fine. *Until a fast-talking, easy-on-the-eyes tightwad showed up at my door. What am I going to do with him?*

She found herself on the waterfront next to the bridge. A gaudily painted galleon lay at anchor by the pier. She stopped to admire it.

"Hey there, young lassie. Fancy a sail on the *Black Raven*?" A young man clad in a frilled shirt and three-cornered hat beckoned her. "We're in pursuit of the dread pirate Blackbeard, who stole our gold. Cap'n Chase be ready to cast off in five minutes." He pointed a finger toward the channel, where a much smaller ship, flying the skull and crossbones, had just set sail. "We shall hunt down *Queen Anne's Revenge* and wrest our treasure from his fiendish hands!"

Treasure? Hmm. The Black Raven *is one of the sites Barnaby's students chose.*

The young man leapt onto the ship's foredeck. "Name's Jamison. You can buy your ticket at the kiosk from First Mate Walker Plankton. Make haste!"

Instead, Philo smiled and waved them off. As she turned toward home, she almost ran into a man standing on the sidewalk. "Oops, didn't see you there. Excuse me." He didn't acknowledge her, but continued to study the laminated map of the city attached to a signpost. *In his own little world, I guess.*

The walk signal flashed. Just as she stepped off the curb, the man raised his head.

He's the guy who bumped our table at the diner. Small world. She pictured the restaurant. *Funny—those tables were at least three feet apart. Not close at all.* The memory of her eyes locked on Barnaby's rushed back. She closed them and let the image whisk her away into a brand-new land of promise.

She didn't hear from Barnaby for the rest of the day and went to bed hoping Joseph would be released soon. *What could have caused his fibrillation? Will he have another episode? Will he have to give up his evening tipple?*

****

Philo's apartment, Wednesday, June 13

If Philo thought she was done with flashing lights in her neighborhood, she was wrong. This time, at least, it turned out to be good news.

She came out on her balcony in time to see two medics unfold an orange wheelchair and help Joseph into it. She ran down and opened the gate, and they carried the old man up the stairs. Philo followed them to Joseph's apartment. One tech unstrapped his patient and helped him onto his bed. Joseph lay there, his face gray. When he caught sight of Philo, he raised a finger. "Won't you come closer, my dear? It's hard to see you in this gloom."

The EMT straightened. "I have to check his vitals, then he's all yours."

Once the techs had packed up and left, Philo sat down on a chair by the bed. "Can I get you some water?"

"That would be lovely. And put a little whiskey in it, would you?"

"I don't know…"

"I think he deserves it, after all he's been through."

She whirled. "Barnaby!"

"In the flesh." He approached the bed. "How are you, Solicitor?"

Joseph waved a languid hand. "Glad you're here. Now I don't have to exert myself in tiresome debate. The Glenlivet is under the sink in the kitchen. There's a good fellow."

Barnaby disappeared, then reappeared with a tumbler in his hand. "What were the results of the new tests?"

Philo straightened Joseph's pillows and helped him sit up. He accepted the glass and took a big gulp of whiskey. "Ah, that's better."

"Well?"

"I refuse to divulge anything until you explain the burnoose." He gestured at the long, hooded cloak Barnaby was wearing.

Barnaby looked down. "This? A Moroccan friend gave it to me. We were trekking across the Atlas Mountains, and a late spring snow squall stranded us." He flung it back over his shoulders, revealing gym shorts and a tank top that read Harlem Globetrotters. "I didn't like to walk the streets *en déshabille* so I tossed it on before I came over."

"Ah."

"Now, what did the doctor say?"

"Doctor Reagle is baffled. Says my blood chemistry is fine, except for a higher than normal level of potassium and some diminution of kidney function. He told me to avoid bananas and suggested I drink a lot more water." He stopped. "Wait. Drink…Eat." He regarded Philo with an anxious air. "I *did* eat something Monday night—it was at the Dog and Whistle. A plate of little fritters made of eggplant." He scratched his head. "Can't think why they slipped my mind. They were delicious. Jimmy—he's the owner and bartender—said it was a new recipe Mabel was trying out."

"Mabel?"

"His wife." Joseph set his drink on the night table. "Mabel runs the kitchen and is always trying to gussy up the place. Makes every dish a work of art. Calls it 'plate presentation.' You know, she runs a knife through the sauce to make a pattern. Garnishes the orders with flowers."

"You were saying about the fritters?"

"They were a rather unexceptional brown color, so she plopped a gay little blossom on top." He chuckled.

"I ate that too. Did you know almost every plant in Florida is edible?" He picked up his glass again.

Barnaby rubbed his jaw. "If I recall correctly, eggplant is in the nightshade family—along with belladonna and the infamous datura plant. Oh, and the hallucinogen mandrake."

Joseph pursed his lips. "Eggplants aren't poisonous though."

"No, but they can cause digestive problems. All nightshades can induce nausea, vomiting, and confusion."

"Does eggplant make the body retain potassium? Doctor Reagle seemed a little concerned about that."

"*Hmm*. I don't think so."

Philo said, "You had heart palpitations, too."

"All right, let me plug in the symptoms…" Barnaby typed a line into the search bar on his phone. "Hah. I think we can rule out the eggplant. Nightshade actually *leaches* potassium. Plus it causes a slow pulse and low blood pressure. You didn't have those." He kept reading. "How about a dry mouth?"

Joseph licked his lips. "Uh-uh. In fact, I remember my mouth felt full of moisture. I figured it was the vomit."

"So…moving on. Are you taking any other medications?"

"Just some water pills the doc gave me for my swollen ankles. Otherwise I self-medicate with whiskey and tea."

Philo nodded. "I'll bet that's the problem, Joseph. The water pills dehydrate you—a lot of nutrients are flushed out of your system."

"But that doesn't make any sense. What does dehydration have to do with a heart attack?"

“We’re not doctors, Joseph.” Philo shrugged. “At least you’re okay now.”

Barnaby didn’t want to let it go. “Well, *something* you ate or drank caused you to fibrillate. Maybe you have an allergy you don’t know about. There is such a thing as late-onset allergies. I can’t eat cashews anymore.” He stuck his lower lip out. “Or pecans. It’s really put a kink in my normal diet of nuts and twigs.”

Philo reluctantly agreed. “Perhaps we should get to the bottom of it before it happens again.”

Barnaby started to the door. “I’m going to the bar and ask the bartender—what’s his name?”

“Jimmy.”

“Jimmy—about his fritters. They might contain another ingredient that did the dirty deed.”

“I’ll go with you.” Philo turned to Joseph. “Will you be all right?”

“Oh yes. I’m feeling much better.” He picked up a newspaper from a pile. “I’ll do the Sunday crossword. I never got a chance to finish it.”

Barnaby flinched. “Crossword…puzzle?”

“Yes. Love them. I can do the daily ones in pen, but Argle Bargle—he who writes the Sunday entry—is considerably more erudite than even I am.” He finished his whiskey. “That reminds me: the fellow I sat next to at the bar Monday evening said he wrote puzzles for his hometown journal. Can’t imagine being able to do that.”

“Yes, well.” Barnaby strode out of the room, leaving the door wide open.

Chapter Eleven

Fashion is like eating, you shouldn't stick to the same menu.

—Kenzo Takada

Dog and Whistle Tavern, Wednesday, June 13

Philo trotted after Barnaby. "You're in a hurry."

"Yes. Well."

"Is that all you can say?"

For answer, he walked faster. By the time they reached the Dog and Whistle, Philo was out of breath.

The man tending bar—short, with a shiny black handlebar moustache—wore a denim shirt with the name "Jimmy" embroidered on it. Barnaby stalked up to him. "Hey, can we talk to you for a minute?"

At that hour there were only a few people in the place, hunched over their beers.

"Sure. You want something to drink?"

Barnaby deferred to Philo.

"I'll take a pilsner."

"Make it two." He pulled out a stool for Philo and sat down next to her.

Jimmy filled two tall slim glasses at the tap and brought them over. "What can I do for you?"

"Our friend Joseph Brighton was in here Monday night."

"Old Joe? Yeah, he's a regular."

“Well, when he went home, he suffered an…incident. They thought it was a heart attack, but now they’re not sure. Do you remember what he ordered?”

“His usual. Shot of Glenlivet and a pint of beer. Why?”

“He said he ate some fritters?”

“Fritters?” Jimmy picked up the bar menu and skimmed through it. “Nothing here…Oh, wait, I forgot. Mabel’s eggplant fritters. Not your average pub food, but she wanted to test the recipe out. Joe’s never loath to be a guinea pig.” He wiped the counter down. “The other fellow—he wouldn’t touch ’em. Hurt her feelings, he did.”

“Other fellow?”

Philo poked Barnaby. “Joseph said he’d met someone here.”

“Yup. Stranger. New to the bar. They seemed to hit it off.”

Philo brought the conversation back around to the pertinent question. “So Joseph ate all the fritters?”

“Gobbled ’em up. Even ate the flower garnish. He must’ve been a bit peckish.”

Flower? Hmm. “What kind of flower was it, do you remember?”

Jimmy laughed. “Me? I wouldn’t know a daisy from a snapdragon. Something bright pink. Not an orchid though. I think orchids are poisonous, aren’t they?”

“Would you mind asking Mabel?”

“No problem.” He went in the back, but returned quickly. “Mabel says orchids aren’t poisonous. Who knew? She says she garnishes plates with them all the time.”

“So it was an orchid.”

"On his plate? No. She says she didn't decorate it 'cause it was only a sample." He went down the bar to attend to another customer, leaving Philo and Barnaby to brood on the mystery.

When he returned, Philo started in. "Tell me, Jimmy. How would a flower get on Joseph's plate if Mabel didn't put it there?"

"Not sure." His eyes went to the empty tables. "There were two young couples in here that night. All dolled up to go to a dance at the college. The girls wore corsages. Maybe a blossom fell off one of them."

"And Joseph picked it up and ate it?" Barnaby was skeptical.

"Wish I could help you."

"It's all right. Thanks for your help." He slid off his stool. "Philo?"

Philo paid the tab, and they left. On the return journey Barnaby walked, if anything, quicker. Philo caught his arm. "What's going on?"

"Joseph said he ate the garnish. Mabel says she didn't put a garnish on the plate. The flower wasn't an orchid."

"So?"

"I want to know if Joseph recognized it."

"Why?"

"Because I'm thinking it was poisonous."

"Poisonous! You don't think...you don't think. What is going *on* around here?"

"Huh?"

"Are you saying someone tried to kill Joseph?"

He stopped abruptly. "That's absurd. No, I'm just trying to determine the cause of his illness. It couldn't be the fritters, so maybe it was the flower. My, what a fertile imagination you have!"

Philo felt a little ridiculous. “I’m sorry. It’s just…all these incidents and…and…deaths.”

“Too much cerebration and not enough animation.” He started to trot. “You know what? Maybe we’ve gotten out over our skis. We’re acting as though these events are somehow suspicious, but it’s more likely the Cottrells and Joseph were simply victims of unfortunate accidents. Nothing to get up in arms about.”

“But what about the Mafia?”

“Mafia! You mean Axel? I told you, he put a stop to the vandalism. And Cottrell was ready to settle anyway.”

“But Harriet wasn’t.”

“No, but even the Mafia wouldn’t break into the Fountain of Youth to drown her. They prefer easier methods—like a bullet in the forehead. Or cement shoes.”

“Cement shoes aren’t as easy as you might think. First, you have to mix the stuff up and then stick her feet in it before it hardens. Then you have to transport her to the river, which would require a van. No—”

Barnaby barked, “The Mafia didn’t kill her, okay? And neither did Axel Zimmer.”

Philo didn’t take offense. She was just happy she’d outtalked Barnaby for once. “Oh, that reminds me. I went past the pirate ship today. Didn’t you say you’d assigned it to one of your students?”

“The *Black Raven*? Yes. Lincoln chose it because he loves ships, but now I think of it, certain lines of the poem could apply.” He recited, “ ‘The first chapter / written in water.’ ”

Philo jumped in. “And another line: ‘Sails pass by night.’ ”

He gave her a high-five. "You're getting into the spirit of the thing. Good for you."

They reached her building. The gate to the upstairs apartments was open. "Did we forget to lock it?"

"Dunno." Barnaby turned to her, dismay in his eyes. "Joseph!" He took the stairs two at a time.

Philo found him panting, hand to chest, before Joseph's door. She knocked. There was no answer. She pounded on it. "Joseph! Joseph! Are you okay? It's Philo."

Barnaby had his phone out and was pressing numbers when the door opened. Joseph looked surprised. "Philo? Why are you yelling?"

She cried, "You didn't answer your door. We thought…we were…frightened."

"That I'd had another attack? No." He chuckled. "I was merely indisposed." He looked over her shoulder at Barnaby. "I see you still have our Barnaby in tow. Won't you come in?"

They crossed the threshold and sat down on Joseph's sofa. "The gate was open."

"Oh? Ed must have forgotten to close it."

"Ed?"

"He was just here. The fellow I met at the Dog and Whistle Monday night."

"The puzzle writer?" Philo felt Barnaby jerk again beside her. *What's eating him?* "What did he want?"

Joseph pointed at a folded paper. "I had left my daily crossword on the bar by mistake. He was at the Dog and Whistle the next day, and Jimmy gave it to him to give to me."

"An old crossword? Why?"

"Well, you, my dear, may be comfortable leaving an unfinished crossword around, but as a serious puzzler,

I'm not. Ed knew I would want it returned. I hadn't had a chance to pick up today's edition, so it was most welcome. He brought me some more of the tea his grandmother used to make as well."

"How did Ed know where you live?"

Joseph chuckled. "I told him. We were commiserating about our aches and pains, and when I mentioned the swelling in my ankles, he offered to leave me some of this special herbal tea of his. Claimed it works wonders." He sat down in an easy chair. "You left here rather precipitously. Any particular reason?"

"About that. We went along to the Dog and Whistle and talked to Jimmy. Barnaby?"

Barnaby leaned forward, his elbows on his knees. "I'm speculating that something you imbibed Monday night brought on your illness. Eggplant's a member of the nightshade genus, but you didn't have the right symptoms. Jimmy said something about a flower garnish."

"Yes, I told you."

"He didn't know what variety of flower it was. Can you describe it?"

"A raucous shade of fuchsia. Shaped like one of those spinning pinwheels." He pinched his lips. "I'm not much good at plant identification."

Barnaby linked to a site on his phone and showed the illustration to the old man. "Did it look like this?"

"Why yes, I think so. Nice peppery taste. What is it?"

Barnaby answered, his tone grim, "Oleander."

"You mean those flowering shrubs that grow all over St. Augustine?"

"Yes. It's from another family of poisonous plants: dogbane. Just as toxic as the *Solanaceae*."

"Are the flowers poisonous?"

"All parts of the plant are." He clicked some keys. "In this article it says people can be sickened simply by grilling food over the branches or by chewing on a leaf."

"And you think that's what brought on the heart attack?"

"Uh-huh. Symptoms of oleander poisoning include gastrointestinal distress, irregular heartbeat, drowsiness, and difficulty breathing, all of which you experienced." He peered at the page. "And excess saliva. You said something about that."

Joseph fell back in his chair. "I—"

Philo interrupted. "Mabel told Jimmy she hadn't put a garnish on the plate. Did you happen to notice where it came from?"

Joseph blinked several times. "I don't remember. It was just there…wait, I did go to the lavatory. Passed some young folks. The women were wearing corsages on their wrists. Perhaps one of them dropped a blossom by accident." He paused. "A lovely old tradition—corsages. You don't see that much anymore."

"That doesn't explain how it got from their table to your plate. Were there any other flowers on the tables?"

"It's a pub, Barnaby. What do you think?"

Philo nudged Barnaby. "There was a vase of flowers at the end of the bar."

Both men stared at her. "Really?"

"Yes. Don't men notice anything that isn't sports- or alcohol-related?"

"I guess not. So, what flowers were in the vase?"

She considered. "A mix. Some daisies, some asters. Yes, I think there may have been some oleander blossoms. One could have fallen onto the plate when Jimmy brought it out."

Joseph turned to Barnaby. "There. Are you satisfied?"

"*Humph.*" Barnaby was only partly mollified.

"An accident." Joseph clapped him on the back. "No harm done this time, but I have learned my lesson. No more flora. From now on, I stick to fauna."

Chapter Twelve

Keep your eyes on the stars, and your feet on the ground.
—Theodore Roosevelt

Philo's apartment, Thursday, June 14

Philo managed to keep Barnaby occupied until the next morning, for which he pronounced himself very grateful. "You have quite an inventive approach to nonverbal communication."

"It's a gift."

He rolled out of bed and bent to gather up his clothes. As he rose, his nose brushed the aquarium. Eyes wild, he yelped and leapt backward, catching his foot on the throw rug. He sprawled across the floor. "Ow ow ow ow!"

"What's the matter? Oh!" Philo giggled and scooped the kingsnake up. Delilah's tongue slithered in and out. " 'Lilah, have you been scaring little Barnie again? Naughty, naughty. Say you're sorry and you can kiss and make up."

Barnaby backed hastily out of the room. "I really must return to my boarding house. The madam expects us to check in at least once a fortnight."

"I see." She lay Delilah back and straggled after him to the kitchen. "You don't have time for breakfast?"

"Would that I did." He pecked her cheek. "I shall see you anon."

"When's anon?"

"A little after now and before then." He looked serious. "Will you miss me?"

"Me? Not at all. I look forward to some R&R."

"Oh." His crestfallen face warmed her heart. "Whatever will you find to amuse yourself in my absence?"

"I have work to do in the store. And you?"

"I am leading the Hebrews on a quest for manna. First, the pirate ship. Then perhaps the fort."

"The Castillo de San Marcos?"

"Is there another one?"

"As a matter of fact, there are three. Fort Mosé is just north of here, and Fort Matanzas guards the southern reaches."

"*Hmm.* I'd forgotten about them. Forts are good places to hide things in. I'll put the other two on my list." He held up his notebook.

"What about the Mission Nombre de Dios?"

"I've soured a bit on it—not enough relevant natural features. I believe Susie agrees."

Philo saw him off, then ate her breakfast and went downstairs. She puttered around for an hour, her eyes drifting regularly to the computer. *What the hell.* She opened the *Secret* website and brought up Image Six. It had been marked with a grid that allowed her to study each small section separately. "Is that a star? No." She flipped to the verse. " 'Stars move by day.' Wait, the fort is in the shape of a star, isn't it?" She switched screens to an aerial view of the Castillo. "Could be…" The doorbell pealed. "We're closed!"

"Even for angels bearing sandwiches?" Barnaby held up a brown paper bag.

"Oh, what good timing! I'm starved." She let him in, got a couple of water bottles from the minifridge, and cleared a spot on a table. "So what about the pirate ship? Did it fit any part of the image?"

"I left Lincoln Nevers to it. He seemed optimistic."

"Nevers. He's the boatbuilder?"

"Yup.

"And this afternoon you're going to the Castillo?"

"Yes."

"May I come along?"

He hesitated. "I'm not sure it's kosher to bring a date to a seminar."

"Oh posh. Tell them I'm a fellow seeker. I finished reading *The Secret*. Did you know the second half of the book describes a whole Tolkien-like pantheon of magical creatures? All with comical names like Maître D'eamons and Freudian Sylphs. They're the Fair Folk who hide themselves from Men, but still live among us."

"Really? I only studied the images and poems. So it's more than a treasure hunt?"

"Uh-huh. The narrative is pure fantasy. It tells of the twelve fairy nations who fled the Old World for the New Found Land."

"They're the ones who brought the twelve jewels, right?"

"Yes. Preiss called them 'wonderstones.' The locals named the creatures the Shining Ones. The Fair People of the First Passage disappeared when humans arrived but offered them the stones if they could find them." She sipped her water thoughtfully. "I get the impression the hunt wasn't the focal point of the book. It was never supposed to become a huge cult. He was just fooling around."

"Huh. Okay, you may come along, if you promise to tell me more. We leave in half an hour." He rose. "Can you meet us in front of the college? I have secured a minivan."

****

Flagler College, Thursday, June 14

Philo made it to Flagler just as Barnaby's students gathered in a gated parking lot. Barnaby stood by the van's bifold door wearing a neon-orange emergency vest studded with blinking lights. He marked off the students on his clipboard as they climbed in. A Reserved sign was duct-taped to a seat in the front. "For you, mademoiselle." Once she was settled, he handed out tickets to everyone, then slid into the driver's seat and pulled out of the lot. Producing a hand-held microphone, he began to lecture, so Philo was left to speculate on which student was which.

Three girls and three boys. Sitting directly behind her was a redhead with ears that jutted out from his head like wings. *Must be Thomas. And the skinny black-haired girl with the sharp face is likely Cleo, the New Yorker. The tall, gangly boy, all legs and arms—Lincoln?* So the other one—fresh-faced Midwesterner with a straw-colored thatch and cornflower blue eyes—would be Kevin. *Or the other way around.* She craned her neck to see the passengers in the last row. A sweet-faced black girl sat next to someone whose only visible feature was the top of her head. *Susie Phelps and...what was the other girl's name?* She shut her eyes. *Oh well, it'll come to me.*

They drove up San Marco Avenue to the Castillo and parked in the space reserved for school groups. The tour guide took them around the interior courtyard and into the various barracks, guard rooms, and kitchens. Barnaby interrupted the docent several times, at one point loudly proclaiming, "So, guys, here we have yet another example of St. Augustine enjoying a monopoly on the oldest stuff. Fort San Marcos is the *oldest* masonry fort in the United States. Oldest city, oldest fort. Kinda makes those English colonists your basic Johnny-come-lately's, what?"

After the tour, the students scattered, some out to the moat, some to the gift shop. Philo and Barnaby climbed to the top of the walls and walked around to the side overlooking the city. *Now's my chance.* "You are aware that the fort is in the shape of a star."

"Of course. I showed you the pictures from my helicopter ride, didn't I?" He pulled out his phone and clicked on the photo. "Oops. That's not precisely accurate. It's actually a square, with four bastions. See? They're those pointy protuberances at each corner. Now if you include the ravelin—the wing that protects the sallyport—it does look like the rays of a star." He gazed at her. "Did you have a point?"

"Yes. I've been thinking about the stars mentioned in the poem. 'Stars move by day / Sails pass by night.' The Castillo may be a better match than the Fountain of Youth." She pointed across the fort to the river sparkling in the distance, where a yacht tacked into the wind. "You can see sails even from this side. What do you think?"

Barnaby shaded his eyes and scanned the battlements. "I *think* someone is watching us." He nodded at a man training binoculars on them from the top of the interior stairway. "What do you suppose is so much more intriguing about us than the fort? Why—" He was drowned out by a shout. "That's Susie Phelps." Philo on his heels, he circled the ramparts to the other side and leapt down the stone stairs. The man with the binoculars had disappeared. Susie stood, straddling the entrance to the fort, her mouth open, screaming.

A guard came barreling through the gate and skidded to a stop behind her. When Barnaby reached Susie, he beckoned the guard. "What's going on?"

The man gently moved the girl aside. Once her cries had trickled down to hiccups, he said, "You Professor Swift?"

"Er…yes." Barnaby's eyes shifted. Philo pondered his reaction. *Is it the form of address? Or something else?* For the second time, she found herself wondering if Barnaby had secrets of his own—secrets she might not like.

The guard gestured at Susie. "If I understood her correctly, this young lady says one of your students took a tumble."

"Oh, Professor!" The girl gulped. "It's Kevin. He was waving at me. Then he…he fell." She burst into tears.

"Is he hurt?"

"I don't…don't know. I ran for help. Lincoln's with him."

"Where are the others?"

"They were on their way when I left to find you."

The guard took charge. "Show us."

They followed him down the sallyport to the entrance and around the walls to the side of the fort facing the river. A young man lay on his back on the grass. *Aha—I was right. The fresh-faced one is Kevin.* The other students clustered around him.

The guard shooed them away and took stock of the boy. He asked—rather brusquely in Philo's opinion—"Is he dead?"

Susie began to yowl. One of the other students, the one Philo thought was Lincoln, said, "No, of course not. He only fell about ten feet. But his leg's all twisted—it might be broken."

At that point, Kevin's eyes fluttered open. He groaned.

Barnaby bent over him. "Kevin? What happened?"

The boy tried to rise but suddenly listed to one side. He screeched, "*Arrggh.* My ankle!" and staggered away, landing with a thump on the ground. His head in his hands, he keened, "Oh God, my parents are going to kill me."

Barnaby stood, hands on hips. "At the risk of repeating myself and boring you all…What happened?"

"I fell."

"Well, duh."

"From there." Kevin indicated a ledge about ten feet up that ran around the walls just below the parapet.

"How did you get up there?"

"I climbed through that hole." Philo could barely make out a thin, vertical opening behind the ledge. "The whole second level is this series of vaulted rooms with little windows. Must have been for the archers to shoot through. Or maybe pour boiling oil from. Anyway, I shimmied through it. Linc was about to snap a picture of me"—the student in question held up his phone—"when I took a header."

Barnaby looked down at Kevin. "You slipped?"

"No." His eyes wide with fear, he stuttered, "Someone pushed me."

Chapter Thirteen

Each person is an enigma. You're a puzzle not only to yourself but also to everyone else, and the great mystery of our time is how we penetrate this puzzle.

—Theodore Zeldin

Castillo de San Marcos, Thursday, June 14

The guard unhooked his phone from his belt and walked away. Soon they could hear sirens. Just as the sound became deafening, it abruptly shut off. Barnaby loped around the corner of the fort, Philo bringing up the rear. An ambulance was backed up to the main entrance. One medic opened the rear doors and pulled out a gurney, while a second approached the guard. A minute later, a police car arrived. Philo said a little prayer that it wouldn't contain Lieutenant Tolliver. To her relief, it was Sergeant Landman who got out and walked over. He cast a quick glance at Barnaby and Philo and glowered. "You again?" He addressed one of the medics. "Got an 11-83 that there's been an accident?"

"Yeah, boy fell off the rampart. Guard says maybe a broken leg." He pulled out a clipboard. "We'll be along after I fill out some paperwork."

The guard led Landman to the grassy area behind the fort. Kevin still sat, his friends grouped protectively around him. When he saw the uniforms, he let himself flop flat on the grass. The guard pointed up. "Kid fell off that ledge."

The sergeant scrutinized the sheer wall. "How the hell did he get up there?"

"Brats do it all the time. We try to keep the casement off limits, but parents let 'em wander anywhere they want." He grumbled, "No control these days."

"So where *are* his parents?"

Kevin said loudly, "I'm an adult, sir. I'm in college. My parents live in Ohio."

Barnaby stepped forward. "I'm his instructor, Sergeant. This is Kevin Magnusson, a student at Flagler College."

"Instructor…What the hell?"

Philo, cringed, fearing the worst.

Landman moved to stand nose to nose with Barnaby. "Don't tell me. You're a professor of paranormal studies, teaching kids all about ghoulies and ghosties at sixty K a pop." He shook his head. "No wonder college graduates end up as baristas."

Cleo and Lincoln spoke together. "Hey! We have jobs. We have goals. We're millennials."

Kevin's voice sounded hollow. "Well, technically, I'm Gen-Z."

Cleo paused. "When were you born?"

"2001."

"Huh." Lincoln tapped his toe, unaware of its proximity to Kevin's head. "So when did the millennial generation end?"

"They say anyone born between 1985 and 2000 is a millennial. After that the Zs take over."

"That makes me a Gen-Z too." Susie seemed pleased with herself.

"Really." Thomas squatted next to Kevin. "I'm only a year older than you. How would you say you're different from me?"

Kevin opened his mouth, probably preparing for a nice, cozy chat about the characteristics of different age groups, when the EMTs arrived. One of them examined Kevin's leg. "With any luck you just wrenched the ankle. We'll see what the X-rays say." He gestured for the other medic to bring the gurney.

Thomas squatted down again. "You were saying about Gen-Z?"

The EMT coughed. "Do you fellows mind putting your discussion on hold so we can take the patient to the hospital? It's rush hour, and traffic's picking up."

Thomas rose, and the others backed away, letting the men lift Kevin onto the gurney and roll him to the ambulance. The sergeant turned to Barnaby. "Tell me why I shouldn't run you in for—I dunno—being a bad role model?"

Barnaby didn't take the bait. He said mildly, "Perhaps I should tell you that Kevin—Kevin Magnusson, the injured boy—claims he was pushed."

"Pushed?"

"Yes."

Landman took his notebook out. "Did he see who did it?"

"No."

"Did anyone else?"

Barnaby turned to Susie and Lincoln. "You were the only ones down here, correct?"

"Right."

"Did either of you notice a person near Kevin? Or behind him?"

They shook their heads. “Kevin was teetering on the ledge. I wanted to take a picture quick before he…before he…”

Philo glanced up. “The opening’s just a narrow slit. If someone were behind him, he wouldn’t have been visible to those below.”

“Right. Wrong angle of sight.” Barnaby turned back to the policeman. “Philo and I noticed a man standing on the steps leading down to the courtyard.”

Philo added, “He was carrying binoculars. If you can find him, he might have seen something.”

Landman spoke to the guard. “Would you please search the fort for a man with binoculars?”

The man frowned. “We’re closed now. All visitors should have left.”

The sergeant’s tone was dry. “You just told me people have been known to disobey the rules.” He headed to his car. “I’ll go along to the hospital and talk to the victim.”

Barnaby called, “I’ll notify his parents and the school.”

The policeman paused. “I wish I didn’t have to say this, but would you mind staying out of trouble for a while? I have a day off coming up, and I’d hate to lose it.”

“Sure thing, Officer!” Barnaby gave him a brilliant smile.

Lincoln approached. “We’d like to go back to our dorm now, Professor.”

“Okay. Come on, everyone.” Barnaby jingled the keys to the minivan.

****

Flagler College, Thursday, June 14

They dropped the students off, and Barnaby parked the van in the college lot. He had taken a step toward the sidewalk when Philo raised a brow. “Are you perchance moonlighting as a crossing guard?” She indicated the neon vest.

“Oops. Thanks for reminding me. It stays with the van.” He peeled the vest off and tossed it on the driver’s seat. Underneath he wore an ivy green Henley shirt that matched his eyes. Something was appliquéd on it.

Philo leaned forward to look. “What is *that*?”

He plucked at the shirt. “I bought it in a souvenir shop. It’s a Tupperwerewolf.”

“A *what*?”

“He’s one of Preiss’s creatures, like the Freudian Sylphs you told me about. You can choose your avatar from any of the elves, sprites, and pookahs in *The Secret*, and they’ll iron it on while you wait.”

“As I recall, their names were all puns.”

“Indeed. Like the Handimanticore. Or Elf S. Presley. Let’s see…” He pulled a flyer from his pocket. “Paltry Geist, Gnome Enclature, Djinn Rummy. Hilarious. When I get my first paycheck, I intend to buy a whole set of T-shirts.” He stuffed it back in his pocket. “Shall we hence?”

She led the way back to her apartment. She was unlocking her door when Barnaby stopped in the hallway. “Let’s check on Joseph.”

The old man came to the door with a pen and crossword in his hand. He perused the couple. “Another adventure I see.”

“How did you know?”

“Disheveled…*that’s* the word!” He scribbled letters down on the puzzle. “And I’m finally done with yesterday's. Now I can tackle today's. The one who writes the weekday puzzles is pretty tough, but not as tough as Argle Bargle."

Philo laughed. "Argle Bargle?" She heard a gasp, and Barnaby bumped into her.

Joseph crooked a finger, drawing them in. "Make yourselves comfortable." When they were settled, he said, "You like crossword puzzles, don't you, Barnaby?"

Barnaby gazed over Joseph's head. A spot of color burned in each cheek. "Of course. Everyone does. They're…entertaining."

"What do you think of Argle Bargle?"

He clicked his teeth. "He's all right."

"He's my favorite. So knowledgeable—even has a sense of humor." He picked up a folded paper. "Like this clue from last Sunday: Broad and strong." He waited.

Barnaby kept his mouth shut tight.

Philo took a stab. "Um, a river? Or a bridge span?"

Joseph chuckled. "Nope. It's Mighty Aphrodite. Get it? 'Broad'? Love it!" Joseph jabbed at the byline with a knobby finger. "Argle Bargle's obviously a pseudonym. Wish I could discover his real name. All it says is he's from New Jersey. Princeton. Must be a professor…or some sort of scientist at the Institute for Advanced Study."

Philo touched Barnaby's elbow. "That's where you're doing your graduate work, isn't it, Barnaby?"

"Yes."

"May I inquire in which field?" Joseph eyed him over the top of his bifocals.

"Semiotics."

"Ah, the study of signs and symbols, together with the manipulation thereof. Fascinating. And I suppose you support yourself writing crossword puzzles." He grinned, teasing.

The spots expanded and merged until Barnaby's face resembled a fully ripe beefsteak tomato. "As a matter of fact, I do." He stiffened his spine. "I confess. I am he. Argle Bargle, the cruciverbalist. At your service."

"Excuse me? Cruci-what?" Philo blinked at him.

Joseph answered her. "Cruciverbalist. The technical term for a crossword puzzle creator. Surely it doesn't surprise you that they would have their own special word for the craft?" He put the pen down. "Wow. It's an honor to shake your hand." He stuck his out. Barnaby's flush went full bore purple. Joseph pulled his hand back. "Don't tell me you're embarrassed? It takes a breathtakingly agile, informed mind to create a crossword."

Philo remained silent, not sure how she felt. *Well, at least I know what his oh-so-shocking secret was. But does this make Barnaby a total geek or a genius? Which would I prefer?* Consorting with a brainiac might enhance her reputation. On the other hand, how could she keep up with an egghead? She peeked at Barnaby. He looked supremely uncomfortable. *I bet he's not sure either.*

"It's no big deal. It's not really enough to make ends meet. There are times I must depend on the kindness of strangers." He didn't look at Philo.

She suppressed the titter. *That's his excuse, and he's sticking to it.*

The phone rang. Joseph hobbled over to the fifties-era princess phone and picked it up. "Hello? Oh, hi, Doctor Reagle. Yes, I had left a message with your nurse inquiring about the effects of oleander?...Right. Can you tell me—since you found no trace of heart disease—if ingesting a blossom could be the cause of my attack? I see…I see…Well, thank you." He hung up.

Barnaby had recovered from his discomfiture and sat forward eagerly. "What did he say? Was I right?"

"Yes. Just as you said, oleander is part of the dogbane family, like periwinkle and allamanda. It has properties that retain potassium in the blood and can cause arrythmia. However, he is fairly certain that one blossom is not enough to induce problems in a healthy adult human."

"But what about those examples I read to you?"

"He says those are anecdotal and likely connected to the victims' size or underlying medical issues." He patted his ample stomach. "For once, my weight served me well. I'd need a lot more than one little blossom to affect me."

"That's it? We're back to square one?"

"He's ordering a few more tests, but he doubts he'll find anything serious enough to warrant readmission."

"Well, it's something." Barnaby seemed conflicted.

"I have to go back to the hospital again tomorrow. Can you give me a ride, Philo?"

"The shop opens at noon. When do you have to be there?"

"Oh dear. He made me an appointment at the lab for eleven thirty."

Barnaby pulled out his phone. "That reminds me. I should check on Kevin's status." He called the hospital. When he hung up, he said, "They haven't released him yet—some talk of possible concussion. They want to observe him for one more night. His ankle injury wasn't as severe as we thought, but he'll be on crutches for a week or so." He laid a hand on Joseph's shoulder.

"Looks like I'll be heading to Shiloh General tomorrow to pick him up. I'm sure Philo will lend me her car and I can take you."

Philo's heart sank. She'd seen Barnaby drive the van and fretted for her little Fiat. "Why can't you drive the college car?"

"It's in high demand—I was on the waiting list for a week before I was able to sign it out."

Philo's objections could barely be heard above Joseph's cries of gratitude. She gave up. A few minutes later, they left Joseph and stood in the hall. Barnaby gazed at her, his expression inscrutable. Finally he said, "I suppose you think I'm a total dork."

"You mean because you write crosswords? Not at all." *I think.*

"Actually, I don't just create the puzzles for money. It's for research."

"Really? Oh yes, the semiotics."

He nodded. "I'm doing my dissertation on the history of crosswords. How it relates to the changing language, to the evolution of humor, to the nexus between the brain and language."

"And that's why you were afraid to tell me what the topic was. I might deduce that you were a…what did Joseph call it?"

"A cruciverbalist. It's really quite interesting. Not at all silly." He peered hopefully at her.

"It sounds fascinating." And she meant it. She looked at Barnaby with new eyes. "You shouldn't be ashamed of your work. Like Joseph says, it's quite difficult."

He brightened. "Oh, great. Then I can stay the night?"

"Huh?"

He didn't miss a beat. "I have to retrieve your car and drive Joseph to the hospital tomorrow anyway. Might as well save some time and leave directly from here." He took her arm and half carried her to her door.

What the heck.

Chapter Fourteen

Damnation seize my soul if I give you quarters, or take any from you.

—Blackbeard (Edward Teach)

Mind Over Matter, Friday, June 15

Philo was sitting in an empty shop when Barnaby and Joseph breezed in. Barnaby announced, “Kevin has been certified concussion-free and has joined his cohorts in the Flagler library for a little research before we sally forth again.” His face took on a strained expression. “His father left several messages for me at my office. It seems he’s holding me responsible for Kevin’s injury.”

“It wasn’t your fault.”

“No, but he is my charge. Mr. Magnusson is threatening to come here and deal with me in person.”

“Well, when he gets here you can just explain what happened. I’m sure he’ll understand.”

“Explain what? That I let Kevin climb all over the fort walls? That I was on the other side of the fort while he was teetering on a two-foot-wide ledge?”

Philo hissed. “Oh, for heaven’s sake. Like Kevin said, he’s an adult.”

Barnaby muttered, “Gen Z. Not sure that qualifies.”

She decided to change the subject. “And how about our other patient. How did that go?”

Barnaby made an effort to recover his buoyant mood. "Joseph here received an Elmo Band-Aid in exchange for not blubbering when his finger was pricked."

"The nurse was quite impressed with my copious flow." Joseph held up a bandaged finger. "I hope you don't mind. I gave them your cell number for a call back when the results are in." He pulled his pockets inside out. "I'm too old for one of those contraptions."

She laughed. "And too young for a pink princess phone."

A customer came through the door, and Philo went to help. Armed with a map of St. Augustine and pamphlets for the Oldest House and Ripley's, he left. Philo's phone buzzed. "Yes? Yes, he's here." She handed Joseph the phone.

The old man spent a minute trying to figure out how to hold it to his ear. "Hi, Doctor…Yes, I can…Preston's pharmacy. What is it again? *Ooph.* I'd better write it down." Philo took a pad of paper from the drawer and held up her pen. "D-i-g-o-x-i-n. Digoxin immune fab." Philo wrote it down. "Got it. Thanks." He handed the cell back to Philo.

Barnaby took the pad and read it. "He gave you a prescription? What's the diagnosis?"

Joseph shrugged. "He says he found neither nerline nor oleandra in my system. They're the toxic chemicals in oleander. He did find an elevated level of digitoxin, but he can't for the life of him put his finger on what caused it. The medication he just prescribed is supposed to bring it down."

"Does oleander contain digitoxin?"

"No." He looked worried. "He's not sure how long the drug's been in my system. Could have been days."

Philo felt a stab of alarm. "Is he concerned about it? Could you have another attack?"

"No. My heart's strong enough to ward off any long-lasting impacts. That is, unless I'm still absorbing it from somewhere."

She shook her head. "I wish we knew what caused your attack."

Barnaby squeezed her shoulder. "Whatever it is, the new medication should counter any effects…Wait a minute. Digitoxin. Digitalis. *Foxgloves*. Of course! I believe it's the only source for the medication." Barnaby faced Philo. "Were there foxgloves in that vase at the Dog and Whistle?"

Philo racked her brain. "I don't think so. They're pretty big. I'd have noticed them."

"Okay." Barnaby regarded Joseph. "Have you been cavorting in meadows recently?"

Joseph chuckled. "Look at me. What do *you* think?"

Philo took the pad back from Barnaby and turned to a new page. "We should make a list of your activities in the last week. Where you went. What you ate."

"I haven't gone anywhere to write home about, I'm sorry to say. I've been working on my memoirs and crossword puzzles. I eat lunch at Harry's, have my pint at the Dog and Whistle every evening, and usually make myself a sandwich for my supper."

"Ah." Barnaby said slowly, "We have to consider the possibility that someone in one of those restaurants slipped digitalis into your food."

"But what on earth for? I've known Jimmy for five years, and Stella—she practically runs Harry's. She—" He stopped and reddened, a sight Philo never expected to see. "Well, she's a little sweet on me. Gives me extra helpings of grits. So, you see, I have no enemies, at least recent ones." Joseph's brow furrowed. "It couldn't be…no."

Philo thought she knew where he was headed. "You were a defense attorney, weren't you?"

"One of the best and most famous in my day." He produced a wry grin. "You think one of my former clients may be after me?"

"Maybe. Were there any high-profile cases you lost? Someone who wants retribution for your failure to get them off?"

Joseph lowered his leonine head. "No."

"Well, then…"

"I *did* defend Ozzie the snitch, though. That was back in 2010." Joseph sat back with a smile. "We put the Jacksonville mob boss, Niarelli, behind bars for thirty years. What a day that was!"

Barnaby went to the window. "We should find out if this Niarelli has been released from prison for good behavior."

"Or escaped." Philo shivered, only partly from fear.

Joseph shook his head. "Last I checked—and I do often—he was making license plates in the Coleman Federal Correctional Facility in Sumterville."

Barnaby stood up. "Okay, you're sure you've only been to the Dog and Whistle and Harry's in the last week?"

"Yes."

He headed to the door. "Let's go, Philo."

Joseph gasped. "Wait—do you intend to malign my favorite establishments?" He cocked his head. "And just how do you expect them to react?"

Philo put the pen and pad on the table. “Um. We don’t have to say anything specific. We could…we could order what you ordered—see if we get sick.”

Joseph sniffed. “Forgive me, but that approach is both reckless and undiplomatic.” He stood and faced Barnaby. “I enjoy my tête-à-têtes with Jimmy, and I would like to continue receiving my double portion of grits from Stella. Since I am feeling in the pink and don’t expect to have a relapse, I must ask you to cease and desist.”

The atmosphere vibrated like a plucked guitar string, and Philo decided to call a time out. She glanced at Barnaby. “Don’t you have a seminar to teach?”

Barnaby checked his watch. “Oh dear. Forgot all about it. Better go. I must gather the troops and mete out assignments.” A second later he was gone.

Philo took a minute to draw a dollop of oxygen into her lungs. Barnaby always seemed to leave her breathless, and it wasn’t always a good thing. Joseph—who had dropped into the chair vacated by Barnaby—heaved himself up. “I’m going upstairs. Thanks for everything, my dear.”

“I think I’ll close early.” She was grateful that Joseph didn’t mention the absence of customers.

****

Philo’s apartment, Friday, June 15

It wasn’t until almost six that Barnaby rang the buzzer. He came up carrying a large pizza. “Students had a pizza party after class. They let me take the leftovers. Although, given their appetites—particularly the girls—I’m surprised there *were* any. Sausage and jalapenos okay with you?” He put the box on the kitchen table and peeled off his sweatshirt.

Philo picked the garment up from the floor and thus was able to see it was printed with an image of a Princeton tiger crouching over a bulldog named Eli. "If I can't have anchovies, sausage and jalapenos are my second choice."

"I presume you have beer."

She put her hands on her hips. "Oh, how sweet. Thank you for asking. Yes, I had a nice day. Quiet in the shop after you scampered out. I read a little more about the treasure hunt. Other seekers seem to disagree with the Fountain of Youth focus."

"Yes, I know. That's why I plan to assign each student two places to research."

"Divide and conquer?"

"Delegation of labor. I'm really very lazy." He picked up a slice of pizza. "Also I wanted to spend more time with you."

Philo blinked. She reached blindly for the beer and knocked it over, spilling it into the sink.

"Well, now you've gone and done it. You only had three bottles in the fridge, and I need two. What will *you* drink?"

Philo was going to argue, but then remembered she'd gone up a size since she met Barnaby. "I'll have seltzer."

"Excellent choice. Very slimming. I'm impressed."

The response to this comment was distinctly unfriendly. Philo retrieved a pack of celery from the vegetable bin and proceeded to gnaw on a stalk while glaring at her companion.

After a while he asked diffidently, "Would you like to hear my list of sites?"

"*Mmm.*"

"Okay!" He took a swig of beer. "Kevin wants to stick with the Castillo. My guess is he hopes to run his attacker to ground."

"Did you settle things with his father?"

"In a way. He showed up right after our seminar and whisked Kevin off for a pow-wow. Kevin didn't seem glad to see him."

"He *was* afraid his parents would make him come home."

"All the more reason to plead for me."

"I'm sure it will all work out. Did the other students have anything to announce?"

He put the beer down. "Lincoln has the *Black Raven.* For his second site, I assigned him Ripley's. Did you know he can bend all his fingers back ninety degrees? I think he'll fit in nicely without drawing too much attention. Let visitors snap pictures of the oddball boy with the hands for a few minutes, and he might be able to slip into areas that are closed to the public." He paused. "My only concern is that they try to recruit him. From what I saw in the Odditorium, they could use some fresh exhibits. Where was I?"

Philo felt her eyelids getting heavy. *Must be from lack of food.* She dropped the celery and picked up a slice of pizza. "Um, I don't know."

"Ripley's, right." He ticked off his fingers. "Then there's Thomas. I had originally given him the Fountain of Youth, but we're going to tackle that as a team, so he gets the Oldest House. Susie has the Mission de Nombre de Dios for the nonce. Since that site seems to have lost its luster, maybe I can stick her with one of the other forts—Mosé or Matanzas. Have I missed someone? Cleo…and the other girl." He squinted. "Agatha. Right.

Cleo has the Flagler dining hall and Agatha the Greek shrine. What are your suggestions for secondary sites for them?"

"Why do you need two per student?"

"In case one doesn't pan out. The seminar lasts another four weeks, and if I don't keep them occupied they'll be enticed down the path to perdition, lured into depraved, debauched, and dissolute hobbies. Not to mention wayward, wanton, and wicked occupations. So…your suggestions?"

"Me?"

"You mean, you don't have any?" He seemed a bit put out.

"Oh, sure. Lots." Philo was still miffed about the slimming remark.

He gazed expectantly at her.

"How about the hot sauce store?"

"You're being facetious. I recognized that right away."

Philo gave up. "I dunno." She pointed across the street. "The Ximenez-Fatio house? The Old Jail? Oldest Drugstore? My store?"

"Your store! What treasures do you have tucked away in Mind Over Matter?"

"Oh, many, many." Sharing the contents of her inventory improved her mood considerably. "I have some of the earliest maps of the Florida coast, as well as the records of explorers like Hernando de Soto and Jean Ribault. I have the diaries of several pirates—including Blackbeard—and a book once owned by Governor Oglethorpe. He was the English governor of Georgia who attacked St. Augustine. Also—"

"But no stones. Or casques." Barnaby was despondent. "You had my hopes up for a minute there."

"Sorry." She took the beer out of his hand and gulped it down.

"*Humph.* I still need spots for Thomas, Cleo, and Agatha."

She thought it over. "You're looking for places that have artwork or a complicated pattern, like a maze, right?"

"Yes—the Odditorium garden, the star-shaped Castillo."

"St. Photios is a good choice then. It has some wonderful icons. Very colorful—much like Preiss's cartoons."

"Yes, that's one reason I let Agatha have it. Ooh, I just thought of something. I'll give her the oldest schoolhouse as well. It's right down the street." He wrote it down. "And?"

"What does Cleo have again?"

"The Flagler College dining room. Cleo's an artist and has studied stained glass." He turned his gaze across the street, where loomed a beautiful white stucco house. "What did you say that was?"

"The Ximenez-Fatio House. In the 1830s, it was a boarding house run by two women."

"I thought everything was from either Ponce de León's or Flagler's time?"

"Actually, no. The influx of northern entrepreneurs who built the railroads and fish camps didn't begin until after Reconstruction. The Fatio house hails from the first tourist boom in Florida, from 1821 to the start of the Civil War. People came here from other parts of the South for health reasons and to escape the Seminole wars."

He scanned it, chin in hand. "Does it have anything worth investigating?"

"Nothing spectacular. I believe they host mystery evenings."

"Murder mystery?" Barnaby's eyes glowed.

"No. Lesser crimes, like robbery. The guests have to find and free a kidnap victim or catch a thief."

"*Hmm.* Mystery. Safes behind portraits. Hidden doors and secret passageways. Sounds promising. We'll give that to Cleo too, and the Oldest Drugstore to Thomas. I do hope he's not tempted by goof balls and chill pills." He put down his pizza and scribbled on his pad. "That takes care of that."

"Wait a minute, what about Kevin? He only has the Castillo."

"Kevin! I've only got six—you'd think I could keep them straight. Yes, Kevin." He tapped the pen on his lip, leaving a streak of ink. "Maybe we'll just see if he can handle the one site since he's still recovering. More pizza? No?" He held out his arm. "Perhaps a stroll in the moonlight then?"

"Okay, but…" She pointed at his chin.

"Oops. Thanks." He rubbed the ink off.

They walked down Aviles Street to the square. Across Avenida Menendez lay the city marina. At the end of one of the floating docks a ship was ablaze with red and green lights. Philo tugged Barnaby's sleeve. "That's the *Black Raven.* Let's go have a dekko."

They walked carefully down the dock, compensating for the slight sway caused by the incoming tide. Just as they reached the ship, the lights winked out, leaving the marina in darkness except for the feeble glow of the gibbous moon. Next to the galleon, tied up stern in, was the *Queen Anne's Revenge.* "That's Blackbeard's flagship."

"So, do the pirates board the *Black Raven* and have their way with the wenches?"

"The only wenches on board are pirates too—Lady Red and Georgia Fury—and they aren't exactly attractive."

"You mean, no man in his right mind would rip their bodices?"

"Something like that."

"Darn. I hope there's at least a mock skirmish."

Philo tried to remember what the young man had told her. "I've never actually gone on the treasure voyage, but—"

"Treasure? Fantastic! Now who did I assign this to?" He snapped his fingers. "Lincoln, that's it. They have a cocktail cruise, which seemed to attract his notice."

She looked over the ship. "How do you suppose they have a proper swordfight if everyone's drunk?"

" 'Any damn fool can navigate the world sober. It takes a really good sailor to do it drunk.' Sir Francis Chichester."

"*Anyway.*" *Why do I even attempt to have a normal conversation?* "Blackbeard arrives on the *Queen Anne's Revenge* and boards the *Black Raven.* He steals their treasure chest and makes off with it. The captain orders the crew—which consists of a couple of college kids on summer break and the paying passengers—to chase him and retrieve it. Which they do."

"And what happens to the redoubtable Blackbeard?"

"I think they make him walk the plank. Or…" She stopped to think. Behind her came a splash. She whirled around. "What was that?"

"It came from the port side." Barnaby walked past the ship's stern and peered into the water. "Probably just a fish jumping."

"It sounded awfully big."

"A big fish then."

Philo scanned the deck. "Someone's up there. I saw a shadow against the moon." She yelled, "Hi there!"

There was no answer, but they heard a bang and another crash. Barnaby ran around to the starboard side. Philo caught up with him. He stood, facing the darkness. "Nothing."

They waited for a few minutes, but all was still. Finally Philo said, "Must be a crew member preparing for tomorrow."

"Okay. Come on."

As he took her hand, she pulled back. "There it is again!"

"What?"

"The shadow."

Before Barnaby could respond, a whistling noise rent the air. A large iron ball attached to a thick rope came swishing down from the mast and crashed at their feet. The entire dock vibrated. Barnaby jumped to one side, but he must have slipped on the decking, for he fell, landing hard. As Philo reached for him, he slid off the slick surface and into the dark water. "Barnaby!"

He surfaced, spluttering. "What the hell?"

"Are you okay?" Philo paced the dock trying to make him out in the faint light. She knocked into something. "Barnaby! I found a ladder!"

"Where?"

“Follow the sound of my voice.”

He let out a bark of laughter. “Yes, my Puck. ‘And we fairies, that do run / By the triple Hecate’s team, / From the presence of the sun, / Following darkness like a dream.’ ” He swam to the side and climbed out. “God, that water’s freezing.”

Philo wrapped her arms around him. “Let’s get out of here.”

“No, wait. I want to know who just tried to kill us.” He took a step toward the ship but suddenly bent down and picked something up.

At that moment a light flashed in their faces, blinding them. “You there. What do you think you’re doing?”

Chapter Fifteen

Not all treasure is silver and gold, mate.

—Captain Jack Sparrow

St. Augustine Municipal Marina, Friday, June 15

"You folks are trespassing."

For once Barnaby was speechless. Philo shielded her eyes from the beam. "Officer?"

A man in uniform approached but kept the flashlight trained on the quaking couple. "The marina is closed to the public after five p.m. You'll have to leave."

Behind them they heard another, much quieter, splash. Philo tried not to scream. "Someone's on that ship."

The guard chuckled. "Come on, you can do better than that. Just a mullet jumping at midges. Admit it—you were trying to sneak onto the *Black Raven*. You tourists are always doing that. Had to run another guy off half an hour ago. Now move along."

"But *sir*." Barnaby had found his voice at last, although his teeth chattered so much it was hard to understand his words. "Someone tried to kill us. Look." He pointed at the ship. The man turned his flashlight in that direction, but the deck appeared to be bare. "Seriously, an iron ball about yea large"—Barnaby cupped his hands—"came barreling down on a rope. It almost hit me in the head."

"Yeah, yeah. Off you go."

"But—"

Philo clasped Barnaby's arm. "The guy must have reeled it back up to the ship. You're soaked. We'll come back tomorrow."

With the security guard herding them along, they reached the avenue and crossed. Philo took Barnaby upstairs. She found a pair of jeans and an old sweatshirt of her father's and gave them to the shivering man. He held them in front of him. "A trifle gaudy for my taste, but I appreciate the gesture."

While he showered and changed, she made tea. "I put some rum in it to stave off any germs."

"That water was pretty rank."

"And cold."

He drank off the tea and rose. "I'd better go home. Don't want to come down with the sniffles and infect you."

"No! What if the killer's out there?"

He kissed the top of her head. "I've been thinking. It's a long stretch to assume we have a killer after us. It was probably the ship's master—we *were* trespassing after all. He wanted to put the fear of God in us."

"What about the other man—the one the guard had to chase off? He was trespassing too. Maybe he never left. Maybe he snuck onto the ship."

"But what earthly reason could he have for trying to bash me in the head?"

"He was stealing stuff. He was afraid we'd see him and call security."

"So he tosses a cannonball at me? Like a body sprawling on the sidewalk with its skull crushed wouldn't draw the guard's attention? No, it must have been an accident. The rope tore loose. I'll bet if anyone was on board he didn't even see us."

Philo didn't agree but couldn't persuade Barnaby. After a few minutes he left. As she picked up his wet clothes to put in the washer, something fell out of a pocket and clanged on the floor. She managed to catch it before it rolled under the table. *What the heck—?*

On her palm lay a gold doubloon.

****

Philo's apartment, Saturday, June 16

"Well?"

Barnaby turned the coin over in his hand. "Honestly? I don't remember. Right before the security guard accosted us, I thought I caught a glimpse of the guy. I tried to get a closer look, but then I heard something hit the ground. Stuck it in my pocket without thinking. Do you suppose it's real?"

Philo shrugged. "Try chewing on it."

"I've had breakfast, thank you very much."

"No, what I mean is, if it's real gold it should be soft."

"So is a cookie." Nonetheless he stuck it between his teeth and bit down. "*Chungh guh.*"

"Huh?"

He took it out. Using a fingernail he peeled the gold leaf wrapping off. "Chewing gum. It's chewing gum."

"Oh, right. I forgot. Besides the cocktail cruises, they have children's birthday parties. This is probably one of the party favors."

"Do you suppose the intruder knew he was stealing candy from babies?"

"Would that make him even more of a monster?"

"Yes." He put it down. "I propose we return to the *Black Raven* and ask the crew if they are aware someone was on the ship last night."

"And if they say no, ask if they're missing anything."

Barnaby's phone rang. "Oh, hi, Lincoln…Yes, all right. Look, do me a favor." He held a hand over the phone. "He's heading to the *Black Raven* this morning." Barnaby related their close encounter of the night before and asked him to question the crew. He clicked off. "That should do it. Now we have the whole day to spend in other pursuits. You'll be gratified to learn that my recent unwarranted immersion doesn't seem to have resulted in the sniffles, much less pneumonia." He took Philo into his arms.

The doorbell rang. She extricated herself and pressed the buzzer. The bell rang again twice. "Must be a delivery person. I'll go see what it is." She ran downstairs. A minute later she trudged back up slowly.

Barnaby held the apartment door open. "What do you have there?"

"A package. It was sent certified mail. The mailman rang because I had to sign for it." She held up the long canister. "It must be a map."

"Who's it from?"

She said, her voice wondering, "The return address says Robert Cottrell."

"Can't be. He's dead."

"I know that." She shook the tube.

"Don't break it."

"How can I break a map?" She swung it around. "I'm going down to the store to open it."

"I'll come with you."

Barnaby turned the shop lights on while Philo slit the top of the tube and carefully knocked the tightly rolled map out. She unrolled it and clamped the corners to the edges of an empty table. They contemplated the picture. It showed a coastline, with a phalanx of tiny ships offshore. Barnaby asked, "Do you recognize the place?"

"It's St. Augustine. There's the inlet that leads to the Matanzas River. The ships seem to be preparing for battle. Or possibly"—her finger tapped a small blue whale in the lower left corner—"a whale hunt."

"It's old, though, right?"

"Seems to be."

"Cottrell's been dead almost two weeks. Why did it take so long to get here?"

She looked at Barnaby. "It must have to do with *The Secret*."

"Then why didn't Cottrell send it to *me*? He died the day you and I met."

"True." She tapped the map. "Unless…unless…My father had an international reputation as a map dealer, and the shop is well known in St. Augustine." She took out a magnifying glass. "I need to examine this."

"Fine. I'm going to go meet Lincoln and get his assessment of the *Black Raven*. See you tonight. What are you cooking?"

Philo laughed.

"*Hmm*. Not a very encouraging response. Don't tell me: you have all your meals catered."

"On the contrary, I make everything from scratch—even ketchup."

"Impressive." Barnaby waited, an anticipatory smile on his lips.

She broke down. "How about a nice frittata?"

"With 'a loaf of bread, a jug of wine, and thou? Ah, wilderness were paradise enow.' "

She pushed him out the door.

****

Philo's apartment, Saturday, June 16

"What enticing aromas fill my nostrils! Do I detect"—he sniffed—"that ambrosia of the gods, bacon?"

"It's in the frittata. Do you want to know what I've discovered?"

"That you want to have my babies?"

She didn't miss a beat. "Where are you keeping them now?"

Barnaby set a baguette and a box of wine on the table. "They didn't have a jug."

"It's okay. I didn't have any eggs."

"I see. So we're having bacon for dinner?" He smacked his lips.

"No—I borrowed some eggs from Joseph. By the way, he says he's stymied by your latest crossword and has cut you out of his will."

"Won't be the first time." Barnaby fussed with the box. "How do you open the spigot?"

"Here, let me. You toss the salad."

When they were settled and had pronounced the wine passable, Barnaby opened the proceedings. "Let me get my report out of the way. I'm dying to hear about the map."

"Proceed."

"Lincoln went to the *Black Raven* and was allowed to join a large troop of Girl Scouts who were celebrating their flying up."

"Flying up where?"

"Flying…" He stared at her, aghast. "Don't tell me. Did you miss out on one of the most important components of any female child's education?"

"If you're asking whether I was a Girl Scout, the answer is no."

"Not even a Brownie? No? See, when you go from Brownie to full-fledged Girl Scout (third class) you get wings. Hence: 'flying up.' "

"Huh. And was Lincoln inducted as an honorary scout?"

"No, but they shared their goody bags with him. Finger puppets, jelly beans, Silly Putty, and Tootsie Rolls. Alas, no bubble gum."

"How come?"

"You remember the chewable doubloon? Turns out it came from the pirate's treasure chest, which according to the script, is stolen by Blackbeard and recovered by Captain Chase during a bloodless but heroic battle."

"Let me guess. The chest has gone missing."

"Correct. Methinks our shadow stole it last night."

Philo laughed. "Believing it held real doubloons? How gullible must he be?"

"He may be gullible, but he's also murderous. I wouldn't want to have seen his face when he opened the chest."

"So the pirates told Lincoln that their treasure was well and truly stolen. Did he enquire about a casque?"

"Yes, and they directed him to the Fountain of Youth. Apparently everybody in St. Augustine knows about *The Secret*." He took a bite of frittata. "This is delicious. A family recipe?"

"From the archives of the Eggland Farms Family."

"I shall write and praise it lavishly. Maybe they'll give us free eggs."

"Worth a shot."

Barnaby put his fork down. "All right, your turn. The map. Will it lead us to our stone?"

Philo guzzled the last of the wine in her glass. "I have to show you."

"Oh? Oh." Barnaby set down his fork and stood. "Let's take the back stairs."

The map lay flat, pegged to the table. "Several patrons inspected it today. One collector I know was very interested. Another fellow badgered me so incessantly I told him it was sold. Caught him trying to unpin it."

"Sounds like it may be valuable."

"Perhaps. I'll have to rate it on some appraisal websites before I price it."

Barnaby brushed the tube with his arm, knocking it over. As it fell, a folded sheet of paper fluttered to the ground. He picked it up. "It's a bill of lading."

"Wait! There's something written on the back of it." Philo took the paper from him. "It's a note from Cottrell. He must not have known Dad passed away. He's asking him to assess its value." She looked up. "He wanted to sell it on consignment."

"Well, that makes sense. He needed money to pursue the hunt."

"But hadn't he decided to sell his liquor business to Zimmer? That would have provided all the means necessary."

"He hadn't made up his mind yet—at least when I last talked to him. Harriet was dead set against it. But…" His gaze returned to the map. "If it *is* a key to the treasure, why sell it?"

Philo suddenly had doubts. "It's a map of St. Augustine all right—but not from Aviles' time. The

English privateer Sir Francis Drake conducted a raiding expedition to the Caribbean from 1585 to 1586, during which he attacked and sacked the city."

"Sir Francis Drake! Wow—he turns up everywhere, doesn't he? A man of many lives, you know."

"What's that supposed to mean?"

Barnaby held an arm to his chest. " 'Nelson was Francis Drake! / Oh what matters the uniform / Or the patch on your eye or your pinned-up sleeve / If your soul's like a North Sea storm?' Alfred Noyes."

This display was met with mystified silence. Finally Philo managed, "Yes, that Francis Drake."

But Barnaby had already moved on. "Can you pull up Image Number Six on the computer?"

She did. He studied it, cocking his head at various angles. "See the horseman on top—the one that looks like Picasso's Don Quixote?"

"Uh-huh."

"The analysis to date presumes he is Ponce de León." He gazed at her. "Could it in fact be Francis Drake?"

Chapter Sixteen

I think that we're pattern-seeking animals, and what we like best is a story where everything fits together, where there's no puzzle pieces left over.

—Noah Hawley

Mind Over Matter, Saturday, June 16

They were interrupted by heavy pounding at the store entrance. Philo cringed. "You don't think it's the police again?"

Barnaby flicked a hand at her while ducking behind her desk. "You'd better go see."

"Don't you dare run away." She went to the door. "There are two people outside. Civilians."

Barnaby came and looked over her shoulder. "Right—that's Cleo, and that's Agatha."

"Oh, now I recognize them from the Castillo. How did they know to find you here?"

He didn't answer, occupied with hand signaling to the two girls.

Finally Philo said impatiently, "Shall we let them in?"

"That might work, too." Barnaby opened the door. "What's wrong, ladies?"

Cleo strode in ahead of Agatha. Philo had a feeling that everyone strode ahead of Agatha. She was under five feet tall, with dun-colored, listless hair and a nose the size and shape of a shooter marble. Her huge, wistful eyes reminded Philo of one of those cat portraits painted on velvet.

Cleo, on the other hand, seemed to be all angles. Sharp elbows, a needle-like nose, and polished black eyes went with a lively, intelligent expression. Even her hair was spiky. She slammed a hand down on the table, knocking a pile of books to the floor. "Professor Swift, you promised me the Flagler ballroom, did you not?"

Barnaby scratched his head. "To tell you the truth, I'm having difficulty remembering who I assigned to what. If you want it, that's fine."

"I do. But Thomas is in there taking photographs. He's supposed to study the Oldest House, but he claims it has nothing of interest and he wants to partner with me. I won't have it!"

Barnaby blinked. "I haven't seen anything from him yet. He couldn't have had time to explore the house complex."

"Of course not. He ambled around the perimeter once and left." Cleo spat out, "He's a parasite—a drone. He wants to piggyback on my research. I won't have it, I tell you!"

Agatha's eyes glistened with moisture.

"All right." Barnaby checked his watch. "Why don't I come talk to him."

Cleo took his hand and tugged him toward the door. Philo, unaccountably miffed at the girl's proprietary manner, called, "I'm coming too."

Barnaby spun around. "Oh, hey. I forgot you were there."

"Why, thanks!"

"Er. Um." He let go Cleo's hand and, bobbing up and down, floundered. "Have you met my students? May I present Cleo Marzetti and Agatha…Agatha…"

The miniature young woman whispered, "Agatha Leonardi, Professor."

"Right. This is my friend, Philo Brice."

Cleo grazed Philo with eyes that were still smoldering from her recent tirade. "We know who she is, Professor. Exquisite, just as you described. Several times. She came with us to the Castillo, or did you forget that too?" She gave Philo an arch look and winked. Philo warmed to her.

Agatha chimed in. "Very pretty." She produced a misty smile.

Cleo opened the door. "Coming?" Barnaby and Agatha ran after her. Philo grabbed her purse and caught up with them at the end of the lane.

They were halfway to the college when Philo remembered she hadn't fastened the shop door. "I'll be right back." As she turned the corner onto Aviles Street, she thought she saw a light flicker in the store window. *I must have left the computer screen on. I'd better turn it off before I lock up.* She went in, but all was dark. She flipped the switch and moved to the laptop. As she closed the lid, she heard a rustling on the back stairs. "Who's there?"

A low mewling answered her. *Must be Joseph's cat Jemimah.* She turned to go and stopped short.

The map was gone.

****

Flagler College, Saturday, June 16

"Barnaby!" She was out of breath by the time she reached the little group at the entrance to Flagler College. The great gates were closed.

He turned. "We can't get in—the campus is shut down."

"Oh, but this is more important—the map's been stolen!"

Barnaby glared at her. "We've only been gone five minutes. What did you do—announce it to the city?"

Philo growled, "I left the door unlocked, okay? Obviously someone was watching the store and slipped in right after we left."

Cleo and Agatha approached. "Did you say a map?"

"It was stolen?"

"Did it show the location of the casque?"

Philo flung her hands in the air. "Who knows? We didn't have enough time to study it. It might have held some clues—or even be itself a clue."

" 'For all sad words of tongue and pen, the saddest are these: it might have been.' John Greenleaf Whittier. A regrettably underappreciated poet." Barnaby flopped down on the curb. "Damn it! We won't ever know now." Philo took out her phone. "What are you doing?"

"Calling the police."

"No!"

She held the phone in front of her. "My shop's been burgled, Barnaby. I've heard rumors of a rash of thefts from galleries recently. Isn't it my duty to notify the authorities?"

"You forget." Barnaby glanced at the girls and lowered his voice. "Me and the police? Lieutenant Tolliver? Sergeant Landman? Do we really want to give them more fodder for distrusting me? I don't want to be banished from the city."

"But—"

Cleo piped up. "We'll help you find it!"

Agatha nodded energetically.

Philo opened her mouth, but before she could refuse their offer, Barnaby interceded. "You guys are great. Tell you what: we'll regroup Monday morning. We can straighten this thing out with Thomas then as well. Tell the others, would you?" Cleo looked disappointed, and Agatha pulled a frowny face. "Please?"

Cleo sighed. "Oh, okay. Can we meet in our seminar room at ten?"

"Perfect." He shooed them toward the sidewalk. "Now get thee to a nunnery."

Cleo blanched. "You want us to join a convent?"

Agatha wailed. "Can't I just go back to my dorm?"

Barnaby stammered incoherently. Philo put him out of his misery. "It's a quote from Shakespeare. He's just joking. Yes, go back to your dorm. He'll see you Monday."

Barnaby watched the girls out of sight and turned to Philo. "Should you have explained that by 'nunnery' Hamlet actually meant a whorehouse?"

Philo was still fuming about the police. "No."

"I'm staying with you tonight."

"Oh yeah?"

"Yeah. Whoever robbed the shop may come back for more."

"I should warn you: I have to feed Delilah in the morning."

A spasm crossed his face. "I shall remain stoic. And in the bathroom."

****

Philo's apartment, Sunday, June 17

"I want to thank you for making me feel welcome." Barnaby didn't sound as though he meant it.

Philo rolled over and snuggled into the pillow. "Oh, fudge. By the time we'd lifted every rock and nosed into every cranny in the store, it was too late for you to go home."

"I see. It couldn't have been that you yearned for another night of unbridled lovemaking, of which only I am capable."

She just grinned. "I'm glad we weren't rudely interrupted by the thief at least."

Barnaby looked over at the aquarium. "The incessant tapping from the reptile was a little nerve-wracking though. Is she hungry?"

Philo leapt out of bed. "Oh dear me. She shed her skin a couple of days ago. Afterward she's starving." She opened the refrigerator, scooped three little mice onto a plate, and placed them in Delilah's aquarium. "There you are, sweetie."

Barnaby watched as the snake pulled one of the pinkies into the plastic log that served as her burrow. "You know, I'm almost getting used to her. She's a lot more benign than, say, an anaconda, or a pit viper."

"Of course she is." Philo sat on the bed. "Are you ready to hold her?"

He shrank back. "Maybe next year."

"Wuss." Philo went to her closet. Her hand floated briefly over the ratty fleece robe on the hook. Instead, she opened the wooden chest her mother had optimistically labeled her daughter's trousseau, drew out a beige silk kimono, and slipped it on. "If you make the bed, I'll make breakfast."

"Deal. After that, I intend to conduct a thorough search of the entire building. There might be clues we overlooked last night." He rose and slung the covers over the pillows with a perfunctory flip.

She straightened the rumpled mess. "Is this your notion of due diligence…or benign neglect?"

He feinted deftly. "Shall I retrieve the newspaper?"

"Newspaper?"

"You don't have a subscription to the St. Augustine *Crier*? My crossword will be in it." His voice trembled. "How do you work it then? Online?"

"Er, no. I don't actually do crosswords."

There was a brief pause. After a moment, Barnaby muttered, "Perhaps I should reevaluate my plans for us." He took in a deep breath. "I'll teach you."

Philo didn't know how to respond to what she considered a threat, so she went into the kitchen. He headed toward the apartment door. She heard a cordial "Good morning, Joseph! I see *you* at least subscribe to your local gazette."

Joseph boomed cheerfully, "I most certainly do—I look forward to the Sunday puzzle all week. Is it up to your usual standards?"

"You'll have to tell me. Say, I understand you have a cat."

"Jemimah? I hope she hasn't been disturbing you."

"No, no. Er…do you let her roam the building?"

"Well, she *has* escaped on occasion."

Philo went to the door. "I thought I heard her meowing last night—about eight?"

Joseph—as usual immaculately dressed in smoking jacket and flannel trousers—shook his head. "As far as I know, she was curled up at the end of my bed from seven o'clock on."

Barnaby and Philo exchanged glances. "It must have been the burglar."

"Burglar! In your apartment?"

"No, in the shop."

"Did you call the police?"

Barnaby paled. "No!"

Philo said more calmly, "As far as we can tell, only a map was stolen."

"Well, some of the maps your father collected are quite valuable. Which one was it?"

"I'd only just received it. It appeared to be an illustration of Sir Francis Drake's raid on St. Augustine. I hadn't had time to authenticate it."

"*Hmm*. Well, good luck." He waved the rolled-up newspaper. "I have my own task to accomplish."

Barnaby drew Philo back into her apartment. "That reminds me. We were speculating whether the *Secret* image might portray Drake and not Ponce de León. Let's revisit the notion after breakfast."

She agreed. "If it does, the map thief *could* be a seeker."

"And—if you are correct about Harriet—he might also be a murderer."

****

Mind Over Matter, Sunday, June 17

Barnaby rubbed his eyes. "Well, it's not definitive."

"You mean, whether the figure is of Ponce de León or Sir Francis Drake?"

"Yes. See—" He pointed at the screen. "Both English soldiers and Spanish conquistadors wore similar helmets."

"Do you have any images of Ponce de León?"

He clicked a few keys. They both studied several screens of portraits of the famous Spanish explorer. After a minute, Barnaby said, "He didn't wear the helmet very often, did he?"

"No, it's usually the hat with the long feather. Doesn't seem very soldierly, does he?"

"Perhaps he was attempting to appear peaceable, as in, 'Hi, there! I'm your friendly neighborhood conquistador. No need for concern.' So as to give the Indians a false sense of security before he brought the hammer down in the form of Franciscan priests."

"Hammer's a bit thick. According to archaeologists, they successfully converted the local Timucuans. A cemetery was recently excavated on the grounds of the Fountain of Youth that held Christian burials of natives."

"Well, I'll be. Another sacred cow slaughtered."

Philo contemplated the screen. "Did you notice that the horse has no saddle? And no bridle or reins—just a rope tied around its muzzle."

"Huh. Curious. I can't imagine a soldier riding a horse bareback."

"Could it be that Drake—or Ponce de León—didn't ride horses? I mean, they were sailors."

"*Hmm.* You bring up a valid point. I've now looked through two hundred portraits of Drake, and never once is he painted on horseback."

"How about de León?"

"Same thing." Barnaby raised his head, his eyes alight. "Maybe this guy is neither Ponce de León nor Drake. Maybe he's Don Quixote."

"The picture incorporates all kinds of images. Could the artist have been making some kind of allusion?"

"Possibly, but to what?"

Philo bit her lip. “Maybe the figure’s just a nobody. One of the Greek settlers. That would explain the lack of a saddle.”

Barnaby said absently, “Not Greek. Minorcan.” He caught his breath. “Minorcan. St. Photios. Aha!”

Chapter Seventeen

In the same way he's fascinated by crosswords, the puzzle of solving the murder is what drives him on.

—John Thaw

Philo's apartment, Monday, June 18

"So you're meeting the class at ten?"

"Right. I'm going to put Thomas's nose to the grindstone and Cleo's shoulder to the wheel."

"Do the rest of them get to ride in the wagon?"

"Ha-ha." Barnaby took his mug to the sink. "Your shop is open this afternoon, correct?"

"Yes." Philo sighed. "I wish we'd found some trace of the thief."

"Well, we know he has a facility with animal sounds."

"You think he was the one who meowed?"

"Indeed. Perhaps I could ask Lincoln to check the Odditorium for cat people."

"Good idea. Oh, and don't forget to tell the students about our hypothetical Minorcan."

Barnaby picked up his briefcase. "Should I? This is their exercise. I don't want to give away too much."

"It's not that we have proof. It's simply a proposition based on an observation of the image."

"I'd rather see if they come up with it on their own first." Barnaby kissed her. "See you this evening."

Eight hours later, as she was closing the shop, Barnaby showed up in jeans, a T-shirt that blared Don't Mess with Massachusetts, and a fishing vest. "We're meeting the kids for a drink at the A1A restaurant." He pulled a string tie with a bolo made from a campaign button that said Courage! Confidence! And Coolidge! out of his pocket and held it up. "In case they have a dress code. Are you ready?"

"Aren't your students underage?"

"Only Kevin and Susie. Linc's twenty-two, and it turns out the others are the full score and one year. The babies can have Shirley Temples." He smiled reminiscently. "That brings back such memories! My grandfather had this marvelous bar with a shiny black floor and a white polar bear rug. There was a brass rail and stools that spun around. He'd set us kids up with Shirley Temples plus our choice of animal-headed glass swizzle sticks. He was a grand old coot."

Philo had by now acquired the knack of continuing whatever she was doing without regard to Barnaby's unremitting jibber jabber. She retrieved her purse. "Ready."

They met the students in the vast second-floor restaurant overlooking the Bridge of Lions. Barnaby observed the swizzle sticks in Susie's and Kevin's drinks with approval. Kevin pushed his crutches aside so Philo could sit down.

Barnaby remained standing. "*Mes enfants*, this is Ms. Philo Brice. She owns Mind Over Matter on Aviles Street. Sells antique maps and books. Let's give her a hearty welcome."

She nudged him. "I've only formally met Cleo and Agatha."

"Oh? Oh. Let's start with Susie. Susie Phelps, Philo Brice." He said in a loud whisper, "Susie's never been to the South before. Her parents wanted her to tap into her roots."

Susie gave him an odd look. "Actually, Professor, my parents come from Canada."

"Oh? Did *not* know that. Well, well. Shall we continue? Thomas Doulton from Otumwah, Iowa." He indicated a youth with pale skin and orange hair. "He claims he's never met Radar, but I don't believe him."

"Radar—the character in M*A*S*H?"

"The very one. You'll remember he hailed from Otumwah."

"Ah."

Thomas, despite his wash of angelic freckles, had a sly look about him. Philo remembered what Cleo had said—that he was adept at wiggling out of work. Next to him sat a gangly young man with hazel eyes. "Hi, I'm Lincoln Nevers. How do you do?"

She almost curtsied.

Barnaby went on. "And Kevin Magnusson you've hovered over."

She smiled at the young man with the pug nose and unruly blond locks. "At the Castillo. I was one of many getting in the way of the medics."

Barnaby said loudly, "What do you want to drink, Philo? I'll get it."

"Gin and tonic, please."

When he returned with a highball and a mug of dark beer, everyone started to talk at once. "Hold it." The ring of authority in Barnaby's voice took Philo by surprise. It quieted the group. "We are here to resume the debate begun this morning, so inconveniently cut short by the power outage."

Lincoln leaned over the table to Philo. "This sophomore wanted to duck out of his exam and pulled the main circuit breaker. Took 'em three hours to pinpoint the problem." He grinned.

Barnaby raised his voice. "To recap. Linc has already discussed the pirate ship. He's been assigned Ripley's as well. Susie, you decided there wasn't much potential in the mission, so I'd like you to research Fort Mosé."

"Fort Mosé?"

"It's a couple of miles north of the city. First settlement of freedmen in the New World."

Susie looked nervous. "Are there soldiers there?"

"Only fake ones. They do reenactments. There may be nothing of interest, but it wouldn't hurt to check it out."

Philo whispered in his ear, "What about the other fort, Fort Matanzas? She could have that if she doesn't want Fort Mosé."

He shook his head. "I considered that. It's a good half-hour's drive south of here. I wouldn't fancy letting Susie go, even if accompanied."

"But—"

"Add to that there's nothing there but this little stone tower surrounded by marshland—nowhere to bury a casque." He turned to Kevin. "Kevin, I know you haven't been able to get back to the Castillo yet—"

Kevin quailed. "I don't want to go back alone, Professor."

"Oh, yes. Well." He pointed at Thomas. "He'll go with you."

"But I want to do the Flagler dining room! Those windows have to have something to do with *The Secret*!"

"We've been over this. Cleo has the Flagler. You have the Oldest House."

"But—"

"I'll go with Kevin."

The group looked up. Standing behind Kevin was a man in a business suit. His hair was cropped short, and his face had the grayish cast of an office dweller who spends his days under fluorescent lights. Kevin twisted around. "Dad!"

Barnaby, whose face had stiffened, said in a tight voice, "Mr. Magnusson."

The man produced a broad smile. "Professor. Kevin told me you would be here. I've come to make amends. He delivered a passionate defense of you and your teaching methods. I had planned to take him home, but once he disclosed the theme of the seminar, I changed my mind." He looked down at his son. "He may have mentioned his mother and I are members of the Ohio *Secret* hunt forum." He added—to the obvious consternation of the young people—"I'd be happy to chaperone!"

"Well, that's mighty nice of you, Mr. Magnusson."

"Call me Runar." He stepped back. "I have to run. Have a teleconference in twenty minutes. I'll give you a call, shall I?"

"Um. Sure." Barnaby clearly didn't know what to make of the elder Magnusson. When he'd gone, he stretched his neck. "Okay, let us continue. Thomas, you were at the Oldest House this afternoon. What did you find?"

Thomas was still grumbling. "Nuthin'. It's not even a house—it's this stupid museum filled with military crap." He thought for a minute. "And a gallery with paintings by local artists—hideous junk."

"What about the grounds? It's reputed to have magnificent live oaks."

"Oh, yeah. Nice and shady." Philo had a feeling he'd spent most of his time sitting on a bench under those trees. "They also have a formal garden. The gardener was pruning back a bunch of tall flowers. 'Dead-heading,' he called it." He sniggered. "Old, whiskery guy. Sure didn't *look* like a Grateful Dead fan."

No one laughed, and several squirmed in their seats.

Thomas was still grousing. "The whole place was a mess—had to wade through this big pile of cuttings." He flushed unexpectedly and pulled something from his pocket. "Did find a pretty flower in it, though." With ardent eyes, he proffered it to Cleo, who recoiled in distaste.

"A crummy weed? Thanks a lot." She waved it off with an exasperated hand.

Philo felt a twinge of pity for the boy, but Barnaby had apparently missed the exchange entirely. He continued. "Once everyone's finished his first site you can go on to your second. Cleo, you have the Ximenez-Fatio house. Find out about their mystery evenings if you can. There may be hidden niches or revolving walls behind which a casque could be secreted." He turned to Thomas. "I know you were supposed to scope out the Fountain of Youth, but I think we'll do that as a class. So, if you're done with the Oldest *House,* I've decided you'll do the Oldest *Drugstore*. That is, if you promise to keep your hands off the merchandise." He smiled. "Just kidding."

Before Thomas could complain, Philo held out her hand. "Wait a minute, Thomas. Your flower. May I see it?" He dropped it on the table in front of her, his face sullen. She turned it over. "This is a foxglove. Were there a lot of them?"

He nodded. "Most of the pile. The gardener said they didn't do well in the salt air and he had to pull out the whole bed. Why?"

Philo tried and failed to ignore the word that had just switched on in her head: murder. She looked at Barnaby. "Joseph."

Barnaby paled. "You don't think…"

Her eyes were wide and fearful.

"He hasn't been in any meadows recently, but he didn't say anything about a garden." He set down his half-empty mug and rose. "Hate to drink and run, children, but we have pressing business to attend to." He took Philo's hand.

"Er. Professor?"

"What?" Barnaby was agitated; Philo knew he wanted to get back to talk to Joseph.

"Aren't you forgetting something?"

"I don't think so." His hand went to his forehead, his crotch, his chest, and his rear pocket, as he recited, "Spectacles, testicles, fountainpen, wallet. Yup, all accounted for."

In the awkward silence that succeeded this speech, Lincoln said, "Um…what about Agatha?"

"Oh, right. Agatha. I didn't see you there. You're St. Photios, right?"

"Yes, sir."

Philo could barely hear her. She waited, hoping Barnaby would mention the Minorcan angle, but he said nothing.

Agatha murmured, "There's one icon that might hold promise, but the shrine closed before I could sketch it. They wouldn't let me take a photograph."

"Well, that sounds great! Yes—" He nodded briskly. "We'll consider it tomorrow. Keep it up, guys. Bye." He practically ran out of the bar. Philo gave the students a helpless smile and sped after him.

She found him rapping on Joseph's door. Philo was taken aback to see the old man in his pajamas. "Are you all right?"

Barnaby brushed her aside. "Never mind that. Have you been to the Oldest House lately?"

"Took a turn about the grounds the other day. Why?"

"I think I know what poisoned you."

Joseph ushered them in and settled back down in his easy chair. A tall glass stood on the table next to him. Philo said, "I thought you were going to lay off drinking for a while?"

"Oh, this? This is a remarkable tincture. It's been very effective in keeping the swelling in my ankles down. Much better than those pills Doc Anderson gave me." He waggled his shoulders. "It does make me feel a bit out of sorts, but Ed says that's from the sugar."

"Sugar? What else does it contain?"

"It's a secret family recipe. Comes in tea bags that I steep in water."

Philo asked, "Ed…your friend from the Dog and Whistle?"

"The very one. He's been bringing me his crosswords. Even though he's on vacation, the editor expects weekly submissions." He winked at Barnaby. "They're good, but they don't hold a candle to Argle Bargle's. Now, it must be something important for you two to appear at this hour. I would expect you to be spooning or at least gazing rapturously into each other's eyes."

"Oh dear, I'm so sorry, Joseph. I didn't realize how late it was."

"Never mind. I've been poisoned, you say?"

"Foxglove. Digitalis. You say your heart is fine, but Dr. Reagle said you have high levels of potassium and magnesium." Barnaby stopped. "High levels…Are you by chance taking a diuretic?"

"If water pills are diuretic, then yes, but as I say, they're only partially effective."

Understanding flashed through Philo's mind. *Ha.* "And Ed's tincture is helping?"

"Very much so."

Barnaby picked up the glass. "Do you mind if we take your friend's concoction for testing?"

"You think—? *Hmm.* By all means, although I'm sure Ed has no idea his drink can cause difficulties. He says his parents swear by it." He went into the kitchen and came out with a small plastic bag. "Here you go."

"I'll take it to the lab tomorrow."

Philo kissed the old man's cheek. "Get some rest!"

Joseph winked. "You too."

They returned to her apartment. Philo retrieved a bottle of water from the refrigerator. "Now, my good man, what's all this about a diuretic?"

"Just a hunch. Digitalis raises blood potassium, but not to dangerous levels. Most diuretics leach potassium from the blood, but there's one class that preserves it.

Joseph thought the tea was relieving the edema, so it likely contains a diuretic."

"And you're thinking it's the kind that retains potassium."

****

Philo's apartment, Tuesday, June 19

"The lab says it won't get results for twenty-four hours. I suppose I'll have to hold the class after all." Barnaby seemed disappointed.

"Well, you *are* getting paid to teach, not solve crimes."

"Not enough. May I have another sandwich?"

"No."

Barnaby's phone buzzed. "Hello? Oh, hello, Mr. Zimmer…Axel, of course. Yes, yes, it's true. Both Robert and Harriet Cottrell are dead. I suppose their liquor store is up for sale…Really? He won't?…No, I don't know him. I wouldn't have any leverage with him. Sorry…Well, I suppose I could…" He checked his watch. "Sure, I can meet you there now, but I have a class at four. All right." He clicked off.

"Who was that?"

"The man I worked for, Axel Zimmer. The guy who wants to buy out the Cottrells."

"He's the one who ordered the vandalism of their store?"

"On the contrary. He's the guy who ordered the vandalism to stop."

"Why does he want to meet you?"

"He says their son is also refusing to sell. Seems Robert told him about the harassment, and he's considering filing a lawsuit against Millstone Brands."

"Well, what can *you* do about it?"

"He's asked me to run interference—see if I can smooth the way to a settlement. Once Cottrell is sufficiently softened up, I can introduce him to Mr. Z." He shook his head. "I suspect he has an inflated opinion of my powers of persuasion."

"You're meeting him at Granada Liquors?"

"Yes, and therefore it is with regret that I turn down your generous offer of another tuna fish sandwich."

Philo didn't feel the need to reply.

He didn't seem put out. "Never mind. I'm sure I can touch Axel for lunch money. He's rich as Croesus."

"Go for it."

A couple of hours later, Philo's phone rang. It was a breathless Barnaby. "Philo? Are you busy? What are you doing?"

"Working."

"Can you come bail me out?"

"What?"

"Bail me out. As in, get me out of jail. Help me, Wan Kenobi—you're my only hope."

"What have you done this time?"

"I'll explain when you get down here. There's a line out the door waiting to use the phone." Which instrument suddenly went dead.

Chapter Eighteen

Once I get on a puzzle, I can't get off.
—Richard P. Feynman

St. Augustine police station, Tuesday, June 19

"I'm glad we cleared that up. Thanks, Sergeant Steve."

Steve rolled his eyes. "If you hadn't been in our sights so often these past two weeks, Swift, we'd have given you the benefit of the doubt."

"I appreciate your indulgence. And I mean that sincerely." Barnaby stuck a hand out. He had to wait a long minute before Steve took it.

Philo put her checkbook back in her purse. "So I don't need to bail him out?"

"No. The other two are still charged with disturbing the peace, but they both affirm that Mr. Swift here was trying to break up the fight."

"Let me guess: the peace disturbers are Mr. Zimmer and Mr. Cottrell."

Barnaby shivered. "I've never seen Mr. Z. so mad. He turned this deep mauve color. And he frothed at the mouth."

"What pissed him off?"

"Cottrell wouldn't talk to him. Threw him out of the store. Asserted that Millstone—and by extension, Mr.

Z.—is an accessory in the deaths of his parents. Ridiculous."

Philo said mildly, "Zimmer admitted his company was hectoring them."

Barnaby cast a guilty glance at Steve. "No, no, that was all a misunderstanding. Everything taken care of. Nothing to worry about. Am I free to go?" This last to the desk sergeant.

"Yes, sir."

Barnaby led Philo outside. He looked over his shoulder. "I told you, Zimmer fired the people who were bullying the Cottrells. He's not the bad guy."

"Then why does Cottrell think he's involved?"

"I don't know. He probably just wants to blame somebody. The police didn't catch the culprits, so Cottrell—his name's Norton by the way, nice chap…at least until he took a swing at Axel…where was I? Oh, yeah, Norton has to cover the repair costs himself."

"That's not fair. Zimmer is the chairman of Millstone Brands, isn't he? At the very least, he should pay for the damage." Philo got in her car. "Do you want me to drop you at the college?"

"Why? Oh my God, will you look at the time! I'll be late for the seminar. Can you step on it?"

"Why yes, Master."

He leaned back on the car seat. "Great."

"I take it Zimmer did not talk Cottrell into selling him the liquor store."

"A rational deduction. Odd though."

"What's odd?"

"Mr. Z.'s reaction. It was way over the top. He kept trying to shove Norton aside to get into the building. I've never seen him so perturbed."

"Maybe he's afraid there's evidence inside linking him to the vandalism."

"The police would have found it."

"Maybe, maybe not…Here you are." She dropped him at the entrance to Flagler College. "Let me know if your students have made any progress."

"Will do."

****

Philo's apartment, Tuesday, June 19

"I wish I'd had time for that second tuna sandwich. I'm starved." Barnaby finished off the peach and threw the pit in the trash.

"No doughnuts at the police station?"

"None left. However, Axel—who has always treated me like a second son—did cough up the bonus he promised me when I left, so it would be my pleasure to squire you to dinner."

"Okey doke." *Better take advantage of it while I can.* Philo tied her sweater around her waist.

"How about Flora's? I have a hankering for chili."

"How about O. C. White's? I have a hankering for food I can eat."

"If you insist." He grumbled while they walked. "Don't understand why you didn't like Flora's. It was so cheap."

"Yes, but she uses plastic beads for the beans and cat food for the beef."

"Do you know that for sure?"

"Absolutely. I read it on the internet." She held the door to the tavern open for him.

Philo ordered drinks while Barnaby went in search of a men's room. "I was forced to fondle several dogs on the way to your place. The big ones drooled, and the little ones had fleas."

When he returned, she said, "So how did the seminar go?"

"Not very productive, I'm afraid. Kevin's still on crutches, so he's doing library research and hasn't returned to the Castillo."

"What news of his father?"

"Runar's busy remote working, but he seems to be hunkering down for an extended visit."

"I hope he doesn't interfere with the seminar."

"We'll see. He's allowing Kevin to stay at the dorm at least, but he keeps dropping by my office to ask questions."

"As long as he doesn't start helping Kevin with his homework." She nibbled on a roll. "Any of the other students have news?"

"As far as I can tell, Thomas spent the day moping. Cleo informed us she's had a breakthrough."

"Oh?"

"Yes. She's been photographing the stained-glass dining hall windows at different times of the day, but today she noticed something she hadn't before."

"That one of them is a perfect duplicate of the sixth picture?"

"Close. When the afternoon sun shone through the stained glass, it made a reverse pattern on the floor. She wants to see if it can be applied to the image."

"Sounds promising. Oh, thank you." She accepted the martini glass.

Barnaby curled his lip. "What's that? A margarita? Real women don't drink soda pop masquerading as alcohol."

"Lucky for me this isn't, then. It's a dirty martini, two olives, with a twist." That shut him up. She raised her eyes to the waiter. "I'll have the bronzed salmon, please." The waiter wrote it down and looked expectantly at Barnaby.

"I'm going to be daring and go for the shrimp and grits."

When he'd gone, Philo sipped carefully from the tippy glass. "What about Agatha?"

"Who? Oh, right. She turned up late. She tends to be rather skittish."

Philo didn't think she would have used that adjective to describe the young woman. *Maybe transparent?*

"She was especially skittish today. She stated that she returned to the St. Photios shrine. While she was investigating the grounds, she became aware that a man was following her."

"You mean stalking? Or tailing?"

"She couldn't tell." His eyes narrowed. "What difference does it make?"

"Stalking means he's after Agatha the girl. Tailing might mean one of the obsessed seekers you've been talking about."

"I see. Someone trying to spy on her so when she unearths the casque, he can move in and purloin it." He spoke to the ceiling. "Could they be that deranged?"

"Did she get a good description of the man?"

"Not really, only that it was a male. He had a hat pulled down so she couldn't see his face, and he hunched his shoulders so she couldn't tell how tall he was."

"Did he follow her out of the shrine?"

"She doesn't think so. He just happened to be in every room while she was there."

Philo chuckled. "He didn't *happen* to be wearing a security uniform, did he?"

"I didn't ask. What I can't explain is how he could even keep track of her. She's like one of those Kalahari bushmen. Or a pixie."

"She does seem to blend into the background, poor thing. Where's she from, anyway?"

"Um…"

Philo took pity. "Why don't I ask her? She hasn't said more than two words in my presence, but she does seem to have a slight accent."

"True." He finished his cocktail. "Perhaps she's from a land of pixies." He brightened. "She could be one of Preiss's Fair Folk in disguise!"

She handed her empty glass to the waiter. "You should have someone escort her the next time."

"I'll put it to the group. It's probably simply her imagination working overtime."

"Uh-huh. Did the other two—Susie or Lincoln—have anything to announce?"

"Nothing yet. I'm beginning to wonder if this was such a good plan."

"The scavenger hunt?"

He nodded. "Maybe we should stick with library work—or choose an entirely different subject."

"Or you could concentrate on the Fountain of Youth."

"Go with the general consensus? Although since the Ponce de León casque was already found at the spring, I still can't see Preiss burying his box in the same place."

"Why not? Maybe he figured that's what everyone would think."

"Reasoning's a little tortuous, don't you think?"

"The whole treasure hunt is tortured."

The waiter brought their dinners. Philo tasted her salmon. "Delicious."

Barnaby didn't move. "So these are grits. Huh."

"What's the matter?"

"I've never actually tasted them. I only ordered them because Joseph waxed so lyrical about the dish. In fact, all you Southerners do. Almost as much as you rave about barbecue." He contemplated the yellowish puddle. "At least barbecue has some color." He played with the grits, swishing a fork around in them, forming them into shapes.

Philo left him to his games and dug in.

"Lookee here." He pointed at his plate. "The state of Texas."

"At least try one bite, child." She considered his creation. "That reminds me: the stolen map. Francis Drake. The idea has merit."

"Oh, so now we've come full circle—or rather, one and a half circles? It's not the Minorcan peasant in Image Six but Sir Francis Drake? Too bad we don't have the map." He twirled the grits into the form of a large-breasted woman. Philo flattened it with her spoon. "Do you suppose the collector who asked about it was the one who pinched it?"

"I called him. He was offended that I'd even suggest it."

"That just makes him sound guiltier."

"Well, if he tries to display it, I have the bill of lading to prove Mr. Cottrell sent it to me."

Barnaby called for the check. When the waiter came over, he pointed at Philo. "She'll take it, thanks."

"Hey!"

He had the gall to look offended. "I was happy to treat you to Flora's, but no. You're too good for chili.

You insisted on haute cuisine. Next thing, you'll be wanting to dine in the Flagler student union." He dropped his spoon into the untasted grits. "When you're ready to come off your high horse and eat with the peons, I'll pay." He took out his wallet. "Tell you what, I'll cover the tip." He riffled through the contents. "Five percent is customary here in Florida, right?"

Philo counted to ten, then rose. She handed the bill to Barnaby. "I'll be in the car." She left him holding it as though it was covered in slime.

When he came out, he seemed chastened. "I apologize, Philo. I'm used to being a poor graduate student. I assume anyone with a job is rich. Tell you what: I'll touch Axel for another bonus and take you out for ice cream." He held up two fingers. "Two scoops. Any flavor."

Philo found she wasn't as aggravated with him as she should be. "All right, hop in."

As she started to make the turn onto Aviles Street, he held up a hand. "I have to stop in at the dorm tonight. The administration requires I make my presence known at least once a week. Drop me off?"

Philo's world suddenly turned chillier. "Sure. Fine."

At the corner of King and Malaga Streets, where a cluster of student dormitories lay, a knot of people milled around on the sidewalk. Barnaby squinted. "Looks like Cleo and some other students."

She pulled to the curb. "Can't be an accident. We're the only car in the road."

"Well, something's stirred them up. Wait here. Let me go ask." Barnaby got out and walked over. He spun around and sprinted back to Philo. "It's Agatha. She's missing."

Chapter Nineteen

If you think you are too small to make a difference, try sleeping with a mosquito.

—Dalai Lama

Flagler College, Tuesday, June 19

"Oh my God…*Agatha*? Wait—do you think the man who was tailing her kidnapped her?"

"I don't know. Cleo says no one really believed her about the man." Barnaby pointed toward the little group. "They're organizing a search party."

"Should I call the police?"

Barnaby hesitated, which Philo thoroughly understood. "What do you think?"

"She hasn't been missing that long. How about if we do some poking around on our own first? Has anyone tried her cell phone?"

"Another question I don't have an answer to. Come on."

Philo locked the car, and together they approached the students. Cleo was barking orders to a rather inattentive audience.

Barnaby took her aside. "Cleo? Did you try Agatha's cell?"

"She doesn't have a cell phone."

"You're kidding."

"I'm not." Cleo shook her fist in frustration. "She doesn't have a laptop either. Or a car. I'll bet she doesn't even have a social security number!"

Philo put a hand on the girl's arm. "Maybe where she comes from she didn't need one. She has an accent. Is she from another country?"

Cleo wailed. "Another country? It's more like she's from another *planet*. I'm sure she doesn't have much money—I mean, look at her clothes."

It's hard to be fashionable when you have to shop at Kids R Us. Philo gave Cleo a sympathetic pat.

She took a gulp of air. "I hope she's okay."

Barnaby took charge. "Where have you searched so far?"

"Nowhere yet. We've only just become aware that she's gone."

"Walk us through it."

Cleo glanced at the others. "We went to a bar after the seminar. We were coming home when I turned around to say something to her, and she wasn't there. One minute she was behind me, the next"—she swished her arm—"nada. You don't think that guy was really stalking her?"

Barnaby didn't answer. He beckoned the others. Lincoln and Thomas joined them. "Where's Susie?"

"She went home early. She's in bed."

"And Kevin?"

Lincoln said, "He's still in some pain from the injury. We didn't want to keep him on his feet unnecessarily."

"Okay. Now, as the good book says: 'Don't panic.' "

Thomas frowned. "I don't remember that being in the Bible."

"The Bible? Of course not. Don't be daft. I'm quoting *The Hitchhiker's Guide to the Galaxy*. Duh."

The students goggled at Barnaby. He shook his head sadly. "What else aren't they teaching you in school nowadays? All right, let's start with her room. Maybe there's a hint there—a note or something—of where she might be."

"This is our dorm." Cleo got her ID card out and swiped it in the key slot. "She's next to me." They trooped up the stairs to the third floor and down the hall. Barnaby knocked on the door marked 315.

"Who is it?"

In unison the posse sighed. "Agatha?"

The little girl opened the door. "Hi, Cleo. Professor Swift." She was licking an ice cream cone.

Cleo curled her hands into the shape you make when you want to strangle someone. "Where the heck have you been, Aggie?"

She held up the cone. "I stopped for ice cream on the way home. I told you I was going to. Didn't you hear me?"

"No, I didn't. How did you get past us?"

"I came in the side door."

Her voice pitched low, Cleo spit out, "We almost called the police."

Philo felt Barnaby quiver beside her.

"Oh, sorry. Say—that guy I thought was following me? He was!" She smiled broadly.

"Oh dear—did he attack you? Did you run away? Why didn't you come get me?" Cleo looked ready to shake Agatha.

"I didn't have to. Guess what? He's my cousin Diego. We haven't seen each other since we were little, and he wasn't positive it was me. Once he was sure, he came up and introduced himself." Her mouth puckered. "I still don't recognize *him*, but then he's a couple of years older than me. Isn't it exciting to reconnect with family?" She held up the cone. "He even paid for the ice cream!" This seemed to elate her.

Starved for attention? Philo took note of the gaggle of students surrounding the tiny girl. *I hope she doesn't take to disappearing on a regular basis, just for the ego boost.*

Lincoln asked, "Does he live here?"

"Diego? No. He's with a tour, and the shrine was on the itinerary. See, our family's Minorcan. My grandfather emigrated after World War II. I didn't get a chance to tell you, Professor, but most of the Greek immigrants to St. Augustine weren't even Greek—they were Minorcan. They started in New Smyrna but ended up settling here. My parents begged me to see St. Photios while I was in town. I thought I'd died and gone to heaven when you assigned it to me."

"You could have just asked for it." Barnaby glanced at Philo. "The Oldest Schoolhouse was built by a Minorcan as well."

"I *know*. Aren't I the luckiest?"

Cleo—who had been steaming in the corner—finally managed in a broken voice, "You're Minorcan? What exactly does that mean?"

Barnaby explained. "Minorca is part of the Balearic Islands. They sit just off Spain in the Mediterranean Sea. Minorcans speak Catalan but were actually British for most of the eighteenth century."

Thomas piped up. "So what brought them here?"

Barnaby answered promptly. "English landowners. See, in the Treaty of Paris that ended the Seven Years' War, the English won both Minorca and Florida. At the time, this part of Florida was underpopulated, so the Brits recruited people from the island to come here."

Agatha scrunched up her nose. "They arrived in New Smyrna as indentured servants to a man named Andrew Turnbull, who owned an indigo plantation, but he treated them like slaves. After nine years, the few who survived escaped and walked all the way to St. Augustine. The British governor—who hated Turnbull—gave them land near the city gates." She glowed with pride. "The Minorcan community has thrived here for over two hundred years."

"So, you wanted to study St. Photios to find out more about your ancestry?"

"Yes, but I also thought the art might have a clue to *The Secret*." A cunning smile crossed her lips. "I found something else instead."

"What?"

"Well, it's probably better to show you. Hang on." She handed the ice cream cone to Cleo, who gave it to Thomas, and went into her room. She came out a minute later with a large atlas, which she set on the bench in the hall. She opened it to a marked page. "This is the entry for Minorca. Here's its flag."

Barnaby gave the picture a cursory scan, then suddenly leaned forward. "At first glance that thing in the middle looked like a gremlin, but it's not, is it? Philo! It's a castle!"

"A square fort with bastions…just like the Castillo."

"A clue! A palpable clue!"

Agatha held up a shy hand. "But wait. I have more." She pulled out a sheet of paper that had been stuck in the pages of the atlas. It proved to be a color print of Image Six.

Before Agatha could continue, Philo tugged Barnaby's sleeve. "Tell them our theory about the soldier."

"Right!" He eyed Agatha. "We may have found another link to Minorca. The soldier in the image is generally thought to be Ponce de León, but Philo—Miss Brice—spotted something." He picked up the printout and showed it around. "See? There's no saddle or bridle, and a rope instead of reins. So…the rider might not be a soldier at all. It *could* be a villager on his dray horse."

"A Minorcan?" Agatha's eyes gleamed.

"Possibly."

"What about the helmet? The fancy duds?" Thomas was more energized than usual.

Philo observed the empty cone in his hand. *Sugar high?*

"He might have stolen them. Or they were left behind by the retreating Spaniards when the English arrived."

Everyone began to talk at once. Philo broke off when she saw Agatha holding the picture. Her mouth was open, but all that issued from it was a cooing sound. Philo shushed the others. "I believe Agatha said she'd found something else."

The girl gave Philo a grateful smile. She held up the picture and pointed at the single rock outcrop next to a palm tree. "I found no rock matching that in Florida in my research. However, it *does* resemble the Rock of Gibraltar, which guards the entrance to the

Mediterranean and is about five hundred miles from the island. And the palm tree in the painting? It's a date palm. Dates aren't native to Florida, but they do grow on Minorca."

Lincoln whistled. "Wow. This means there's a relationship between Minorca and *The Secret*."

Barnaby was skeptical. "There's nothing in the literature about Preiss traveling outside North America."

Catching everyone by surprise, Thomas made a suggestion. "How about this? The link could be between the casque and the Minorcan community here in St. Augustine."

Lincoln nodded sagely. "St. Photios."

"Or the Oldest Schoolhouse."

"Both definitely on the top of the list now." Barnaby beamed at Agatha.

She smiled shyly. "So I did good?"

"You did good."

"But don't vanish like that again." Cleo was clearly still upset with her. "You gave us quite a fright."

Philo wondered whether anyone else was thinking that it would be more unusual if Agatha *didn't* fade into the woodwork.

Barnaby clapped his hands. "All right, everybody. Go to your rooms. Agatha, I want you to hit the library tomorrow and start researching Minorca and that flag. Cleo—"

"Pardon me, but could I go back to St. Photios? There may be more clues."

"All right, but take Cleo with you. I think we should buddy up from now on."

"But Professor, I haven't finished with the reflections in the dining hall yet! I want to create a panoramic photo."

Barnaby sighed. “Okay, who wants to go where?”

Everyone except Thomas started to talk. Barnaby singled him out. “You, Thomas. You go with Agatha tomorrow.”

“But…”

“No buts.” He opened his arms wide. “We’ll reconnoiter Thursday. Now off you go.”

Thomas handed the empty cone back to Agatha. The last thing Philo saw as she went down the corridor was the girl staring at it.

Chapter Twenty

To approach a poem as if it is a puzzle to be understood is to miss the point.

—John Cooper Clarke

Joseph's apartment, Wednesday, June 20

"Thank you, Miss Jones." Barnaby hung up. Joseph and Philo, sitting at Joseph's kitchen table, watched him apprehensively. "It's lucky you aren't in the hospital again, Joseph."

"Ed's tisane?"

He nodded. "That was the lab technician. Your pretty purple tea consists of a powerful diuretic called amiloride, mixed with a hefty dose of digoxin, a drug made from *Digitalis purpurea*—foxglove leaves. Both the diuretic and the digitalis raise your potassium and magnesium levels and impair your kidney function, leaving you more vulnerable to a heart arrythmia."

"This amiloride is a diuretic? I was already taking one for the edema. Could that have exacerbated the problem?"

"Yes. When Dr. Reagle received the results, he ordered Miss Jones to tell you to stop the water pills immediately and continue with the digoxin immune fab. Also, you're to consume at least sixty-four ounces of water a day for two weeks. And it goes without saying: stop drinking the tea. He wants to take more tests at the end of that time to see if the poison's been purged from your system and your chemical levels are back to normal."

"I'll start right now." Joseph went to the sink and filled a water glass. "I ought to tell Edmund."

"The sooner the better. When will you see him again?"

"He said he would drop by tomorrow when his crossword comes out."

Philo asked, "Do you have his phone number?"

"No."

"Does he live in St. Augustine? He could be in the phone book. What's his last name?"

Joseph pursed his lips. "Greer. I believe he told me he's on vacation. I want to say he's from Ohio, but I could be wrong. I only met him that Monday…No, wait, I'm right. It *is* Ohio. His crossword puzzle is published in the Cleveland *Post* on Thursdays. He took a couple of months off to visit Florida. I'll ask him about the tea tomorrow, shall I?"

"Okay." Philo didn't like to wait, but at least Joseph would be off the stuff.

Barnaby added, "And you might ask what particular ailments his family used the formula to treat. It could be it was meant for an entirely different issue."

"Will do."

They parted at Philo's door. "I have work to do in the store today—I'm way behind on the inventory of seventeenth-century memoirs."

"That reminds me." Barnaby kissed her absently. "I thought I'd bone up on Sir Francis Drake. Who knows? Maybe we're wrong and the man in the image isn't some peasant but Drake himself."

"Since Drake sacked and burned St. Augustine, you'll hardly find a monument to him here. No monument, no casque."

Barnaby shrugged. "You won't spoil my fun no matter how hard you try. Remember, I'm not really out to win the gem—I just want to train my kids in fieldwork, to wean them off their dependence on secondary sources." He headed to the door. "Got to get cracking at my crossword as well."

"When is it due?"

"It goes to the publisher on Fridays."

"*Hmm*…Crosswords." She grabbed Barnaby's sleeve. "Could the *Secret* riddles be crossword clues?"

Barnaby stopped short. "Now that's a new one. Most seekers employ the poem as a kind of linear map—providing step-by-step directions to the casque's burial spot. My approach has been different—I've been treating the riddle as an array of disparate clues leading to the same spot."

"Like a star?"

"More like a black hole. Your idea of crossword clues is intriguing. I could write clues to the lines—"

"Or make the *lines* the clues."

His eyes lit up. "Better. And the finished crossword serves as the guide to the casque's location. *Hmm*. I shall postpone the Drake research to cogitate upon this new concept." He kissed her again. "See you soon."

****

Mind Over Matter, Wednesday June 20

"This is fantastic!"

"What is?"

Barnaby dropped his umbrella on the floor and, sticking a manila folder under one arm, hugged Philo with the other. "That I've found someone both beautiful and intelligent who is remarkably informed on all things chili and hot."

Philo looked over his shoulder. "And did you bring her with you?"

"No, silly. It's you." His green eyes narrowed. "You do not agree?"

Philo was tempted to turn sideways so he could admire her pudgy silhouette, but decided against it. *Let him have his little fantasy.* "Is that all? Has something else come to light?"

"Not exactly, but I may be on to something. Or rather, you may have put me on to something. The crossword."

"Ah." Philo had no clue what he was talking about but was fairly sure he would tell her soon enough, with a lot of excess verbiage thrown in. She picked up the umbrella and stuck it in the umbrella stand. "Is it raining?"

"No. Why?"

"Never mind. Would you like a beer?"

"Indubitably. Yes. 'Twould constitute the acme of an already perfect day. The keystone to complete the arch. The cherry on the whipped cream. Will you have one too?"

"Don't mind if I do." She got two bottles from the mini refrigerator and locked the shop door. "Let's go upstairs."

They settled themselves on the balcony. Philo didn't bother to say anything. She knew she'd only be interrupted halfway through her sentence. Sure enough, Barnaby started up halfway through his own sentence. "There I was in my cramped quarters, only a pillowless cot to sit on and a bare light bulb to illuminate my tenpenny composition notebook. Quill pen in hand, I was poised to sculpt my latest creation for my overlords." He lowered his eyes to her face. "Now, with my crosswords, I prefer to begin the process by selecting a theme—it makes it easier to choose the answers."

"You go from the answer to the clue? Isn't that backward?"

"Not for me. Usually, that is. Anyway, I said to myself, 'Barnaby old thing, let's review the poem that goes with the sixth image.' " With a great flourish, he pulled a sheet of paper out of his folder. "Here are the first couple of lines: 'The first chapter / Written in water / Near men.' As you opined, these were clues, not answers. So how to work with them? Then it came to me. Aha! The same way the average puzzler does, of course. So: 'The first chapter.' " He licked his lips and waited.

She stared back at him.

He sighed. "All right. I'll help you. 'Prologue' or possibly 'Act One.' Next: 'Written in water.' " He didn't wait for her. " 'Whirlpool' or maybe 'eddy.' Now you try."

The fact was, Philo loathed puzzles. Her father had once told her it was because she was too competitive. If she couldn't be the best, she didn't want to try. *True or not, I hoped I'd never have to admit it to the king of cruciverbalists.* There was nothing for it but to confess. "I don't know. I don't want to play, Barnaby."

"Oh, come on. Just one, and I'll leave you alone."

She studied the next lines. "How about 'behind bending branches' is 'shade'?"

"Excellent!"

"Oh, and 'a green picket fence' could be a yard, or maybe a garden?"

"You're on a roll, dear one."

She was beginning to enjoy herself. " 'Stars move by day' has to be celebrities."

Barnaby started to fidget.

"And the honking is geese. Or car horns." She read on, her fingers grazing the words.

Barnaby cautiously slid the page from under them. "You've…uh…given me enough for now. Very helpful. I'll just slip this back into my folder, shall I?"

"What did I do wrong?"

"Wrong? Nothing. I can take it from here, that's all. I'll…er…get back to you."

The store bell rang. Philo went to the top of the stairs. "Shop's closed. Who could it be?"

"One of the students? It's only been twelve hours—somebody's bound to have gotten into mischief again." He toddled down the stairs and went through the back door into the store, Philo hot on his heels. Nobody's face filled the glass front. All seemed quiet. Philo went to the entrance and turned on the outside light. "It's a package."

"Let me. Just in case." Barnaby opened the door and took hold of the brown cardboard cylinder. "Did you order a fluorescent bulb? A window blind?"

"Perhaps it's a donation."

They unrolled it. Barnaby whistled. "Well, whaddaya know?"

Lying on the table before them was the stolen map of Francis Drake's raid on St. Augustine.

****

Philo's apartment, Thursday, June 21

Barnaby and Philo were still speculating on the return of the map the next morning over coffee. "Buyer's remorse?"

"Wrong map?" Philo took a sip.

"Or the thief's mother found it and made him give it back."

"And hopefully turned her son over to the police."

"You're a cruel sort of person, aren't you? You can't expect criminals to be rehabilitated unless you show some mercy."

She was firm. "He'll relapse if you go easy on him."

"You don't know that. In fact, you don't know who it is, so why condemn him out of hand?"

Philo put down her cup. "This is not a productive conversation. What is on the agenda today?"

"I have to work on my puzzle, and no, I don't think I'll use the poem, at least not for this one. I don't have time. The kids are supposed to announce their progress, if any, this afternoon."

"Are you going to discuss Agatha's discovery?"

"Naturally. Oops, I wonder if Kevin and Susie have heard the news. They weren't with us that night." He picked up his phone.

Someone knocked. Philo opened the door. "Joseph?"

The old man stood on the threshold. "Edmund is coming by in a few minutes, and I thought you'd like to meet him."

Barnaby jumped up. "We'll be right with you." He punched in a number and went into Philo's bedroom.

Philo accompanied Joseph across the hall. They had just sat down when the downstairs buzzer sounded. "That'll be Ed."

A minute later a rather nondescript man in his fifties arrived. Balding, he stooped as though he'd spent his life bending over a desk. Thick-lensed glasses obscured eyes waxy with myopia. He had thin lips, and he seemed vaguely familiar.

He directed a broad smile at his host. "Hello, Joseph. How are you feeling today?"

"*Mens sana in corpore sano*, knock on wood. Edmund Greer, I'd like you to meet Philo Brice. She owns the shop downstairs."

The man blinked. He said nothing to Philo but turned to Joseph. "I've brought my latest opus for you."

"Great, great. Sit down. Would you like a cup of tea?"

"That would hit the spot. Some of that Darjeeling if you have it." While Joseph was pottering in the kitchen, Edmund watched Philo. She had the distinct impression that he didn't want her there. He called, "Will you have some of your tisane, Joseph?"

"Not today. As a matter of fact, we'd like to talk to you about it."

"We?" Greer's voice had an edge to it.

Joseph didn't answer the question. "I'll be with you in a trice."

Barnaby walked through the door. "According to Lincoln, both Kevin and Susie are up to speed on Agatha's adventure. Social media working its magic. You must be Ed."

The man rose slightly from his seat. "Edmund Greer. And you are?"

"Barnaby Swift. I don't live here."

"I see."

Barnaby sat down next to Philo, and they waited in silence for Joseph.

After a minute, he bustled in with a tea tray. "I think I'll forgo the formal tea ceremony this once. Philo?"

She shook her head. Barnaby refused as well. Joseph poured a cup and passed it to Ed. When Greer had stirred in sugar and begun to sip, Joseph cleared his throat. "Barnaby? Will you take the floor?"

Barnaby stood up. "Mr. Greer—"

"Ed."

"Ed it is. This potion of yours. Do you know the ingredients?"

The man's puffy face tightened. "Of course I do, but as I told Joseph, it's a secret family recipe. My great-great grandmother concocted it from plants in the Minnesota woods where she grew up."

Barnaby spoke casually to the wall. "Do foxgloves grow well in Minnesota?"

Greer's glance shot from Joseph to Barnaby. "Foxgloves? I don't know. Why?"

"Foxgloves and…amiloride?"

"What the hell is amiloride?"

"A powerful diuretic."

Ed rose all the way and stood a foot from Barnaby. "What are you insinuating?"

Barnaby's eyes dropped to Ed. "That you're trying to poison Mr. Brighton."

Chapter Twenty-One

Shall I let in the stranger
Shall I welcome the sailor?
Or stay till the day I die?
Hands of the stranger and holds of the ships
Hold you poison or grapes?

—Dylan Thomas.

Joseph's apartment, Thursday, June 21

Ed's jaw dropped. He stood stock still for a full minute, then burst out laughing. "Why on earth would I do that? Joseph's my friend. And one of my few fans, although he seems to have high regard for Argle Bargle. Don't see it myself."

Barnaby made a sound that closely resembled "Argle Bargle."

Joseph leaned forward. "That's what I told Philo and Barnaby, but they were concerned about my recent attack. The doctors are at a loss, and Barnaby surmised that something I ate or drank was the source of the reaction. They took one of the tea bags to the lab, which found it contained a concentrated form of digitoxin and the diuretic amiloride. The combination put me in the hospital with symptoms of atrial fibrillation. How do you explain that?"

Greer seemed bewildered. "I can't. Look, I'll tell you the ingredients if you promise not to divulge them to anyone else."

They all nodded.

He recited, "Three parts dried chamomile flowers, two parts dandelion root, five parts sugar. The dandelion root has a mild diuretic effect which works to reduce the swelling in your ankles."

Philo was deciding whether to believe him or not when he took a plastic bag out of his pocket. Inside were several small bundles wrapped in cheesecloth. "Here, I brought you a fresh supply. You can have these tested too if you like."

Joseph took the bag. "These don't look like the first ones you gave me."

"It's the same stuff."

Joseph went to the kitchen. He brought out a similar plastic bag, but the contents were packets of a different color. "You didn't leave me these purple ones?"

Ed shook his head. "My tea is always yellow due to the chamomile. Where did you get those?"

"They were in my mail box. I assumed they were from you."

Ed straightened. "I didn't mail anything to you."

"I know, but the Monday we met you said you were going to leave the tea here for me."

Ed's face cleared. "Oh, I see why you're confused. No, I didn't drop it off that night. When I got home I realized I didn't have any on hand, so I made up a batch and brought it round to you Wednesday along with your crossword."

Barnaby took the sack of purple bags from Joseph. "Did this come in a package?"

"Just a plain brown manila envelope. It wasn't addressed, but the label on it said 'Medicinal tea.' "

"Well, we seem to have a new mystery on our hands. Joseph, do you have any enemies?"

"We've been over this. As a former defense attorney, I have my share."

Philo had a thought. "The mobster…what was his name? Niarelli. You're sure he's not out of prison?"

Beside her, Greer made a slight movement. "Niarelli? The gangster from Jacksonville?"

Joseph turned surprised eyes on him. "Yes. Do you know him?"

Greer drew in a deep breath. "I know *of* him. I remember reading about his trial."

Barnaby repeated the question. "Is the guy still in the jug?"

"He'd better be. He was sentenced to thirty years to life."

Philo said firmly, "We have to take the purple tea to the police. They're the only ones with the facilities to investigate. They can find out if any of your former clients have been freed lately. That's probably it." She looked at Greer. "I do apologize—on behalf of all of us—for accusing you."

He weighed her words. "I accept your apology. I'm glad I was able to clear it up." He smiled sadly at Joseph. "And here I was congratulating myself on finding a new friend."

Joseph slapped him on his back. "Well, there's no reason we can't continue our most diverting conversations. That is"—he beetled his brows at Greer—"if you're able to let bygones be bygones?"

"By all means." The other man pulled a spiral notebook out of a tote bag. "I brought my latest creation for you. Let's see how long it takes you to solve. I'll wager it's a lot more difficult than the over-rated Argle Bargle's Sunday puzzle."

Philo opened her mouth to enlighten Edmund, but Joseph beat her to it. "Before you go any further, I think you should know you are in the presence of the inimitable Argle Bargle himself."

"You?"

"No." He gestured at Barnaby. "Mr. Swift can claim that honor."

Edmund had the grace to blush. "Forgive me. I wouldn't have been so blunt had I known."

Barnaby growled, "No harm done," which, Philo reflected, was most charitable of him.

"So…" Greer spread out the puzzle. "Why don't you both see what you think?"

Barnaby stood. "I'm afraid I don't have time. Friday is my deadline, and I want to test a new angle using the *Secret* poems." When Joseph looked at him inquiringly, he said, "It's possible the texts are in fact crossword clues."

Edmund twitched. "Poems? Secret? What are you talking about?"

Barnaby paused. Philo knew he wanted to keep it to himself. He said, his manner offhand, "Poems…in a book of…er…puzzles. Pretty obscure really."

"Oh. Well." Edmund stood. "Actually, I have just remembered I have an appointment and must take my leave as well. Joseph, why don't you inspect my work, and I'll call you later?"

Before anyone could speak he was gone.

Joseph closed the door after him. “Whew. Despite his assurances, he may still resent our allegations. That’s too bad.”

Philo snickered. “More likely he’s ashamed of his snarky comments about Argle Bargle.”

Barnaby was noncommittal. “He’s entitled to his opinion.” He put his hand on the knob. “I’ll see you later.”

Philo pulled him back. “Where are you going?”

“Remember? I have to write my own puzzle.”

“Don’t go just yet. We need to talk about this.”

Barnaby came back and sat down. “Shoot.” He checked his watch ostentatiously.

Philo glared at him. “We’ll try to make it quick.”

“Thanks.”

Joseph shook the bag. “It *is* strange about this purple tea though. If Edmund didn’t leave it for me, who did?”

Philo stood.

“Where do you think *you’re* going?”

Philo would have laughed at Barnaby’s unrighteous indignation if she weren’t so irritated.

“I’m going to call the police. Give me the bag please.”

Joseph gave it to her. She went across to her apartment. Five minutes later she was back. “Lieutenant Tolliver says they’ll check with the post office, see if the mailman remembers the package.”

“It wasn’t addressed. I’d venture someone just stuck it in the box.”

She threw up her hands in frustration. “I don’t know what else to do.”

Barnaby had been tapping a pencil on the table. "Someone must have it in for you, but it's definitely not Greer."

"Why not? I mean, I agree, but what's your reasoning?"

"You had the attack and went to the hospital on June 11."

"Right."

"The same night you met Edmund Greer."

"Right…oh. He said he didn't give me his tea until Wednesday."

"When did the purple stuff show up?"

"*Mmm*. Come to think of it, it was in the box when I returned from the Dog and Whistle. It could've been there all day. When Ed brought his packet on Wednesday, I didn't pay any attention to the color—just put his behind the purple bag, planning to use up the older batch first." He shivered. "To think I've been drinking poison all this time."

"You've also been taking the digoxin immune fab. Otherwise you'd be back in the hospital now."

Philo mused, "Both teas contain a diuretic."

"Yes, but I hadn't touched the yellow one yet."

"Oh, then—"

Barnaby interrupted. "You weren't drinking Greer's tea, but you *were* on your doctor's prescription—what was it?"

Joseph went down the hall. He came back with a white bottle labeled triamterene.

Barnaby looked it up. "As I feared. Both amiloride and triamterene are potassium-conserving diuretics. Together with the digitalis, they caused your potassium to shoot up to critical levels."

"Wow. Whoever made up the purple tea must have known I was already on the other stuff."

Philo gave Joseph a worried look. "Maybe you should go away for a few days. Hide."

Joseph tittered. "Go to the mattresses?"

"I thought that referred to a stakeout."

Barnaby shook his head, "No, it means preparing for war."

"Huh." Joseph's gaze went to the television. "You know, I've never watched *The Godfather.*"

Barnaby threw up his hands. "How could you not have seen it? It's part of our national culture, for Christ's sake. Plus, innumerable phrases and words from it crop up in crossword puzzles."

Philo rolled her eyes. "Hello? We were talking about Joseph's safety."

The old man sat down. "Look, I understand your concern—and appreciate it—but I'm on the alert now. This may have been merely a shot at revenge from an old adversary. He won't try again." He winked at Philo. "On the other hand, it could simply have been a mistake. A pharmacy delivery gone AWOL." He waved Barnaby away. "I thought you were working under a deadline. Hadn't you better head out?"

"Oh, yeah." Barnaby opened the door. "After I submit the crossword, I'm meeting with the students. They're keen on this new connection between Minorca and St. Augustine."

Philo stayed in her seat. Joseph smiled at her. "I don't think there's any cause for concern, my dear."

"*Hmm.*"

"I promise to be careful."

When she continued to sit, Joseph said, "Really, Philo, you don't have to babysit me. I'll be fine."

She rose reluctantly. "All right. I'll go. But keep your door open. I'll be listening."

"In case I scream or you hear a mysterious thud?"

"Not funny."

Chapter Twenty-Two

Let schoolmasters puzzle their brain
With grammar, and nonsense, and learning
Good liquor, I stoutly maintain
Gives genius a better discerning.

—Oliver Goldsmith

Philo's apartment, Thursday, June 21

"Can you hear me? You're cutting out."

Philo dropped the red nine she was about to place on the black ten and held the phone to her ear. "I'm here."

"Better. We decided to hold the seminar at a local watering hole at five. Agatha—or rather Thomas—wants to update us on their activities. Care to join us?"

She gathered the cards into a pile and took her purse off the hook. "I'll meet you there."

"Don't you want to know which bar?"

"A1A?"

"Uh-uh. We thought we'd try one the Flagler students hang out in. If it's too noisy, we'll repair to the little café in the student union. No one ever goes there." His voice faded, then came back. "The place is called the Culture Club. Maybe I should wear a tie."

Philo could hear Cleo in the background. "Ha-ha, no! It's a football pub, you ninny…I mean, Professor."

Barnaby returned to the phone. "It's on Cuna Street."

"I know it. I'll see you in fifteen."

The tavern occupied the ground floor of a dingy gray Victorian, half of the space taken up by the bar and the rest by four two-tops. The students had pushed the tables into a square so they could all sit together. Barnaby's voluminous chartreuse- and vermilion-checked circus clown pants spread out over two chairs.

"Hey, Philo! We're over here." He flipped the pink polka dot tie and snapped his rainbow-hued suspenders. "I opted for formal to set an example for the children."

She laughed. "I almost didn't see you there." In one stride she was upon them. Barnaby tucked his trousers under him, freeing the last seat. She sat down and gazed around at the cheerful faces. "What did I miss?"

"Well, Linc took Susie with him to the Ripley. Sounds like it was a total bust." Kevin made a face and mumbled something inaudible.

Philo regarded the boy. *If I had to guess, I'd say his attitude has more to do with Lincoln and Susie than with the Ripley.*

Lincoln shook his head. "Not a *total* bust, Kev. Most of the displays are completely preposterous, true. It's almost *too* kitschy…but the contortionists were worth the price, weren't they, Susie?"

She bounced eagerly. "So was the clock made entirely of clothespins. And the six-legged cow. And how about the man who could pop his eyeballs out? Oh, and—"

"Thank you, Susie. I think we get the picture," said Barnaby hastily.

Kevin's expression turned even more sour.

Lincoln continued. "But I feel it has little potential as a site for the casque. See, it's actually a chain. There are lots of Ripley's Believe It or Not museums across the country. Mr. Preiss would have chosen a unique spot—not one that could be in any of twelve different states."

"That's Linc's opinion." Susie wasn't ready to give up. "But I read that this one is the original Ripley's. That should count for something."

"Eh." Lincoln shrugged.

Barnaby looked his charges over. "Anyone else? In that case, let's vote. Shall we dispense with Ripley's?"

All hands went up, Susie's last. Barnaby gave her an encouraging thump on the back, which left the poor girl gasping for breath. "All right, any other sites we can discard?"

Thomas drawled, "We can drop the Oldest Drugstore too."

"Why?"

"It's a nothing burger. Just a shack that sells coffee and tea. It's not even the oldest. It's just *old*."

"Was it ever a pharmacy?"

"Yeah, but it was a tavern first. It sat around empty for like a hundred years until some guy from Charleston opened a drugstore. He made his own 'medicine.' " He curled his fingers to simulate double quotes.

"You mean, elixirs? As in, Professor Marvel's Magick Medication, a toothsome combination of lemon flavoring and alcohol which cures all ills in humans, goats, and snails?"

Thomas gawked at Barnaby.

Philo put in, "There's also the Oldest Store. Maybe you should give that a try." The gawk did not falter, only now it was directed at Philo.

Barnaby harrumphed. "Okay, moving on. Anyone else?"

Cleo cleared her throat. "The reflections from the windows on the dining hall floor were intriguing, but the only place the casque could be buried is *under* the floor. I doubt whether the school will let me tear up their beautiful hardwood planks."

Lincoln wagged a finger. "That's a nonstarter anyway. The hotel was built in the 1880s. Preiss wouldn't have been able to bury the casque under the floor a hundred years later."

"Okay." Barnaby paused while the bartender dropped six full mugs on the table.

Agatha opened her mouth, but Cleo held a finger to her lips. "It's only beer," she whispered. "*Shh.*"

Agatha pressed her lips together, but her eyes darted from Kevin to Susie. The bartender turned to Philo, his pencil poised on the order form. She said, "Vodka gimlet please. Straight up."

"Any particular vodka?"

"No, the rail is fine."

The young people were visibly impressed. "Wow, you sound so sophisticated," said Thomas admiringly.

Philo thought "Thank you" would sound pretentious, so she just contrived to look the part. Barnaby ordered an IPA.

When everybody was settled with their drinks, he turned to Kevin. "Your turn. Anything?"

Kevin opened a notebook. "I've been reading up on the history of the Castillo de San Marcos. Agatha's story of the Minorcan community gave me something to search for. As far as I can tell, they weren't conscripted into the Spanish military, although they did provision the garrison there."

"That's it?"

"Well, I haven't had a chance to delve deeper. I thought I'd spend some more time in the library tonight." He hesitated. "My father's been at the Castillo every day. He's going over every inch of it."

Barnaby swung his head angrily. "This isn't a third-grade science experiment, Kevin. You have to earn your own grade."

"I told him that. He says he just wants to help while I'm on crutches. He'll leave as soon as I'm walking again."

"Good." Barnaby pinched his lips together. "All right, let's move on. Anyone else?"

Agatha twitched in her seat. The small movement brought the group's attention to her. She wilted. "I…uh…"

Barnaby said affably, "Thomas says you two had quite a day. Do you want to do the honors?"

She looked confused. "We did? Oh, I mean…it was at least…" She appeared to choose and discard several words, finally settling on "worthy of mention."

Thomas said impatiently, "We may have found another tie to Image Six in the gardens at St. Photios."

Philo sat forward. "Foxgloves?"

"No." He gave her a baffled look. "What do foxgloves have to do with *The Secret*?"

Barnaby jiggled a dismissive hand. "Never mind. What about the gardens?"

Agatha burst out, "There's a whole bed of purple asters! Just like in the picture."

Kevin put his mug down and wiped his mouth with a napkin. "The asters in the picture aren't in a garden—they're wild. And they're growing out of a rock."

"I don't see that that's significant." Thomas glowered at his colleague.

Susie remarked dreamily, "Asters grow everywhere in Maine. They bloom in the fall."

Barnaby said mildly, "Actually, there are hundreds of varieties of asters. The ones in Image Six are purple—I believe they're New England asters."

Philo focused on Thomas. "What color are the asters in St. Photios?"

"I'll show you." He clicked on his phone and passed the photo around. "They let us take pictures in the garden."

"*Hmm*. They do look right."

Barnaby handed the phone back. "So, we have asters, and a possible nexus—as yet unexplored—between Minorcans and the Spanish garrison. Anything else?"

"The Minorcan flag? The palm tree? The Rock of Gibraltar?"

"Yes, yes, but is that all you have that's new? The asters? *That's* what you consider 'worthy of mention'?" He scowled.

The sudden silence brought the bartender out from behind the bar. "Problem, folks?"

Agatha took a sip of beer and made a face. Cleo said kindly, "You don't have to drink it if you don't like it."

Agatha looked pointedly at the two underage drinkers. "Well, if they're going to…"

Her eye on the bartender, Cleo said quickly, "Never mind them. Could we get a root beer please?"

When he returned with it, Kevin graciously commandeered Agatha's beer. Barnaby, moving restlessly, repeated his question. "Well?"

Agatha cast a furtive glance at Cleo and muttered, "No, there's more. We…uh…we saw Diego again."

"Your cousin?"

"Uh-huh. He's staying at a hotel and has been spending time in the shrine. But—"

"But what?"

Thomas prodded her. "Tell them."

"See, my family went back to Minorca every summer until I was six, and I was hoping he'd have news of my other cousins. My mother mentioned in a letter that one of them, Victoria, had died." She paused to take a sip of root beer. "He didn't seem to know anything about it. I mean, she grew up right next door to him." Her gaze went from face to face. "He told me he was back there last year, but she died *two years ago*. How could he not know?"

Cleo offered, "Maybe they were estranged."

"Wouldn't he have said so then? And another thing. He wouldn't tell me how he got the scar."

"Scar?"

"On his cheek. He seemed offended when I asked him." She was quiet. "He was much more interested in what Thomas and I were doing than in family gossip."

Thomas added, "*Very* interested. I got the feeling he was dogging us, just like he did Agatha the last time. Like maybe he's looking for the same treasure we are. I even caught him taking a picture of us by the asters."

"You think he may be a seeker?" Susie leaned forward eagerly. "We haven't actually met one yet."

Barnaby frowned. "Nothing in the literature about *The Secret* refers to St. Photios as a possible site."

"Really? Then why did you assign it?"

"Because," he said earnestly, "as you recall, this is an exercise in historiography. You're supposed to be using *The Secret* as an instrument to help you learn research methods and field work techniques. The scavenger hunt was an attempt to liven it up."

No one spoke. Finally, Lincoln mumbled, "I guess we got carried away."

"It's easy to do. It's a puzzle. Anyone who likes puzzles will be drawn to it, but I don't want you guys to become emmeshed in its coils and lose perspective. I don't expect you to solve Image Six, just use it as a kind of template."

The reprimand only worked for a minute before a grin broke out on Kevin's face. "It would sure be a coup if we did solve it though, wouldn't it? We could win the stone—I think it's a sapphire. Probably worth a fortune—"

"For its celebrity alone." Thomas was so aroused he spilled his beer.

Cleo's eyes sparkled. "Professor, you said the Fountain of Youth is the site the seekers favor the most. We should drop everything else and concentrate on it. I'll bet if we put our heads together, we could find the casque in a jiffy. What do you say, Professor?"

Barnaby closed his eyes. "I say…" Philo wanted to interrupt, afraid Barnaby was about to endorse what would surely be a course fraught with danger, but she was stumped for the right words. "I say, no."

Whew.

A chorus of "whys" met this declaration.

"Why? Number one, for the reason I just stated. This is a course on sources and methods. I'm being paid—albeit not much—to teach them to you. Look at you." He took in the table. "One second you've calmed down and the next you've all gone gaga again. This is an academic pursuit, not a game. And"—he held up a hand to quell the rebellion—"*and*, the second—and more consequential—reason, is because two people have already died while seeking the casque, and another may be the victim of a murder attempt. It would be irresponsible of me to put you at risk."

"Died? Who died?"

Philo realized the students had no knowledge of Barnaby's association with recent events. *We should probably avoid explaining too much.* She put a hand on Barnaby's arm. "A couple of people had...accidents while they were searching for the key. One of the accidents was at the Fountain of Youth. That's why it's closed."

Lincoln said, "Right—remember, guys? The guard said a woman had been found dead there." He gave Barnaby a quizzical look. "You didn't tell us she was a seeker."

Barnaby opened his mouth. Philo eyed him meaningfully. He raised an eyebrow, then, in an offhand manner, said, "Yes, it's true. The police are still investigating. And that's why we stick with our syllabus. That's final."

A lot of grumbling and a lot more drinking consumed the rest of the evening. When the students finally straggled off to their dorm, Barnaby and Philo strolled back to her apartment. "I'm going to check on Joseph."

"I'll come with you."

The old man was settled in his recliner with Barnaby's crossword. He put the pencil down. "Don't tell Edmund, but yours is markedly more difficult than his. I do hope he's sticking with his day job."

Barnaby's hand flew to his mouth. "Oh damn, I still haven't finished next Sunday's puzzle, and it's due tomorrow." He swung on Philo. "We'll have to postpone our lovemaking until I've sent it in. You do understand, don't you?" He didn't wait for an answer but flew out the door. They heard the downstairs gate slam.

Joseph said, "He's a bit of a kook, isn't he?"

"You noticed that too?"

Chapter Twenty-Three

[A] riddle wrapped in an enigma tucked in a mystery deep-fried in a conundrum slathered in hickory-smoked puzzle sauce.

—*Axel Hirsch*

Philo's apartment, Thursday, June 21

Philo didn't get much sleep that night, but it wasn't the treasure hunt that made her curl into a fetal ball. It was Barnaby. *Is he serious about me?* He was by turns grave and flippant. Flighty—like a honey bee that knew it didn't have long to live and couldn't stop gadding from flower to flower. *It's like his mind is always on the move.* She was sure he was extremely intelligent and well-read. *Couldn't create the hardest crossword puzzles in the world if he weren't.* So where did that leave her? *I can't compete with his brain. What does he see in me? Pollen?*

She had to admit she'd grown increasingly fond of him. Never much of a talker herself, she didn't mind Barnaby usurping the conversation. *Although I seem to have picked up the habit of speaking in long, convoluted sentences.* On the other hand, the constant hustle and bustle didn't give her a chance to wind down, and she knew herself well enough to acknowledge she needed time off. *It's not like I'm his student. I don't have to join in his whirlwind of activities.* She refused to examine the other elephant in the room: *where do we go from here?*

He was only in St. Augustine for the summer after all. He'd be gone soon. Back to...*where? Did he say where home base is? Oh, yes. Princeton.* That was in New Jersey. Miles and miles away.

She gave up about six in the morning and went to the kitchen to make coffee. Her cell phone rang. She was going to let it go to voicemail, but nowadays it was as likely to be a crisis as a salesman. "Hello?"

"Hey, you won't believe this. Axel Zimmer called."

"Is he in jail again?"

"Huh? No. Why would you think that? The man's a millionaire. He can afford bail. That is, if he needed it. Which he doesn't. Why do you keep interrupting me?"

Philo figured if she remained silent, he'd have to fill the void.

"So...He's still on about this Cottrell thing. He wants the store badly. Claims no other independent liquor store in northeast Florida meets his standards."

"What does he think *you* can do about it?"

"Evidently Norton's a big crossword puzzle fan." There was a momentary silence. "Not like *some* people I won't mention. He loves Argle Bargle—"

"Small world."

"Well, Norton's parents were puzzle freaks, so it must run in the family. Say, do you suppose he has a finger in the *Secret* pie too?" As usual, he didn't wait for an answer. "Anyway, he promised that if he could meet me, he would consent to sit down with Axel. Axel will pay me to cozy up to the guy, sign an autograph, maybe give him a T-shirt. It would mean I could pay my own bar tab. What do you think?"

"You have souvenir T-shirts?"

"Doesn't everyone?"

Philo considered. "If you give me a T-shirt, I'll support you in whatever decision you make."

"T-shirt, mug, pen—whatever you like. If you marry me, I'll give you a signed first edition puzzle as a wedding gift."

Philo couldn't breathe. Finally she wheezed out, "Excuse me?"

"Just an expression. So, your store's open today, right? I'll go catch Mr. Zimmer then." She heard his fingers snap. "And finish that puzzle for the editor babe. Kiss, kiss." He hung up.

****

Mind Over Matter, Friday, June 22

"Done!" Barnaby swung from the transom above the store's doorway.

"And buried?"

"I think in fact that is slang for news the paper doesn't see as fit to print. No, it should be 'it's in the hopper.' Maybe 'in the can.' Or is that for a movie? *Hmm*. This could make a great clue." He whirled around and started to leave.

"Barnaby? Are you saying you submitted Sunday's puzzle?"

He whirled back. "I thought that was obvious. Are you closing up or what?"

She turned the sign to Closed and beckoned him inside.

He swaggered in. "I have something to show you."

I'll show you mine if you...Stop it, Philo. "Okay."

He opened his wallet and took a wad of bills out. "See? Mr. Zimmer came through. I can take you out for even better chili than Flora's."

"Did you contact Norton Cottrell?"

"I did. We are set to meet on Monday. I'm going to open my archives for him."

"Archives? Of your puzzles?"

"Yup. He's all agog. He also wants a mug." He looked down at the money. "I hope I'm not expected to spring for that. They're like eight whole dollars. It should be the responsibility of the publisher, shouldn't it?" He appealed to Philo.

"I've got an idea."

"Well, that's grand. You should have one of those at least once a day."

"Let's buy some steaks and cook out."

He went very still. "Out? Where?""

"We have a patio behind the building with a communal hibachi. You grill the steaks, and I'll make a salad."

His face sagged. "*Grill*?"

"What's the matter?"

"I…I don't know how. I know every man is supposed to be adept at cooking with fire, but I never learned."

"Your father didn't teach you?"

"He said he'd done enough eating *al fresco* in his days as a Boy Scout and then in the army. We also weren't allowed to have Spam. Or creamed chipped beef on toast. He called it 'shit on a shingle.' Of course my mother would yell at him and explain to us kids he meant to say 'slop on a shingle' or 'gruel on a shingle.' At any rate, I never tasted it. Nor did I ever learn to grill meat."

"I see. Well, there's a nice steak place over on Ponce de León Boulevard. You can take me there."

"I'll do you one better."

****

Harvey's Family Buffet, Friday, June 22

An hour later they were settled in a booth with unartfully torn leatherette benches in Harvey's Family Buffet, and Philo was uneasy. Her qualms were confirmed when the waitress—a skinny woman of about fifty whose name tag read Gladys—brought a triple caddy of relishes over before she even poured water into their glasses. She tentatively asked her if they served wine.

Gladys's response: "We got red, we got white."

Barnaby scanned the placemats printed with ads for dentists and dry cleaners, set with aluminum utensils wrapped in paper napkins. Next to the ketchup and mustard stood salt and pepper shakers in the form of Charlie Brown and Lucy. "Isn't this *great*?"

Philo read the laminated menu. Accompanying each entree was a photograph, the colors faded to a hazy sepia tint. As she feared, the steak options were chicken-fried or cubed. Sides consisted of French fries, pickled beets, and applesauce. She peeped at Barnaby. His face was aglow.

"Wow. Will you look at this menu?" He lowered the plastic sheet. "When I was growing up and we went on a road trip, we'd pass Harvey's all the time. It's a chain, you know. They have them all over the country."

Why am I not surprised?

Barnaby picked up Charlie Brown and turned him upside down. A little pile of finely ground pepper formed on the table, giving off a slightly musty aroma. Philo gently extracted the shaker and set it back down. "In their commercials they always boasted about having a whole bank of candy bars at the cash register. My father would never stop. He claimed it wasn't the candy, but what else could it be? Anyway, I swore when I grew up I'd betake myself to a Harvey's. And here I am." He bounced on the bench. "Take that, Dad!"

Philo could only sigh.

He signaled Gladys. "I shall order for the both of us." He did. "And a bottle of your finest."

Philo hoped she wouldn't take that to mean Dr Pepper.

Gladys dispatched, Barnaby put his elbows on the table. "Now I shall tell you about my day. As I said, I deposited my latest creation with Phyllis. It was okay."

"Only okay? She wasn't satisfied with it?"

"Oh, Phyllis adores all my puzzles. It's me. I confess I've been preoccupied with this question of using the *Secret* riddles as clues. It's worth pursuing, but I haven't been able to follow through on it."

Gladys plunked down two minuscule carafes of red wine and two empty plastic cups. "You want ice?"

"Er. No. Thanks."

"Be right back." Two minutes later, she appeared with a large tray and set it down on a folding table. Philo resigned herself to a meal that with any luck would soon be forgotten. Dementia didn't look so bad when faced with sweet potatoes baked with marshmallows, green beans swimming in cream of mushroom soup, and a slice of ham that resembled pressure-treated plywood.

Barnaby dug in with gusto. When he'd popped the last marshmallow into his mouth, he asked for the dessert menu. "Wow! Red Jell-O! Or maybe Mississippi mud pie? Ice cream? You like ice cream—I've seen you eat it."

Philo wasn't sure if that was a statement or an accusation. "I'm really not hungry, after all that…that…food."

"Jell-O it is, then."

She let him take a bite of the shimmering red block before asking, “What are your students doing today?”

“I’ve packed them all off to the library. It’s time they spent a few hours on their buttocks rather than sashaying around monuments. We’ll regroup on Monday.”

“Aren’t you supposed to meet Norton Cottrell on Monday?”

“I am quite capable of executing more than one transaction per day.” He signaled the waitress. “Would you box up this Jell-O for me please?”

“By the way, when is the summer session over?”

“Middle of July, but I had to rent through August, so I thought I’d stick around.” He wiped his hand on a napkin and reached for her. “You shall have me underfoot for another two months.”

By then I should be well over him.

****

Philo’s apartment building, Sunday, June 24

Philo was coming home, the Sunday newspaper under her arm, when she saw Edmund Greer enter the alley to her building. She reached the top step as Joseph was letting him into his apartment. The old man noted her approach. “Good morning, Philo. Edmund and I are going to work on Barnaby’s crossword together. Maybe it won’t take me a whole week to solve this time.” He bowed. “Will your illustrious swain be calling upon you today?”

Philo hadn’t heard from her swain since Friday night. After leaving her on her doorstep, he’d said something about getting a head start on next week’s puzzle while he savored his Jell-O. That apparently took the entire Saturday. She didn’t mind. She’d searched her cookbooks for recipes and experimented with them on the ancient hibachi someone had left on their patio. After several setbacks, she'd finally produced a passable hamburger. The rest of the weekend had been occupied with planning a banquet of grilled dishes for Barnaby.

Joseph prodded her. "Philo? Hello? Are you with me? You seem to be daydreaming. Where's Barnaby?"

She shook herself. "I don't know. He said he was going to work on next week's puzzle."

"Oh?" Greer elbowed Joseph aside. "Did he say if he'd come up with a theme?"

A new voice intruded. "I have indeed." Barnaby put his hands on Philo's shoulders and spoke over her head. "I have combined business with pleasure. I have come up with a way to use *The Secret's* images as crossword clues. Pretty clever, eh?"

Greer seemed perplexed. "Secret images as crossword clues? What secret images?"

This time Barnaby couldn't avoid revealing the truth. He described Preiss's book and the twelve paintings and poems. "Many of the players think Image Six refers to St. Augustine—and the casque is buried somewhere in the city."

Philo added, "Barnaby has his students researching the potential hiding places for the treasure."

"Huh." Edmund stifled a yawn. "What does all this have to do with your crossword?"

"I'm thinking I could use the lines from the poems as clues. Even if it doesn't solve the mystery, at least it will make a great puzzle."

"I see." He pondered. "It could be a nice gimmick. I'd like to make a little wager with you."

"I never bet more than a nickel."

"I have another prize in mind."

"All right. What's the stake?"

"We'll each work on our own puzzle and present the finished product to your editor anonymously. If he likes mine, you persuade him to publish it."

Joseph said carefully, "You're a good friend, Edmund, but I don't think it would be a fair fight."

Edmund bristled. "You said my puzzles are very difficult. You called them works of art."

"Um. They *are* works of art. Technically. But that doesn't mean they're in the same league with Argle Bargle's." He gave Edmund's back a friendly pat. "Sorry, old sport."

Edmund stood. "I don't have to sit here and—"

Barnaby cut in. "Actually, I like his proposal. It'll keep us both on our toes. I suggest we meet back here on Thursday with our results. How's that?"

"All right." Edmund bowed to Joseph. "I'd best get started on my entry if I'm to outwit the great Argle Bargle." He left.

Joseph regarded the closed door. "I fear, Barnaby, that you may have made a mistake."

"Oh?"

"I think Mr. Greer may be taking advantage of you."

"How so? We're just doing puzzles. Each puzzle is unique."

"In your case, yes, but I've noticed that Edmund's often seem…unoriginal."

"You mean, prosaic? Dull? Derivative?"

"I'm saying that I believe Mr. Edmund Greer is a plagiarist."

Chapter Twenty-Four

Rally 'round the flag, boys.

—Max Shulman

Philo's apartment, Monday, June 25

"I'm meeting Norton for lunch—then we'll go back to his store to sift through my archives." Barnaby opened his briefcase and took out a small box. "The mug almost didn't come in time. Maybe I should have the Flagler school store stock them."

"I'm not sure they'd be amenable, since you're not full-time faculty."

"Surely they want to flaunt their puzzler-in-residence." He blew on his fingers. "I'm like a poet laureate, only more winsome."

Philo wasn't so sure. "What are you going to do about Joseph's accusation?"

"You mean, that Greer's a plagiarist? Nothing."

"Nothing! Isn't that copyright infringement?"

"Possibly, but Joseph didn't say Greer was ripping *my* stuff off. If it's someone else's crosswords, I don't have standing. And anyway, do you have any idea how difficult it would be to prove? I mean, they're just one- to two-word clues, not whole paragraphs."

Philo wasn't ready to yield. "What if he stole an entire puzzle?"

"Again, if he stole one of mine, the puzzle world would know immediately. It's as close-knit a group as the casque-seekers. And my publisher would haul his butt into court in a New York minute."

"But—"

Barnaby's phone rang. He pulled it from his pocket. "Hi, Agatha. Oh? Where are you now? I see." He checked his watch. "Sure, I'll meet you guys there in fifteen minutes, but I have a lunch date so I have to leave by noon." He clicked it off.

"What was that about?"

"Agatha and Thomas are at the St. Photios shrine. They claim they've uprooted another clue. They got hold of Kevin, who was heading to the Castillo, and he's going to meet them there. They want me to come too."

"To St. Photios?"

"No, to the Castillo. They must have found something connecting the two." He put his phone in his pocket. "She sounded agitated."

"Agatha? Agitated?"

"I know. This could be big. Coming?"

"Try to keep me away."

****

The Castillo de San Marcos, Monday, June 25

They met Agatha and Thomas at the entrance to the Castillo. Agatha rushed forward. "Oh, Professor Swift, we really think we're onto something."

Thomas, lounging against the stone wall, flicked a bored hand. "Well, *she* thinks so."

"Where's Kevin?"

Just then, Kevin stepped off the red trolley and limped toward them.

Philo asked before Barnaby could. “Is your father joining us?”

“He said he had to attend an office party—some kind of luau.” He held up a small notebook. “I’m to record any new developments for him. So what’s this about?”

Agatha led them to a wide bench. She took a large roll of paper from Thomas and spread it out. Kevin set rocks on the corners to hold it flat.

“That’s the flag of Minorca.”

“Right.” She pulled a brochure from her purse. On the center page was a map of the Castillo. “See the two castles—the one on the flag and the fort? They have exactly the same layout.”

“Yes, we know.” Kevin tapped a foot. “What’s your point?”

Agatha’s exhilaration overruled her normally modest demeanor. “When we went back to St. Photios, Thomas found something in the library. Thomas?”

The boy’s eyes radiated excitement. “Okay. As you know, a substantial Minorcan community settled in Florida in the late eighteenth century.”

Barnaby was showing signs of impatience. “What does that have to do with the Castillo?”

“Nothing.”

“That’s it. I’m off.” Kevin started to turn away.

Agatha, with some effort, raised her voice. “Wait! We haven’t gotten to the important part yet. See, what Thomas discovered was that this wasn’t the first time Minorcans had showed up in the New World.”

An exuberant Thomas exclaimed, “There were Minorcan sailors on Ponce de León’s ship! They were with him when he landed in Florida in 1513.”

"*Hmm*. So, Minorcans were in the New World much earlier than we suspected. Does this confirm my hypothesis that the figure in Image Six is a Minorcan peasant—or not?"

Agatha demurred. "Sort of. You thought he might be a farmer, but the man is wearing standard armor for the time. If it's not Ponce himself, it could be one of his Minorcan soldiers."

"And you're postulating that the soldier in the picture is standing on top of the Castillo?"

For the first time Agatha faltered. "I…don't know. The fort is identical to the one on the Minorcan flag. It can't be coincidental."

Breaking the uncomfortable silence, Philo said, "Wait! The fort is *also* on the flag in Image Six."

"It is?"

"Hang on…" She pulled up the picture on her phone. "The soldier is holding a flag or banner, right? See what's on the flag?"

"A fort. Just like the Castillo."

Kevin cried, "Up there on the battlements! See? There's a flagpole."

Barnaby took out his wallet. "How about we go in and take a look at it."

They bought tickets and moved across the courtyard toward a flight of stone steps that led to the ramparts. Kevin began to fall behind. "Guys? My ankle's still sore. Why don't I stay here on the parade ground and wait for you?"

"Sure. While you're sitting, think."

"About what?"

Barnaby just looked at him.

They reached the open air on top of the wall. Thomas led the way. "We have to take this path all the way around the castle to get to the flagpole on the city side."

Barnaby said absently, "It's called an allure, sometimes a wall walk." He pointed at various parts of the castle. "The continuous wall is the parapet, and the bits that stick up are called merlons. The holes the cannons poke through are crenels. That's where you get the word 'crenellated.' " He patted a large cannon. "We're standing on the terreplein."

"Huh." Philo felt Thomas spoke for all of them.

They'd gone halfway around when they heard a shout. Kevin was waving his arms at them. Barnaby cocked an ear. "I can't hear what he's yelling, can you?"

Philo shook her head. "Whatever it is, it will have to wait until we get back to the courtyard."

They reached the flagpole. A banner flew from the top. "Damn. It's too far away to see what's on it. We'll have to check online or ask the guide."

Thomas leaned over the parapet. "So we know the fort's pictured on the Minorcan flag and on Image Six, but unless the Castillo's banner is identical, I say we stick with St. Photios."

"But…but it's *got* to be the Castillo." Agatha gazed up at the pole. "Otherwise it doesn't make sense that the banner looks so much like the one in *The Secret*."

Barnaby turned away. "Let's go back down. I have a lunch date, and Philo needs to open her store. You kids put your thinking caps on. We'll regroup at five thirty."

They arrived at the bottom of the stair to find Kevin standing, hands on hips. "Didn't you hear me?"

"We did, but we couldn't make out what you were saying."

"Well, they're gone *now*." He seemed frustrated.

"Who's gone?"

He pointed up at the battlements. "I saw the same guy who was here the day I was pushed."

Barnaby followed his finger. "Could you identify him?"

"No, he was too far away."

"Okay. Do you still believe he was the perpetrator?"

"Dunno. See, he kept showing up while I was wandering around. He always faced away from me, but I had the feeling I was in his sights." Kevin studied the courtyard. "It's strange to see him here again, that's all."

Philo had a thought. "He could be a member of the staff."

"Nah. He was dressed like a tourist—you know, Hawaiian shirt, binoculars." He wrinkled his nose. "Socks and sandals."

"Well, it may only be that he's especially attracted to the Castillo."

Kevin shrugged. "But that's not the creepiest part."

Thomas, who had been kicking pebbles into the grass, pricked up his ears. "Creepy?"

Kevin nodded. "He was being shadowed."

This got everyone's attention. "How do you know?"

"Who was it?"

"What did he look like?"

"If you'll be quiet, I'll tell you. This other guy was short. Tough-looking. He kind of moseyed along—like he wasn't in any hurry. He kept like ten feet behind the first guy—"

"The guy in the Hawaiian shirt?"

"Yeah, but whenever the first guy looked over his shoulder, the second guy ducked behind a cannon. Then, when number one started walking again, he'd tag behind."

Philo asked, "Were they up on the wall walk?"

"Yes. In fact"—he frowned—"I could have sworn the first guy was tailing *you* all."

Thomas giggled. "Sounds like a comedy sketch."

Barnaby ordered, "Stay here." He climbed the steps and panned the fort. He returned to the waiting group. "Nobody up there now."

"Maybe they went down a flight to the casement level. Shall we wait and see if they come out to the courtyard?" Philo hoped the others would disagree.

Kevin nodded strenuously, but the rest were dubious. Thomas said, "We have to get back to school. I want to toss around ideas. We have all these threads and no blanket."

"And I have to get to my luncheon." Barnaby crooked his finger. "Let's go."

They trooped toward the entrance. As they waited for the trolley, Agatha looked back. "Wait!"

"What?"

She blinked. "Never mind. It's all these mysterious comings and goings. My imagination is running wild."

"Did you see the stalkers?"

"No. But…but I think I just saw Diego, my cousin."

Chapter Twenty-Five

For slow centuries, the exotic Dracs and Fadas from the Riviera had sported and dozed on the beaches of new-found Florida. Perhaps the metal-clashing landfall of the Conquistadores took them by surprise, and they fled without taking time to disenchant their Fountain of Youth.

—Byron Preiss, The Secret

Castillo de San Marcos, Monday, June 25

"Diego?" Barnaby shaded his eyes, but the fort entrance was empty. "I thought you doubted whether he *was* your cousin?"

"I know. I'm still not sure. I wrote Mama asking her if she knew he was in Florida."

"She hasn't emailed you back?"

Agatha gave Barnaby an inscrutable look. Philo whispered, "Remember? Cleo says she doesn't have a computer. Or a phone."

"Oh? Well." He faced Agatha. "Why do you suppose he's here?"

Agatha glanced nervously over her shoulder. "Thomas thought he was following us at St. Photios. He could be doing the same here."

Kevin checked the sidewalk. "Did he happen to be wearing a Hawaiian shirt?"

"No."

"What does Diego look like?"

She locked her hands over her head. "He's…uh…taller than me."

"That doesn't really help."

"Brown hair. Brown eyes." She looked hopefully at Thomas. "Can you describe him any better?"

Thomas blew out his cheeks. "I dunno…He walks like a prize fighter—kind of bow-legged. Didn't get much of a look at him."

She blurted, "I almost forgot. He has a scar on his cheek."

"*Hmm*. Well…He told you he was in St. Augustine on a tour. No reason to think he was doing anything other than sightseeing." Barnaby straightened. "I need to go."

As they watched him running to catch a bus, Philo turned to Agatha. "You said Diego was touring St. Augustine. Did he mention where he came from?"

She hunched over, making her seem even tinier. "I assumed he still lives in Minorca. But no, he didn't actually say."

"*Hmm*."

****

Mind Over Matter, Monday, June 25

"Hi there, how was your lunch?"

"Fine. I brought a doggy bag back with me." Barnaby stepped aside.

Philo beheld a young man attired in designer slacks and a burgundy Lacoste polo. His thinning hair was pulled back in a man bun. His vivid blue eyes reminded her of Kevin. "Hello."

"This is Norton Cottrell. He wanted to meet you."

"He did? Why?" Philo shook herself. "Oh dear, that was rude. Barnaby has a tendency to speak for people, and I'm afraid I've come to expect it. How do you do, Mr. Cottrell?"

"Please, call me Norton." Cottrell's voice was high and shrill, acting like a brain freeze on Philo. She winced. He didn't seem to notice. "It's nice to meet you. Barnaby was telling me about you at lunch, and I realized you must be the daughter of Oscar Brice—owner of this shop. Is it true?"

Philo bit her lip. "I'm his daughter, yes. He passed away three years ago. I inherited the store."

"Oh? I'm sorry to hear that." A cloud crossed his face, reminding Philo that he had recently lost his parents as well.

"I'm sorry about *your* parents also. A terrible tragedy."

He closed his eyes, then opened them, the blue if anything more intense. "Another thing we have in common: I inherited my parents' business too—Granada Liquors. However, I was asking Barnaby about you for a different reason. Since their…deaths, I've been assessing the inventory and reviewing the financial records. I haven't decided whether to put it on the market or keep it in the family."

"Oh, you haven't decided?" Philo glanced at Barnaby, but his face showed no emotion. "Do you live in St. Augustine?"

"I've been in Jacksonville for the past five years, but I grew up here. I wouldn't mind moving back."

"I see."

"Anyway, while I was sorting through a storage closet, I came across a package addressed to your father. A long, thin, cylinder. I went ahead and mailed it. Did you receive it?"

"Ah, the map." Philo and Barnaby nodded at each other.

Barnaby asked Norton, "Did you happen to look inside the package before you sent it?"

He shifted on his feet. "Why…no. Was it something important?"

"A map of Sir Francis Drake's expedition against St. Augustine." Philo watched the young man carefully, hoping for a hint of how much he knew. *Is he a seeker like his parents? Alternatively, is he aware of the map's value?*

He shrugged. "Oh. I don't have much truck with maps. Didn't know my father did. I'm an accountant."

Barnaby said deliberately, "It was stolen."

"Stolen? When? From here?"

"Saturday, June 16. Yes, from the store."

"Huh." His lashes fluttered.

Philo didn't trust him. *He looks kind of—what's that word Gollum used in Lord of the Rings? Tricksy. Did he take the map? Then why bother to give it back? And why admit he sent it?*

Barnaby continued. "It was returned Wednesday, June 20. Care to make any conjectures on why?"

"Not me. Like I said, I didn't know what it was. I was simply clearing out the office."

Philo persisted. "Your father wanted mine to sell the map on consignment. Would you like me to go ahead with that?"

He shrugged. "I don't really care what you do with it." He smiled. "Consider it a gift. You'd be doing me a favor by taking it off my hands." He turned to the door. "Look, I really have to get going." He looked at Barnaby. "I'll see you tomorrow, right?"

"Right." They watched him walk swiftly down the lane. "That was odd."

"You don't think he stole the map, do you? It doesn't make any sense."

"With seekers, very little makes sense." Barnaby gazed after the retreating form. "It did strike me that he was hiding something."

"Like what?"

"No clue. Perhaps he sent the map to your father for authentication. He may have been eavesdropping the night we examined it. When he heard what it was, he snuck in and stole it."

"Then why return it?"

Barnaby threw up his hands. "Who knows? You said yourself you hadn't had a chance to research its value. Perhaps he enlisted a second expert who told him it was worthless."

Philo had had enough speculation. "What else did you discuss at lunch? Norton seems open to selling the store."

"Maybe, but he's still stewing over the vandalism. He refuses to meet with Zimmer, but he's accepted my invitation to a puzzle-writing session. I'll try to soften him up that way. Perhaps the *Secret* clues would make a good project." He winked. "Do you suppose it's cheating to have him assist me in the competition with Greer?"

"Yes."

"You're a hard woman, Philo Brice."

****

The Culture Club, Monday, June 25

"We're meeting the children at the Culture Club again. It's Susie's birthday, and they want to disport themselves."

"How old is she?"

"Twenty-one." He chuckled. "Do you think the bartender will be shocked that she's turned twenty-one a second time?"

"He won't care, since she's legal now."

"Let's hope that's the case."

As they strolled toward the pub, Barnaby kept up a stream-of-consciousness conversation. Philo had lapsed into comforting thoughts of alcohol when he suddenly burst out, "Why do you suppose all these people are following us?"

She surveyed the street behind them. A group of teenagers pushed and shoved each other, laughing. An older woman in an elegant sheath dress and high heels was folding up the sandwich board in front of her store. "I don't see anyone taking an unhealthy interest in us."

He stopped short. "What? No. I mean the Hawaiian shirt and Diego. Maybe Norton."

"Nothing else to do?"

"It just seems as though queer little things keep happening. Like your map being stolen."

"And returned. Yes."

"Joseph being poisoned."

"But not by the obvious suspect."

"Agatha meeting her cousin, who may not be her cousin. I tell you, I'm spooked." Barnaby opened the door for Philo. He held a finger to his lips. "Not in front of the you-know-whats."

The students had pushed together the same four tables. Lincoln stood to give Philo his seat. "Kevin's been regaling us with the mysterious events at the Castillo."

The bartender slid a mug under Barnaby's nose and grinned at Philo. "I took the liberty of preparing your usual, miss." He handed her a vodka gimlet.

She accepted it gratefully.

Barnaby held up his mug. "And now, lads, let us cry huzzah and happy birthday to Susie!" Everyone cheered. Susie smiled happily. When they'd finished the toast, she took a sip from her mug and blinked. "Wow. This is strong."

Lincoln nodded proudly. "I ordered it for you. It's Guinness stout. Now that you're all grown up, no more pussyfooting around with wine spritzers and light beer."

She gingerly took a second sip. Her hand flew to her mouth, and she stood up quickly. "Excuse me. I'll be…right back." She headed to the ladies' room.

Barnaby drank off his beer. "Now, have you come up with any conclusions concerning our assorted mysteries? Agatha? Thomas? Kevin?"

The boys looked at Agatha, who kept her head down. "We believe…the casque must be in the Castillo somewhere."

"Why not the shrine?"

She spoke just above a whisper. "It's the image. There's nothing in it that resembles St. Photios, but both the soldier and his banner point to the fort. St. Photios helped us fix on it, but I—we—don't think it's the actual site."

"Is everyone agreed then? We direct our energies to the Castillo?"

Kevin said, "If we do, we'd better get going on it right away."

"Why is that?"

"Because I'm betting those two scumbags are after the casque too, and they're riding our coattails to get to it." He flushed. "Dad's getting impatient with our lack of progress."

His words reminded Philo that Kevin's father was a seeker too. She hoped he wasn't pressuring Kevin too much.

Lincoln was asking, "How can we stay a step ahead if we don't know who they are? You never saw their faces."

"Yeah, but the first one had on the same Hawaiian shirt I'd seen the day I was pushed. The other guy was wearing a windbreaker with a picture on the back of a juggler. If I see that jacket again, I'll know it."

Agatha spit up her root beer. "The jacket—was it tan?"

"Yeah."

"And the picture. You're sure it was a juggler?"

"Couldn't miss it. It was bright red."

"Could you make out what he was juggling?"

Kevin shook his head.

"Oh dear." Agatha set her soda down.

"What is it?"

"Diego was wearing a tan jacket like that when I first met him at St. Photios." She turned frightened eyes to Barnaby.

"Then he's still following you. I don't like this." Barnaby was grim.

Agatha began to wail. "I'm scared."

Barnaby looked around the table. "Okay. The Castillo is our primary objective—but wherever you go I want you to buddy up."

Susie, her face a bit green, returned, carrying a tall glass of lemonade. She quietly pushed her mug toward

Lincoln. Barnaby signaled for a new round of beers. Philo gave a thumbs-up to the bartender. "Another gimlet, please."

Cleo raised a hand. "Before we drop everything for the Castillo, I'd like to present my findings on the Flagler dining room."

Susie raised her hand as well. "And since we took the Mission off the list, I've been researching that fort you told me about. Fort Mosé. It has potential."

Cleo nodded at her. "You go first."

Barnaby acknowledged the gesture. "So Fort Mosé has potential?"

"Well, I'm going by the image rather than the verse. Fort Mosé was established as the first freedman settlement in North America." She smiled. "It turns out there was an underground railroad moving runaway slaves long before the famous one."

"Really?" Kevin jiggled his chair closer. "Where'd it go?"

"It went south from the Carolinas to Spanish Florida. The Spaniards welcomed the escapees as long as they agreed to convert to Catholicism. Then, in 1738, the governor allotted them land for their own village. It was called"—she consulted a pink quilted notebook—"Gracia Real de Santa Teresa de Mosé. The settlers formed a militia and helped the Spanish beat back the British invaders in 1740." She broke off. "An ancestor of mine escaped from South Carolina. He married a Creek woman and settled somewhere in Florida." Her eyes lit up. "I was thinking maybe it was at Fort Mosé."

Kevin gave a little whoop. When no one joined in, he blushed and bit his lip. "Well…I think that would be swell."

"Fascinating, but what makes you think the fort's a likely spot for the casque?" Barnaby accepted the fresh mug.

She extracted a copy of Image Six from her purse and passed it around. "See, over on the left side of Image Six. It looks to me like a black person in a uniform."

"Huh."

"Don't see it." Thomas was blunt.

Philo could tell Susie was really stretching. *She would probably love to find a link to her heritage.* "It's as good as any other explanation."

Barnaby put his hands together in a time-out signal. "I'm proud of all the research you've done, Susie. I look forward to the written report. But, again, I think we should be centering our efforts on the Castillo for now."

"Hold on. You haven't heard my verdict on Flagler yet." Cleo didn't sound particularly enthusiastic.

"Okay. Shoot." Barnaby signaled the barkeep, who brought over two baskets of tortilla chips and a bowl of salsa. "Susie? May I treat you to a second lemonade?"

Philo caught herself before she fell off the chair. *Did he actually use the word "treat"?*

Susie seemed chastened. "No, thanks." She pushed the half empty glass away from her.

Cleo spoke with determination. "As you know, Flagler College contains seventy-nine Tiffany glass windows, mostly in the ballroom."

Kevin spoke. "It really is the neatest place to eat. You feel like you should be wearing thigh-high boots and a velvet waistcoat. And carrying a riding crop."

"You're thinking of the eighteenth century." Barnaby curled his hands around imaginary lapels. "Flagler and Plant and the great hotels and railroads flourished in the late *nineteenth* century. Theirs was called the Gilded Age."

"Oh?"

"Men wore top hats and cutaway coats and spats, not thigh-high boots."

Philo took a moment to imagine her clothes-horse boyfriend in a frock coat and spats. *It would make a nice change from the polka dots and clown pants.*

"Yes, well." Cleo dismissed the subject. "I found some early photographs of the construction of the hotel. The foundation is solid concrete—nowhere to bury a casque. So I think we should move on."

"What about the Ximenez-Fatio house? That was your second site."

She frowned. "It's closed for renovations. The woman told me they tore all the drywall down. If a casque was hidden there, they'd have found it."

"So…two swings and two misses, but we're not out yet." He raised a fist. "All righty then. Back to the Castillo?"

Lincoln spoke for the first time. "Aren't we forgetting the Fountain of Youth? I thought we were saving that for last." He took a sip of beer. "I've been reading *The Secret,* and it's actually referred to in the text."

"Oh yeah?" Cleo seemed surprised. "What did it say?"

"Preiss wrote about these magical little people, the Fair Folk, who brought twelve 'wonderstones'—the jewels—to the New World. Those who settled in Florida were called Dracs and Fadas—"

"Dracs…as in dragons?"

"I'm not sure. Anyway, when the Spanish conquistadors arrived, they fled. The book says they left their enchanted Fountain of Youth behind."

Thomas seemed to wake up. "I read that they reopened it today. The Fountain of Youth. All except the spring where they found that dead woman."

"I don't understand." Philo accepted the second gimlet. "Why keep it closed for so long? The spring's the most visited part of the site."

Barnaby added, "The entire raison d'être for the park, in fact."

"According to the local paper, the police are keeping it closed while they examine some new evidence. They no longer believe her death was due to accidental drowning. They're now considering it a homicide."

"Homicide!" Agatha's eyes were huge.

Cleo leaned forward eagerly. "Did the article say what they found?"

"No." Thomas's eyes gleamed. "I imagine they don't want the murderer to know they have it."

Barnaby stood up quickly, knocking his chair over. "Well, I'm all tuckered out. Gonna call it a night. Philo? May I escort you home?"

They walked out to general sniggering.

Chapter Twenty-Six

He puzzled and puzzled till his puzzler was sore.
—Dr. Seuss

Cuna Street, Monday, June 25

"What was that all about?"

Barnaby said over his shoulder, "No need for the kiddies to know about my brush with a certain murder victim."

Philo stopped short. "So I was right all along. Harriet was murdered."

Barnaby said heavily, "I was hoping you wouldn't be. That screech I heard inside the park? I didn't want to admit it before, but it was definitely human."

Philo took a deep breath. "Thomas said the police came across something at the spring that changed their minds. Do you think it was whatever Harriet planned to show you?"

"You mean Robert's brochure? I specifically asked the detective about it, but he said it wasn't on her person. Either she left it at home or the murderer took it."

"But then what did the police find?"

"You got me. They seem to think it's significant at any rate."

"Wait." Philo stopped again. Barnaby gave her arm a tug, but she stood firm. "Didn't she change your meeting place from Ripley's to the Fountain of Youth?"

"Yes. We had originally planned to meet at a bar near Ripley's."

"So it's more likely she had uncovered something about Ripley's, not the Fountain of Youth."

Barnaby's voice rose. "You're suggesting someone tracked her to Ripley's."

"Yes, so she changed the venue to throw him off the scent." Her nostrils flared like a lioness on the scent.

"But he caught up with her."

"And killed her."

"And stole the brochure. By George, I think we're onto something."

His enthusiasm only served to cool hers. "Or maybe not." Philo resumed walking. "If the information were that earth-shattering, it would have allowed the killer to solve the puzzle, and he would have announced it."

It was Barnaby's turn to stop. "If he announced it, he'd be confessing to murder."

"He'd hardly disclose how he'd come by the solution. No, he'd lie and claim he found the clue on his own."

Barnaby thought that over. "He would be taking an awful risk then. Robert Cottrell wrote in our online forum that he'd discovered something. That's why I contacted him. The St. Augustine forum has about forty members. Somebody else undoubtedly saw Cottrell's post."

"I'll give you that and raise you. If the police found something, then maybe the murderer didn't."

"And it couldn't have been the brochure, because Sergeant Steve would have told me." He stepped around an open manhole. "So how do we get them to spill the beans?"

"Call your best friend, Detective Tolliver."

"*Or* I could try the good sergeant."

"Better." They had arrived at Philo's building. She expected him to open the gate for her, but he pivoted and started loping down the cobblestones. "Barnaby?"

"Gotta go. See you tomorrow."

****

Mind Over Matter, Tuesday, June 26

"It pays to have friends in low places."

Philo looked up from her computer. The store was closed, but Barnaby had somehow managed to appear at her elbow. She sighed. "I wish you'd stop doing that."

"Doing what?"

"Sneaking in."

"I did no such thing. Your door was open."

She glanced at the entrance. "No, it isn't."

"It isn't *now*. You should really keep it locked except during store hours. Any kind of riffraff could ooze in."

She looked him over. Today he was clothed in golf pants dotted with swaying hula dancers, and a T-shirt sporting a picture of a Puritan, complete with Pilgrim hat and ruff collar, swilling from a bottle of Providencia rum. She pointed to a map of Caribbean pirate lairs hanging on the wall. "You do know Providencia is where Henry Morgan's base was, right?"

"The pirate? Yes. Did *you* know the island was settled by Puritans in 1629? Who, finding the terrain untillable, turned to the slave trade?"

Rather than answering, she went back to the computer.

He read the screen over her shoulder. "That's our Francis Drake map. Are you selling it on eBay?"

"Are you nuts? My reputation would go down the tubes if my customers found my stock on eBay. It'd be like selling a first edition of Boswell's *Life of Johnson* at a yard sale."

"Well then, what *are* you doing?"

"I'm trying to get an estimate of its worth." She indicated the screen. "This guy is offering two thousand dollars."

"Not bad. Say, we never settled the question of why the thief brought it back. Guilt? Or stupidity?"

"I won't care when I'm two thousand dollars richer." She clicked on the Contact Us tab.

"Wait!" He held her wrist. "It could be part of our mystery. What if the thief is our stalker?"

"That's crazy. We've established Francis Drake had nothing to do with the casque."

"No, we haven't. It's only because I've been too busy to delve into his history—if any—with Minorcans. Could be something there. Did the British own the island in the sixteenth century?"

"I don't know. I can't believe it matters." Philo was irked to see her glorious vision of dollar bills winging their way into the ether. She closed the laptop lid. "You mentioned low places?"

"The St. Augustine constabulary is situated in a swampy area off King Street. It is there I disinterred the inimitable Steve Landman, policeman extraordinaire. He was loafing in his office. I do believe we're currently best friends. He has asked me to call him Steve."

"You've dethroned Norton Cottrell without so much as a how-de-do? I'd advise you not to be fickle until we've solved our puzzle."

"I'm not prone to fickleness, thank God. But I do tend to collect best friends, and sometimes they bicker amongst themselves. I shall try to keep Norton and Steve in separate cubicles."

"Two best friends? Could you perhaps be sucking up to them because they both have something to offer you?"

"Could be. Could be. At any rate, the lordly Steve apprised me of the evidence the police have regarding the demise of Harriet Cottrell." He paused. "Shall I share it with my other bestie? Nah."

"Evidence?" Philo prompted.

"According to an anonymous tip…Great balls of fire! It may have been Norton himself! He was keeping this from me." He pounded the table. "I must mull over my allegiance to him."

"Anonymous tip?" Philo couldn't think of any other way to pry the information out of him short of applying a can opener to his brain.

"Yes. The police were on the verge of shutting the investigation down when one sharp-eyed underling extracted a wadded-up piece of paper from under the grating. Although it was quite damp, a rough ink sketch of a prancing horse was still decipherable."

"A horse. Like the one in Image Six?"

"No, that one is standing—you might even say drooping. Both horse and rider appear to be exhausted. The picture the police found is of a very lively animal. In fact, I'll show you." He took Philo's elbows and, lifting her out of the desk chair, sat down. Opening a new screen, he searched for a few minutes. "Ah hah!"

The Ripley's website appeared. He clicked on a menu. "This is the garden. There are all sorts of sculptures on display—a family in an ox-cart made entirely of white concrete, a full-size metal crocodile, a replica of Michelangelo's David…and this." He pointed. A rearing stallion stood on a pedestal. It was silver and very shiny. "This was created to honor the Denver Broncos' Super Bowl appearance in 1987. It's made of vintage chrome car parts. It weighs a ton and stands twenty feet nose to tail. But the key point is, it looks exactly like Harriet's drawing."

"And you think the casque is buried under it?"

"Harriet must have thought it was at least a clue."

Philo considered. "Okay, so the clue, or possibly the casque itself, is at Ripley's. Why suggest the bar then?"

"The museum was closed, but the sculpture is on the grounds outside the building. Ripley's outer fence is a low, wrought-iron railing. The horse is visible through the pickets."

"Well, then, why redirect you to the Fountain of Youth? Surely she'd know that park would also be closed."

"It's not far from Ripley's." Barnaby clapped an imaginary thinking cap on his head. "Aha. We return to our earlier premise: she knew she was being followed and wanted to lose the tracker." He rubbed his chin. "She must have known a secret way in—perhaps someone in the forum found it." Barnaby's eyes crinkled. "Those guys can ferret a ferret out of its burrow."

"And the man slipped in behind her."

"Or woman. Yes. And killed her. Just like we speculated."

Philo gazed at Barnaby. "Then why didn't he take the drawing?"

"He didn't know she had it," he returned promptly. "He only knew she was on to something. He overheard her call me and had to find out what it was about."

"Then why not wait for the two of you to meet and eavesdrop on your conversation? Why knock her off before she revealed to you what she had discovered?"

"Because the guy's an idiot. Nobody ever said criminals are smart." When Philo appeared unconvinced, he tried again. "Maybe…she caught him sneaking into the park and confronted him."

Philo still wasn't buying it. "Is that reason enough to kill her?"

"She catches him in the dead of night? In a shuttered park? If she threatened him, yes, he might feel murder was the only viable course of action." Barnaby didn't give Philo a chance to object. "Or how about this? It was the killer who'd got wind of something, and when he found her in the Spring House, he was afraid she'd beaten him to it. He had to silence her."

"You're treading way out in left field now."

"You're saying my idea's like a high fly?"

"More like a foul ball."

Barnaby leapt up. "Wait…'anonymous tip.' Sergeant Steve said the police received a phone call directing them to the spring. If it *was* Norton…" He turned troubled eyes on Philo.

"You're not intimating he killed his own mother?"

"This quest does peculiar things to people."

"It makes no sense. Why not form an alliance with his parents? The prize isn't that valuable, at least intrinsically."

"Not sure what it would bring on the open market." He flopped down again. "It would behoove us to learn what the other stones were appraised at."

"You mean the three that were discovered? What kind of gems were they?"

"Lessee…an emerald. The Boston one was a peridot. Cleveland? What was Cleveland?" Barnaby grabbed his satchel. "Lots to check. I'm meeting Norton to work on the crossword this afternoon. I'll make some discreet inquiries."

"And get back to me?"

"Tomorrow. We're going to the Alligator Farm, remember?"

"No."

He regarded her sadly. "I'm going to have to start jotting the program down on sticky notes and plastering them to your refrigerator." He walked out the door, leaving the bell ringing merrily.

****

Philo's apartment, Wednesday, June 27

"I have beer and pretzels. What are you bringing?"

"To what?"

Barnaby's expression perfectly mirrored the picture on his T-shirt of a smiley face with squiggly black brows and a round O for a mouth. "That's it; we're going to have you tested."

Philo snorted. "When last you updated me on your schedule, you were going to work with Norton Cottrell on your puzzle. I did not anticipate that would involve beer and pretzels, let alone me."

He put down the six-pack, sat down across from Philo, and looked deeply into her eyes. She was about to pucker up for the kiss when he said gravely, "We're going to the Alligator Farm."

Philo did in fact remember, but still felt she deserved some explication. "Why?"

"Why not? I understand they exhibit all known species of reptile. Besides, it's one of Florida's oldest amusement parks. Older even than the mermaids of

Weeki Wachee Springs." He whistled. "Oh dear, I didn't mean to imply the mermaids were old. Well, I don't really know. Real mermaids are of course immortal…but one must presume that the damsels in sequined tails blowing bubbles through breathing tubes have an age limit. Or am I being ageist?"

He seemed to expect a response, but Philo wasn't playing. "It's kind of expensive. The Alligator Farm."

"No matter. I'm rolling in dough, thanks to Mr. Zimmer."

"Has Norton Cottrell agreed to meet him?"

"Not yet, but I have high hopes. The puzzle's going swimmingly. He has a devious little mind—very helpful in coming up with clues."

"Do you still think the *Secret* verses might be used to plot the casque location?"

"At this juncture, I'm only trying to use the lines in a puzzle. Verse Nine isn't long enough to provide the number of clues I need for a proper crossword, so we've had to include the other poems, as well as the site candidates for the other casques." He frowned. "That may mean the crossword can't solve any one location."

"I thought you weren't really trying to solve it."

"Well, I don't want the kids to. It's okay if I do."

"That doesn't seem fair."

"And your point?"

Philo gathered her things and put them in a tote bag. "I suppose we have to take my car."

"Since I don't have one, that would be yes."

They bought some fried chicken and coleslaw and, crossing the Bridge of Lions, drove down A1A to the Alligator Farm Zoological Park. The parking lot was empty when they entered. Philo braked. "Is it closed?"

"No. See? The door's propped open."

A few hours later they pulled the cooler from Philo's car and sat at a picnic table under live oaks heavy with Spanish moss. Philo dug her spoon into the coleslaw. "That wasn't so bad. The albino thing was pretty cool."

"The gavial? Yes." Barnaby put down his beer and ruminated on the bucket of chicken pieces.

"I didn't realize they had lemurs and birds as well." Philo sipped her beer. "The stuffed alligator was somewhat unnerving."

"Indeed. I wonder how the live ones feel about him."

"I doubt they're aware he's dead. Probably assume old Stinky's just been napping for two years."

Barnaby licked the salt off a pretzel. "Which was your favorite?"

"Has to be Maximo."

"Me too. I loved the underwater viewing window." They'd both spent a long time watching the enormous saltwater crocodile as he floated in his private pool. "I must say, I'm warming up to these cold-blooded creatures. I may even have a go at Delilah when we get home."

Philo just smiled, but a little bun of warmth started to grow somewhere behind her sternum. After a minute, she remarked, "So how did Maximo end up at an alligator resort in Florida?"

"The sign said he hatched from an egg some aborigines found in Australia." Barnaby began to gnaw on a chicken leg. "Why do you suppose they gave it up? Must've been a pretty big egg. Why not just make an omelet?" He didn't wait for her to reply. "That sitting Buddha—"

"It's a Hindu god—Shiva, I believe."

"Whatever. It reminded me of the one in Ripley's garden. *Hmm…*"

"Oh, for heaven's sake, you see hints of buried treasure under every rock."

Barnaby stuck his nose in the air. "Forgive me, but I believe in the *maxim*—ha-ha, see how I did that?—that there are merely two degrees of separation between everything."

"People maybe, but not clues."

"Especially clues. How do you think I write the crosswords? Oh, by the way, I sent the kids to Ripley's to inspect the grounds. They should be calling in any moment." His phone tinkled. "Aha…Linc? What's the matter? Well, did they do anything? Okay. Leave Ripley's at once. We're at the Alligator Farm. We'll meet you at the college in twenty minutes. My office." He hung up.

"What happened?"

"They were poking around the gardens when Agatha screamed."

"Oh dear. Was she attacked?"

"No, no. A rat ran across the path in front of her."

"And that's it? That's why you told them to leave?"

"No, of course not. When they gathered to help her, they saw the same two guys who were at the Castillo. Agatha identified one of them."

"Who was it?"

"Diego. Her so-called cousin. He's definitely not sightseeing."

Chapter Twenty-Seven

For me, the most enjoyable part is the puzzle, the process of solving, not the solution itself.

—Erno Rubik

Barnaby's office, Flagler College, Wednesday, June 27

"Now compose yourselves and tell us what happened."

Agatha sat in the one chair, Cleo hovering around her. "She'll be okay, Professor. Just give her a minute." Cleo shivered. "It was a *huge* rat. Yuck."

It looked like Agatha wasn't going to relax anytime soon, so Barnaby turned to Lincoln. "Setting aside the rat for the moment, did you all see the two men?"

Lincoln and Thomas shifted uneasily. Cleo said, "Not me. I was tending to poor Agatha."

"We didn't either."

"What about Susie?"

Cleo answered. "Susie wasn't with us. She went up to Fort Mosé."

"Alone? What did I say about sticking together?"

"Kevin wanted to go with her, but she said she'd be fine. She took her cell phone and went by taxi."

Barnaby was livid. "If anything happens to her…"

Lincoln's phone rang. He clicked Talk. "Oh, hi Susie. You're where? The dorm? No, we left Ripley's and we're meeting with the professor. Come on over."

Barnaby scratched his head. "Where were we?"

Philo answered promptly. "Who observed what. We've established that Cleo, Lincoln, and Thomas saw nothing."

Agatha whispered. "I did, though. There was a man in the garden who was wearing a Hawaiian shirt."

"The same shirt as Kevin's guy?"

"Um…"

"But you are confident you saw Diego?"

"Yes."

Barnaby steepled his fingers. "So, bottom line, we don't know for sure if the man in the Hawaiian shirt at Ripley's is the same man who shadowed us at the Castillo. Lots of people wear Hawaiian shirts. This is Florida after all."

Embarrassed silence. Finally, Lincoln said, "Kevin recognized him."

"Kevin…" Barnaby made a show of looking around the tiny room.

Philo asked the obvious question. "How did you know he was the same man if Kevin wasn't there?"

"I was."

She spun around, bumping into Thomas, who knocked over a table lamp. Kevin limped into the room.

Cleo opened up space for him. "Where have you been, Kevin?"

"You all skedaddled so quickly that I couldn't keep up with you. I decided I might as well wait at the entrance to Ripley's in case the men came out."

"Did they?"

"No. I waited as long as I could."

"Could one or the other have tagged you?"

Kevin's brow furrowed. "You know, I hadn't thought of that. No one else was around, so I was probably pretty conspicuous."

"Can you confirm the Hawaiian shirt was the same one the man at the Castillo wore?"

"Affirmative. It's yellow, with big red flowers all over it."

"Can you describe him?"

"That's the thing. In all the times I've seen him, I've never been close enough to see his face. He's sort of medium height, medium build. Wears a hat. Always carries the binoculars."

"White? Black?"

"His legs are pasty white, and he has knobby knees." He looked hopeful. "Does that help?"

"Hardly." Barnaby frowned. "There isn't much to go on. The second man could simply be a tourist, hitting all the sights. Diego's the one we need to watch." He winked at Agatha. "Unless he's been sent by your family to marry you."

Agatha's eyes went wide. "But…but…"

"I certainly hope not." Philo heard a touch of regret mixed in with the humor in his voice. She was afraid Barnaby held out little hope that Agatha would ever find a mate, related or not. "I don't approve of intrafamilial unions. Besides, it's illegal in the United States, if not Minorca."

"No, you don't understand," Agatha burst out. Even with her voice raised, they had to strain to hear her. "There's no way he's my cousin. He couldn't be."

"Well, then, why is he following you? Why did he claim to be a relative?"

"I…I don't know."

Philo went to the door. “Let’s not fuss over this now. Until we have an identity for the Hawaiian shirt guy, and/or Diego makes a move, we should go about our business.”

All except Kevin seemed relieved. “I still want to know if it’s the fellow who pushed me.”

“I don’t see how we’ll ever find out.”

As the students shuffled out, Susie appeared, panting. “Did I miss the meeting?”

Kevin took her arm and led her to the bench by Barnaby’s office door. “I’ll bring you up to speed.”

Barnaby said sternly, “Susie, I’m very disappointed in you. I thought I’d made it clear you were all to have a buddy on your outings.”

“But I—”

Kevin stood up to him. “Susie wasn’t with us when you said that, Professor. Anyway, she’s capable of taking care of herself. You shouldn’t treat her like a baby.”

“A baby?” Barnaby took a step back. “Oh, dear, no. I just want you all to be safe.” He bent his gaze to the girl. “You went to Fort Mosé?”

“Yes.” Her lower lip protruded. “There’s no way the casque could be buried there.”

“How so?”

“There are no historic buildings left—it’s empty except for an exhibit building. The park wasn’t designated until 1994, so Mr. Preiss wouldn’t have found any landmark to hide a casque under in 1982.”

“Okay, we can take it off the list.”

Kevin said, “I’m sorry, Susie.”

“It’s okay.”

They left him patting her hand solicitously. Philo faced Barnaby. “Now what?”

"I have some work to do on the puzzle. I'm meeting Norton tomorrow to finalize it."

"Oh."

He checked his watch. "You have a few hours to pretty yourself up. I suggest a facial."

"Huh?"

****

Philo's apartment, Wednesday, June 27

"Wow, you look terrific. So you took my advice?"

"What advice?"

"The facial." He made a circular motion with his hand. "Your features manifest the supple elasticity of cosmetic manipulation."

"It's called health."

Barnaby took Philo's hand and led her toward the bedroom.

"What are you doing?"

"I want to see if it glows in the dark."

****

Philo's apartment, Thursday June 28

"Don't get up. I can make my own breakfast. Let's see…toad in the hole sounds nice."

"Good thing you know how to make one." Philo rubbed her eyes. "Can you wash your own dishes?"

"If forced to, yes."

Barnaby was putting a plate covered in crumbs and spattered with egg into the dishwasher when Philo came into the kitchen. "What the hell are you doing?"

He turned. "Obeying the instructions in the commercials. The fellow pretending to be an appliance says not to scrape."

She took the plate and thrust Delilah into his hands. He flinched but kept mum after a glimpse of her expression. He cupped the snake on his two palms, his eyes glittering with fear. Delilah coiled herself into a tight scroll and went to sleep. After a minute, he looked up. "She's not slimy."

"I told you."

Delilah woke up and unfurled her slim body. She raised her head to look at Barnaby, and proceeded to wrap herself around his arm and slither up to his shoulder. He went rigid, his face frozen. "Is she…is she…"

"No, she's not going to choke you to death." Philo carefully unwound the snake from Barnaby's arm. "She likes you."

He drew in a huge breath. "Well, that's reassuring."

Philo took Delilah back to her aquarium and returned. "What's on the docket today?"

"I told you. I'm meeting Norton in an hour. See you for lunch?"

"Okay."

Philo frittered three hours away rearranging piles, picking at imaginary bumps on her arm, and playing with Delilah.

Precisely at noon, Barnaby showed up. This time he knocked. Which was unnecessary because he'd apparently located a shirt that played "It's Not Easy Being Green" when you pressed the little frog on his chest pocket.

"Wherever did you dig that up?"

"Like it? I gleaned it in the fields of Goodwill." He plucked at the fabric. "I'm dumbfounded that anyone would discard such a unique piece of apparel."

"Me too. Lunch?"

"That's why I'm here." He held out an arm. "Harvey's?"

"No. And not Flora's either."

"Ooh, ooh. I found this little hideaway that serves Polish food. Pierogis, cabbage rolls, the works. It's mostly for carry-out, but they have one table." He peered at her. "You don't mind choosing your meal from the menu board above the counter, do you? They have assured me it's the way they do it in Poland."

"You apparently got your taste buds at Goodwill too." She headed to the door. "We're going to Catch 27."

They walked to the old stucco-fronted house on Charlotte Street. The place was busy, but the hostess found them a corner table in the spare, blue-washed dining room. The waiter announced they could call him Karl—"with a *K*"—and recited the specials.

Philo's mouth began to water. "Ooh, the deviled egg with fried oyster sounds scrumptious. And the shrimp roll. They aren't rock shrimp, by any chance, are they?"

"As a matter of fact, yes." Karl was impressed. "Most customers have never heard of them."

She leaned toward Barnaby. "They're small, but have this wonderful flavor. Yummy." She closed her menu. "I'll have those, and iced tea."

Barnaby had been perusing the menu and deliberately ignoring the two people waiting for him. He muttered, "Apropos of nothing, Norton and I have completed the puzzle—he has a real knack for crosswords. I think this could be the beginning of a very beautiful friendship."

"Aw, you say that about everyone."

"Untrue. I am exceedingly choosey about my companions. You may not have noticed, but I sized you up for an entire quarter of an hour before asking you out. If that isn't discrimination, I don't know what is." He turned to the waiter. "What's in the chowder?"

Karl, by this time noisily tapping his foot, rose to the occasion. "Mullet, sir."

"Mullet? Isn't that a haircut?"

"That too, sir. In this case—unless you find a hair in your soup—it will be fish."

"I see today's floor show features a comedian." Barnaby handed the menu to Karl. "I'll have the green tomato sandwich and a cup of the Minorcan chowder, please." He stopped. "Minorcan…Gee, do you suppose this place is—"

"No, and stop it. Like Agatha says, there's a large Minorcan community here. Now, what were you saying about Norton?"

"That he has a knack for crosswords. Puzzling must be in his genes. Or maybe not puzzling per se, but an ability to see patterns." He scratched his head. "Or could he simply have a prodigious memory?"

Philo cut through the morass of words. "More important, did you talk him into meeting with Mr. Zimmer?"

"I think so, yes. I've buttered him up with honest compliments. He loved the T-shirt and mug, by the way." He rubbed his hands. "I am hoping Mr. Z. will give me a nice little check for my services. Then I'll get you that steak I've been promising. Do you prefer cubed or chicken-fried?"

"Neither." Philo accepted the appetizer. "Deviled eggs and oysters. Who invented such a magnificent combination?" She dug in.

Karl brought Barnaby's soup. An orchid floated in it. Barnaby propelled his chair backward from the table and pointed a wobbly finger at the bowl. "Please! Take it away! Take it away *now*!" The waiter started to remove the cup, but Barnaby bleated, “No! The flower! The flower!”

“Okay. Right away, sir. No need for alarm, sir.” Karl snagged the blossom and retreated.

Philo prayed he’d return. “Has Agatha recovered?”

“Cleo tells me she’s taken to her bed. Between the rat and the other rat she’s afraid to go out.”

“What about the rest?”

“They seem to be able to keep themselves occupied.” A shaft of foreboding sliced through his mobile features. “I don’t like the way Thomas looks at Cleo. I think he has a crush on her.”

“She knows. She’ll take care of it.”

“That’s what I’m afraid of.”

They finished lunch and walked back to Philo’s shop. Joseph called from his balcony. “Can you two come up to my apartment?”

They climbed the stairs and went past Philo’s door to Joseph’s. He was leaning over a table on which lay a copy of Preiss’s *The Secret*. He pointed. “See that?”

The book was open to Image Six. Philo said, “Yes, that’s what we’ve been studying all this time.”

“I know.” He prodded the picture with his finger. “Take a gander at that.”

She studied the picture, finally shrugging and moving aside. Barnaby traced his finger down the side of the rocky edifice. He twitched and bent closer.

Joseph grinned. “It’s an alligator.”

Chapter Twenty-Eight

How doth the little crocodile
Improve his shining tail
And pour the waters of the Nile
On every golden scale!
How cheerfully he seems to grin
How neatly spreads his claws
And welcomes little fishes in
With gently smiling jaws!

—Lewis Carroll

Joseph's apartment, Thursday, June 28

"You may be on to something, Joseph. See—" Barnaby showed Philo. "There are the nostrils, and up there is its tail. The jaw is this line. *Hmm.*"

Philo squinted. "But it's upside-down!"

"I don't think it matters. Everything is topsy-turvy in these paintings." Joseph put a hand on Barnaby's shoulder. "Are you thinking what I'm thinking?"

"A reference to St. Augustine? I'm not sure." Barnaby seemed dubious. "Alligators abound in Florida. The artist could simply be directing seekers to the state."

Joseph rubbed his chin. "On the other hand, if the casque *is* in St. Augustine, it might depict a specific animal."

Barnaby straightened. "Maximo."

That got Philo's attention. "The huge creature at the alligator park? The one with an enclosure the size of a basketball court?"

"The very one."

"You do know he's a crocodile, right? Not an alligator."

Barnaby was not to be deterred. "Well, maybe the one in Image Six is a crocodile too. Which would pinpoint the hiding place even more precisely." He headed to the door.

"Where are you going?"

"To the Alligator Farm, of course."

"Shouldn't you collect the troops?"

"No time. Besides, I just want to snap a photograph of Maximo for now. We can explore the park later if the images match."

Joseph tied a scarf around his neck. "I'm going with you."

"Are you sure?"

"I'm invested in this now."

The three of them took Philo's car across the bridge to the farm. The lot was empty except for a red sedan parked at the far end. The cashier recognized Barnaby and Philo. "Hi, there. Back again? Did you forget something?"

"No, no. As a matter of fact, we were extolling the virtues of the park and our friend here"—Barnaby indicated Joseph—"had a question about one particular exhibit. Could we possibly nip in and see it? We'll only be a minute."

She considered. "Well, the zip line's down, and the whole park will close in half an hour. I guess you can go in—but be quick about it."

"Perfect. Do we have to pay?"

His puppy dog impression did the trick. She batted her eyes. "Nah, if you're back in five minutes."

"Thank you! We promise we'll be in and out before you have to put your shoe back on."

As they went through the turnstile, Philo looked back. The cashier was gazing at them, slack-jawed, a fire-engine-red three-inch heel dangling from her left hand. She nudged Barnaby. "How did you know about the shoe?"

"She was rubbing her foot when we came in and grimacing. I deduced her feet hurt. The only logical conclusion was that she was wearing shoes that are inappropriate for work." He winked at her. "Probably has a hot date this evening."

Philo ran smack into Joseph, who was standing in the middle of the sidewalk, consulting a map of the park. "Maximo is to the left down this trail."

"Come on." They reached the animal's pen. Maximo lay half submerged in a pool. The part that was visible was the size of Philo's Fiat.

Joseph read the sign. "Says here he's over fifteen feet long and weighs twelve hundred and fifty pounds." He eyed the creature. "That's more than half a ton. How much must he need to eat per day to keep up his strength?"

Barnaby roamed along the fence snapping pictures. "That's enough I think. Let's go."

As they approached the path that led toward the entrance, they were met by a barricade that completely blocked the way. Weighted cones supported a heavy iron gate that swung out from a stanchion. Philo tested it. It didn't move. "Was this here before?"

"We couldn't have come this way if it were."

"True." Joseph checked his watch. "They must be closing up the park early. It's still ten to five."

Barnaby swung around. "Maybe this path is a loop that will take us around to the main walkway." A few steps later, they turned a corner, passing through a small grove of thick bamboo. The trail came to an abrupt end at a brick wall. "*Hmm.*"

Joseph slapped his forehead. "I forgot—the map. This path is strictly for Maximo viewing."

Philo frowned. "Do you think the cashier forgot to tell the staff we were here?"

Behind them, Joseph gasped. "I don't know, but we'd better find a new exit strategy *quick.*"

"What the—" About ten yards away—its jaws stretched wide, revealing rows of craggy, bone-crunching teeth—crouched a huge, hungry-looking crocodile.

Philo screamed. The crocodile turned its head to regard her with an amber eye as cold as it was calculating. Barnaby threw an arm in front of her. "Back up slowly."

"Back up *where*?"

Joseph yelled, "Split up. I'm going to try to scare him." He ran straight at the reptile waving his arms and shouting.

Barnaby cried, "Hit him on the nose!"

Philo pulled at his shirt tail. "No! He can't reach its nose with its mouth open."

"Then jump over him!"

Joseph halted. "You're kidding, right?"

Time stood still while the three humans stared at the animal, who stared back at them. In Philo's fevered brain, he seemed to be casually taking their measure. *Is he deciding which one looks juiciest? Which of us will put up the least fight?* "I think we should link arms and march on him. Maybe that'll disconcert him."

The two men dragged their eyes from the behemoth in front of them to focus on the idiot woman beside them. "Huh?"

"Hey, you!"

Their heads went up like dogs at the word "walkies."

Philo saw him first. A dark-haired man in a blue uniform stood on the other side of their attacker, observing the situation. "Hi! We're stuck." She didn't think she needed to explain further, considering the reptile currently swishing his colossal tail between them.

Suddenly the man pivoted and galloped off.

"Wait! Don't leave us!" Joseph blew out his cheeks. "I can't believe he abandoned us."

"Maybe he went to get help."

"How long will that take? We could be dinner by then."

"Yikes!" Barnaby took a step back, probably because Maximo had moved a foot forward.

Philo cast a quick glance backward. The end of the path loomed just a few feet away. "How about you try to boost me over the wall?"

"It's an idea."

Barnaby had linked his hands and Philo was about to step into them, when Joseph called. "He's back."

"The man?"

"Yes."

The keeper appeared, carrying a large hunk of raw beef and a long pole. "Just keep calm, folks. Don't move." He unlocked the gate and swung it open, then shut it quietly behind him. Hooking the meat on the end of the pole, he waggled it. "Come on, Maxie," he cooed. "Lookee what I brought you. A special early treat."

The croc lumbered around, saw the bloody lump, and snatched at it. The keeper held up the pole and sidestepped. "Come on, kid. Let's go back home." He gradually coaxed the animal into his enclosure, threw the meat in, and slammed the gate shut. He wiped his neck with a bandanna. "Whew!"

The three erstwhile victims rushed toward him. The man rolled the barrier aside, allowing them to trot out, then locked it behind him. Barnaby slapped him on the back, Joseph pumped his hand wildly, and Philo kissed him.

He squirmed out of their clinging embrace. "What the hell were you people thinking? That croc is in a cage for a reason. Why'd you let him loose?"

"We did no such thing. He cornered us." Joseph glared at the man.

"Don't look at me! No keeper would let any of the animals—let alone Maximo—out this close to feeding time."

"F…f…feeding time?"

"Five o'clock. Five minutes from now." He tipped his cap. "Bet he thought you were the blue plate special. You're lucky you're not in bite-sized pieces."

Philo put her hand on her hip. "Well, *somebody* opened his cage. And *somebody* lowered the barrier."

The man was still peeved. "Oh, all right. I'll check the latch." He fiddled around with the closing mechanism. "Seems in order."

"You don't lock it?"

"Of course I do, but I usually leave the key in it. Saves time when I'm in a hurry." He gave Barnaby a meaningful look. "Like now."

Joseph volunteered, “We came in a few minutes before the park closed. Someone else could have as well.”

“Huh.” The keeper started toward the main entrance. “I’ll escort you back to the register. We can ask the cashier if anyone came in after you.”

They walked back to the lobby. When the woman saw the guard, she straightened, presenting a significant bosom.

He grinned. “Hey, Patsy, lookin’ good. Say, did anyone come into the farm after these three?”

Patsy blanched. “They said they were only staying a couple of minutes. I thought it’d be all right. I didn’t let nobody else in after them.”

He gave her arm an affectionate squeeze. “S’okay, hon. Turns out ole Maxie got loose and gave ’em a run for their money.”

Her lipstick fell from a limp arm, hitting the floor with a crack. “Oh no!”

“Everything’s shipshape now. Gave him an early snack. Still, reckon I’ll give the park a quick scope before I close up. See if any stragglers are wandering around. Back in a few.” He winked at her.

She smiled a little damply at him. “Okay, Jocko.”

The hot date?

He opened the entrance door and ushered Barnaby, Joseph, and Philo out. Philo shook his hand. “Thanks again for saving us.”

“No problem. I’ll check with my boss. Maybe we should do a full recon of all the cages.”

The red car still sat in the parking lot when they came out. It appeared to be unoccupied. Barnaby pointed at it. “At least one person’s still inside.”

"Parked way over there? It's more likely Jocko's or some other employee's." As they made the turn onto A1A, Philo checked her rearview mirror. The sedan was right behind her. She could make out a blue shirt. "I was right. Probably just finished his shift."

"Uh-huh."

When they reached Aviles Street, Joseph leaned forward between the two front seats. "Fancy a drink?"

"God, yes."

Philo parked the car, and they walked up to the Dog and Whistle. Jimmy hailed Joseph. "How you doin', old man?"

"Just fine, young lad." He grinned. "My usual, please. And a round of beer for my friends."

When they were settled with drinks at one of the high tops, Barnaby asked Joseph, "So why were you examining the image today, anyway? I thought you'd dismissed *The Secret* and the seekers as humbug."

"What? Oh, Edmund picked up the book in your shop and brought it round yesterday. We were chatting about you and your students, and I opened it to Image Six to show him what you were working from. He asked which spots were currently in your sights. I said I wasn't sure, that you had taken the day off to visit the Alligator Farm. The words were barely out of my mouth when the outline of the gator jumped out at me. It's like when you're cloud-gazing and before your eyes the cloud transforms into an elephant. Edmund couldn't see it."

Philo murmured, "To be fair, I couldn't see it either until you traced it for me."

"True." Joseph drank off his whiskey. "It wasn't until you two showed up today that I could share what I had tumbled to." He patted Philo's hand. "Although, in light of our recent encounter, maybe I should have kept the news to myself."

At that moment, a hand descended on Joseph's shoulder. "Why, Joseph, fancy meeting you here. This isn't your usual cocktail hour." Edmund Greer stood behind the old man. He was breathing rather heavily and drops of sweat beaded on his forehead.

"Well, well, hello, Ed. Have you been running?"

"What? No. It's warmed up out there. Thought I'd duck in and cool off with something tall and chilled." He undid the top button of his chambray shirt. "Mind if I join you?"

"Not at all."

Greer pulled a chair from another table and sat down. "I'm glad to find you here too, Mr. Swift."

"Oh?" Barnaby's brows went up.

"Today is the deadline for our little crossword puzzle contest." He plopped a manila envelope on the table with an eager smile. "I was going to drop it off at your office, but I might as well leave it with you now."

For a moment, there was dead silence. Then Barnaby coughed. "Oh, dear. I must apologize. I completely forgot about our bet. I've been partnering with someone on a…business deal, and I couldn't put him off. You do understand?"

Edmund's eyes narrowed. "I see." He rose, ignoring Barnaby's protestations.

Joseph picked up the envelope. "Wait, Edmund. I can testify that Swift has indeed been swamped with work. Tell you what: I'll take your submission now, and when Barnaby finishes his, I shall compare them myself."

Edmund stood, clearly vacillating. Finally he rapped, "All right. I'll leave it with you." He glared at Barnaby. "At least I can count on an unbiased evaluation." He bowed and left.

Joseph watched him go. "My, my. He didn't even wait for his drink."

Philo felt sorry for the man. "He's disappointed. He expected to go head-to-head with the great Argle Bargle, and the great Argle Bargle dissed him."

Barnaby said absently, "I truly did forget. Thanks for covering for me, Joseph."

The old man grinned. "The only downside is now I have to solve his puzzle before I can get to yours. Can I treat you two to another drink?"

The others nodded vigorously. While they waited, Barnaby began to tap out a tune on the table. While Philo tried in vain to identify it, he said, "I've been thinking. Maximo is a crocodile, not an alligator. A 'saltie.' "

Philo snapped, "I pointed that out before we went."

Barnaby went on as though she hadn't spoken. "Most of the other clues in the images are nonspecific—in the sixth one, there's a palm tree, a generic soldier, asters that grow everywhere. So if the picture shows an alligator…maybe I was right after all. It's only an icon, designed to direct attention to Florida."

"Does that mean we can discard the Alligator Farm as a potential cache?"

"I think so." He gulped down his beer. "To be honest, I'd rather not go back there. Hazardous to one's health."

"*Humph.*" Philo signaled to Jimmy. "Could we get some peanuts, please?"

The bartender grinned. "You sure you're not in the mood for eggplant fritters?"

Philo didn't feel the need to respond. She picked up her beer. "I wish Maximo was the *only* near-death encounter we've had."

Joseph demurred. "If you're referring to my heart attack, I'm sure it was a simple mistake. The mailman meant to deliver the medicine to someone else on his route."

Philo refrained from reminding him that the package hadn't been addressed. *He's probably right*. "Besides that, there was Kevin—"

Barnaby shook his head. "Who claims he was pushed, but we found no one nearby and no sign of a second person."

"The pirate ship? That iron ball nearly decked you."

"Could've been left untied and rolled off the deck."

"But someone stole their treasure chest!"

"A prank—the thief knew it was filled with candy. A practical joke."

This wasn't going well. Philo had to make Barnaby accept the dangers they faced, and he seemed increasingly skeptical. Desperate for a surefire rebuttal, Philo blurted, "All right, how about the Cottrells? I mean Robert and Harriet? You can't deny their deaths are suspicious."

"I won't. But what does that have to do with us? They both died before the seminar convened and before the students began their research. I don't see a connection." Barnaby gave her a reproachful look. "You sound almost as though you *want* there to be a killer on the loose."

"The seminar hadn't started, true, but you were communicating with the Cottrells about *The Secret*."

"I'll give you that, but it's not as though I'd met them in person or we'd exchanged anything of value."

In the simmering atmosphere, Joseph ordered another whiskey. "Jimmy, has Mabel concocted any new culinary delights? Despite my recent medical misadventure, I don't mind being a lab rat."

"All I've got is eggplant dip. You game?"

"No!" Barnaby's voice cracked with horror. Joseph guffawed.

Jimmy shrugged and refilled the bowl of peanuts.

Philo wasn't finished. "If there *is* a killer out there going after seekers, you have a duty to protect the kids. Their safety is in jeopardy."

"My students? Why?"

"The Cottrells were seekers, and your students are seekers."

His voice crisp and firm as a Granny Smith apple, Barnaby said, "Philo, my students are conducting an academic exercise. They do not constitute a threat to the actual hunters."

"Ah, but do the hunters know that?"

Chapter Twenty-Nine

Keep your friends close; keep your enemies closer.
—Niccolò Machiavelli

Dog and Whistle, Thursday, June 28

At this point, Joseph cleared his throat. "Barnaby, Philo has a point. The young folks could be in danger. The real seekers have no way of knowing they're not seriously pursuing the prize."

Barnaby reluctantly agreed. "You've convinced me. Maybe we should put a hold on the research."

"Hey! How come you take Joseph's advice and ignore mine?"

Barnaby's eyes opened wide. "It's the same advice, isn't it?"

"Ye…es."

"Then what's the problem?"

Philo found herself speechless.

Joseph filled the silence. "Or you could find some other project entirely. You shouldn't be putting the class at risk."

Philo, still seething, got up and stalked toward the ladies' room. As she passed the bar, Jimmy leaned over it and whispered, "It's nice to see young people showing deference to age and experience." He gave her a meaningful look.

Sigh. When she returned, she was feeling much more generous toward Barnaby. Which brought to mind another issue. She sat down next to him. "I've been thinking. If it does turn out that the Cottrells were murdered, the killer may feel he has to do away with *you* as well."

Barnaby looked up. "What's that?" He popped a peanut in his mouth. "You're suggesting *I'm* the next victim? That makes no sense. Besides, I have friends in the police department now."

"I don't think Tolliver likes you."

"Ah, but Steve does. Always butter up the underlings. In fact, I might invite him along."

"Along?"

"To the Alligator Farm."

Joseph's jaw dropped. The peanut he'd been chewing fell onto his napkin. "You're going *back*?"

"A minute ago you said it was too dangerous." Philo couldn't keep the desperation out of her voice.

"That I did, but I've been thinking. If someone tried to kill us—or at least scare us off—it stands to reason he thinks the casque is there. I aim to find it."

"What about the students?"

"I shall set them up in the library for the weekend. They'll be safe there." He stood and took his glass to the bar. "I've got to meet Norton and finalize the crossword before we submit it tomorrow."

"I thought you finished it this morning."

"We did, but I always like to let it stew for a few hours, then take a last look. I usually catch a typo or something. Are you going to be all right?"

She wasn't sure if the last was directed at her but tried to act upbeat. "Of course!" She refused to brood on the prospect of another night without Barnaby.

Her cheerful dismissal seemed to bother him. He bent down and whispered in her ear. "Later?"

She glanced at Joseph, who chuckled. "Maybe."

After Barnaby had gone, Joseph paid the bill and he and Philo walked home. As they entered Aviles Street, Philo spotted two familiar forms standing in front of the store, the street lamp illuminating them like the tractor beam from a flying saucer. Or God. As usual, she was struck by the physical dissimilarities between Cleo and Agatha. Yet they seemed to be close friends. *Cleo is quite protective of Agatha.* Her solicitude was heartening; Agatha was the type who was always left behind, and Cleo was the border collie who herded her back to the fold. The two girls turned at their approach. "Hi there, Cleo. Agatha. Were you looking for me?"

"Actually, we hoped to find the professor. He's not with you?"

"He's working on his crossword puzzle."

"Crossword puzzle? In the midst of all this?"

"Well, it's his job."

Agatha's eyes bugged out. "You mean he writes crosswords for a *living*?"

Oh dear—was I supposed to keep that a secret? Philo suddenly remembered how mortified Barnaby had been that his alter ego was a nerdy puzzler. She stammered, "I mean, just as a hobby. Yes. And sometimes they publish them. He's really quite good." She had no idea if that were true, but according to Joseph, he was the greatest of them all, and if Joseph thought so, that was good enough for her. Fortunately, the old man didn't say a word. "May I give him a message?"

Cleo spoke. “Agatha here has been really affected by the stress. We were thinking maybe we could lie low this weekend—do online research.”

Philo sighed, relieved. “Yes, in fact he told me that for now he’d like you all to stay indoors until we unravel what’s going on.”

“Great.” Cleo seemed curious. “We couldn’t find him anywhere today.”

“We…uh…did a little sightseeing.”

“Where’d you go?”

“The Alligator Farm. And before you ask, I wouldn’t recommend it.”

****

Philo’s apartment, Thursday, June 28

“Boy, when things start to move, they move quickly.”

Philo jerked awake. “When did you come in?”

“Half an hour ago—I hated to wake you, but when it looked like you were down for the count rather than taking a brief forty winks in order to be fresh when I arrived, I had to act.”

She sat up and rubbed her eyes. “Okay, *how* did you get in?”

“That other neighbor of yours—the old lady? She let me in.”

“Ida Kink?”

He said meditatively, “Didn’t seem happy. Is she always in such a foul mood? Maybe it’s the late hour. No…that dismal I-detest-everything-and-it’s-your-fault expression of hers appears to be permanently pasted on. You really should remember to lock your apartment door.”

By the time he'd finished, Philo had risen, brushed her teeth, and changed into a shift. "What moved quickly?"

"You *were* listening. Good. Norton has agreed to sell the liquor store to Zimmer. Champagne corks are popping everywhere—I'm surprised you didn't hear them."

"I was deep into REM."

"REM? Is he a rival for your affections? Just kidding." He gestured at her dress. "Why did you clothe yourself? I had intended to slip between the sheets and spoon while we talked."

"You said you had news."

"I've given it to you. Norton has agreed to sell the liquor store to Millstone. My work is done; I expect remuneration any day."

His cell rang. "Hello? Oh, hi, Mr. Zimmer…Okay, Axel. Really? No, I didn't hear anything. It's too late to talk to Norton tonight. Well, I'm sorry, there's nothing I can do…Right. First thing tomorrow." He clicked off. "Sheesh. It's not my fault, much as your neighbor would like it to be."

"What isn't?"

"That was Axel Zimmer."

"I know."

An eyebrow went up. "Wow, you're good. Anyway, he says Norton sent him a text saying the deal was off."

"That didn't take long. Did he give a reason?"

"No. My mission, should I choose to accept it, is to glean the answer tomorrow. Now, where was I?"

She got under the covers. "Slipping between the sheets."

"Your memory is improving."

****

Philo's apartment, Friday June 29

"This does not bode well for my finances."

Philo put down her mug. "Oh, there you are. I must say, I do not approve of you disappearing as precipitously as you appear."

"Would you like me to wear a bell around my neck?"

Philo reckoned saying yes would not be taken in the spirit in which it was intended. "I take it the good news from last night has taken a turn for the worse?"

Barnaby—clad today in green denim overalls and a red and blue gingham shirt, took his straw boater off and laid it on the table. "Yes. I've just been to Granada Liquors. With tears in his eyes, Norton Cottrell informed me that his parents had died intestate." He gave a little skip. "That is *such* a useful puzzle word! So many vowels."

"You mean they didn't leave a will?"

"Correct. It seems Mr. Norton Cottrell—only child of the late lamented Robert and Harriet—may not inherit their millions. Of bottles, that is."

"If he's their only son, surely he inherits no matter what."

"I would assume so, but I'm no lawyer. Say, shall we consult the eminent Mr. Brighton, Esquire?"

"I'm right behind you."

They walked down the hall to Joseph's door. A sharp rap brought the old man out. "Ah, Joseph, you're up."

"I usually am at ten in the morning."

"Good. We have a legal question for your steel-trappy mind."

He beckoned them inside and sat down in his easy chair. “Shoot.”

“When a couple die intestate and only have one child, does said child automatically inherit their goods and chattels?”

“Oh dear, I’m a trial lawyer. Never did wills and trusts.” He pinched his lips together. “As I recall, it depends on the state, but it likely goes to probate. An administrator is appointed, who distributes the assets. Is this someone you know?”

“It’s the Cottrells—the two people who died earlier this month. Robert and Harriet.”

“Robert Cottrell? Wasn’t he the jumper at the Lightner?”

“Uh-huh. And Harriet died at the Fountain of Youth.”

He took a sip of tea. “So they left no will. And they have a son?”

“Yes, and he wants to sell their liquor store.”

“Well, he’ll just have to wait. These things can take up to a year. All creditors must be given time to step forward and submit their claims.”

“Axel Zimmer won’t be pleased to hear that. He wants to buy the store.”

“Zimmer? Who’s he?”

“He owns Millstone Brands, headquartered in Milwaukee.”

Philo clarified. “He makes gourmet liquors, like pear-infused vodka and banana bourbon. He needs an outlet to sell them in St. Augustine.”

Joseph turned to Barnaby, confused. “Why not just ask Cottrell to stock his products?”

“Zimmer likes to own his own storefronts.”

"I see. And where do you come in?"

"I used to work for him. At first, Norton Cottrell refused to negotiate with Zimmer. Axel asked me to intercede on his behalf."

"This sounds like a commercial issue, not a legal matter."

"Not anymore it isn't. They had agreed on the sale last night before this no-will thing came up. Now Norton can't sell the property as promised, at least not yet."

"Sorry, I can't help you. The younger Cottrell should retain a firm with estate expertise."

"I'll tell him."

"Well, then." He heaved himself out of his chair. "Time for my morning constitutional. I'll see you out."

"You're exercising?" Philo hoped her astonishment hadn't leaked through.

"Doctor's orders. I walk along the quay to the Kookaburra coffee house, where I partake of a healthful snack—usually a cup of mocha latte and a blueberry scone. I understand blueberries are loaded with antioxidants." He winked.

Barnaby and Philo watched him leave, his cane tapping on the stairs. Barnaby led the way to Philo's apartment and flopped morosely on the sofa. "Mr. Z. is going to hit the ceiling."

"As long as he's not mad at you."

"Are you kidding? He's the type who takes it out on the nearest body. He once canned the delivery boy because the restaurant put mayonnaise instead of mustard on his sandwich."

"He could fire the delivery boy?"

"No, but no one wanted to tell him that. The restaurant simply switched services."

Philo hoped she wouldn't ever have to meet Mr. Zimmer. "Why is he so bent on buying the store?"

"I told you—he wants an outlet for his boutique vodkas."

"Yes, but he seems awfully keen."

"He's one of those manic businessmen. Acquisitions are mother's milk to him." He pulled out his phone. "I'd better call him."

She put a hand on his arm. "Before you do, Agatha and Cleo were here yesterday. They'd like to stay in this weekend. I told them that was your plan as well."

"Great. I won't have to chain them up."

"Agatha's a bit overwhelmed."

"Should I call her too?"

"No. Cleo is watching over her." She smiled. "For all her tough New York exterior, I think she has a soft spot for Agatha."

"And the feckless Thomas has a soft spot for the headstrong New Yorker."

"Won't get him anywhere. She has his number."

Barnaby said dreamily, "I wonder if any of the other students have amorous intentions? Methinks Kevin looks with affection upon Maid Susie."

Philo pictured the boy with the Swedish features and the young girl with the creamy caramel skin. "They are sweet together—I don't know if they're sweet *on* each other."

"Time—spent in each other's company—will tell. Ah, summertime, the juice that fuels countless dalliances."

"Yes—which are tucked away in diaries with tiny padlocks and forgotten by October."

"You, my dear, are not a romantic."

Philo went to her bedroom. “I have to open the store. Will I see you tonight?”

“Only if Mr. Z. decides not to execute me. I go to lay my head on the block.”

“Don’t make it easy for him.”

“She does care!” He kissed her and left.

Chapter Thirty

The best defense is a good offense.

—Jack Dempsey

Philo's apartment, Friday, June 29

"He was ominously quiet."

"Mr. Zimmer?"

"The one and only. I fear for my vitals." He plucked at the T-shirt that said "Millstone Brands—Try a Threesome" under a picture of a juggler juggling tiny liquor bottles. "If I hoped wearing his logo would help, it didn't."

"It's not your fault the Cottrells didn't leave a will. It's not even your fault they died."

"Well, I'm not so sure about the latter. I was basically the last person to have contact with them. It's possible I contributed to their untimely end."

"Tell you what." Philo carefully laid her fork down. "Why don't you go tell Lieutenant Tolliver that and see what happens."

"Oh, he knows." Barnaby spoke casually. "He hasn't arrested me yet."

"Maybe Diego is an undercover cop. He's trailing us to get confirmation before they lower the boom."

"*Now* you're putting me off my feed." Barnaby took his plate to the sink. "Excellent stew, by the way."

"It's a good thing you managed to put away three helpings before you lost your appetite."

"Yes, indeed." He came back to the table with a fresh baguette. "Perhaps I should wash my hands of this whole Cottrell debacle."

"While you're at it, wash your face. You have a dab of sauce on your chin."

"I'm serious." He pretended to pick something up off the floor while swabbing his face. "I only intended to do research on *The Secret*. I didn't expect to be ensnared by the treasure hunt."

"And now we have our hands full with whoever is playing these tricks on us."

"Agreed. By the way, I returned to the Alligator Farm." At her gasp, he said quickly, "It was closed."

"Good."

"Don't you want to know why?"

Philo tore a hunk from the baguette. "Shoot."

"Evidently, Jocko and Patsy were caught *in flagrante delicto* in the mud pit."

"Jocko and Patsy?"

"You mean to tell me those memorable names aren't etched in your memory? Jocko—our savior, the crocodile tamer. Patsy, she of the carmine stilettos and easy ways."

"Oh yeah…" She put the bread down. "They were caught *where*?"

"In the mud pit at the Alligator Farm."

"With all those alligators?"

"No, no. According to the caretaker I ran to ground, the two inamorati, under the influence of what must have been *at least* a case of Boone's Farm, decided to unfetter their charges so the creatures could gambol freely about the grounds. To their chagrin, the animals chose instead to run amok."

"That's awful. Were the humans harmed?"

"No. I think they were so well-known to the inmates that they were ignored. Unfortunately for Jocko and Patsy, the gendarmes were not as blithe."

Philo giggled. "Thus ending what could have been the beginning of a beautiful friendship."

"Hey, that's my line." He had started to pour more wine into his glass when his phone buzzed. "Why, Lieutenant Tolliver, are your ears burning? No? Because we were just talking about you. All nice things, of course." He listened. "Yes, I can come down, but doesn't he have someone closer—family or friends? I see." Barnaby put the phone back in his pocket. "Gotta go."

"I'm coming with you."

"You don't know where I'm going."

"The police station. What does he think you've done now?"

"There's been a break-in at the Cottrell liquor store. They've arrested Norton Cottrell."

"For breaking into his own store?"

"You forget. It doesn't belong to him."

"Maybe so, but he must have a key. Why would he break in?"

"The store has been closed and cordoned off by the police while they investigate the two deaths. Nobody is supposed to be inside."

Philo drove Barnaby to the station. Tolliver was in the lobby, the ever-present stogie stuck between his teeth. "There you are. We're waiting for Cottrell's lawyer, but he wants to talk to you."

"The lawyer?"

The detective glared at him. “Don’t be cute. Cottrell. He’s asking for you.”

“Happy to oblige, but why arrest him? Seems pretty innocuous to go into the store your parents owned, even if it *is* sealed off.”

“It’s not that, although technically he was breaking and entering. When we caught him, we decided to go ahead and hold him for murder. Two counts.”

“You’re talking about his parents?”

Philo gasped. “Matricide? Patricide?”

Barnaby nudged her. “Or more comprehensively, parricide.”

The detective rolled his eyes. “We here in the less rarified levels of the atmosphere just call it homicide.”

“But…but what happened to the suicide theory?”

“Forensics is convinced it wasn’t suicide. Something about angle of the fall and position of the body. Our second theory—of a business deal gone bad—seemed promising until we traced the anonymous call about the horse drawing. It led us to Norton Cottrell’s phone number.”

“How did you jump from that to murder?”

“The only way Norton would know about the sketch is if he was with his mother when she died. We first assumed he killed only Harriet, but then we learned he was booked on a plane from Anchorage to Jacksonville the night before his father fell to his death. He could easily have been in St. Augustine on June the fourth to do his father in as well. The motive for both being the same, the case is open and shut.”

A visibly angry Barnaby exclaimed, “And exactly what motive would that be?”

"The store, of course. We have indications that the harassment and vandalism were instigated by Norton Cottrell himself."

Philo burst out, "Why on earth would he do that?"

"He knew Millstone Brands wanted to buy the store. He thought by fixing the blame on them he could jack up the sale price."

"But he refused to sell it to them!"

Barnaby elbowed her aside. "Never mind that. How is that a motive for murder?"

"Cottrell's mother—Harriet—adamantly refused to sell. Norton needed money—"

"For what?"

Tolliver shrugged. "Who knows? Do you know anyone who *doesn't* need money?"

Barnaby looked like he wanted to spit. "That's outrageous! Police malfeasance. Conduct unbecoming a professional. Why, I've a mind to—"

Philo, who had taken a moment to think while Barnaby ranted, interrupted softly. "It sounds as though you have a murder charge looking for a suspect."

Tolliver grimaced. "You caught me. We now know both Robert and Harriet were murdered, but that's all we've got. CSI could only determine cause of death—not who did it."

A police sergeant came through a door. "Mr. Cottrell's asking if Mr. Swift has arrived yet."

"Take him back."

Philo tugged his sleeve. "May I go too?"

"I guess so."

Norton sat on a hard bench, his face in his hands. He raised his head at the sound of Barnaby's voice. A purple welt colored his forehead above his left eye. "Hey, Barnaby. Long time no see." He attempted a weak grin.

Barnaby reddened. He turned to the sergeant. "There's no way this fellow could have murdered his parents. Let him out at once!"

The sergeant remained impassive. Norton leapt up. "What did you say? They think I murdered Mummy and Dad? Oh my God, that's crazy!" He shook the bars.

The officer unlocked the cell. "You two can go in and talk to the prisoner, but when his lawyer arrives, you'll have to leave."

They sat next to Norton on the bench. Barnaby said, "You remember Philo Brice."

He looked her over. "You're the map lady. May I ask what *you* have to do with all this?"

Barnaby was offhand. "She's just a friend. Now, tell us what happened."

He took a deep breath. "You know they shut down Granada Liquors while they conduct their investigations, and I told you about the will—or lack thereof. I know I'm not supposed to, but I've been checking on the store every day in case the earlier attacks had resumed."

"But both your parents are dead! What would be the purpose?"

Norton threw up his hands. "Who knows? I couldn't risk any more costly damage."

Barnaby whispered, "The police think you did the damage yourself."

"Huh? That's absurd." He glanced at the sergeant. "So today I go by there. I still have a key—"

The officer made a sharp movement.

"I know, but I felt it was my responsibility until everything's resolved to protect the business. Anyway, someone was inside when I got there."

"About what time was this?"

"Maybe four. Before five anyway."

"What did you do?"

"Not what I should have done. I should have called the cops. But no. I told myself it would take them too long, plus they might quiz me as to what I was doing there myself. Norton, I sez, Norton, my boy, you can take care of this yourself. So I went in. The burglar was in the office rooting around. He must have had an accomplice, though, because when I challenged him, someone cracked me on the head from behind."

"From behind you say? How did you come by the goose egg on your forehead then?"

He rubbed it. "I think I hit the desk as I fell."

"Okay. So then what happened?"

"When I came to, I called the police. By then the crooks were gone."

Philo said, "But why would the cops arrest *you*? Obviously you'd been knocked out by somebody. And you did call them eventually."

"That detective with the cigar told them to arrest me." He gazed at Barnaby, his blue eyes terrified. "I inferred it was for breaking in, but now you say it was for murder?"

"I don't think Tolliver's ready to charge you yet. They're holding you while they gather evidence."

"Can they do that?"

"I think so. By the way," Barnaby asked casually, as though it had just occurred to him, "do you have your phone with you?"

"Funny you should ask. I lost it a few days ago. I thought I'd left it by the cash register when I was going through the receipts, but when I went back to look, it was gone. I have a new one on order."

Philo interrupted. "Then how did you call the police?"

"There's an office land line. I used that."

A rumpus at the door caught their attention. A round little man in a shabby three-piece suit, one hand clutching a scuffed leather briefcase, rushed in, brushing off policemen like flies. "Let me through. Cottrell? You're out of here. They got nothing. Come on."

At a nod from Tolliver, the sergeant opened the cell door. The three inside shuffled out. The lawyer took Norton's arm and propelled him out of the building. Barnaby stopped before the detective. "What now?"

"It was worth a shot. Hoped for a confession or at best some extra time to investigate. We'll keep working on it."

"But if he's telling the truth, someone else broke into the store. Did you get fingerprints? DNA?"

Tolliver bit his lip. "What a great idea. We here on the squad don't usually dust for prints, but I'll certainly take your advice and suggest it to the forensics unit. Now, if you'll excuse me, I have to go find that criminal investigation manual and bone up. Unless you have time to give me a lesson?"

"There, there, Lieutenant. No call for sarcasm. We'll…uh…we'll leave you to it, shall we?"

Tolliver was gracious enough to agree.

Barnaby stomped out of the station, Philo on his heels. "Where to?"

He stopped so short she had to veer off to avoid hitting him. "Joseph."

"Joseph? Is he ill again? Oh dear, let me call—"

"Joseph is a defense lawyer. Let's ask him what we can do to protect Norton."

Philo was feeling cross. "Since when are we responsible for a virtual stranger's problems?"

"Since we know he's innocent."

"And how do we know that?"

"Because I happen to know he was out of town for at least Robert's and possibly Harriet's deaths."

"You have proof?"

"Yes."

"Why didn't you tell Detective Tolliver?"

"I need the emails."

"Emails."

"Yes. Between me and Robert. I hope I haven't deleted them." He walked faster. "Can you drop me at the college?"

He's leaving me again? A catch in her voice, she whispered, "No problem."

He kissed her. "If I succeed, I shall appear at your door tomorrow and sweep you off your feet and into the bedroom. Be prepared."

"Okay."

Chapter Thirty-One

Dead Men Don't Wear Plaid *was my favorite of all the things I ever did, because it was like doing a Sunday crossword puzzle and beating it.*

—Carl Reiner

Philo's apartment, Saturday, June 30

"The one message from Cottrell in my phone merely confirms our appointment."

"Remind me: you thought you had emails exonerating Norton Cottrell?"

"I wasn't sure. If I remember correctly, Robert mentioned that his son was away on a business trip. I thought if I could find that message, we'd be home free."

"Didn't you keep the whole thread of emails?"

Barnaby shook his head. "I only saved the last one."

"Well, that's a bummer."

He tapped his fingers on the table, nearly knocking over the glass of grapefruit juice. Philo caught it before it spilled into his lap, currently covered in seersucker and a sleepy Delilah. "You've become altogether too fond of my pet."

He stroked Delilah affectionately. "I can't help it. Once I touched her, the irrational fear humans are born with dissipated. She's really a cutie pie."

"Yes, well." Philo took the snake back to her bedroom.

When she reappeared, Barnaby took up the conversation as though there hadn't been any interruption. "We have to find a way to get into the Cottrells' store. The emails will be on Robert's computer for sure."

"How do you know? He may have contacted you from home."

"His email address is Robert@Granada.com. That's from the business website. Wait here." He went into the hall and came back a minute later. "Ready?"

"You found a way?"

"Uh-huh."

"Did you ask permission from Lieutenant Tolliver?"

"We're meeting Norton at the store. He'll slip in through the alley."

"So that's a no."

Barnaby said defensively, "I only want to check his computer."

"But surely the police have already confiscated it."

"Norton says no. Look, it'll just take a minute. Are you coming?"

Philo slipped off her indoor shoes and put on her sandals.

****

Granada Liquors, Saturday, June 30

Norton let them in the back door. "No police around. We should be okay for a few minutes."

Barnaby sat down at the clunky old office desktop. He turned it on. A cursor blinked. "What's the password?"

"Should be 'robandharrietcottrell.' All one word."

"Not very hard to hack."

"They weren't exactly tech savvy."

"Okay…" Barnaby started clicking keys. The other two went out into the store. They heard a rap on the front door.

"Oh shit, I hope that's not the cops." Norton slipped behind the register and knelt down. "See who it is."

Philo peered through the glass. Two men stood outside. She raised her voice. "Who are you?"

"Axel Zimmer. Open up."

From behind her came the whispered, "Axel Zimmer! What the heck does *he* want?"

"More to the point: how did he know we were inside?"

"Does he look hostile?"

"No."

"I guess you should let him in." He stood up.

"If you think so." She unlocked the door.

The man who marched in was gargantuan. Philo immediately thought of a Sherman tank. His shoulders were stiff and broad, and his hands were the size of hub caps. His gray hair grew in a thick mat on his head. A short, stocky man with a long scar down one cheek slid in and stepped to one side, hands behind his back. Philo recognized him as the muscle. *I hope that lump in his pocket is a pickle and not a gun.*

Zimmer halted at the sight of Norton. "Cottrell, what are *you* doing here? I thought you were in jail."

Norton said sullenly, "I didn't do anything wrong. They had to release me. And I might ask the same question about you."

"I saw a light on. The police have roped off the premises, and I was afraid there might be a looter inside."

"What's it to you? It's not your store."

"Not yet, no, but it represents an investment. I don't like it being left unsecured any more than you do." He beetled his brows. "Why did you kill them anyway?"

"Kill them? How dare you!" Norton launched himself at Zimmer.

The shorter man jumped between the two. For a feverish second, the three stood immobile, but the standoff quickly lost steam. Norton took a nonchalant step to the left, and Zimmer swaggered to the right, leaving his bodyguard, slightly abashed, rocking from foot to foot. Barnaby came out, stuffing a crumpled sheet of paper in his back pocket. "What's all this?"

Norton, his face purple, pointed a shaking finger at Zimmer. "This…this bastard is accusing me of murdering my parents."

"Well, he's wrong."

Zimmer looked surprised. "Can you prove it?"

"Yes."

"*Hmm.* Pardon me, but I'm going to wait to hear it from the police. If they declare Cottrell innocent, I'll apologize."

Norton sneered. "Gee, what a saint. When we're through probate, I'm keeping the store. You're not getting your mitts on it."

Zimmer didn't say anything, but a tic started up in his cheek. *He wants this store as much as a toddler wants his brother's toy. It's not normal.* She caught Barnaby's sleeve. "Let's go. Come on, Norton."

He balked. "Get out, Zimmer."

The man left unwillingly. His companion—who hadn't said a word during the exchange—went with him. Once on the sidewalk, Zimmer turned and yelled, "I'm not done with you yet, Cottrell! I'll get this place one way or another."

"You stay away from the store and me, or it'll be you sitting in the slammer."

Norton made sure Zimmer had driven away before he left the store. As they came out of the alley, Barnaby said, "I want to consult our lawyer friend before we proceed."

"Did you find something in the computer?"

"Hopefully proof of your innocence."

He sprinted to his car. "Right behind you."

****

Joseph's apartment, Saturday, June 30

Joseph was home. "You seem to be multiplying."

"Hi, Joseph. This is Norton Cottrell."

"Ah." He regarded him with sympathy. "The son of Harriet and Robert?"

"Yes."

"Come in. Come in. So sorry for your loss." He stood aside to let the three enter his living room.

Before he had a chance to close the door, a woman's voice rose in a high-pitched shriek from the hallway. Philo recognized it as belonging to Ida Kink, the other occupant of the second floor. Nasal and twangy, hinting at adenoidal issues, it suited its owner well—an unpleasant, unhappy woman in her sixties. "Joe! You get out here!"

Philo happened to know that he hated being called Joe, except by Jimmy the bartender, who was grandfathered in due to the free drinks on All Saints' Day. *I don't trust either Ida or Joseph to keep it nonviolent.* "I'm going with you." Barnaby made up the rear guard.

Ida stood in the hall, wearing a dirty terry cloth housecoat and hefting a brick. She shook it in Joseph's face. "Someone threw this through my window." Seized by a fit of coughing, she wiped her mouth on the frayed sleeve, leaving a pink stain. She rasped, "Know anything about it?"

Joseph drew back, bewildered. "How would I know who did it? Your apartment's on the other side of the building."

"Thought you might have seen something. You're always skulking around." She coughed again, causing a drop of spittle to fly through the air and land at his feet. He shifted slightly. "My ex is back in town. He has a whatchacallit—a vendetta—against me. Just 'cause I took him for all he was worth. Teach him to run around with that slut." Her face twisted with frenzied scorn. "It'd be just like him to throw a brick at me." She peered at Joseph and then at Philo. "You sure you ain't seen a squirrely kinda guy around? Balding? Pot belly? Thick glasses?"

Joseph said firmly, "I remember what Arlen looks like, and no, we haven't. I promise to keep an eye out for him, though. Now, if you'll excuse me, I have to attend to my guests." He gently closed the door in her face.

Barnaby whistled. "I had a run-in with Miss Ida a while ago. Is she a piece of work or what?"

Still, Ida's accusation disturbed Philo. "You don't suppose her husband is really after her?"

Joseph shook his head. "Arlen is too rabbity to be dangerous—just the type of cringing jellyfish Ida would marry, if you'll pardon the mixed species."

"O...kay."

"Now, what can I do for you all?"

They sat down. Barnaby explained about Norton and the detective's suspicions. "When Robert wrote me to set up our get-together, he mentioned that Norton was at a convention in Alaska, but that his flight home was canceled. In that case, he couldn't have been here in time to kill his father." He handed Joseph a folded sheet. "I couldn't find his original email, but I printed out my response. Do you think it'll be enough to exonerate Norton?"

The accused gazed at Joseph, his expression imploring.

"Let me see it." He read slowly. "All it says is, 'I hope your son isn't stuck in Anchorage for long.' When were you supposed to meet Robert?"

Barnaby answered promptly. "Monday, June fourth." Philo—who could barely keep the days of the week straight—was amazed he could remember the date so clearly. Barnaby kissed her cheek. "It's stuck in my mind because it's the same day I met Philo."

Oh.

"This was written on the Sunday before—June third. Mr. Cottrell could have returned to St. Augustine that night."

"I didn't, though!" the young man cried. "A 6.2 earthquake hit a few miles from Anchorage, and the airport shut down. It took me six more days to get out of Alaska."

"Do you have the flight information? Hotel receipt? Anything?"

Cottrell shook his head miserably. "The conference wasn't tax-deductible so I deleted everything when I got home."

Barnaby sighed. "You're saying it doesn't look good, Joseph."

Philo had been quiet, trying to put her finger on the item nibbling at the back of her cerebral cortex. "Wait. Barnaby, that's not the same note I saw you tuck in your pocket at the store. I didn't say anything then with Zimmer there, but it must be important. What was it?"

Barnaby chuckled. "I forgot all about it." He drew a balled-up sheet of lined paper out of his pocket. "Sorry to disappoint, but it's merely an idea I had for a crossword puzzle theme…arising from my newly minted attachment to a certain Delilah." He smoothed the paper out. "Idiomatic expressions using reptiles. Like a snake in the grass."

Norton, his eyes alight, added, "Or crocodile tears."

Joseph joined in, his voice burbling with mirth. "A lounge lizard. Naming no names, of course."

Barnaby was not to be outdone. "Nurturing a viper in one's bosom. Snake oil salesman." Suddenly his face fell. "I hadn't realized there were so many derogatory phrases referring to the overly maligned creatures. Maybe this wasn't such a good idea."

"Well, it's a lot more amusing than Edmund's contribution to your erstwhile contest," said Joseph. "I had to put it down half finished."

Before the conversation went too far off track, Philo hissed, "Gentlemen? We were talking about Norton's exoneration?"

"Oops—we puzzlers are easily led astray." Joseph turned to Norton. "You say you were at a convention in Alaska during the time period in question. Surely someone there can vouch for you. Try to get in touch with your fellow attendees. Or with the convention organizers."

Barnaby added, "Perhaps the airline will still have its manifest. You'd be on the passenger list."

Norton dropped his eyes. "I guess it's all I can do," he whispered. When he looked up his eyes were blurred. "I've lost both parents in the space of a few days. To be suspected of murdering them is pretty hard to handle."

Barnaby patted him awkwardly on the back. "I say, why don't you help me with next week's puzzle? We'll do the reptile theme. It'll take your mind off your troubles."

"That's very kind of you, but I'd better get cracking on proving my innocence."

"Oh, all right. How about a spot of lunch then?"

"Sure." Norton got up. "I'm going to go home and clean up. Shall I meet you somewhere?"

"Glad you asked." Barnaby puffed out his chest. "There's this divine chili place—it's off St. George Street. Flora's. You know it?" Norton shook his head. "Well, you're in for a real treat. Meet me downstairs when you're ready, and we'll walk over."

Philo would have said something, but she hated to rain on Barnaby's parade. *Who knows? Maybe Norton will* like *the food.*

When Cottrell had gone, Barnaby sat down. "So where do we go from here?"

"How about we leave poor Joseph alone and go to my apartment?"

Joseph was content to see them go. "I'm not used to this much company, pleasant though it is."

They settled on her couch. Barnaby drew Philo to his side. "Where were we?"

"Deciding what to do about Norton. Although I still think it's a matter for the police."

"The police didn't check Robert's computer—"

"We don't know that for sure."

"No. True." He rallied. "But they sure botched the arrest. Tolliver should have had the goods before he brought Norton in. If he were guilty, it would only serve as a warning to him. He'd likely bolt."

"But he's innocent. At least that's what you claim."

"I do believe he's not guilty, but I doubt if he'll cooperate with the police after this." Philo got up and went to fill Delilah's water bowl. When she returned, he muttered, "Besides, whoever set the croc on us *made* it our business."

Philo had almost forgotten their recent pas-de-deux with Jaws. "All right. Who else has a motive?"

"Maybe it has nothing to do with *The Secret*. Maybe the police were right before: a business competitor killed the Cottrells."

"Maybe...oh, dear." She gazed at Barnaby, concern creasing her brow. "Mr. Zimmer? He does seem excessively anxious to buy the place. And finding out the estate's going to probate hasn't diminished his desire."

"No, no! I didn't mean him. He'd be too obvious. Axel's made no secret of the fact that he wants the store—and he did stop the vandalism. He wouldn't risk becoming Suspect Number One."

"Okay."

Barnaby was quiet so long Philo thought she might have to pinch him awake. Finally he said, "No one. I can't think of any other suspects."

"Then the working hypothesis must still be that someone wanted to beat them to the casque." She steepled her fingers. "The seeker world is huge, and we're not insiders. You never actually met the Cottrells, and they were your only contact with the hunt. It could be one of thousands."

Barnaby straightened. "Rather than search for other suspects, then, perhaps we should look for a different motive in the same one."

"Same suspect? As in Norton?"

"No."

"You mean Zimmer? What sort of motive other than profit could he have?"

He looked down at her, his eyes concerned. "Maybe Axel Zimmer is a seeker."

Philo scoffed. "That makes no sense. What could possibly make you believe that?"

"I hadn't really focused on it before. Diego."

"Diego. Agatha's cousin."

"She says he's not."

I'll bite. "Okay, what about him?"

"The scar."

"Scar…" It meant nothing to Philo.

"She said he had a scar. So did the fellow with Axel."

"Lots of people have scars. His was on his cheek. Did Agatha say where Diego's was?"

His shoulders slumped. "I don't remember." He sat tapping his knee. "I've got it!" Barnaby was positively glowing. He grasped Philo's hands. "His clothes. Remember? Agatha described them."

Philo threw her mind back. "Was he the one in the Hawaiian shirt?"

"No, that was the other stalker." Barnaby let her go, pulled out his phone, and began to type something in the Search box. "Agatha said Diego wore a jacket with a picture of a juggler on it."

"So?"

"That's the logo of Millstone Brands. Remember my T-shirt? They gave one to all us interns."

"Could it be a souvenir? He bought it in the company gift shop?"

"No. The logo was on the back, but I happened to descry a name embroidered on the front. It didn't really register until now."

"What do you mean you saw a name? On who? Diego? How? You've never met him—only Agatha and the other students have seen him."

"Actually, I saw him today. At the Cottrells' store."

"You mean, on that guy with Mr. Zimmer?"

He nodded. "Diego."

Chapter Thirty-Two

So this was the big secret historians keep to themselves: historical research is wildly seductive and fun. There's a thrill in the process of digging, then piecing together details like a puzzle.

—Nancy Horan

Philo's apartment, Saturday, June 30

"Diego!" Philo sat up straight. "Thomas speculated Diego has been pursuing Agatha because he's after the treasure too."

"And we shot him down. But what if Thomas was right? And if Diego works for Axel Zimmer…" Barnaby went to her desk. "Where's your laptop?"

"It's being upgraded. Someone used up all the memory. Shop says it's loaded with thousands of photographs."

"Can we use the one downstairs?"

"Yes."

They fought each other to be first down the back stairs to the store. Philo turned on the overhead light, and Barnaby booted up the computer. "There. Look."

He had pulled up the website for *The Secret*. Philo expected to see Image Six, but instead a different image appeared on the screen. "What am I looking at?"

"Image number ten. Believed by many seekers to refer to Milwaukee, Wisconsin."

She examined the painting. What appeared to be a castle atop a high crag filled the background. In the foreground a man in medieval raiment juggled several curious objects. “I get it. A juggler. The logo for Millstone Brands…but what’s he playing with?”

Barnaby pointed at the various items. “The gemstone is an amethyst. Then a cane, a primrose, a key, and a millstone.” The last was a round, gray object with a square hole in the center. “Some speculate that the image is a rebus: “mill” plus “walk” for the cane, plus “key.” Zimmer comes from Milwaukee. His company is Millstone Brands.”

“He couldn’t have chosen his logo at random.”

“No. It contains all the elements of Image Ten. He’s a seeker all right.”

Philo wavered, not quite ready to commit. “He could simply be using it for advertising purposes.”

“In that case, he wouldn’t be here in St. Augustine.”

“He’s here to buy a liquor store.”

“Owned by two seekers. Now deceased.”

“But liquor is his business. The fact that the Cottrells were associated with *The Secret* could be mere happenstance.”

“*Humph.*” Barnaby swung the chair around. “From what I’ve read, seekers aren’t limited to only one image. They go wherever the most promising site is.”

Philo considered. “It’s the thrill of the hunt, not the kill?”

“Er, yes. Kill…Someone out there wants both. Diego has been shadowing the students, and he works for Zimmer. He’s definitely Axel’s hired gun. Is it his job to eliminate the competition?”

Philo felt a lump in her throat. “Ulp.”

Barnaby rose. “I have to meet Norton. I’ll ask him if he knows Axel is a seeker. That will clinch it.”

****

Philo’s apartment, Saturday, June 30

It was a long afternoon. Finally Philo heard the bell and buzzed Barnaby in. “What happened? What did Norton say?”

He dropped a duffel on the floor. “He declared Flora’s chili to be the finest in St. Augustine.”

“He couldn’t have.”

“You’re right. He had a similar reaction to yours. We opted for a street hot dog.” He looked her up and down. “Are you a relish girl? Onions?”

“On my hot dog? Everything except ketchup.”

“Good to know.”

Philo thought about waiting for him to get around to it, but didn’t have the patience. “What did Norton say about Zimmer?”

Barnaby sat down on the couch. “He didn’t know anything about his hobbies. Hadn’t picked up on Diego’s name tag—I guess he’s one of those guys who looks you straight in the eyes, which is a good thing. Shows the man has integrity. A dishonest person looks anywhere *but* the eyes. That’s why they’re called ‘shifty.’ Now, Diego didn’t make eye contact, but then he’s a lackey, so I don’t think they’re supposed to. Where was I?”

She joined him on the seat. “What did Norton know about Diego?”

“Nothing, but I’m still of the opinion that Zimmer sent Diego to follow the students.”

“Well, to be specific, he only followed Agatha.”

“Hard to tell. She may have been his first mark—a way to insinuate himself into the group.”

"Then why did he back off? Why not talk to us when we were at the Castillo?"

"Kevin thought he was spying on somebody else—the guy in the Hawaiian shirt."

"Oh, for heaven's sake. I think if you're assigned to tail a person you're supposed to stick with them, not go haring off after anything that moves."

"Well, if I'm right and he's a seeker, he'll keep track of all those involved. Robert and Harriet Cottrell. Agatha." He stopped. "I wish we knew if the Hawaiian shirt guy is an active participant or just a tourist."

"Now we have *too* many suspects."

"Why do you say that? Right now we're only considering Axel Zimmer and Diego." He leapt up. "Perhaps we should confront them."

Philo scoffed. "Whoa. Now *there's* a great idea. You're going to buttonhole a man who may have killed two people? While you're at it, why don't you ask to meet him in a dark alley? Tell him to bring his gun."

"Now you're just being silly." His phone dinged. "Hi, Cleo. You're where? Oh, okay. I'm glad you're staying close to the college…What? All right, but I don't want you students to go alone. Let's plan to go together tomorrow. Ten a.m."

Philo waited.

"Cleo says the Spring House at the Fountain of Youth has reopened, and they want to go check it out."

"I thought we'd fixed on the horse at Ripley's?"

"Not at all. And you're forgetting that the Castillo is still in the running as well. As to the fountain, Cleo's reasoning goes like this: it's top of the list for most of the participants, so we have to at least eliminate it before we move on."

"But we've done so much research on the other two sites!"

"I'm just the messenger. Anyway, it won't do any harm to see what the spring has to offer." Barnaby picked up the duffel.

"What's the bag for?"

"This?" He hefted it. "In case we rouse an enemy and must hole up for protection."

"An extra set of clothes?"

"And a mask. I intend to disguise myself so masterfully that even you won't be able to spot me."

Sigh. Philo was beginning to tire of the game. She longed to get back to her books and maps and her own little kingdom. "I would remind you of what you told the students—the task is *not* to find the casque, but to conduct an instructional exercise."

"Right, right. Still, we only have two weeks left in the semester. I would like to have something to show for it." He tented his fingers. "That's it: I'll ask the students to write papers on their particular sites."

Philo felt improvement on the proposal was in order. "They've kind of skipped around and reshuffled responsibility. Maybe a collaborative effort—a joint paper—would be more effective?"

"Perhaps. There are only six of them. Could work." Barnaby seemed pensive. He dropped the duffel again.

"What's wrong?"

"I'm missing something."

"A clue?"

"No. A body."

"Another one? Don't we have enough?"

"I don't mean a dead body. I mean a live, warm, soft, cushiony body. Like yours. It's been two whole days."

Philo saw no reason to continue the conversation in the living room.

****

Philo's apartment, Sunday, July 1

"I am refreshed." Barnaby rolled over and kissed Philo. "Also famished. Do you have any food?"

"Eggs and bacon. English muffins."

"Perfect. I shall await your summons."

"Can you cook *anything*?"

"Have you forgotten my memorable toad in the hole?" He beamed with pride.

"Well, at least you perform well in other categories."

He reached for her. "I do, don't I?"

She pulled away. "I'm going to make breakfast."

"And I shall make my ablutions. I'll be with you momentarily. Where did you put my duffel?"

"The bag? It's in the closet."

"Aha. A neatnik? Or do you enjoy my company?"

Philo didn't reply, mainly because she wasn't sure of her answer. She was pouring coffee into her mug when he joined her. "Where on earth did you find *that* outfit?" She indicated his orange plus-fours and a T-shirt that said "Par Tee Animal."

He looked down. "Oh, these old things? Found 'em in the bottom of my trunk."

Okay. She handed him a plate filled with scrambled eggs and bacon. The toast popped up, and she buttered them and brought them to the table. "You're still going to the Fountain of Youth today?"

Barnaby spoke with his mouth full of egg. "*Mm-hmm.*"

"I'm coming with you."

He swallowed. "I expected no less."

****

Fountain of Youth, Sunday, July 1

They met the students at the entrance to the Fountain of Youth. Word hadn't yet spread that the spring house had reopened, and there were only a few people waiting to get in. Barnaby surveyed the line. "Good. It will be easier to explore without wading through scads of tourists." He bought eight tickets and handed them out. "Okay, where to first?"

Philo was the first to respond. "The spring, of course. That's where they found the horse drawing. Mrs. Cottrell must have wanted to meet you there for a reason."

The students peered first at Philo, and then at Barnaby. "Mrs. Cottrell?"

"She was the one they found dead here. That's why the spring's been closed."

"But…but…" Cleo stammered. "Professor, you were meeting with her? Why?"

For once Barnaby had no answer. Philo took over. "He was interviewing seekers before the seminar began in order…um…to prepare a dossier on demographics—you know, age, weight, profession."

Barnaby found his voice. "Also, how long they'd been seekers and what got them hooked on it."

"You compiled research for us." Lincoln seemed disappointed. "We should have done that."

"I was gathering background information to gauge whether my approach would work for the seminar. In this case, it was lucky I did. You wouldn't have wanted to be talking to Mrs. Cottrell while she was dying."

Agatha yelped. "Were you?"

"Well..." Barnaby looked to Philo for help. "Not exactly. I was outside, and she was inside. It was dark."

Thomas burst out, "So she *was* murdered! Did you see anything? A cloaked figure? A blood spatter?"

"My heavens, where do you dredge up these ghoulish fantasies? First of all, she drowned, so there wasn't any blood. And no, I didn't see anyone but the police, and even that was much later."

"Did they arrest you?"

"No. Now let's get going."

The students led the way in a close clutch, whispering to each other. They stopped in front of a small building. "This is it: the Spring House." Kevin read the plaque. "It says it's built of coquina, a limestone comprised of ancient shell fragments. Resilient and extremely hard."

Philo nodded. "Just like the Castillo."

"The fort? I thought that was stone."

"No. The Castillo de San Marcos was the first fort ever built of coquina. When the English attacked in 1702, everyone expected the walls to crumble, but instead the cannonballs actually *bounced* off them."

Cleo laughed. "Bounced, huh. Too funny."

"Shall we?" Lincoln led the way inside.

They crowded into the room and surrounded the spring. Kevin pointed out the obvious. "There's a grate over it." He looked at Barnaby. "How could Mrs. Cottrell drown if she couldn't get to the water?"

Barnaby bent down and nudged the grate. It moved aside easily. "She was found prone on the floor with her head in the water. A trowel lay nearby, and they believe she was digging in the spring for the casque."

Thomas said cheerfully, “Mrs. Peacock in the spring house with the trowel.”

Agatha said timidly, “Could it have been suicide?”

Barnaby shook his head. “When she contacted me, she was all atwitter, insinuating that she had discovered something about the casque. How could she go from euphoria to suicidal depression in the space of a few minutes?”

Philo mused, “She thought it through and concluded she was wrong. That’s why the drawing was crumpled.”

The others perked up. “Drawing? What drawing?”

Lincoln said, “You referred to a horse. Was that it?”

“Police recovered a piece of paper near where she died. It contained the picture of a horse.”

Philo added, “A picture that closely resembles the chrome sculpture of a rearing stallion on the Ripley grounds.”

“We think she might have deduced the casque was under, or near, the horse.”

“Is that why you sent us to Ripley’s? We wondered why you only said to examine the garden.”

“Yes.”

Cleo put her hands on her hips. “I don’t understand. If she thought the casque was at Ripley’s, why come here? And what did she see here that made her decide she was wrong about the horse?”

Agatha’s voice rose plaintively. “If she hadn’t gone to the spring, she wouldn’t be dead, would she?”

“She…she…” Lincoln rubbed his temples.

Barnaby said resolutely, “We have no way of knowing what she was thinking. It’s none of our business. Now, let’s get back to work.”

The students ignored him and huddled together. “Say it was an accident and she didn’t commit suicide, how would her head stay under water long enough to drown?"

Lincoln declared, "That's why it couldn't have been accidental. Someone had to have held her down until she died."

"That would be pretty tough to do."

"Not necessarily." He crouched on the floor. "If the killer kneeled on her back, he'd squeeze the air out of her lungs and she'd probably lose consciousness before she drowned."

"Killer? Murder?" Agatha's voice was even squeakier than normal. She sat down, her face in her hands. Cleo sat down next to her and put an arm across her shoulders.

Thomas was irrepressible. "So were there other people around? Was it during the day, Professor?"

"Excuse me? Did you not hear me? Anyone care to state our real objective? Anyone?"

Philo answered for him. "It was at night, Thomas. The park was closed. She was supposed to meet Barnaby—Professor Swift—at the entrance. He heard a yell, but he couldn't get in."

"Well, someone *else* did." Lincoln turned to Barnaby. "You said there was no one in sight?"

"No." Philo could tell Barnaby was getting frustrated.

"So…" Thomas, his eyes riveted on Barnaby, said, "It seems that *you* were the only one in contact with her that night. *Hmm*."

Chapter Thirty-Three

Tell the truth so as to puzzle and confound your adversaries.

—Henry Wotton

Fountain of Youth, Sunday July 1

"Hey!" Barnaby went from cranky to irate. "I didn't see anyone here, Thomas. I didn't even see *Harriet,* okay? This is beyond the pale. If you don't stay on track, I'll flunk the lot of you."

"*Urp*. Sorry, Professor." Lincoln crooked a finger at Thomas and made a slicing motion across his throat. "We're just messing around. Of course you didn't kill the lady." Before Barnaby could respond, he called the others. "Let's split up and hit the exhibits, guys." The students left the building single file without looking back.

Barnaby leaned on a railing over the spring, gulping for air. A Dixie cup dispenser was attached to a pole next to him. Philo gestured at it. "Want a cup?"

"No!…Well, okay." She filled two and handed one to him. He took a tentative sip and made a face. "I'd forgotten how execrable this stuff is."

She read the plaque. "It says here the water comes up from the Floridan aquifer and contains some sixty minerals. Says it's good for you."

"Well, it wasn't good for Harriet."

A new voice intruded. "Are you talking about Harriet Cottrell? What do you know about her?"

They turned to the door. Axel Zimmer stood there, flanked as usual by Diego. The little man's scarred, expressionless face reminding Philo eerily of a gargoyle. She noticed they blocked the entrance. Barnaby opened his mouth and shut it again.

Philo said, "What do *you* know about her?"

"I know she didn't want to sell the store to me. And that she was killed here."

"How do you know she was killed here?"

"I read the papers same as everybody else. She was found by security on June eighth, drowned." He peered at Barnaby. "You sound as though you have more information than that."

"Don't play dumb. You knew I was meeting Harriet here that night."

Zimmer blinked. "I beg your pardon?"

"You followed me—"

"Or Harriet." Philo was thinking fast. "You tailed her from Ripley's to the Fountain of Youth. You saw what was in her hand. She recognized you and hid the drawing. In a fit of rage, you murdered her."

Zimmer blinked again. "Rage?"

"Face it, Axel. It's over." Barnaby had found his voice.

"Boss? Want me to flatten him?"

They'd forgotten Diego. He muscled in, blocking Barnaby from Zimmer, and raised a fist.

Zimmer reddened. "No. At least, not yet." He waved him off and stepped closer to Barnaby. "To be clear, you are accusing me of murder?"

Barnaby hesitated. The tension was tight as a coiled Slinky. Philo said quietly, "Why are you here anyway, Mr. Zimmer?"

Instead of pacifying him, the effect on Zimmer was cataclysmic. He pivoted toward her and shouted, "I can be here if I damn well want to! You people are *way* out of line." He whirled back to face Barnaby. Out of the corner of his mouth he grunted, "Diego, whack him."

Diego grinned. "Sure, boss." He swung his arm back, obviously preparing for a roundhouse punch, and screamed.

Philo raised her chin to peer over his shoulder.

Lincoln stood there, holding Diego's wrist in what appeared to be an exceedingly uncomfortable position. "Mister? You wanna reconsider?" Behind him Kevin, Thomas, and Cleo all had raised fists. Behind *them* Susie and Agatha tried to look menacing.

Susie had a phone to her ear. "Yes, Officer, in the Spring House. Thank you."

Lincoln said pleasantly, "Now, while we wait for the police, how about if you answer the question?"

Zimmer was still incensed. "I'm not answering anything until you let Diego go."

Lincoln looked toward Barnaby, who nodded. Rubbing his arm, Diego turned to identify his tormentor but stopped at the sight of the crew backing him up. He blanched. "Agatha?"

The little girl, normally meek as a newborn fawn, had two bright red spots on her cheeks. Her murky eyes flashed. "You…You." She gulped. "You are *not* my cousin!"

Diego, hardened roustabout that he was, blushed. "I'm sorry, Agatha. Mr. Zimmer"—he waggled a thumb in the direction of his boss—"he came up with the idea.

It's true that my mother's side of the family is Minorcan. They've just never been back to the island."

"Is your name really Diego?"

"Uh huh. It's a common name in Minorca, and we assumed you'd have at least one relative called Diego. I didn't figure on you asking so many personal questions." He paused a second, then blurted, "Mullet on the beach!"

This was greeted by dead silence. Finally, a slight snuffle came from Agatha, which turned into a full-fledged crow of delight. "Aha! You do know!"

The girl lifted a hand, which Diego took. She gave him a curtsy, and he gave her a bow. They might have waltzed out of the room had Susie not called, "Er…Agatha? You probably shouldn't leave. The police are on their way."

"Oh? Oh!" The little girl prodded Diego. "We'd better stay here. You're in awful trouble. You should confess."

"More important, Axel should confess." During the conversation Barnaby had moved and was now standing between Zimmer and the exit. "You're a seeker, aren't you?"

Zimmer studied the determined faces. His body sagged. "All right, I admit it. I set Diego on your trail. I don't know how you organized such a dedicated crew, Barnaby, but I had to keep you under surveillance in case you came up with a solution. Yes, I'm a seeker."

"For the casque?"

"For *all* the casques. I've been searching for them since 1984. I was drawn into it right after those kids discovered the first one in Chicago. My second wife…" He paused and closed his eyes for an instant. "God, she was gorgeous! She got this bee in her bonnet that she had to have one of the stones. Didn't care which one; she only wanted something unique to lord it over her girlfriends with."

From the others' expressions, Philo guessed they were all thinking the same thing. *Whipped.*

"But you haven't found one."

"No. I was a step behind the Cleveland lawyers in 2004 and was homing in on the one in Boston when some local guy claimed it. It's been no end of frustrating. The worst part is, Liz cleared out two years ago. Took off with a gigolo she met in Aruba." He paused as though he expected some murmurs of sympathy. When none came, he gamely continued. "Even with her gone, I can't bring myself to stop. It gets into your blood." He sat down on a bench and put his head in his hands. "Diego, make yourself scarce."

Barnaby said, "Let him go, guys." Without a word, the man melted into the group. They heard a door slam. "Go on."

Zimmer took a deep breath. "You students now have a taste of the obsession that comes with this hunt. Imagine how bad it is for me—thirty-five years of poring over the images and the poems, traveling the country chasing after this theory or that, always coming up empty. My business suffered. My family even tried to have me committed so my son could take over Millstone Brands."

"*Humph.*" Philo couldn't decide if any of his story was true. *Maybe a sprinkle or two of fact in a sea of fiction?*

Axel was still talking, his words tumbling out. "When I read that Robert and Harriet thought they'd located the burial spot of the sixth casque, I hightailed it here. I presumed they'd keep the proof in the liquor store—on their computer, or in their files. I didn't want to break in, so I tried to buy the store. You all know how that went."

Philo cried, "But you did break in! You—"

"As I *told* you, I was monitoring the store while it was sealed off." He glanced quickly at her, then away.

Barnaby's eyes narrowed. "You claimed yesterday you were merely monitoring the store. Did you sneak in the night before? Did you knock Norton out?"

Zimmer didn't answer for a minute. "Yes. I'd become desperate. We were rifling through the files when Norton came in. Diego hit him over the head." He attempted a casual shrug. "I considered it self-defense; after all, if he killed his parents, he'd have no compunction about killing me."

"Are you insane? Norton is innocent."

"Oh yeah? Prove it."

Barnaby's mouth snapped shut.

"You pushed Robert from the gallery." Philo's gaze was penetrating.

"No! I read about that. I wasn't anywhere near the Lightner that night."

"Can *you* prove it?"

His eyes dropped. "Um."

"And Harriet?"

"Yes, I was here, right across the street. I watched you"—he gestured at Barnaby—"try to get in and fail. When I heard the sirens, I decamped."

"But you never actually saw Harriet?"

"No. I missed her at Ripley's, but then I glimpsed Barnaby walking toward the Fountain of Youth and figured they had a change of plans."

Now's the time to get the full confession. "How—or when—did you find out Barnaby and the Cottrells were communicating?"

"When he called me about the harassment."

Barnaby asked abruptly, "You did order it, didn't you?"

He nodded. "I didn't expect it to go that far, though. I canned the thugs I'd hired when I heard the extent of the damage."

Kevin cracked open the door. He whispered, "The police are coming up the path."

Zimmer faced Barnaby, his voice pleading. "Please, Barnaby, I've confessed my weakness—can't we just forget the whole thing?"

Philo cried, "No! He knocked Norton out. For all we know, he may have tried to poison Joseph. There's no reason to cut him any slack."

Barnaby studied Axel. "Tell you what, do you promise to cooperate with the police? Tell them everything you know about the Cottrells?"

"Absolutely. I staked them out for weeks." He brightened. "Come to think of it, I might have seen or heard something that will expose the killer."

Philo still wasn't sure how much of Zimmer's story she believed. "And if it's you, so be it."

Unfortunately for Barnaby, it was Lieutenant Tolliver who arrived first. He saw Barnaby, turned to Sergeant Landman, and said, "Cuff him."

"Hey! I was the one who called you."

"Oh, so now you can imitate a woman's voice on the phone? Someone named"—he checked his notebook—"Susie Phelps spoke to Steve. That your alter ego? Or are you gender fluid?"

"She's my student."

Cleo stepped forward, Susie cowering behind her. "We're Professor Swift's students. We called you." She glanced at Barnaby. "I'm afraid that we…er…may have misinterpreted the situation."

Barnaby pushed Zimmer at Tolliver. "This is Axel Zimmer. He's also a seeker, and knew the Cottrells. He was relating his…er…experiences. He may have seen something of use to your investigation."

Zimmer bit his lip. "To be precise, Officers, I don't know whether I did or didn't, but I'm happy to relate all my encounters with them."

Tolliver continued to glare at Barnaby. "You got anything to add?"

Barnaby maintained an innocent expression. "Nope. We happened to run into Mr. Zimmer here. The students were prattling about *The Secret*, and he was providing them with some background when the subject of the Cottrells came up."

Tolliver wasn't buying it. "And that was enough to motivate you to dial 9-1-1?"

Cleo took the lead. "As I said, sir, Professor Swift and Mr. Zimmer were engaged in a very…lively discussion when we arrived, and we jumped to an inaccurate conclusion." Behind her, Susie gave the policeman a perky smile and a thumbs-up.

"All right, if that's how you want to play it." He turned away. "Zimmer, will you come with us?"

"Now? Oh, oh, sure."

When Axel and the police had gone, Diego emerged from the bushes at the entrance. Philo took a step down the path, intending to call the cops back, but Barnaby put a finger to his lips. "If he's indeed guilty, Axel will spill something to the detective. In the meantime, we'll have

Agatha keep an eye on Diego." He cocked an eyebrow at the girl, and she grinned. Philo watched her stroll toward Diego. They took the path to the gift shop and disappeared from view.

Philo felt better. At least they were doing *something*.

Barnaby gathered the students. "Let's meet tomorrow afternoon. We'll recap our experiences. Then I want you to get started on a paper."

Lincoln asked, "Who should do which site?"

"I think"—he winked at Philo—"a joint effort is in order. You've visited all the sites alone or together. You each have input. There are two weeks left in the session, so after tomorrow, I'll let you guys divvy up the work yourselves."

At the entrance, the class hopped on a trolley, waving goodbye. When Philo turned to Barnaby, she saw Agatha standing a few yards away on the sidewalk. "Agatha? What happened to Diego?"

The little girl seemed to wake from a trance. She walked back to Philo. "He went to the station. He thought he should be there when the police let Mr. Zimmer out."

"Why didn't you go with the others then? Did they forget you?"

"I guess so. It's my fault. I went up the street to watch the merry-go-round." She pointed.

Philo shaded her eyes. A couple of blocks away, a carousel twirled. Carnival music blared along with the delighted cries of the passengers.

"I'd forgotten it was there. It's a nice, old-fashioned ride for the children, isn't it?"

"Yes." Agatha sighed. "I love carousels. It's one of the few rides I'm allowed to go on."

"Allowed? Oh, because of your height?"

The girl nodded. “Maybe I’ll see if Cleo will go with me next week.”

Just then Philo glimpsed that particular person running toward them. Cleo skidded to a halt, panting. “Agatha! We thought we’d lost you again. Come on. The conductor’s holding the trolley for us.”

Barnaby and Philo watched the two girls dash down the street. “Maybe we should have the others cover Agatha while she’s guarding Diego.”

“She has a phenomenal ability to evaporate before your very eyes, even when you’re looking straight at her.”

“A redundant comment, but a good quality in a sleuth.”

Chapter Thirty-Four

There's no perfect answer to the puzzle, and creativity is a renewable resource.

—Biz Stone

Philo's apartment, Sunday, July 1

"Well, this sucks."

"It's a straw. It's supposed to suck. Let me demonstrate." Philo stuck one in her own glass of lemonade.

"I mean, that Zimmer isn't guilty."

"Just because he professed his innocence doesn't mean it's true."

"There's that. One can only hope."

"A bit mean-spirited, but okay."

Barnaby took a bite of pizza. "The thing is, without him, we don't have any suspects."

"And yet only yesterday we had too many. Anyway, I thought you were going to let the police handle it."

"I feel responsible. If I hadn't contacted Robert, and then Harriet, they might be alive today."

"That's hogwash. If someone killed them because they solved the mystery, it has nothing to do with you. They'd be victims anyway."

"I don't know. I brought attention to them. These seekers seem to be all over the place, prying into each other's affairs. If the Cottrells had published their answer before I got in touch with them, there would be no reason to kill them."

"That's assuming they had the solution. Robert didn't actually state he knew where the casque was, did he?"

"N-no." Barnaby took another slice from the box. "Not enough anchovies again. Why don't they ever put enough anchovies on pizza? I mean, just because sixty-five percent of Americans don't like anchovies, that's no reason to deprive the ones who do." He bit into it. With his mouth full, he lisped, "Tyranny of the majority, is what it is."

Philo had to set him straight. "I adore anchovies, but it turns out you can have too much of a good thing. I once ordered triple anchovies on my pizza."

"And? Did they supply you with a decent number of little fishes?"

"No. Well, yes—too many. It was inedible."

"Huh." She knew that was Barnaby's way of saying he disagreed but was too hungry to take up arms.

"We were talking about Robert Cottrell."

"It's true, he didn't specifically claim that he'd found the burial site. He only said the brochure he'd come across at the college held a clue, but he hadn't followed up on it yet."

"Harriet must have, though."

"Why?"

"Because she was excited and because she changed the venue for your meeting. That must count for something."

"Doesn't mean it had to do with the brochure."

Philo put down her lemonade. "Wait a minute. Didn't Harriet agree to bring it with her?"

“Yes, but it wasn’t found on her at the Spring House.”

“So you never saw it. Aha. The killer took it. The horse drawing means nothing. Maybe it was he who crumpled it up and not Harriet at all.” She smacked the table, rattling the glasses. “The brochure holds the key.”

Barnaby didn’t debate the point. “Damn. Now where do we stand?”

Philo took her plate to the sink. “I propose we relegate the game to the designated hitters.”

“It’s not a game to Axel. He was not above ransacking Granada Liquors and attacking Norton Cottrell.” He paced restlessly. “Which leads us back to him. He’s a clever one, isn’t he? He talked me out of pressing charges, but he may be playing the police to mislead them.” He stood up and went to the window. “I’ve been a chump.”

Philo said placidly, “It’s late. Why don’t we take this up tomorrow?”

He looked at his watch. “It’s only nine o’clock.”

“Right.” She gave an elaborate yawn. “I need a distraction. You coming?”

He said, “I should be working on my crossword.”

“Tell you what, I’ll supply the clues.”

****

Mind Over Matter, Monday, July 2

“The students are beavering away, and I thought I’d come help you close up shop.”

“Well-timed.” Philo looked Barnaby up and down. “I must say I like the USA theme—you should wear those on the Fourth.”

He hitched up white slacks decorated with tiny American flags and eagles. “Not to worry. I’ve got something even more star-spangled for Independence Day."

Uh oh. Philo turned the sign to Closed. "I'm ready for a drink."

"My thoughts exactly." His chest expanded. "I feel as though it's been a productive day."

"By productive you mean you delegated work to six other people?"

"It's my job, Philo. I'll have to read their magnum opus after all."

"When is it due?"

"Next week. It has to be marked by that Friday so I can deliver the grades to the registrar. Thus, we have some leisure time. Dos Chicas?"

"How about the Dog and Whistle? I saw Joseph go out earlier. He was probably on his way there."

"Sounds good."

They walked up the street. Sure enough, the old lawyer occupied a stool at the bar. He had a jigger and a mug in front of him. "Well, fancy meeting you two young'uns here. Set a spell, as they say in the South."

They sat on either side of him. "How have you been, Joseph? In fine fettle?"

"Oh yes, full of piss and vinegar, as my old nanny used to say. Although"—he held up his folded newspaper—"this crossword of yours is a doozy. Was Norton Cottrell any help?"

"Oh, yes. As I told Philo, he has the perfect mind for esoteric metaphors."

"Is he working with you on the reptile-themed one?"

Barnaby accepted the lager from Jimmy. "Begged off. He has too much on his plate, what with a murder charge hanging over his head."

Joseph knocked back his whiskey. "I may have to call Edmund in on this one. By the way, I shamelessly complimented his puzzle even though it was, shall we say, not a winner."

"He's still coming by?"

"Uh-huh. He's taken to calling them 'wellness' visits." Joseph laughed. "He was asking about you the other day, Barnaby. I confessed that your 'business deal'—the reason you'd forgotten your little bet with him—was a collaboration with Norton Cottrell on a puzzle."

"I was only working with Norton because Axel asked me to." Barnaby stopped and repeated slowly, "Axel asked me to. Huh." He leaned back to peer at Philo behind Joseph. "To keep us out of the way?"

"Or to keep tabs on Norton?"

Joseph straightened, blocking their view. "You want to tell me what's going on?" Philo and Barnaby took turns narrating their latest adventures. "So basically, you haven't solved a single one of our mysteries—including the attempt at my liquidation."

"It's very disheartening. I might have to set the problem aside in favor of the crosswords." Barnaby didn't look happy.

"Something will crop up. This criminal is exposing himself—"

"Or herself."

"Or herself—with every assault. He—or she—is bound to make a wrong move."

"Let's hope we recognize it when he does."

****

Philo's apartment, Tuesday, July 3

Barnaby put down the magazine. "I give up. This is purported to be the go-to bulletin for the St. Augustine social scene, and I can't find anything on it." He appealed to Philo. "What *does* St. Augustine do, if anything, for Independence Day?"

Philo and Barnaby sat in the morning sun among the potted plants on her balcony. Below them clumps of tourists ambled by on the ancient pavement. Many took pictures of the flowers cascading from the railing. Barnaby deadheaded a petunia and only Philo's quick action prevented him from tossing it down on a large woman's hat. He gestured at the view. "You really are in the center of everything here, aren't you?"

"I love it. It's busy during the day, but the evening activities—by which I mean the noise—are all across City Square and up St. George."

"You mean every night, or just on the Fourth of July?"

"Every night during the season, but on the Fourth they go all out. Concerts in the square. Fireworks over the river. It's almost as big a holiday as St. Patrick's Day."

"St. Patrick's Day? Here? Last I checked, there weren't a whole lot of O'Learys in this city."

"Don't have to be. ICYMI: the very first celebration of St. Paddy's Day was right here in St. Augustine in 1601."

"ICYMI?"

" 'In case you missed it.' Haven't you learned anything from your students?"

"I asked not to be made privy to their secret language. So, the first St. Patrick's Day was here? Before even Ireland?"

"Uh-huh. Dublin's first parade wasn't until 1931, almost two hundred years after New York and Boston.

And we beat both of those cities by nearly a hundred and fifty years. Take that, Yankees."

Barnaby refilled his mug from the carafe. "So who was here in 1600? The Spanish or the British?"

"The Spaniards. Patrick was their patron saint."

"Now, that's downright weird."

"Not that weird. Many Irish priests fled to Spain to escape Protestant rule in Britain. The Spanish sent them on to the New World. It was…hang on a minute." She clicked some keys on her phone. "Yes, Richard Arthur." She read, " 'Of Irish descent, he was a priest posted to St. Augustine from 1598 to 1606.' He was probably the one who organized the first parade."

"And it continues to this day?"

She grinned. "Best parade ever."

"Okay, so I missed the big event. Can you make it up to me? Will you take me to see the fireworks tomorrow?"

A voice called from the street. "Professor! Miss Brice! May we come up?"

Philo buzzed the door open, and soon Cleo and Agatha, trailed by Thomas, arrived at Philo's door. The two girls were panting with suppressed emotion. Thomas feigned indifference. Cleo cried, "You'll never guess!"

"Probably not. Let's go inside so we can all sit down."

When they were distributed among the furniture, Cleo announced, "Agatha has made a breakthrough."

"Agatha?"

With all eyes upon her, Agatha turned the color of a damson plum. Her voice came out in a guttural whisper. "Cleo and Thomas and I took the bus to the carousel."

Cleo elaborated. "The J & S Carousel. It's just north of the Fountain of Youth."

Thomas chirped, "Open seven days a week, ten a.m. to nine p.m., year-round. A dollar a ride."

"But—"

Agatha interrupted Cleo. "*But*…you have to be under five feet tall to ride it." She smirked. "It's the only time in my life I could do something my friends couldn't. It's not easy being four feet eleven."

And almost invisible.

"Yes, well." Agatha's obvious pleasure seemed to grate on Cleo. "So Thomas and I had to stand behind the railing, and Agatha got to ride the merry-go-round."

"Which is why," said Thomas bitterly, "she saw it and I didn't."

"See what?"

"The horse."

Barnaby shook his head. "I've been to the carousel. All the rides are horses."

"Yes, but one horse is special."

Agatha's tone was triumphant. "It looks exactly like the one in Image Six!"

Philo held a hand to her mouth. "Oh gosh, she's right! The pinto!"

Barnaby's brow creased. "Pinto…pinto…You mean the painted pony?"

"Right! The one with brown and white splotches. I'd forgotten all about it. It does look exactly like the one in the painting. Good catch, Agatha."

The girl said proudly, "And it's the only one without a bridle or saddle. Just like the image."

Thomas added, "It's not prancing either, the way the Ripley's horse is."

Cleo prodded. "Don't forget the streamers."

"Right. One streamer from the roof of the carousel is identical to the one the rider is holding."

"But what about the other items in the picture? The palm tree?"

She nodded feverishly. "There."

"And the big rock? The one that looks like Gibraltar?"

Agatha considered. "There's a big pile of sand on the playground. It's maybe ten feet high."

Thomas added, "And it's dark brown."

Barnaby leaned forward, his whole body quivering. "Okay…how about the man?"

Cleo was ready for that one. "We think he's just a symbol of St. Augustine. The whole Ponce de León bit."

"After all, someone has to hold the flag."

Barnaby tapped his chin. "Okay, I'm on board. Get the others up to speed, and we'll all go tomorrow. Where do you think the casque is buried? Under the carousel? That would be tough to get at."

"Or in the machinery?"

"Maybe Preiss managed to slip it inside the pony itself."

The three chorused, "We can spread out and nose around when we get there."

"Okay. We'll meet tomorrow at…nine?"

The young people fidgeted. "Maybe ten?"

"All right."

"Let's hope it's open on a holiday."

Thomas chanted, "Seven days a week, 365 days a year."

****

Davenport Park, Wednesday, July 4

“Is everyone here?” Barnaby, decked out like Uncle Sam—complete with top hat and tails, striped pants and fake beard—counted heads.

Lincoln let out a belly laugh. “Wait a minute. Aren’t you supposed to be leading the Independence Day parade?”

Barnaby had his answer ready. “They bumped me for a guy with a real beard. Where’s Agatha?”

“Here I am.”

Philo could just see the top of her head as the girl hopped behind Lincoln.

“All right. I’ve secured the minivan for the day. Let’s head up to the carousel.”

They drove up bustling San Marco Avenue, passing Ripley’s Believe it or Not and the arched entrance to the Fountain of Youth. Just beyond lay a large rotary. Cleo called, “It’s over there in Davenport Park on San Carlos Avenue.”

Barnaby parked the van and let the others off, then hopped out after them. He took a step and bumped into Thomas, who was standing stock still. “Do you mind moving?”

“It’s not there.”

“What’s not there?” He followed Thomas’ pointing finger. Beyond the fence were picnic tables, a playground, and a big open space. “Where’s the carousel?”

Thomas’s hand dropped to his side. “It’s gone.”

Cleo opened the gate, and they trudged in. The only thing left of the merry-go-round was a steaming pile of rubble. A driverless backhoe sat next to it. Philo walked over to a sign. “Over here, guys. It says the owner of the carousel died suddenly, and his heartbroken widow decided to dismantle it and move it to Port Charlotte."

"No!" Agatha's mouth was a perfect circle.

Lincoln asked, "What do we do now?"

Barnaby began to pick his way over the broken cement blocks and metal cables sticking up through the soil. He bent down suddenly, rising with a flower in his hand.

Philo moved closer. "What's that you've got there?"

"It's an aster."

Chapter Thirty-Five

Seek and ye shall find.

—*Matthew 7:7*

Davenport Park, Wednesday, July 4

"See?" Agatha stood straight. "The final clue."

Barnaby wasn't ready to concede. "Without the actual evidence—the banner, the horse, etc.—I don't think we can prove this is—or was—the site of the casque. An aster just isn't enough."

Cleo disagreed. "I've downloaded pictures of the carousel horses and of the streamers. We don't have to have the actual objects, do we?"

"Maybe not, but in order to win the prize, we do need to have the casque in our eager little hands. If it's on its way to Port Charlotte…"

"The professor's right," said Lincoln. "The casque doesn't hold the actual gem—just a key. We're supposed to present the key to Mr. Preiss in order to get the sapphire."

Cleo piped up. "I read there was a mix-up, and the Cleveland guys got the sapphire instead of the aquamarine."

"Oh no! A sapphire is way cooler."

"But…*but* they're willing to trade if we find the St. Augustine casque."

Kevin said gloomily, “Doesn’t matter. Preiss died in 2005 and a law firm took control of the safe deposit box. We’d have to take the key to them.”

“Lawyers?” Thomas picked up a chunk of coquina and threw it at the fence. “Then we’re screwed. You can’t trust lawyers—they’ll come up with some excuse to weasel out of giving us the stone.”

Barnaby held up an index finger. “Once again, folks, we’re drifting far afield. This is the final week of our seminar on historical methodology. Before we go off all half-cocked hunting the casque, I would like for you to take stock of our findings. There must be some pedagogical conclusions we can draw from this exercise. Anyone?” His gaze went from student to student, landing on Thomas.

The boy cringed and poked Kevin. “You go first.”

Kevin said slowly, “It appears that hands-on, in-situ research is the best kind.”

Cleo volunteered, “Keep your eyes and ears open.”

Lincoln chimed in. “And your mind. Keep your mind open. Don’t presume the prevailing theory is right; wait for the facts. I for one don’t think I was as skeptical as I could have been.”

“To be fair, the professor made us look at a whole bunch of sites—potential or not.” Susie smiled at Barnaby.

“Yes,” Barnaby agreed. “I wanted to train you to consider and analyze the full spectrum of opinions and evidence you may face during the research process.”

Cleo stood up and wiped her hands on her skirt. “All well and good, but I want to find the casque. If it was under, rather than on, the merry-go-round, it’s still here. Who’s with me?”

The other five jumped up. Lincoln waved at the pile of rubble. “Let’s sift through some of this. Who knows? The backhoe might have dredged it up.” They spread out, climbing over mounds of dirt, tripping over loose wires, and generally getting in each other’s way.

An hour later they were back at the bench. “We’ve raked through the debris. Nothing.”

Barnaby nodded. “Therefore, the casque must be hidden inside the structure. Maybe even in the spotted horse. In that case it’s no longer in St. Augustine.”

Cleo wasn’t about to give up. “I’m going over to the playground. If it’s not there, I intend to drive to Port Charlotte.” The others trotted after her, Thomas lagging behind.

Philo slapped her knee. “The drawing. Harriet’s horse. It must have been of the carousel horse and not the Ripley one.”

He shook his head. “Uh-uh. Like Thomas said, her drawing was of a rearing horse. It only shows Harriet was wrong about Ripley’s.”

“Right, but she crumpled the paper.”

“Proving she realized her mistake.”

“And then asked to meet you at the *Fountain*. Not at the merry-go-round. If she’d solved the mystery, why not meet here?”

“She knew she was being watched. She didn’t want to draw attention to the carousel.” Barnaby’s eyes blurred with tears. “All she wanted was to keep her discovery a secret—instead she was murdered.” He gazed down the street toward the Fountain of Youth. “Why didn’t she tell me? I could have protected her.”

"You shouldn't beat yourself up over it." Philo tried to cheer him. "How could you have known she was in danger?"

"I guess so." He rose. "I can't dwell on it now. I've got to round up the kiddies." He made a megaphone with his hands. "Guys!" When they'd reassembled, he said, "Right. Okay. I want you to go home and write the report. If, after that, you want to continue searching, be my guest, but my part in this is over."

Cleo cried, "I'm still driving to Port Charlotte once we hand in our paper."

Agatha stepped up beside her. "I'll go with you."

After a minute, all but Thomas agreed. He tossed another rock, narrowly missing Kevin's head. "Not me. I'm sick of the whole thing. I'm heading home to Otumwa as soon as I get my grade."

Kevin started for the gate. "Will you take us back to school, Professor?"

Barnaby shook his head. "I have something I have to do. Lincoln, would you mind driving them back? Turn the minivan in at the student lot."

Lincoln dithered. "Am I allowed to do that?"

"All you have to do is park the van and drop the keys in the slot. Look like you know what you're doing, and no one will ask questions."

"Okay."

Once they had seen the students off, Barnaby slung an arm around Philo's shoulder. "They'll be fine. We can flag down a trolley when we're ready to go home. For now, I propose we adjourn for lunch."

"Agreed."

They rose and, hand in hand, began to stroll across the park. They had reached a copse of shrubs and trees when Barnaby shaded his eyes. "I can see a river over there. Is that the Matanzas?"

"No, it's the San Sebastian. It rises just a few miles up and empties into the Matanzas."

"Huh. So St. Augustine is an island?"

Philo was about to answer when a man in a yellow Hawaiian shirt appeared, clambering over the rocks. "That's Kevin's father. What's he doing here?"

He saw them and waved his arms over his head.

Barnaby muttered, "God, what a helicopter parent! He tails Kevin more assiduously than Diego does."

Magnusson reached them. "Where are the kids?"

"I sent them home."

He wiped his forehead. "Then what the hell are you two doing here?"

Philo bristled. "What business is it of yours, Mr. Magnusson? It's a free country."

"No! Um…" He seemed to reconsider. As they watched, he grew more and more agitated. "Look. I'm only going to warn you once. Beat it. This is my prize."

"*Your* prize? Just how do you come by that conclusion?"

His eyes narrowed. "I solved the riddle before you did. The casque's in the carousel, and I'm going after it. I suggest you back off." He put his hand in his pocket. A bulge appeared, resembling nothing so much as the snub nose of a .38 police special. "I mean it. Get out of here. *Now*."

Barnaby held his hands up. "Okay, okay. We're leaving." He took Philo's arm and marched toward the closest entrance.

She whispered, "So it's been Runar Magnusson all along."

"All along what?"

"He must be the one—the murderer."

Barnaby halted. "Oh my God. It all fits, doesn't it? But wait: he didn't arrive until after Kevin's accident."

"We only have his word for that." Philo pushed him. "Let's get out of here." When they reached the gate, she looked over her shoulder. Magnusson was standing in the middle of the playground. While she watched, he began to rotate slowly, shading his eyes.

"It's locked."

"What's locked?"

"The gate. We'll have to find another way out."

"Hurry—before he decides to come after us." She cast frightened eyes behind her.

They took a side path that wound through a dense hedge. Tall bushes hemmed them in on both sides. "Here's another gate." Barnaby started to open it. "Ouch! Ow! What the hell was that?" He clutched his leg.

Philo knelt down. "There's something sticking out of your calf. Oh my God, it's a jackknife! Magnusson!"

Barnaby reconnoitered. "I don't see him. He must be on the other side of the hedge. We'd better keep moving."

"Wait." She pulled the knife out. Blood immediately spurted from the wound. "Uh oh." She pulled the belt out of his pants.

"Hey!"

"*Shh.*" She wound the belt around his thigh and cinched it tight. "I'm going to call 9-1-1."

"No, you aren't."

They looked around. "Who said that?"

Edmund Greer emerged from the trees. "I did." He glanced at Barnaby's leg. "He'll be all right. It's only a flesh wound. Let me have the knife." Philo gave it to him. He folded it closed and stuck it in his pocket. "Come with me."

"Where? To the hospital?"

"No." He led them through a gap in the hedge. They found themselves in an alley, empty but for a couple of dented garbage cans. A maroon Honda with tinted windows blocked the exit. Greer produced a pistol and two pairs of handcuffs. Keeping the gun trained on Barnaby, he handed one set of cuffs to Philo. "Put them on him."

"But—"

"Just do it." When she had, he snapped the other pair on her wrists.

"Where are you taking us?"

"To my car."

Barnaby said carefully, "I think you should be aware that we're not seekers."

Greer laughed. It was an ugly laugh. "Right. You're Uncle Sam. Got it. Now keep moving."

"No, seriously. I'm a…professor of historiography. Those youngsters are my students. They're participating in a seminar at Flagler College."

"What does *The Secret* have to do with historiography?"

"I set it as an exercise in research methods. My purpose had nothing to do with solving the mystery."

"Like I believe you. I've been tracking you for the last month. You guys are as much participants as I am."

Philo blurted, "You're a seeker? Why didn't you say so?"

Greer gave her a "how dumb *are* you" look. "Why would I identify myself? Might as well stick a neon sign over my head. If the others knew I was here and on the scent, every seeker in the US of A would've descended on me." He gave her a little shove.

"What made you think we were seekers?"

"Joseph joked about you the night I met him. He didn't take it seriously, but I kept an eye on you. When you ordered the little tykes to do your legwork, I thought to myself, Edmund, you're a smart fellow. Let the minions do their thing. The more you went round and round, back and forth to every site in St. Augustine, the stronger the chance you'd come across something significant. That's when I planned to swoop in. It'd be like taking candy from a baby." He spat. "You were all *so* naïve."

"But why act now? How is kidnapping us going to help you?"

"In the last few days you were clearly getting close—all those frantic meetings. Had to stop you."

"You're wrong." Barnaby grimaced in pain. "We weren't close at all. We still don't know where the casque is."

He snarled, "The hell you don't. Once the kids picked up on the Minorcan link and the painted pony, it was only a matter of time."

"We led you to the carousel."

He touched his nose. "Bingo. I was here at dawn, but it was already dismantled. Fortunately, they broke it up into large sections rather than wrecking it. Chances are the casque is still inside one of the horses, on an eighteen-wheeler heading across the state." He grabbed Barnaby's elbow. "Let's go."

"Where?"

"To Port Charlotte."

"Port Charlotte? Now?"

"I've got to get there before the kids do. I'm not about to lose out again. I almost had the box in Cleveland, and those assholes nabbed it from right under my nose."

Philo had a thought. "If you know where the casque is, what do you need us for?"

He didn't answer but hustled them toward the red car. He gestured at Philo. "You—get in back."

Philo helped Barnaby into the shotgun seat, then sat in the rear. Edmund leaned in and took their phones from their pockets. "We don't want any butt calls, now do we?" He tossed the phones in a trash can. Then he slid into the driver's seat and pulled a map from the glove compartment. "Let's see—I think we'll take Route 207 through Palatka. Everyone will be lining San Marco Avenue for the parade, so I don't expect any traffic on the byroads. We should make Port Charlotte by midafternoon." He snickered. "Lots of nice empty country along the way. Pretty."

Empty country? Philo's heart sank. "What are you planning to do with us?"

Again, he didn't answer. He took side streets, making several quick turns, and eventually left the city behind. They were driving through scrub country, a landscape of Spanish moss-shrouded oaks and small ranches on a two-lane highway, when he began to talk. "How'd you figure out the casque was in the carousel anyway, Swift?"

"One of my students is short."

"So? Oh, I see. She could ride the horses. See them up close. For me, it was the streamers from the roof." He beeped his horn at a bicyclist. The rider wobbled and ran into a ditch. "I knew my competitors were wasting their time with Ponce de León and his fountain, but every time I was on to something, you jerks would be there ahead of me. Thought if I knocked the kid off the ledge, you'd back off."

Philo gasped. "It was *you*. You pushed Kevin."

"Yeah. Lucked out there. The fort's second story is closed off. Saw him sneak under the rope and head down past the casemates. Nipped after him, stuck my arm through the embrasure, and whoops a daisy! Down he goes."

"Surely someone would have seen you."

"Who? Most law-abiding citizens would respect the Do Not Enter sign. I tiptoed back out to the top of the stair. The only ones in sight were you two over on the west wall, and you were too far away to get a good look at me."

"You were the one with the binoculars." Barnaby sounded fretful. "But how did you get out of the fort? You had to have walked right past us."

Edmund chuckled. "The minute the girl started screaming, I sauntered out the entrance. I was long gone by the time you arrived." He coughed. "You know that kid's from my home town? His parents are seekers too. When he made a beeline for the fort, I suspected his father had given him a hint. Had to take him out of commission."

"You tried to kill him?"

Greer shrugged. "Nah, but if he'd landed on his head it would have been no skin off my nose."

"You're a monster! He's only a child."

"All I cared about was scaring you off. You should've been scared, too, but you were like leeches. There you all were, back on the hunt before I could say Jack Rabbit."

Barnaby murmured, "Jack Robinson. It's Jack Robinson."

Greer snorted. "Who in hell is Jack Robinson?" He didn't wait for an answer. "I picked up on the flagpole at the Castillo and thought I'd have the place to myself, but damn all if you and the whole crew weren't there too. With you scrabbling like army ants all over the castle, I couldn't get a break to look for myself."

Barnaby growled. "By any chance, do you own a Hawaiian shirt?"

He smirked. "Kevin has a good memory."

Despite her agitation, the irrelevant thought crossed Philo's mind that a Hawaiian shirt was the one item of clothing she'd never seen Barnaby wear.

"Did you try to knock me out with the iron ball?"

Greer slammed his hand on the steering wheel. "Stupid, stupid. Did you know that treasure chest is full of bubble gum? I couldn't believe it. If they'd caught me on the ship, I would have been arrested for stealing *bubble gum*."

Something's not right. "How could you know we'd decide to check the *Black Raven* out that night?"

"Didn't. Saw one of your toadies—the tall one—at the ship, asking a lot of questions. It was a new one on me, so I popped down to see what the fuss was about. I came across the chest just as you two arrived."

Philo bent to check the sideview mirror. *Red sedan.* "And the alligator park. We saw this car there. You let the crocodile loose."

He snickered again. "The look on your faces was priceless. The fact that it was feeding time made it even more delicious. My bad luck that keeper changed his normal inspection route and happened on you before little Maxie could turn you into gator kibble."

"But how did you manage to lock us in? It was broad daylight."

"Pure chance. After Joseph's little revelation, I scooted down to the farm. I was in the underground viewing area when you literally walked over me. Slipped out while you were snapping shots of Maxie."

Philo felt a tiny prick of hope. "All those times—you were just trying to frighten us off? You weren't trying to kill us?"

He waved a nonchalant hand. "Either way, as long as you ceased being an issue."

Barnaby was quiet. Philo leaned forward as far as the seat belt would let her. "Are you okay?"

"Just aches a little." He glanced at Edmund's face. "The students saw you at Ripley's, too."

"Did they? Actually, I was following Diego that time."

"Why?"

"I know he works for Axel Zimmer, another seeker."

Barnaby whistled. "It's a small world. He was tailing you, too."

Greer slammed on the brakes and veered to the curb.

Chapter Thirty-Six

Writing a mystery is like drawing a picture and then cutting it into little pieces that you offer to your readers one piece at a time, thus allowing them the chance to put the jigsaw puzzle together by the end of the book.

—Ashwin Sanghi

Route 207, Wednesday, July 4

Greer turned to Barnaby. "Diego was following me? Where?"

"At the Castillo."

Greer relaxed and, putting the car back in gear, pulled out on the road again. "I doubt that's true. No one knows I'm after the stones. Most of the seekers trade information online. I never do, but I monitor all the forums and pages so I'm privy to everyone's latest conjectures."

Philo was temporarily distracted from her terror by indignation. "It's supposed to be a club—people working together, sharing their findings. It's supposed to be *fun*."

"This isn't some charity, lady. Do you know what those stones are worth?"

"That's not the purpose of the hunt though."

"It is for me."

Barnaby muttered, "You'll be disappointed then."

"Why's that?"

"Some of the gems—the diamond, the emerald—may be worth a few thousand, but most are semi-precious. They were amulets—like the totems of a tribe—brought to the New World by the Shining Ones from their twelve countries of origin. They weren't supposed to be treasure *per se*."

Greer gave a short bark of laughter. "Fat lot you know. The value of an object corresponds more to its rarity or unique history than to its intrinsic worth. A jeweler might appraise the whole lot at ten thousand dollars, but I could auction just *one* of those babies off for a fortune."

"Oh? What did, say, the Boston peridot fetch?"

He didn't respond for a minute. "Stupid gits won't sell it."

"How about Chicago? That was an emerald."

"Fools left it lying around, so of course it was stolen." He snorted. "You can bet if I'd won 'em, they'd have been on eBay in nanoseconds."

Barnaby sucked in a breath. "You killed the Cottrells."

"Damn straight I killed them. Nobodies. Got into the hunt a year ago. Not in it for the long haul. Then just like that"—Greer snapped his fingers—"they make a major breakthrough. Had to silence them before the news reached the national forum."

Philo stifled her anger. "If you knew then that the casque was in the carousel, why didn't you just go and dig it out?"

He shook his head. "I only knew they had come across a lead—the brochure—that brought them to the brink of solving the mystery."

"And then when Robert made the appointment with Barnaby, you guessed he had solved it. You had to act quickly."

"Right. Wow, that old swimming pool is cool. And no safety net." He stopped at a red light, then took a left on a four-lane road marked Route 301.

Barnaby broke his silence. "You made a mistake when you didn't take Robert's wallet. If it was missing, the police might have chalked his death up to a mugging gone awry."

Greer shot a glance at his prisoner. "You think that would have been smart? Not me. See, then they'd be looking for the mugger. If they ruled it a suicide, there wouldn't be any investigation. All I did was sneak up behind Robert and push. I had intended to go back to the store with plenty of time to look for the brochure. It wasn't until I saw the detective with it that I realized he'd brought it with him."

"Wait a minute. You *saw* the detective with Cottrell's body? You were still there in the museum?"

"Do I look like a fool? Hot-footed it out the other entrance and came around the building. Mingled with the crowd of rubberneckers. When they brought the body out on a gurney, the detective was holding his wallet and the brochure." He wagged his head. "I should have knocked Cottrell out and emptied his pockets before throwing him over the railing. It cost me time and another risky foray to get it from Harriet."

Philo sat up. "The brochure. Then I was right—it did hold the clue!"

"Nope, you're dead wrong." Greer rolled the window down and spat into the wind.

"What do you mean?"

"Turned out to be a sightseeing flyer about things to do around St. Augustine. It listed all the usual attractions. None of them were circled or marked. If it had any significance, it was lost on me." Barnaby shifted in his seat. Greer eyed him. "What's with you?"

He jiggled his arms. "The cuffs are digging into my back."

"Tough shit."

Hoping to take Barnaby's mind off his discomfort, Philo asked, "How did you kill Harriet?"

He had the gall to chortle. "Pulled a fast one on you, Swift. Caught up with her at the entrance before you arrived."

Barnaby muttered something.

"What's that?"

"I should have galloped instead of cantered."

Greer shrugged. "Told her I was the night watchman and had a message from you to meet inside the park. Brought her in through the staff entrance and took her to the Spring House. Dumb broad never questioned me. Knocked her over and held her under the water till she stopped struggling. Lucky for me she was so old and frail."

"You monster!"

"Sheesh. Can't you come up with another epithet? Something tells me you couldn't solve a crossword puzzle if you had the answers tattooed on your arm." He looked at her in the rearview mirror. "You can't make me sorry, lady. Treasure is treasure."

Philo kept still.

Greer groused, "Even so, I cut it too close. The security guard makes his rounds every thirty minutes, and I'd already taken too long scrabbling through her purse for the brochure. Didn't think twice about the wad of paper in her hand. Assumed it was trash. That is, until I got home."

"How did you get out of the park?"

"Same way I got in—by the back gate. Simple combination lock." He slowed down to go through a small town. "Now smile at the nice pedestrians. Since you can't wave. Ha-ha."

Once they'd returned to open fields and a clear road, he took up the narrative again. "I meant to exit through the front entrance, staying a step ahead of the guard, but Swift was standing under the security light at the gate. So I hid in the bushes till the coast was clear, then made my escape." He rolled the window back up and put the air conditioner on but too low to reach Philo. A drop of sweat dribbled down her forehead and landed on her lip. "Toyed with the idea of calling 9-1-1 to warn them of an intruder at the Fountain of Youth."

Barnaby's voice was startled. "You mean me? Why?"

"You were still loitering outside. With luck they'd glom onto you and not bother to check inside the park."

Philo was confused. "But you decided against calling them. Why?"

"Ah. What happens if Swift here tells them he was supposed to meet the Cottrell woman?" He gave Barnaby a sidelong glance. "They'd find the body in the Spring House, and I might have left something incriminating there. No, sir, couldn't take the chance." He honked his horn at a hay truck attempting to move into his lane. "It wasn't until later that I remembered the paper."

"Did you go back for it?"

"No. The park was closed for the investigation. So I made an anonymous call."

“It was you!”

“It was the only way to find out if it was significant.”

Philo was perplexed. “Didn’t that open you up to renewed scrutiny? The police might have traced the call to you.”

“I’m not an idiot. Used Cottrell’s phone.”

“That’s right. The police said the anonymous tip came from Norton’s number, and Norton told me his phone had been stolen.” Barnaby twisted his neck around to Philo. “Well, at least we have proof that Axel and Norton are innocent.”

Philo didn’t think that was a reason to rejoice. “I never really believed either one was guilty.”

They were silent, absorbing the horrific tale. The dark clouds that had been threatening made good on their promise, and rain poured down in a torrent. Edmund hunkered over the steering wheel. “Can’t see a thing in this crap.”

One last question popped into Philo’s head. “Why did you try to poison Joseph? He’s not a seeker.”

“Didn’t. Ah, here we are.” Edmund slowed the SUV and exited at a two-lane road marked EC470.

“What do you mean, you didn’t? You tried to kill everyone else. Why spare him?”

“Would you shut up, lady? I don’t have time to answer your dimwitted questions.” They passed a ramshackle gas station, its ancient pumps missing their hoses. She saw a sign in the distance but could only make out the word *Corrections* before Edmund swung onto a dirt lane.

Barnaby peered out the windshield. “Where are we?”

“Familiar territory.” Greer drove along the rutted track through thick woods. The downpour filled the spaces between the trees. At the end of the lane, they came to a wooden shack. The porch listed to the right, and the roof had lost many of its shingles. A rusted Chevy sat on blocks next to it. "Home sweet home."

"You're kidding."

"Of course I am. I have a comfortable apartment in Cleveland, to which I intend to repair to plan my relocation to paradise. This"—he rolled up to the front and braked—"will be *your* final dwelling place."

"But why? Why kill us?"

"Diversion. While the hounds are on the scent of the missing couple, I'll be cruising to Port Charlotte free as a bird." Greer pulled Barnaby roughly out of the car, eliciting a groan from the injured man. He manhandled him up the sagging steps and into the shack. A few minutes later, he came back out and did the same with Philo. Once inside, he spun her around to face a large, single room, its floor laid with unfinished, splintered planks. A Franklin stove took up one corner. The only furniture was a sofa, its broken springs piercing through the worn corduroy. Philo hoped Greer wasn't going to make her sit on it. Barnaby lay hogtied on the ground.

"I think I'll put you in the kitchen. Don't want you too near each other. 'Social distancing,' that's the ticket." He giggled. "Just like in the last plague."

A small room at the back of the hut boasted an antique black iron range, a white enameled sink, a rickety wooden table, and two straight-backed chairs. The rain pummeled the roof, seeping through the holes and making the floor slick. Edmund raised Philo's manacled arms and draped them over the back of a chair, then forced her down on the seat. He took a length of rope from a hook on the wall and tied her ankles to the chair's legs.

He started to leave, but Philo called through cracked lips, "At least leave us some water."

He snarled, "It'll just prolong the time till you die."

"Please."

"Oh, all right." He left. A minute later she heard a splashing sound and Barnaby choking. Greer appeared in the doorway with a bottle half filled with water. He tipped it into her mouth, spilling half of it down her front. "Oops, sorry about that." He threw the empty bottle in the corner. "Bye now."

She heard the car start and tires crunching on gravel. "Barnaby?"

"Philo? He didn't hurt you, did he?"

"No. I wish I could see you."

"Me too."

"Let me see what I can do." She wiggled and rocked until the chair moved a fraction. She tried again and almost toppled over but managed to right herself. Ten minutes later, she'd reached the center of the kitchen. She inched slowly toward Barnaby, resting every few minutes. She could see his face now. His expression was blank, his mouth slack. "Barnaby! Are you awake?"

"Just…need…to…close my eyes…cat nap…"

"Oh dear, I hope you're not going into shock." She peered at his pants. "I don't think you're bleeding anymore. Barnaby? What's wrong?"

"Starving. Haven't eaten since breakfast. I always get sleepy when I miss a meal—hypo or hyper-something. Forget what it's called."

Barnaby can't remember a word? We are *in trouble.* She peered through the one window, its glass cracked and brown. "It's hard to tell what time of day it is with the rain."

"Must be late afternoon. I think we were on the road for about two hours."

Their involuntary departure from the park seemed a long time ago now. "Barnaby? Greer didn't mention Runar Magnusson."

"You're positing that he's unaware he has yet another rival in his quest for pecuniary reward? *Hmm.* Possible. There'd be no reason for their paths to cross."

"Greer knew he was a seeker."

"Yes, but he didn't know he was in St. Augustine." He mumbled something.

"What was that?"

"If Magnusson beats him to the casque, it will come as a rude shock to the poor schmuck. I only wish we were in a position to enjoy the schadenfreude."

"I see Yiddish is the tongue du jour."

" 'Schmuck' is Yiddish. 'Schadenfreude' is good old-fashioned German."

She was thoughtful. "Interesting that Greer didn't actually admit the Hawaiian shirt was his. Do you think—"

"That it was Runar? Kevin did mention he had to go to a luau…but wouldn't he have recognized his own father?"

"He never got a good look at the stalker. The two men are a similar height. If…Poor Kevin!"

"That's the least of our worries at present, my dear."

She stretched her back. "Ooh, I ache. You're probably more comfortable than I am."

"Yes, indeed. This is all very restful." He managed a weak chuckle.

"I think I'll close my eyes too—just for a little while. Then I'll try to move some more."

The shack was silent except for the pinging of the raindrops on the range. When even that faded, Barnaby raised his head. "Sounds like the storm's passed. I'm going to try to turn over. If it works, I'll roll myself out of the shack and onto the porch."

"And then what?"

"There must be some life around here."

"We're deep in the woods, Barnaby. I didn't see any houses on the way—just the one shuttered gas station…Wait. There was a sign just beyond where we turned. It said Corrections." She gulped. "We must be near a penitentiary."

"Great—this is probably the local hole in the wall for escaped prisoners." He twisted his body, ending up on his face. "*Mmph.*"

She tried not to laugh, but he looked so funny with his hands and feet tied together. "You look like a trussed pig."

"*Mmph.*"

"Can you turn back over?"

His voice muffled, he spluttered, " 'Fraid not. Stuck." She watched helplessly as he lurched and swayed. He finally hooked his feet on the base of the Franklin stove and rotated onto his side. "That's better." He spit out a dust ball.

"So…any advice on how we get out of this?"

"In fact, I do. While I was occupied with a minute examination of these Southern yellow pine boards, I was able to cudgel the old gray cells. First order of business was to extirpate the discouraging lines winging through my head: 'Ashes to ashes, dust to dust.' Although I believe the actual quote is 'For dust thou art, and unto dust shalt thou return.' Genesis 3:19."

Philo had learned to sift through the trivia and tweeze the essence out of the salad of references. "And once you did?"

"I considered the possibility that, if this is in fact a hiding place for runaways, and there's a breakout, it would be the first place the guards will look. We'd be rescued."

"Right. So all we have to do is sit tight and wait for the next escape. Which could happen any minute now."

"You're a bucket-half-empty kinda gal, aren't you?"

They were quiet, pondering their predicament. Philo remembered something. "Edmund said this was 'familiar territory.' I wonder…"

"If he was incarcerated at the prison? That would make him a—"

"Convict."

"But he must have been released. He wouldn't be parading around St. Augustine if he were a fugitive."

"I don't know. He's from Ohio. If they're looking for him, it's there, not in the prison's backyard."

Barnaby managed a wan smile. "We may never know the answers."

"That's the spirit." Philo felt the knot in her stomach tighten. She closed her eyes.

Chapter Thirty-Seven

Even the smallest person can change the course of the future.

—Lady Galadriel

Shack near Sumterville, Wednesday, July 4

The sound of a car bumping over the dirt road jarred Philo awake. She whispered urgently, "Barnaby! Someone's coming."

"Wha—? Who?" He struggled to rise. "Oops, forgot I was in such *straitened* circumstances." He attempted a laugh, which fizzled into a cough.

"*Shh.* I think he's coming back. Maybe he's had a change of heart." She looked at Barnaby hopefully.

"Change of heart? More likely he's resolved to accelerate the imminence of our extinction."

Philo began to wail.

"*Or—*" He attempted to speak over her. "It could be a patrol from the prison, scouting for escaped convicts. We could end up in an even worse situation."

The wailing stopped abruptly. "They won't think we're escapees."

"Why not?"

"We're tied up, dummy. Plus, if we were, we'd be wearing orange jumpsuits. *Plus*, we haven't committed any crimes."

"*Shh.*"

They listened. Two people were whispering outside. A female voice said something too softly to understand. Her companion—a male—rasped testily, "No! You're staying outside. That's final."

Barnaby looked at Philo. "I recognize that voice. It's Axel Zimmer. Oh shit, do we have to contend with yet *another* seeker out to dispose of us?"

Philo finally let the terror take over. "Why is this happening? I don't want to die. Barnaby!" Her voice reached a crescendo in a howl of despair.

The door burst open. Axel Zimmer strode through, a revolver in his hand. He yelled, "Greer! Let her alone!" He halted and surveyed the room uncertainly before spying Philo in the kitchen. "Where's Greer?"

Philo took a deep breath. "He's gone."

From the floor, Barnaby asked, his tone composed, "Uh, Axel? Would you mind moving? You're blocking my view."

Zimmer's head lowered, and he jumped back. "Oh! Sorry, Swift. I didn't see you there."

Even to the still frightened Philo, his reaction was comical. As the minutes ticked by and he continued to stand, silently contemplating the man on the floor, she felt the need to provide some guidance. "Could you please untie him?"

"Huh? Oh, yeah. I was a bit thrown by the tailcoat and beard." Zimmer bent down and picked tentatively at the ropes around Barnaby's legs. He must have noticed the dried blood. "Are you hurt? Did he shoot you?"

"No. He stabbed me. I'm okay for now. Go free Philo. She's in worse shape than I am."

Zimmer pocketed his gun. "First things first. Greer left you here?"

"Yes. He's on his way to Port Charlotte."

"Ah. The casque."

"You knew?"

He nodded. "I've—of course—been trailing you and your students."

"The police let you go?"

Axel scratched his ear. "They didn't arrest me, if that's what you expected. I told them what I knew and left. Spent all of fifteen minutes at the station."

"You saw us combing through the carousel grounds."

"Yes. We must have all come to the same conclusion at the same time. I was about to go after the kids when I saw Greer stuffing you in his car. We've been pursuing you since you left St. Augustine."

"Who's we? Who's outside? We heard a female voice."

"Agatha." He turned and whistled. "Agatha! It's safe to come in."

The little girl marched in, an angry frown plastered across her face. "See? I told you he was gone. There was a double set of tracks." She paused when she saw Barnaby. "Professor! You're tied up?" She looked through the door to the kitchen. "You too, Miss Brice?"

"Afraid so," Barnaby said wearily. "I promise to recount our tale if you would kindly loosen our bonds."

"Sure." She bent to the task while Zimmer watched. Philo couldn't help it. "Tell you what, Mr. Zimmer, why don't you stand a little closer to Agatha. That way you can be not only useless, but counterproductive."

"Hey." He patted his pocket. "I'm standing guard."

"Against what? A nosey raccoon?"

As Agatha removed the rope from Barnaby's hands, she sucked in a breath. "Oh, dear. He handcuffed you as well?"

"Yeah. We'll need a hack saw to get them off."

"No, we won't. Hang on." She rummaged through her purse. "Ah, here it is." She held up a metal pick four inches long and about the width of a bobby pin. "I always carry one of these in case we want to stuff a turkey." While Barnaby held his hands out, she stuck the pin in the keyhole, bent it over, and pushed down with her thumb, depressing the part that held the ratchet in place. The cuff slid open. "There you are." She went to Philo and released her as well.

Barnaby carefully pulled the fake beard off, wincing as it ripped a bit of flesh from his chin. "Thank you, Agatha. You're not only a saint, you're a very resourceful cookie."

Philo added her two cents. "Crackerjack. Boffo. Top drawer."

Barnaby beamed at Philo. "Way to go, *mon amour*."

Rubbing her wrists, she asked, "What time is it?"

Zimmer checked his watch. "Six o'clock. We would have been here sooner, but we took Route 4 west toward Tampa."

Agatha added, "We should have caught up with Mr. Greer by the time we got to Brandon, but he wasn't there. Then Mr. Zimmer pulled out an old road map."

"There was another possible route that went through Palatka and down 301."

Barnaby nodded. "That's the one we took."

"Right. So we backtracked."

Barnaby sat down on the sofa and immediately jumped back up. "Ouch!" He rubbed his backside. "This place is a death trap, even without the killer!"

Philo indicated the other kitchen chair. He sat down gingerly. "You were saying you headed back up 301. How did you know where to get off the highway?"

Zimmer smiled. "When I saw the exit to EC470."

"Oh, yeah? What does EC470 mean to you?"

"You didn't notice? Oh, maybe it's only when you're heading north. See, just before the off-ramp there's a sign for the Coleman federal penitentiary. I surmised this was where Greer would head, since he's acquainted with the area. The compound is the only occupied place for miles around."

" 'Familiar territory.' So you knew he'd been a prisoner here?"

He nodded. "Us seekers know everything about each other. He was convicted of mail fraud and served five years."

Greer was living in a fantasy world if he thought the seeking world didn't have his entire resume on file.

"But how did you know we'd be in this shack? It's a quarter mile off the road."

"You can thank Agatha for that." He patted her shoulder.

"Agatha!" It occurred to Philo that she hadn't asked how the girl had come to be with Zimmer. *Once again she faded into the background like a ghost or the last beam of sunlight. How does she* do *that?*

Zimmer was saying, "She came back to the playground—"

"To get my hat. I'd left it on the bench." Her hand flew to her mouth. "Oh dear. Mr. Zimmer, the others don't know I left the dorm. Cleo is going to be furious."

"I don't think we need to fret about Cleo. We'll let her know you're safe once we've finished here."

"But—"

He cut her off. "When I ran into Agatha at the park, I convinced her to come with me—"

She sniffed. "On the contrary. I *insisted* on coming with you."

Agatha—it seemed—was developing a spine.

"Oh, well, whatever. I thought her presence would restrain Greer. We didn't want any unpleasantness."

She refused to be muzzled. "I pointed out as well that, if we found you, you would surely assume Mr. Zimmer was an enemy too. I could vouch for him."

Barnaby waved that aside. "You still haven't explained how you knew about the shack? It's not exactly marked."

The girl opened her mouth, but Zimmer interrupted again. "I was hell bent to get to the prison, but she caught a glimpse of this lane going off. The rain made it nice and muddy. A set of tire tracks—"

"Two. Two sets of tire tracks." Agatha wasn't going to let it go.

"Yes, two, were clearly visible. We took a chance."

"And it paid off for us. We are most grateful." Barnaby gave them a smart salute.

Philo added, "Otherwise, we probably wouldn't have been discovered until, well…" She petered out.

Axel inspected Barnaby's leg. "I suppose we'd better get you to a hospital."

Agatha tugged on Zimmer's sleeve. "Um…can we call the police now?"

"What? Oh, yes, of course." He turned to Philo. "He was driving to Port Charlotte, you say?"

"To find the carousel. I don't know where in the city they would have delivered it."

"Well, it would be hard to miss." Axel smiled at Agatha and handed her his phone. "Would you like to do the honors? Give them directions to this place, but also a heads-up on Greer's destination."

Barnaby half rose. "No! Send them straight on to Port Charlotte. Greer may not stay there long, and even then, he'll lie low somewhere."

"Nonsense. He'll have to locate the merry-go-round and find a way to gain access so he can search for the casque. Anyway, it's too late tonight, so he's bound to stay at least another day."

"Okay, but do we really need the police here? I mean, you've already rescued us."

"This is a crime scene, Barnaby. Greer is guilty of attempted murder."

His words brought home how close they'd come to catastrophe, and Philo began to cry. Agatha hesitated, obviously torn between comforting her and making the phone call. Barnaby put his arm around Philo. "Go on, Agatha. We'll be all right."

The little girl nodded and went outside. When she was out of earshot, Barnaby whispered, "Not just *attempted* murder, Axel. He admitted to us that he killed both Cottrells."

Zimmer didn't seem surprised. "I'd guessed that. All the more reason to get the cops here quickly. You'll have to tell them the whole story."

A few minutes later Agatha returned, a bemused expression on her face. "The police are already on their way."

"You're kidding! How did they know we were here?" Barnaby rose from his chair. He took a step toward Agatha and stumbled.

Philo pressed him back down. "Stay put. You don't want to reopen the wound."

"Yes, yes. I'll be good." He brushed her off. "Did they catch Greer?"

"No."

"Do they…" Philo choked on the words. "Do they think he's on his way back to finish us off?"

Agatha held up a hand. Her voice could barely be heard above the sirens. "They were unaware of Greer or that he'd kidnapped you. Evidently there's been a prison breakout. A gangster named Niarelli escaped. They're searching the area."

"Niarelli?" Philo glanced at Barnaby. "Where have I heard that name before?"

Barnaby shivered. "Niarelli. The Jacksonville mob boss Joseph put away. Remember? He was sent to the Coleman correctional facility. Right down the road."

Philo said slowly, "If Greer knew about this shack, then it's likely everyone in that prison knows about it."

"And a dangerous convict could be headed this way." Axel pulled his pistol out of his pocket.

The sirens were getting closer. Barnaby cocked his head. "Out of the frying pan into the fire?"

Chapter Thirty-Eight

If there was crime, there should be punishment. If the specific criminal should be involved in the punishment process then this was a happy accident, but if not then any criminal would do, and since everyone was undoubtedly guilty of something, the net result was that, in general terms, justice was done.

—Terry Pratchett

Police station, Wildwood, Thursday, July 5

The party didn't stop until the wee hours of the morning. Niarelli had been apprehended only five hundred yards from the shack and remanded to the prison. The troopers took the four witnesses to the nearest police station, ten miles away in Wildwood. When the sergeant saw Barnaby, he guffawed. "Hey, look, fellas, it's Uncle Sam! Must be fresh from the parade. There's the striped pants and tail coat. He's only missing the beard and the top hat."

Barnaby gingerly touched his chin. "I did have them—the hat must have fallen off when we were attacked." He frowned. "Darn, it was a rental. I hope I don't have to pay for it."

The same cop sniggered. "Not to worry: Uncle Sam always gets someone else to pay."

Philo said stiffly, "It's impolite to mock our nation's mascot, you know."

The cop sobered. "Yes, ma'am." Still, she detected an undercurrent of mirth among the officers until they finally let them return to St. Augustine.

Zimmer took Agatha back to her dorm. The girl wanted backup to defend herself from a predictably volcanic Cleo. The other two went to the emergency room. Philo sat by Barnaby while the nurse applied gauze to the wound. "Poor Agatha. Cleo is going to give her hell for disappearing again."

Barnaby winced. The nurse, bent double to reach his calf, growled, "Sir, if you'd stop wiggling I could finish faster."

She's asking the wrong man to stay still.

He muttered, "Sorry, Nurse Ratched…or is it Miss Nightingale? I always confuse the two. As for Cleo, she should be accustomed by now to Agatha's wandering off. At least this time she didn't get in trouble."

"In fact, she got us *out* of trouble. You should find a way to reward her for her bravery."

"I intend to." He unconsciously patted the nurse's head. "What made her trust Axel, anyway? The last time they met we'd called the police on him."

"A good question. We'll ask her tomorrow."

The nurse pulled her gloves off. "You're all fixed up, sir. You can go home."

"Thank you, Nurse Betty." When Philo pinched him, he replied, "What? It's her name."

****

Philo's apartment, Thursday, July 5

The sun pouring in from Philo's window woke her. She stretched and watched the sleeping Barnaby for a minute before heading to the bathroom. As she was toweling off, the phone rang. It was Steve Landman, the police sergeant. "I'm looking for Barnaby Swift. One of his students at Flagler told me I'd find him at this number. Is he there?"

"Yes. He's resting. Do you have news?"

"Depends. To whom am I speaking?"

"Philo Brice. We met at the Lightner museum. And again at the Castillo. Oh, and also at—"

He interrupted hastily, "Right. Got it. You're his girlfriend."

"I…uh." *Am I?* The policeman's next few words dissolved in swirling clouds of tentative joy. "I'm sorry, officer. What did you say?"

"I said, I thought you'd like to know that the state police nabbed Edmund Greer in Mango. That's about half an hour from Port Charlotte. He was in a restaurant eating oysters and drinking champagne."

"Celebrating a little prematurely, what? Or did he happen to have a white urn in a clear plastic box with him?"

"No, but he had a top hat in his car with Swift's name on a card stuck inside. He also had a pistol in his glove compartment. When they ran his name through the system, they learned he was a convicted felon, so that alone allowed them to arrest him. They popped him in the brig in Brandon, but he'll be extradited to St. Augustine today or tomorrow for arraignment."

"What are you going to charge him with?"

"Kidnapping, assault, and battery for starters. With your testimony, we should be able to nail him for the Cottrell murders. Maybe attempted murder as well."

"Barnaby."

"And you."

"Yes, but Greer tried to kill Barnaby at least one other time. He was the one who swung the iron ball at his head."

"Excuse me?"

"It was a few weeks ago. We were standing on the dock by the *Black Raven*—you know, the pirate ship?—when we heard someone prowling on the deck. It was Greer, stealing their treasure chest. Since we were scoping out the ship, he concluded that the casque was hidden there, or at least that we suspected as much."

"Huh. You say he stole the treasure chest? What on earth for? I took my twin eight-year-olds to a birthday party on that ship. The chest is filled with candy."

"He found that out, but not before he let a cannonball loose. It barely missed Barnaby's head."

"I see. One thing's clear: we'll have to bring you in again. Apparently there's a lot more to this case than the Brandon cops reported last night. We'll reexamine the other incidents too—the student who claimed he was pushed for instance. I gather Greer was at the Castillo that day."

"Yes. He was in a Hawaiian shirt."

"And all this was because he wanted to beat you to a box?"

Philo wasn't in the mood to elucidate. "It would seem so." Barnaby came into the living room, yawning. "Well, thanks for the information, Sergeant."

"Sure. Hang on a sec." She heard him speaking to someone away from the phone. "Lieutenant Tolliver says plan to come in at three."

At this point, Philo just wanted it over. "I suppose we have to." She rang off as two arms went round her and squeezed.

"Good morning."

"How are you feeling?"

"Better. Famished. That was the esteemed Officer Steve?"

"Uh-huh. They caught Edmund. Lieutenant Tolliver wants us at the station this afternoon."

They jumped at a loud bang on the door. She opened it. "Joseph!" The old man was a mess. His hair was rumpled and his eyes bleary. He was still wearing his pajama top but had pulled on his trousers. The suspenders hung uselessly from his waist. "What's happened? Are you ill?"

"Me? No!" He lunged at her. She staggered back, throwing her arms up, prepared to repel an attack. To her shock, he gave her a bear hug. "I'm so glad you're safe! Where have you been? How did you get home? Are you hurt? What on earth have you been up to?"

She held up a palm to slow the questions. "We're fine now. We'll come tell you all about it after we get some breakfast."

An hour later, they knocked on Joseph's door. The latter had taken the time to make himself more presentable. He wore a summer-weight flannel suit, a repp striped tie—and slippers. His tailored appearance contrasted sharply with Barnaby's baggy fleece sweatpants and T-shirt picturing the rapper Pitbull wrestling a mermaid. "Come in, come in. Coffee?"

"No, thanks. Already had my morning dose."

"I'll have some." Philo scowled at Barnaby. "*Someone* drank the last cup."

"Hey! It was two days old. I tasted more dregs than coffee."

Joseph handed a mug to Philo, and she and Barnaby sat on the sofa. Joseph edged his easy chair closer. The couple described the prior twenty-four hours, ending with their rescue from the shack.

Joseph sat, stunned. “I take it back.”

“What do you take back?”

“Edmund. Here I thought he was merely a plagiarist. In reality he’s a cold-blooded killer.”

“You’re the only one he didn’t try to harm.”

Joseph chuckled. “That young lady—Agatha—sounds like a real pip.”

“She’s certainly grown a lot more confident since the beginning of our story.”

“I’m pleased your old boss is not the murderer, but my heavens! It gives me the willies to think I sat here with Edmund all those afternoons, blissfully unaware that I was in the presence of evil.” He stopped. “You’re positive he didn’t try to poison me?”

“He says no. He probably just milked you for news of us.”

“So the mystery of the purple tea remains unsolved.”

Barnaby said, “Now it’s your turn. Why were you so overwrought? You couldn’t have known what happened.”

He smiled a little lopsidedly. “That was part of the problem. I had been up all night trying to solve Argle Bargle’s latest creation. As I was finally heading to bed about two a.m., the phone rang. I didn’t answer it, allowing the answering machine to take the message. It was Edmund.”

“Edmund! What did he say?”

“I’ll let you listen.” He pressed a button on the answering machine.

A tinny voice gabbled incoherently at first, but the last words rang out clearly: “Joseph! Joseph Brighton! I need your help. I'm under arrest. I want you to be my lawyer."

Joseph pressed the Stop button. "That was it. He left no number, no explanation for his predicament." The old man sipped from his cup. "I've had phone calls like that before, so I knew there was no point in trying to get hold of him at that hour. I went to bed. It wasn't until I picked up my paper that it registered that you two had never come home. I had a horrible premonition the two things—his arrest and your absence—were connected. I was frantic." He patted Philo's knee. "I'm glad I didn't know just how bad it was."

"Sergeant Landman called this morning. Edmund Greer was caught near Brandon. They're bringing him back to St. Augustine today. We've been asked to go to the police station for another interview."

"I'm coming with you."

Philo choked on her coffee. "You're not going to be his lawyer, are you?"

"I haven't decided."

****

St. Augustine police station, Thursday, July 5

They arrived at the police station half an hour early. The lobby was crowded. Philo spied Steve and Lieutenant Tolliver in deep conversation. Another figure rose as they entered. "Look, Barnaby, it's Norton Cottrell." Today he was dressed in a conservative navy blue suit and paisley tie.

He came toward them. "Did you come down to congratulate me?"

"Congratulate you? For what?"

"You haven't heard the news?"

Barnaby goggled at him. "Heard? We *are* the news. Why are *you* here?"

"The lieutenant asked me to come down to the station." Norton tucked a stray curl into his man bun. "See, yesterday I dropped off the list of staff and attendees at the convention I went to in Alaska. They got hold of the event planner. He not only confirmed I was there but told them the airport had been shut down from June third to the ninth due to the earthquake. I was stuck in the terminal when my parents were killed." He beamed. "I'm off the hook."

Barnaby snapped, "We already know that. Edmund Greer is our man. We've come to deal the coup de grâce."

Steve must have caught the last sentence and glared at Barnaby. "Do not take this lightly, Swift. You're lucky to be alive."

Norton's eyes had bugged out. "What are you talking about? Who the hell is Edmund Greer?"

Philo almost laughed. "It's a long story." She went over to the line of chairs against the wall and sat down. Norton sat on one side of her, Joseph on the other. Tolliver went to his cubicle. Barnaby and Steve remained standing. Philo faced Norton. "Greer is a seeker like your parents."

"And he killed them?" Norton's eyes filled with tears. "For the love of God, why?"

"Because he believed they'd figured out where the casque is hidden."

This got his attention. "And had they?"

Philo pictured the brochure. *Greer thought it was a dead end.* "Maybe."

"And exactly what place had they settled on?"

"We have reason to believe it was in, or under, the J & S Carousel."

"The one up on San Carlos Avenue?"

"The very one. Only it's in Port Charlotte now."

"Huh." Norton's brow furrowed. "I don't think my parents ever mentioned that one."

"They may not have, you know." Barnaby was thoughtful.

"They may not have what?"

"Settled on the carousel. They both died before I had a chance to discuss it with them. Other than the brochure, the only evidence we have is the drawing of the horse."

Norton craned his neck at Barnaby. "Horse?"

"A picture found near your mother. It's either the chrome stallion in Ripley's garden or one of the merry-go-round ponies."

"Oh, yeah. Mom was convinced the casque was buried at Ripley's."

"Really?" Philo was getting muddled. "Then why did she throw the drawing away?"

"I think I know." Barnaby pulled Norton up and sat down next to Philo. "You asked me yesterday why she wanted to meet me at the Fountain of Youth rather than the carousel. I'm guessing she didn't."

"Didn't what?"

"Want to stay at the Fountain. In fact, Harriet asked to meet me there because it was convenient, and she knew I'd be able to find it. Then she planned to lead me up the street to show me the carousel and the pinto pony."

"That doesn't explain the stallion drawing."

"It explains why she crumpled it up." Barnaby nodded at Norton. "He just told us. His mother was sure the casque was at Ripley's. Somehow she figured out that she was wrong. That's when she switched our assignation from Ripley's to the Fountain."

Joseph interrupted. "Was it the brochure that changed her mind? You say Greer killed them for it."

"He did, but it turned out to be useless. Greer said it listed all the major sightseeing attractions in St. Augustine, but none of them were marked or tagged or had anything indicating special interest. If Robert and Harriet had one of the sites in mind, they didn't write it down."

Norton was looking from Philo to Barnaby, his eyes wide. "Brochure?"

Barnaby explained. "Your father told me he'd found an old brochure in the basement of the Flagler College library. He said it held a clue."

"So *that's* what he was talking about." He rocked back on his heels.

Barnaby stood up and grabbed the lapels of Norton's jacket. "What. Are. You. Saying?"

"He told me he'd found a flyer from 1994 in the college archives. He hoped it would pinpoint the spot. He didn't specify what spot he meant."

"1994? What happened in 1994?"

Joseph pushed himself off the chair. Wheezing with the effort, he said, "I believe I may have the answer, if the good desk sergeant will allow me to use his computer."

Steve nodded at the officer. "He'll be happy to."

"Thanks." A few minutes later, he was back. "I thought so—1994 was a banner year for the children of St. Augustine."

"Why?"

"That was the year the J & S Carousel, newly restored by James Soules and Carl Theel, opened for business in Davenport Park."

Norton nodded sagely. "The brochure was dated 1994. What do you want to bet it mentioned the carousel's arrival?"

Joseph agreed. "And very likely some other fact that led Robert Cottrell to believe the casque was buried there."

Barnaby, who had been staring into space, started. "Why didn't he tell Harriet?"

"What makes you think he didn't?"

"When I called to offer my condolences on his death, Harriet said she had the brochure but had no idea what it meant. The night of our rendezvous—"

"And her death."

"She brought both the brochure and the horse drawing. I believe it wasn't until that moment that she understood what Robert had guessed."

"But *how*?" Philo knew she sounded plaintive, but they didn't seem any closer to a solution and she had to pee.

"Hang on." Barnaby went back to the desk. "Do you still have Harriet Cottrell's effects—what you found on her at the scene?"

Sergeant Steve came over. "They're in the evidence room. I'll get them."

Now's my chance. "I'll be right back."

"Where are *you* going?"

"Never mind."

A few minutes later Steve returned to the lobby with a cardboard carton. Philo sidled back in behind him. Norton reached for the box.

Steve brushed his hand aside. "Sorry—we need them for the trial."

"May I at least look at them?"

"I suppose."

Before Norton could open it, Barnaby snatched it from him. "If you don't mind…" He rummaged through the items. "Aha!" He held up a folded piece of stiff paper. When he unfolded it they could see it was a full page photograph.

"That's Image Six."

"Right. Harriet brought this, and the brochure and horse picture with her. When she examined them together, she must have realized that the two horses—in the image and the carousel—were identical. She called me, then walked up to the Fountain of Youth. You all know the rest."

He handed the box back to Norton, who whistled. "Amazing."

Philo's exhilaration fizzled with a fresh thought. "Wait a minute. Hold your horses."

"Ha-ha."

"Yes. Well. Byron Preiss buried his twelve casques in 1981 or 1982. The carousel wasn't here then."

"Right." Joseph agreed. "The website says it was built in 1927 and moved from a barn in Mystique, Michigan, to a children's zoo in Fort Wayne, Indiana, before arriving in St. Augustine."

"In that case, the casque would be hidden wherever the merry-go-round was in 1982."

The four were silent, unsure how to proceed. Finally, Barnaby said, "How about this? Preiss somehow hid the casque in the carousel itself. The casque moved with it from Indiana or Michigan."

Joseph frowned. "What about the painting, then? And the poem? Everybody thinks they point to St. Augustine. Wouldn't it reflect Fort Wayne or Mystique instead?"

"Maybe it does." Something tickled the back of Philo's mind. "Wait. Horse."

"The pinto?"

"No." She leaned forward eagerly. "Ripley's!"

Barnaby shifted irritably. "We've established that the image's horse refers to the carousel, not to Ripley's."

"No, we haven't. Remember what Susie told us? That Ripley's has parks in thirteen other states. Or was it fourteen?" She wrinkled her nose. "Anyway, if the horse symbolizes Ripley's.... and there's a satellite park in Michigan or Indiana..."

Norton sniffed. "I think we're getting a little out there."

Barnaby clicked his phone on. "Before we start battering the proposition to death, let's see if there's a Ripley's in either of those states." He scrolled. "Huh. Damn."

"Nothing?"

"Looks like only twelve states have parks. The good folks of Michigan and Indiana will have to find alternate sources of entertainment."

"That's it." Norton slapped a knee. "We go back to the drawing board."

Exhaustion enveloped Philo like a sodden, dark mist. "You know what? I don't care. I'm sick of the whole thing."

Norton gasped. "But...my parents! They died not knowing if they were right or not. We owe it to them to try to find the key."

Barnaby blew a long breath out. "Okay. There's no way the casque would be in Indiana or Michigan. Or anywhere except Florida."

"Why not?"

"Like Joseph said. No alligators. No Spaniards. No palm trees."

Norton threw up his hands. "So where does that leave us?"

"With an unmarked flyer."

Philo added, "And without notes or some kind of hint, we can't decipher what was significant about the brochure."

"Any more than Edmund could."

Philo stood. "Robert never said he had the answer, and neither did Harriet. It doesn't take much to get seekers frothing at the mouth. For all we know, they were only onto a good clue."

"Or—alternatively—they were wrong," Barnaby said glumly.

She gazed sadly at Norton. "Which means…that Greer didn't have to kill them after all."

Joseph spoke. "*If* he killed them."

Chapter Thirty-Nine

The law is an ass.

—Charles Dickens

St. Augustine police station, Thursday, July 5

With one voice, Barnaby and Philo shouted, "*What*?"

In a calm and deliberate tone that Philo failed to appreciate, Joseph said, "This great nation is founded upon the premise that you are innocent until proven guilty." Before they could respond, he knocked on the lieutenant's door. Tolliver opened it. "I'm Joseph Brighton. Edmund Greer has asked me to represent him. May I speak with him?"

The detective pointed at the front desk. "Sergeant Miller can take care of you."

While Joseph busied himself filling out forms, the door to the cells opened, and a man appeared. Philo shook Barnaby's arm. "Look who's here."

Barnaby whistled. "Runar Magnusson. I guess the police caught both crooks. Good for them."

Magnusson spoke to the desk sergeant, then turned his steps to them. Philo resisted the impulse to hide behind Barnaby. She said as boldly as she could, "So, why aren't you in handcuffs?"

His eyebrows went up. "Me?"

Barnaby raised an arm. "Officer! Arrest this man. He threatened us yesterday. I believe that calls for a charge of assault."

Philo added, "He has a gun."

The sergeant laughed. "Of course he does. He's a federal agent."

"A…a fed?" Barnaby seemed to be having trouble grasping the concept.

"Special Agent Runar Magnusson, FBI, at your service." He showed them his badge. "I've been tracking Edmund Greer across the country, from Ohio to Chicago to Boston and now here. He's wanted in the suspicious deaths of four people." He offered Barnaby a hand. "I do regret my behavior yesterday, but I had to get you guys out of there. We'd received a tip that Greer was at the carousel. If he believed you had the casque, I wouldn't have given two bits for your chances of survival. I didn't realize he'd kidnapped you until it was too late."

"A…a fed. A gumshoe. Flatfoot, G-man. The fuzz."

Philo put a gentle hand over Barnaby's mouth. "Now is not the time for flaunting your prowess with synonyms."

Magnusson grinned. "At least those adjectives are benign."

She wracked her brain, trying to put all her questions into some kind of logical order. Instead, she blurted, "Did you really go to a luau?"

"No. Oh, you mean the Hawaiian shirt? It's new. Hadn't packed appropriately for this Florida sunshine."

"You didn't wear it to confuse us?"

"Why would I do that?"

"We kept seeing Greer in one."

Runar chuckled. "I forgot. It's his signature costume—evidently his dream was to settle on the Big Island." He headed down the corridor.

Philo called him back. "Just a minute, Agent Magnusson. Are you really Kevin's father?"

"Yes."

"So is it just serendipity that you and he are here at the same time?"

"No. In fact, it was a stroke of luck. I'd lost track of Greer, but when I heard of Kevin's mishap at the Castillo, I had a feeling there was a connection." His face was grim. "I was right."

"You used your own son as cover for a hazardous operation?" Philo was fuming.

"Absolutely not." He lowered his voice. "There's no reason for him to know I was here in my capacity as FBI. We don't want him—or any of your students—to have any inkling they were in danger. Capiche?"

"It's a little late for that, isn't it?"

At that moment, Axel Zimmer arrived, Agatha on his heels. Magnusson, holding a finger to his lips, ducked behind the desk.

Zimmer asked, "Did we miss anything?"

Joseph held up his clipboard and blocked their view so Magnusson could slip out the door. Philo said loudly, "Mr. Brighton is going to represent Edmund."

"Mr. Brighton?"

They introduced Joseph. Zimmer scanned his three-piece suit and silk tie. "Why would you defend him? He tried to kill your friends."

"I'm just going to talk to him."

Norton said, "Are you allowed to do that if you're not going to be his lawyer?"

Joseph glanced over his shoulder at the two policemen. “Since I’m retired, I can only recommend someone to him. I just want to assess the man’s attitude.” He paused. “Everyone is entitled to a defense.”

As the door closed behind him, Philo sputtered wordlessly. A full three minutes passed in astounded silence. Barnaby recovered first. “So…Agatha. Did you regale the rest of the crew with your feats of valor?”

“I told Cleo, so they all know by now.” She smiled at Axel. “She was pretty rattled, but Mr. Zimmer managed to placate her.”

“My pleasure, my dear. If it weren’t for you, we’d never have located Barnaby and Philo.” He grinned. “I made sure to emphasize the two sets of tracks.”

“That reminds me.” Philo took Agatha aside. “Yesterday, you hopped into Mr. Zimmer’s car without so much as a cavil or a quibble. Considering the altercation at the spring house, what made you trust him?”

“Diego.” She glanced shyly at Axel. “Mr. Zimmer is like a father to him. See, Diego was in a street gang. That’s how he got the scar—the gang attacked him when he tried to quit, and Mr. Zimmer rescued him. He didn’t tell me before because it’s a part of his life he wants to forget. Anyway, Diego is fiercely protective of Mr. Zimmer. He says he has suffered a lot and needs affection in his life. I was glad to help.”

Looks like I owe Axel Zimmer an apology.

Barnaby came up to them. “Aren’t the others coming, Agatha?”

“No. They’re expecting you back at the college when you’re done here.”

"Tell Cleo I want them to keep working on the paper."

"Should we include the carousel?"

"You can make your case, but I'm afraid we'll never know if it's the actual resting place of the casque."

"Why not? We can go to Port Charlotte, can't we?"

Norton piped up. "What's in Port Charlotte?"

Agatha—who with her recent exploits had grown emphatically bolder—replied, "The casque! I found it. Or rather, I solved the mystery." She gave Barnaby a pleading look.

He shook his head. "Sorry, my dear. If it's there, it's a pile of pottery shards now."

"What?"

Barnaby hesitated. Then, with a sympathetic expression, he said, "Lieutenant Tolliver got hold of the carousel owner's widow. Apparently, it didn't make it to Port Charlotte in one piece. The tractor trailer carrying it overturned, and the sections—including the horses—were broken and scattered. They've retrieved some, but they're in such bad shape that she doesn't think they can be repaired. The merry-go-round will never go around again."

Agatha burst into tears. "It's so unfair!"

Philo hugged her. "We may not have the casque, but we're all so proud of your detective work. Yours will be the lead name on the paper."

She snuffled. "Do you think so, Professor?"

"Undoubtedly. And I believe—yes, you most definitely deserve an A."

"Thank you!" Agatha skipped toward the water fountain.

When she was out of earshot, Philo took Barnaby's hand and led him off to the side. "Lieutenant Tolliver didn't say anything about a crash."

He whispered in her ear. "I know."

"Not only that, the casque couldn't have been in the carousel anyway. The timing is way off."

"Yes, but Agatha doesn't need to know that. I had to spike any inclination on the part of the students to go to Port Charlotte." He pointed his chin at the girl. "If her theory is debunked, it will only crush her just when she's coming out of her shell."

Zimmer said something to Steve in a low voice. Steve nodded and knocked on the police chief's door. He came out a minute later and called the group over. "Mr. Zimmer here has suggested, and Captain Westwood agrees, that the little lady, and I do mean little"—he smiled at Agatha—"deserves a citation for her extraordinary efforts in tracking and liberating Mr. Swift and Miss Brice. Miss Leonardi, can you be here tomorrow at noon?"

Her lips shut tight, Agatha looked to Barnaby for approval. He said, "Sounds fine. We'll round up the usual suspects, by which I mean her fellow students."

They were attempting to soothe a blubbering Agatha when the door to the cell block opened and Joseph strolled out. Philo called, "What did Greer tell you? What are you going to do?"

Joseph sat down on a plastic chair and let out a whistling breath. "I am not authorized to tell you what he said in our private conversation. What I can say is, he's changed his mind. He wants to defend himself."

Barnaby quoted under his breath, " 'He who represents himself has a fool for a client.' "

Joseph laughed. “Abraham Lincoln.”

Barnaby shook his head. “That’s the word on the street. However, the first known instance of the quote was in 1795, and even that cited it as an old adage derived from an Italian proverb.”

“Thus proving that some truths are eternal.”

“*Plus ça change, plus c’est la même chose*.”

“So true. Once again, you best me in the trivia department, *mon cher* Swift.”

Joseph turned to the policeman. “I shall not return unless the prisoner asks for me. But rest assured, I am not going to represent him.” He left.

Zimmer had been tapping his foot. “Norton? May I have a word?” The two men went out to the sidewalk. When they returned, they were all smiles. Axel clapped Norton on the back. “Mr. Cottrell has consented to come work for me while the estate is sorted out. My manager can run the store.”

Barnaby’s eyes narrowed. “You’re not just angling for a chance to continue your search of the premises? After all, we still don’t know if Norton’s parents had any more evidence.”

Zimmer’s expression held steady. “It wouldn’t do any harm to go through their files.” He turned to Norton. “Would you consent?”

Norton shook his hand. “Now that I’m no longer under suspicion, I’d like to resume my parents’ research.” When Zimmer twitched, he added, “In collaboration with you, of course.”

“Wonderful. Fancy some lunch?”

“Don’t mind if I do.”

Barnaby watched them depart. “At the risk of being redundant, that may be the beginning of a beautiful friendship.”

"I thought you and he were going to work on the puzzles together?"

"One was enough. That reminds me: I presume the contest with Edmund is null and void. Never cottoned to the idea anyway. I'm not a betting man, even if it's a sure thing."

"So you've discarded all your puzzle partners."

"I prefer to work alone." He kissed Philo's cheek. "On puzzles, that is."

****

Philo's apartment, Thursday, July 5

After a tedious two hours with Special Agent Magnusson and Lieutenant Tolliver, Barnaby and Philo were finally let go. If they hoped for a quiet afternoon on the balcony (or elsewhere), they were to be disappointed. No sooner had they turned the corner onto Aviles Street than the sirens and flashing lights struck at them like the crash cymbals in Tchaikovsky's fourth symphony.

"Am I getting a migraine?" Barnaby held his head. "Oh, the tintinnabulation of the bells, bells, bells."

"They're at my building."

"Of course they are. Where else would they be?" He regarded her warily. "I may have to meditate upon this infatuation. You're a high-risk environment."

Philo was resigned. "We might as well find out who they're here for. I hope Joseph hasn't been swilling toxic beverages again."

They reached the building as a stretcher, on it a body covered with a sheet, was carried out of the alley. Philo—dread clamped like a vise on her heart—ran up to the EMTs. "It's not Joseph Brighton, is it?"

"No, ma'am. It's a woman. Name of"—he checked his clipboard—"Ida Kink. You know her?"

"Not well. I've only lived here three years." *And she's barely spoken three words to me in that time.* "Is she…is she—?"

"Deceased, I'm afraid. You happen to have any next-of-kin information? We couldn't find anything in her apartment."

Philo conjured an image of the shrewish old lady. "I only recall her mentioning an ex-husband. They were not on friendly terms. Do you know how she died?" *Did you find a brick lodged in her forehead?*

"Not precisely, no, but all the signs point to a massive heart attack. The lab will have to take blood samples and analyze them before the ME can certify cause of death."

"Where are you taking her?"

"To the morgue." She could tell he wanted to add, "Duh."

Joseph leaned over his balcony and sang, "Ding dong, the witch is dead."

She called up. "That's not very nice of you."

"Do you beg to differ?" He crooked a finger. "Come on up. I have champagne."

They climbed the stairs. The door to Ida's apartment was open, and they could see forensic agents going over it. One of them came out of the kitchen holding a metal box in a gloved hand. Another one spied them peering in and closed the door.

"In here." They followed the pop of a cork.

Barnaby said, "I'd go easy on the festivities. You could become a suspect."

"Lucky for me she died of a heart attack then. Anyway, probably half of St. Augustine would be a suspect. Ida was widely despised, and in some cases—for example, by her family—abhorred."

"She wasn't so bad." Philo didn't like to speak ill of the dead.

"You weren't here for the great wars. She and her now-ex got into ear-splitting arguments that often morphed into brawls, sometimes even spilling out into the street. Police were called on a regular basis." The ambulance siren started up outside. He chuckled. "Alas, that particular tradition continues unabated."

"What happened?"

"To the Kinks? They finally divorced. The minute the papers were signed, Ida started living like a queen—packages delivered every day, new clothes, cruises. Turns out she'd created an offshore asset protection trust and had been pouring their money into it. When hubby found out, he was livid, but there wasn't much he could do."

"Couldn't he sue her?"

"I suppose, but it would have cost him a fortune. Now, there's a motive for murder if I've ever seen one." He tittered. "I'd be happy to represent *him*."

"Did they have any children?"

Joseph tapped his forehead. "I believe so. Yes, a son. Must be in his thirties by now. He left for boarding school when he was thirteen, before they moved here. I don't think he even came home for vacations." He took a sip from his flute. "I trust he didn't take after his mother—surely there couldn't be two such ugly pusses in Florida."

"You really didn't like her."

"Does it show? She would leave nasty notes on my door, claiming I was noisy. Me!" His eyes blazed. "She even tried to kill Jemimah once. She caught her in the backyard and held her down in the fountain."

"That's criminal!"

"Indeed. However, she did not reckon with a cat's ablutophobia." He waited, grinning.

Barnaby mumbled, "Fear of baths."

"Aha. I knew you wouldn't disappoint. Anyway, Jemimah fended her off. You may have noticed the jagged scar on Ida's arm?"

"Good for Jemimah!" Philo raised her glass.

Barnaby clinked hers. "And here's to Jemimah's 'ineffable effanineffable deep and inscrutable singular name,' whatever it may be."

"T. S. Eliot. Thank you." Joseph poured more champagne. "And a second toast to whoever's responsible for her elimination."

Barnaby murmured, "It was a heart attack."

"In that case, to God."

Chapter Forty

The best laid schemes o' Mice an' Men, Gang aft agley.
—Robert Burns

St. Augustine police station, Friday, July 6

"We are so proud of you, Agatha!"

"Here, let me see that." Diego took the medal from Agatha. He rubbed it and pretended to chew the edge. "Yup, it's real." He gave it back to her. When she blushed, he blushed too.

He stood gazing down at her until Cleo gave him a nudge. "Come on! Give the rest of us a chance."

They were gathered outside the police station. All six students were in attendance, as well as Axel Zimmer, Diego, Philo, and Barnaby. The ceremony had been brief, but someone had notified the St. Augustine *Crier*, and a reporter took pictures. He handed Barnaby a card. "It'll appear in our 'Neighbors in the News' section."

Barnaby turned the card over to Philo. "Now would be a great time to buy that subscription." He opened his arms wide. "What shall we do to mark this grand occasion?"

"I vote for the Culture Club."

The rest agreed, and Lincoln led the way.

As they crossed the street, a police cruiser pulled up. The officer opened the rear door and led a manacled man into the station. The prisoner wore a rumpled suit and his hair was mussed, but his expression portrayed more fury than fear. A battered Toyota screeched to a stop behind the police car, and a young man jumped out. His eyes swept the sidewalk before sprinting through the door. Philo pointed. "He must be a relative of the one in handcuffs."

"Either that, or an experienced pettifogger."

"Pettifogger?"

"Ask Joseph. It's a legal huckster, a shyster."

She watched the door swing shut. "I wonder what they arrested him for."

Barnaby took her arm and tugged. "No idea, but the way our luck is running, we'll be asked to testify against him. Let's hoof it."

****

Babushka's House of Pierogies, Friday, July 6

They left the students on their third beers and headed toward home. Barnaby stopped before the Polish take-out restaurant near her apartment. "Shall we pick up some lunch here?"

Philo was too hungry to argue. *It can't be worse than Flora's…can it?*

They were at the counter waiting to order when Barnaby took a call from Steve. "*Again*? We've got to stop seeing each other like this, Officer…Yes, it was a joke. Say, didn't you have some vacation days coming up? Canceled? Too bad…All right, we're on our way." He hung up. "I was right—the prisoner? He's Ida Kink's husband. They haven't booked him yet, but they're holding him for questioning."

"What do they want us for?"

"Not us. You."

"Me?" She checked her watch. "I have to open the store. Call Steve back and see if it can wait."

"I didn't get the impression it could. Our sweet Ida appears to have been one-eighty-sevened."

"Excuse me?"

"Street slang for murdered. I learned it at the sergeant's fatherly knee."

Philo waved off the cashier—*at least I dodged one bullet today*—and had reached the restaurant door when his words sank in. "Ida didn't die of a heart attack?"

"No. She tested positive for—get this—digitoxin overdose."

"Oh, my God. That's what made Joseph sick. Do you suppose…"

"The purple passion tea was meant for her? Let's run it up the flagpole and see who salutes."

When they arrived at the station—Barnaby grumbling about setting up a tent there—Tolliver greeted them, his expression nearly, but not entirely, jovial. "It's nice to be interviewing Miss Brice for a change instead of you, Swift."

"I couldn't agree more."

He led them into a small conference room. The two men they'd seen earlier rose at their entrance. One was a younger version of his companion: both had wispy beards, bulbous Roman noses, and beer bellies. The older man wore rimless glasses. Tolliver introduced them. "This is Arlen Kink, Ida Kink's ex-husband, and Duncan Kink, their son."

"How do you do."

The son immediately started complaining. "When are you going to let my father go? He hasn't done anything. This is an outrage. I'm calling my lawyer."

"Your father already called his own. Why don't you sit down, Mr. Kink?"

When Duncan had settled back in his seat, spewing grunts and curses, Tolliver directed Philo's attention to Arlen. "Do you recognize him?"

"No."

"You haven't seen him hanging around the apartment building recently?"

"I've never seen him before in my life."

"I see." He seemed disappointed.

Is he simply fishing? How much does he actually have to go on?

He escorted them to the lobby. "Well, thanks for your time."

"No problem. Give my regards to Sergeant Landman." They left. On the drive home, Philo was quiet.

Barnaby said cheerfully, "Maybe Joseph can shed some light. He's home most of the day. He might have seen Mr. Kink sneak in and stir poison into her soup."

Philo woke from her reverie. "He told Ida he hadn't seen her ex."

"Oh, that's right. Of course, she was brandishing a brick at the time. He might have fibbed to avoid a drubbing."

"*Hmm*. It's true, I'd never seen the older one, but his son—Duncan? He looked familiar. Now where…?" She rolled the window down and sucked in a breath of fresh air. "I've got it. He came into Mind Over Matter a couple of times. He was most intent on my collection of early maps, especially the sixteenth-century ones."

"Think he's a seeker?"

"Maybe. Everyone else in this town seems to be. Although I got the impression he was angling more for an estimate of the *market* value than the *historic* value.

He kept picking one or another up and asking how much it would sell for at auction."

"Did he buy anything?"

"Nope."

"Probably just browsing investment possibilities." Barnaby bounced on the seat. "I'm hungry—too bad we hadn't got our sandwich order in before we were summoned by the authorities."

The one thing that's gone well today. They were driving by the Lightner. "How about a midafternoon snack at the Café Alcazar?"

"I'm game."

It wasn't until they were sharing a curried chicken salad in the nearly empty café that Philo connected the dots. "The last time Duncan Kink came into the store, I had just pegged the Drake map to the display table." She set her tea cup down. "He was the one who tried to unpin it."

Barnaby dropped his fork. "Are you thinking what I'm thinking?"

"Uh-huh. Now where did I put that cardboard tube?"

"Why? Oh—in case he left his fingerprints on it?"

She folded her napkin and set it on the table. "You primed for another waltz with Lieutenant Tolliver?"

"He's going to think I have a crush on him."

****

St. Augustine police station, Friday, July 6

Tolliver wasn't as impressed as they had hoped. "You say the map was stolen, and then returned? That's hardly worth my time. Is it valuable?"

"I don't know. Probably. Look, it means that Duncan Kink has been in the neighborhood. I'd at least check his fingerprints against those on the map case.

There's been a rash of thefts from galleries recently." She looked at him with shining eyes. "You could crack the case."

The detective sighed. "All right. I'll ask Mr. Kink to come in. He's not going to be happy."

"Tell him you need his prints for your database. You don't have to let on that you suspect he's a burglar."

"I don't. Not yet." He gave her a reluctant smile. "At this rate we may have to recruit you." Tolliver didn't say it as though he meant it.

****

Philo's apartment, Saturday July 7

"You were right. Alongside Norton Cottrell's and your fingerprints, we found Duncan Kink's on the map container. We're reviewing the evidence boxes of the other burglaries now."

Philo juggled the phone closer to her ear. "Thank you, Lieutenant Tolliver. If Duncan is the culprit, you should be able to clear a slew of unsolved crimes off your books."

Tolliver didn't respond for a minute. Finally, he growled, "The police are always grateful for assistance from the public." He hung up.

Barnaby came into the kitchen. "Was that Tolliver?"

"Uh-huh. Duncan Kink's a match. He's the thief. In fact, they think he might have been responsible for several robberies of fine art both here and in Jacksonville."

"Huh. Does Tolliver have any idea why Kink returned our map and not the others?"

"I forgot to ask."

"They won't be able to interrogate him until they arrest him. Reckon he and his father have flown the coop yet?"

"I don't see why they would. Duncan doesn't know he's under suspicion, and the police couldn't find anything tying Arlen to Ida other than mutual hatred. *Hmm.*" She rose. "I want to ask Joseph something."

"I'll come along to keep you honest."

They found Joseph working on a crossword. He held it up. "I've finally gotten around to finishing Edmund's contribution to your contest. It's not only not very impressive, but several clues are identical to the one in last week's *Crier*. Imagine—stealing crossword clues. To what unfathomable depths will a man stoop?" He shook his head. "Edmund is a thoroughly despicable character."

"Plagiarism is indeed despicable. How about murder?"

He shrugged. "Eh." He put down the paper. "To what do I owe the honor of your presence?"

Before Philo could speak, Barnaby barked, "Were you lying to Ida when you said you hadn't seen Arlen Kink recently?"

"No." The old man shook his head. "I make it a habit to tell the truth to harridans wielding weapons. Like I said, Arlen made tracks after the divorce and hasn't been back since."

"How about his son, Duncan?"

"I never met him. The Kinks moved here after he'd gone off to boarding school."

Philo sat down across from him. She spoke earnestly. "Joseph, do you still have the manila envelope the purple tea came in?"

"No, I threw it away. Why?"

"Damn. It was marked 'medicinal tea,' right?"

"Right. That's why I assumed it was from Edmund."

"It didn't have an address on it though, did it?"

"No…but it was in my mail slot." He arched an eyebrow. "What's with the third degree?"

Barnaby jerked upright. "I see what you're getting at, Philo." He leaned toward the old man. "Which cubby's yours, Joseph?"

"The middle one. Philo's is on my right, and Ida's is on the left."

"Come on." They trooped down to the building entrance. Philo pointed at her mail box. "I pasted my name above mine, but the other two are only labeled with the apartment number."

Joseph studied the wall of cubbies. "You think the murderer put the tea in the wrong box?"

"I'm thinking that Ida Kink was the intended victim. Not you."

"Why would Edmund Greer want to kill *her*? As far as I know, he'd never met her."

Suddenly it all became clear. "That's not it." She headed back up to her apartment. "I have to call the detective back."

Tolliver was in. She put the phone on speaker. "Detective? This is Philo Brice."

"What is it *now*?"

"Yes, it's good to hear your voice again too…Lieutenant? Do you still have the bag of purple tea that sickened Joseph Brighton?"

"It's in the evidence room. Why?"

"You might want to check it for Duncan Kink's fingerprints as well."

"Oh? Wait—you think he might have killed his own *mother*?"

"You had no problem believing Norton Cottrell killed *his* parents."

He sighed. "I'll be glad when I retire. Or you do." He hung up.

Chapter Forty-One

Unraveling the threads of a good…story is like solving a well-crafted puzzle. After a lengthy, sometimes difficult journey, the pieces click into place, and you're rewarded with the satisfying payoff of a job well done.

—Jason Schreier

Philo's apartment, Sunday, July 15

"I am prepared to certify that this past week was a great improvement over the previous one."

Philo kissed the top of Barnaby's head and sat down next to him on the balcony. "Agreed."

"The students presented their thesis Friday morning. Agatha read it for the group."

"Oh my. She has definitely grown."

"Yes, in fact she says she shot up a couple of inches this month alone. At this rate, she should be tall enough by next year to ride that super-duper roller coaster in the famous amusement park where life-size cartoon characters walk among us. You know, the one with a statue of a man and a mouse."

"I certainly hope she's got more sense than that. Have you graded the report yet?"

"Yes. I was tempted to make it an A minus, just to give them something to aspire to, but the paper was really very good. It was well-constructed, with a summary, sections for each site, and a conclusion. The research was detailed, the assumptions reasonable, the progression logical, and the final determination very persuasive. Agatha need never know she was wrong about the carousel."

Philo pursed her lips. "We can't assume she was wrong. Perhaps we simply didn't delve far enough into possibilities. The casque could still be in Indiana or…what was the other state? Michigan."

"Not to worry on that score. Evidently Lincoln posted their theory on the main *Secret* forum. A lively debate ensued, culminating in several seekers packing their Matildas and hopping a CSX car to seek their fortunes in the Hoosier state. The latest school of thought places the casque in the Indiana Dunes."

"Matildas?"

"Rucksack. Knapsack. Australian for backpack."

A tune floated through Philo's head. *"Waltzing Matilda." Barnaby whistled it the first day we met.* "Well, that should at least diminish the ranks of fanatics infesting the streets of St. Augustine."

They sat quietly for a minute, listening to the cheerful conversations of the tourists wandering along the street below. Barnaby put his arm around Philo's shoulders. "And what of your day? Productive?"

"I had a long talk with Detective Tolliver. He's gotten over his annoyance at our interference and was really quite communicative."

"*Hmm.* He has finally learned to appreciate your beauty and perspicacity."

"It must be that. He said Duncan Kink confessed when he was presented with the fingerprint evidence."

"To the murder?"

"Yes."

"So Duncan Kink killed his mother." He picked a geranium blossom from a potted plant and tossed it over the rail. It landed at the feet of a young woman in a pink sundress. She picked it up and stuck it in her hair. "Granted, she was not the most maternal of women."

"In fact, she could give Joan Crawford a run for her money."

"Or Mary Ann Cotton."

"Who?"

"English lady who poisoned eleven of her thirteen children, all four husbands, and a couple of passers-by."

He reached for another flower, but Philo moved the pot to another table. "It's also possible Ida was a bad wife but a good mother."

"Unlikely. Still, one usually requires a transcendent reason for matricide. Did he provide Tolliver with a motive?"

"He was incensed at Ida's shabby treatment of his father. He'd been sending Arlen money regularly, but then he lost his job. When the unemployment benefits ran out, he began stealing rare books and maps, selling them, and giving Arlen the proceeds."

"An admirable show of filial loyalty."

"Oh, now larceny is a good thing?"

"They're just maps and books. It's not like he was stealing anything valuable."

She knew Barnaby was baiting her and stifled the retort. "On the contrary, maps can fetch a pretty penny. The Drake map? I just sold it for five thousand dollars."

"Five thousand smackers, huh?" He stood up and did a little tap dance. "That should be good for several nights of chili and ice cream. Although I hear Flora has been shut down by the food inspectors. Can't imagine why."

She pulled him back down. “Rumor has it her meat supply came from a stable in Palatka. Merely vicious slander from her competitors, I’m sure.”

“I shall ignore the insult to a good woman and a great cook. But let us hark back to the subject of money. Don’t you have to deliver the swag to Norton? It was his map after all.”

“You’ve forgotten. He relinquished his claim—washed his hands of it. It was mine to dispose of.”

“A noble soul, that Norton.” He paused. “You know what this means?”

“What?”

“That Francis Drake is not the man in Image Six.”

“The map had nothing to do with *The Secret*. Yes.”

“Whew. All right, moving on. If what was no more than a bit of glorified graffiti is worth a potful of wampum, why did Duncan return it?”

She was ready with the answer. “Because he’d decided to kill Ida.”

“Begging the question: why did the good son stoop to homicide?”

“The black market for antique books and maps wasn’t steady enough to keep Arlen in the style to which his son felt he should be accustomed. So Duncan came up with the peachy idea of offing Mumsy to inherit her millions. He planned to transfer the funds to his father.”

“Likely justified it as revenge for her sins. And with that accomplished he would no longer need to steal to keep his father in cognac and Cuban cigars.”

“Correct. According to Lieutenant Tolliver.”

Barnaby rubbed his chin. “Now that’s an original twist. Altruistic murder. Would make a good story. By the way, how did he come to mix up the mail slots?”

"That was his first real mistake."

"Surely the theft of the map was his first mistake. His fingerprints ultimately led us to the murder weapon."

"An error, yes, but not a fatal one."

"I don't understand."

"If he hadn't mixed up the slots, Joseph wouldn't have been poisoned, and we never would have known Ida didn't die of a heart attack. We might have eventually pegged Duncan for the art thief, but not the murderer."

Barnaby leaned over the railing to watch a family of four. A teenage girl marched sullenly six feet in front of her parents, staring at the ground, while a boy of about seven scuffed his shoes six feet behind them. "I'm a tad concerned about our lad's evolving career path—from petty theft to homicide. I mean, sure, he would be able to look forward to a sizeable estate—but as we know from Norton's predicament, that could take months. Why not sell the Drake painting to be assured of a supply of ready cash in the interim?"

"Because of where his mother lived."

"Huh?"

"See, Duncan had never been to Ida's apartment. He was sent to boarding school before the Kinks moved here, and after college he landed a job in New York. He didn't return to Florida until his parents were divorced and his father had moved out. When he stole the map from Mind Over Matter, he was unaware that she lived above the store. His father must have mentioned her address sometime after that. He fretted the police would connect the burglary to the Kinks, so he returned the map."

"And without the map to sell, he found himself in an impecunious state. That's when he decided to bump off the mater earlier than scheduled."

"That's about how Tolliver sees it."

Barnaby got up and went into the kitchen. When he returned, he held two old-fashioned glasses filled with whiskey. He gave one to Philo. "You were explaining about the mail slot switcheroo."

"Like I said, he'd never been to his mother's apartment. When he brought the poison, he was confronted with three slots, only one of which was labeled. He took a chance."

"I see. I'll go out on a limb and propose that life is not as precious to the Kink child as it is to us. He didn't care who 'shuffled off this mortal coil.' "

Philo disagreed. "He most definitely wanted Ida to die. He told the police he assumed if he chose the wrong cubby, its owner would simply pop it in the other slot."

"Granting that somewhat iffy scenario, how did he know the tea would kill the delectable Ida?"

"Ah, that part is diabolical. His father had informed Duncan that Ida suffered from heart failure—"

"I'm sure he said it with sufficiently somber regret."

"His tone was more likely salivating and vindictive. Duncan told Tolliver that Arlen had on numerous occasions declared he hoped 'the old bag' would run out of her medicine and kick off."

"An offhand remark by the father inspired the son. He must have read up on symptoms of digitoxin poisoning and mixed up a lethal batch. While it only made Joseph ill, it was enough, given her heart condition, to do the trick for Ida." Barnaby sipped his drink. "Have the police charged Arlen Kink as an accessory?"

Philo shook her head. "He knew nothing about it. Duncan claimed he only mentioned he was going to try to see her—to reconnect. Arlen's response was to grunt that he was wasting his time. That was the end of the conversation." She sucked on a piece of ice. "Lieutenant Tolliver believed Duncan, since Arlen would have known which mail slot belonged to Ida."

"Ah." Barnaby cackled. "So how did our would-be assassin feel when his mother continued alive and kicking cats?"

"Nonplussed, no doubt. He decided to try again—this time delivering the tea in a Bigelow tin—to her door. He wrapped it and attached a card saying it was a gift from her bank, thanking her for being a loyal customer."

"Considering her lavish life style, she probably didn't question it."

"And that was *her* fatal mistake."

The red trolley trundled down the street, the docent's spiel drowning out any possibility of conversation. When it had passed, Barnaby resumed. "By the way, oh Fount of Knowledge, what's happening with Edmund?"

"They found his DNA at the two crime scenes."

"Not definitive. The Spring House and the Lightner are both public places, heavily frequented."

"They have security videos of visitation at the Fountain of Youth. Edmund never showed up on them. Also, the Spring House was cleaned before the park closed that night and remained closed while the police investigated. His DNA could only have been deposited the night of the murder."

"What about the museum?"

"Fresh DNA was retrieved on the gallery balustrade that matched his. *Plus*—" She raised her voice to drown out his interruptions. "Plus, he left wads of evidence around his hotel room. Tolliver says it's open and shut now."

"Nasty man, Edmund." Barnaby clicked his teeth.

"He was nice to Joseph though. And we now know he wasn't the one who tried to poison him."

"To be fair, no one tried to poison Joseph. And no one will. He's finally put his name on his mailbox."

"What's that expression about a horse and the barn door?"

"Don't try to bail the boat until you've plugged the hole. Why *was* he nice to Joseph, anyway?"

"I was half right: he needed a way to keep tabs on us, but he also simply enjoyed doing crosswords with him."

Barnaby raised his phone and took a picture of a line of schoolgirls in plaid skirts and white blouses, marching single file down the road. " 'In an old house in Paris that was covered with vines, lived twelve little girls in two straight lines.' " He pointed. "The littlest one must be Madeline." He put the phone down. "Greer didn't just pump Joseph for information; he also followed us. Remember the guy at Dos Chicas?"

"The man who spilled his drink when I talked about murder? That was Greer?"

"I think so. And after the Alligator Farm, he showed up at the bar all hot and bothered."

"In a blue shirt like Jocko's. *Hmm*. Makes sense."

"He was indeed desperate. He had lost out to a bunch of students in his hometown of Cleveland, and he was determined to win this time."

"Determined may not be a strong enough word. He was willing to resort to murder." Philo gazed out at the sky. "What makes a person so obsessed that he loses his humanity?"

"Don't you mean, that he doesn't see others as human?"

"No. At the end—when Edmund kidnapped us—he was no longer rational—he was like a beast. Inhuman. Remember his eyes? The way he looked at us? Almost…hungry."

"*Hmm*. Say, do you have any crackers?"

"Really, Barnaby?"

"Hey, you brought it up."

"I haven't had time to shop for anything. Want to go to A1A?"

"Sure. Nice night for a stroll. Let's come home by way of the pirate ship."

"Cheating death once again?"

"It's just nice to know no one's going to knock me down with an iron missile this time." He stood up and held out a hand.

"Oh! I almost forgot! They found the chest of bubble gum in Edmund's hotel room. Depleted by half."

"He didn't strike me as a gum-chewer."

"Everybody has at least one nasty habit."

"And Edmund Greer was blessed with a boat load."

Chapter Forty-Two

You can have anything you want in life if you dress for it.

—Edith Head

A1A restaurant, Sunday, July 15

They arrived at the restaurant just as happy hour came to a close. Barnaby checked his wallet. "Oh dear, I find myself *sans* funds. Can I touch you for a glass of Chablis?"

She waited just long enough to disconcert him. "Yes, but only one."

"*Humph.*"

They ordered appetizers and sat gazing out at the traffic along Avenida Menendez and beyond it to the darkened marina. Barnaby chewed on a mozzarella stick. "By the way, I heard from Norton. He and Axel Zimmer have really hit it off. He says Axel left his business in the capable hands of his CFO and he and Norton have gone on safari."

"To Africa?"

"No, to look for the eighth casque. They're positive Image Eight refers to Texas."

"Good luck to them. What about the kiddies? Are they still here?" Philo accepted the balloon glass filled with golden liquid.

"Scarpered off yesterday for the remainder of the summer. Most of them will be back for their senior year in the fall."

"Where'd they go?"

"Well, Lincoln has been bitten by the seeker bug and is on his way to New Orleans. Evidently that's where the seventh casque is. And Susie's happy as a clam at high water, ensconced in her tiny Maine village." He signaled for another drink. "I gave A's to all of them, even Thomas."

"I think Thomas really came through at the end. Could it have anything to do with Cleo finally warming up to him?"

"Sometimes it just takes a little positive reinforcement to goad a person into action. They do not, in my opinion, make a cute couple."

"Not like Kevin and Susie." Philo giggled. "They're adorable."

"The beginning of a beautiful friendship?"

"You were redundant the second time you said that. Now you're just being repetitive."

"I can't help it. For once, I'm at a loss for words."

"That'll be the day." As the waitress placed the fresh drink on the table, Philo snatched it from Barnaby's reaching hands.

He gaped at the waitress, who shrugged and walked away. "Sorry, who were we discussing? I was lost in the contemplation of my empty glass."

"Kevin and Susie. Cleo told me he went home with her to meet her parents."

"And what of Kevin's father? Smokey done got his man. What is there left for him to do?"

"Kevin says Runar's taking some time off. He and his wife are headed to Montreal."

"The preferred site for the ninth casque." As Barnaby's fingers inched toward Philo's wine, she picked it up. He sighed and noisily slurped the last drops of alcohol from his glass.

"I am not moved." She sipped her wine, Barnaby's eyes fastened on her lips. "Speaking of romance, I must say, I was not expecting Agatha and Diego to hit it off like that."

"Bless the little darlings, they're going to be spending a lot of time together. Axel has offered her an internship. She'll be helping bring Granada Liquors into the Millstone family. I mentioned the complimentary T-shirt that comes with the position, and she was all agog." Barnaby caught the hem of the waitress's apron. "Sally, wine. *Stat*."

Sally deferred to Philo, who shook her head. "Have a fried pickle." She nibbled an olive. "Diego really isn't the tough nut he pretends to be."

"Yes, one little smooch on his cheek, and he cracked like a pistachio."

"I can't imagine where she drummed up the courage to even do that."

"Love gives you powers even the angels can't fathom."

"That's pretty."

"Thank you. It's probably a quote."

"Speaking of, did you submit your crossword on Friday?"

"Yes, to rave reviews from all but Joseph, who says he's sworn off Argle Bargle for the nonce. Too stressful." He rose. "Since it appears another drink is not in the cards, I shall await you downstairs."

When Philo had paid the check, grumbling about grifters and skinflints, but in a desultory fashion—*he really is so cute*—she joined Barnaby and they strolled across the avenue. The *Black Raven* rode at anchor, the only sound the lapping of water against its high wooden sides. Barnaby said, “One day I’d like to take the cruise and fight off Blackbeard and his crew.”

Philo remembered his kilt and white ruffled shirt. “You’ve already got the proper ensemble.”

He took her arm. “Shall we hence?”

“Lead on, MacDuff.”

****

Philo’s apartment, Monday, July 16

Philo came into the living room, sifting through flyers and envelopes. “Did you pick up your mail? You were expecting a check from your publisher, weren’t you?” She looked up and dropped the pile. “What on *earth* are you wearing?”

He blushed furiously. “I had no choice. I could no longer ignore the fetid state of my wardrobe.”

“Let me guess: your socks are now classified as a pet-food product.”

“Flora wouldn’t even put them in her chili. I was forced to dip into my Sunday-go-to-meeting regalia.” He straightened the red Ferragamo silk tie and shot the cuffs of his Brooks Brothers shirt. The black Versace suit fit him like a glove.

She bent closer. “There’s a monogram on your pocket where I usually see a cartoon character.” She gazed up at him. “It says BAS. What does the A stand for?”

“Never you mind.”

He tried to pull her into his arms, but she backed off, a hand on his chest. “None of that until you tell me.”

His hands fell to his sides. His mouth worked. Finally, he mumbled, "Aloysius."

"What was that?"

He sighed and said loudly, "Aloysius. My middle name is Aloysius."

Philo took a moment to compose herself. When she had successfully stifled every joke that reared up like the Ripley stallion, clamoring to pass her lips, she stuttered, "So…did you bring your mail?"

He scrutinized her face. She held it as still as she could. "Yes. The landlady has been holding it for me. She gave me what I believe is called the 'fisheye.' Or is it perhaps a 'gimlet eye'? *Hmm.* At any rate, she disapproves of my continued absences." He gazed around the living room. "I never paid much attention before, but this is a singularly small space."

"It's big enough for one. And it's free. Comes with the store."

"Free is good." Barnaby slit open a large envelope. "I hope the publisher sent a contract renewal along with the royalty check. Flagler hasn't coughed up the bonus they promised me yet." He read. His eyes grew wider and wider. He slumped back in his chair. The paper drifted to the floor.

Philo picked it up. "What does it say?" She skimmed the letter. "It looks like you've won some sort of prize. Did you enter the Publishers Clearing House sweepstakes?"

"N…no." He jumped up, took her in his arms, and danced a polka around the room. "Remember my reptile-themed crossword? It's won me the Gordon prize!"

"Well, that's nice."

He slowed. “You don’t understand. The Gordon is *the* most prestigious award there is for cruciverbalists! It comes with gobs of money. See?” He picked up the letter and ordered, “Read that sentence there.”

“ ‘As part of the prize, you will be receiving a check for’…oh my God, Barnaby! A hundred thousand dollars. You won’t be destitute anymore!”

“And we can afford a whole house!”

“Huh?”

“To live in.”

“Huh?”

He showed signs of mounting irritation. “When we’re married.”

“But…but…don’t you have to go back to Princeton?”

“Oh, that.” He sat down again. “I haven’t told you yet. I was saving it for some time when you’re really pissed at me, which happens more often than I’d like. On the strength of stellar recommendations from my students, Flagler has offered me an assistant professorship. I can finish my dissertation here.”

Philo felt a catch in her throat. She had deliberately put off thinking about Barnaby’s impending departure, so she wasn’t prepared for the joy at learning it wouldn’t happen. But then, the other thing…that word. What was it? She wracked her brain. “Married.” *Married.* She wiped her brow of the sudden perspiration. *Maybe if I ignore it. Concentrate on the other stuff.* “That’s…that’s great.”

He sat up. “You don’t sound happy.”

“I am. It’s just…so sudden.”

“Sudden?”

“I…I wasn’t expecting you to stay on here. I—”

"That's not what you meant by 'sudden,' is it?" Barnaby rose, stepped toward her, and stood inches from her face. "You're wrong, you know. We've been in love since the first day we met."

She shook her head, trying to hold back the tears. "I…I…"

He put a finger under her chin. "You're just being stubborn. Admit it. That first night at Flora's? The way you scarfed down that disgusting chili without blinking? You would only do that for love. And the fact that you refrained from commenting on my eclectic choices of apparel—at least some of the time. And listened raptly to all my longish diatribes. Yup. You're in love."

It occurred to her that he was right. And that she—for once—was happy to let him have the last word.

More on *The Secret*

For readers who may be interested in learning more about Byron Preiss's *The Secret*—perhaps even dip a toe into the hunt—here are some resources and links.

Byron Preiss, Ted Mann, Sean Kelly et al., The Secret. Ill. by John Jude Palencar. NY: Bantam Books, 1982. Republished 2015 by IBooks.

For aggregated information on the hunt, the main website is https://12treasures.com/

The Secret was featured on Discovery channel's *Expeditions Unknown.*
https://www.discovery.com/shows/expedition-unknown/episodes/the-secret

For current news on the treasure hunt, *The Secret Podcast* on Apple.com:
https://podcasts.apple.com/us/podcast/the-secret-podcast/id1319433512

Spotify:
https://open.spotify.com/show/4ZwNR1XqDjrlrEuX01ScsY

Facebook Pages:

The Secret: A Treasure Hunt by Byron Preiss. Administered by John Jude Palencar. https://www.facebook.com/groups/thesecrettreasures/

The Secret Podcast: https://www.facebook.com/12treasures

There are Facebook pages for every city as well. For information on the St. Augustine hunt:

Mysterious Writings: An interview with George Ward. https://mysteriouswritings.com/in-search-of-the-st-augustine-casque-of-the-secret-armchair-treasure-hunt-six-questions-with-george-ward/

Facebook group: The Secret by Byron Preiss (St. Augustine). https://www.facebook.com/groups/thesecretstaugustine

A word about the author...

Librarian, anthropologist, Congressional aide, speechwriter—M. S. Spencer has lived or traveled in five of the seven continents. She holds a BA from Vassar College, a diploma in Arabic Studies from the American University in Cairo, and Masters in Anthropology and in Library Science from the University of Chicago. All of this tends to insinuate itself into her works.

Ms. Spencer has published fifteen romantic suspense and mystery novels. She has two fabulous grown children and an incredible granddaughter and currently divides her time between the Gulf Coast of Florida and a tiny village in Maine.

http://msspencertalespinner.blogspot.com

Thank you for purchasing
this publication of The Wild Rose Press, Inc.

For questions or more information
contact us at
info@thewildrosepress.com.

The Wild Rose Press, Inc.
www.thewildrosepress.com